A GROWING SEASON

A GROWING SEASON

Sue Boggio
Mare Pearl

University of New Mexico Press · Albuquerque

17 16 15 14 13 12   1 2 3 4 5 6

Library of Congress Cataloging-in-Publication Data

Boggio, Sue.
  A growing season / Sue Boggio, Mare Pearl.
    p. cm.
  ISBN 978-0-8263-5224-8 (pbk. : alk. paper) —
  ISBN 978-0-8263-5225-5 (electronic)
  1. Farmers—Fiction. 2. City and town life—Fiction.
  3. Endangered species—Fiction. 4. New Mexico—Fiction.
  I. Pearl, Mare.   II. Title.
  PS3602.A395G76 2012
  813'.6—dc23
                              2012013981

Composition: Maya Allen-Gallegos
Typeset in 11.5/15 Warnock Pro
Display type is Charlemagne Std

We dedicate *A Growing Season*
to family farmers everywhere
and especially to the family farmers of New Mexico,
whose chile we cannot live without.

ACKNOWLEDGMENTS

We would like to thank the loyal readers of *Sunlight and Shadow* (New York: New American Library/Penguin, 2004) for their support and for insisting the story of Esperanza must continue.

For our research into the issues involving chile farming and the Rio Grande, we found excellent information from Southwest Farm Press; numerous articles in the online edition of the *Valencia County News-Bulletin* (News-Bulletin.com); the Middle Rio Grande Conservancy District; the Chile Pepper Institute of New Mexico State University; and *The Chile Chronicles: Tales of a New Mexico Harvest*, text by Carmella Padilla, photography by Jack Parsons (Santa Fe: Museum of New Mexico Press, 1997).

In our research on the silvery minnow and the Rio Grande, we appreciate the information garnered from "Why the Silvery Minnow Matters," a *Santa Fe Reporter* article by Laura Paskus that was reprinted on AlterNet.org (November 10, 2003); the work of research biologist Steven Platania with the U.S. Department of the Interior, Bureau of Reclamation; the Interstate Stream Commission of the New Mexico Office of the State Engineer;

Chris Altenbach and the City of Albuquerque Biological Park's Rio Grande Silvery Minnow Rearing and Breeding Facility; the Los Lunas Silvery Minnow Refugium; the Middle Rio Grande Endangered Species Act Collaborative Program; New Mexico State Senator Pete Domenici, who proposed the silvery minnow sanctuary; the New Mexico Water Resources Research Institute; the Alliance for the Rio Grande Heritage; and the U.S. Fish and Wildlife Service.

We gleaned much information and inspiration from all of the wonderful books by Stanley Crawford, especially *Mayordomo: Chronicle of an Acequia in Northern New Mexico* (Albuquerque: University of New Mexico Press, 1988).

We exhaustively used *A Dictionary of New Mexico and Southern Colorado Spanish* by Rubén Cobos (Santa Fe: Museum of New Mexico Press, 2003).

Our *dichos* came largely from *It's All in the Frijoles: 100 Famous Latinos Share Real-Life Stories, Time-Tested Dichos, Favorite Folktales, and Inspiring Words of Wisdom* by Yolanda Nava (New York: Fireside, 2000).

In our research regarding Jewish history in the New World, we studied *HaLapid*, the quarterly journal of the Society for Crypto-Judaic Studies; material in the Leona G. and David A. Bloom Southwest Jewish Archives at the University of Arizona, Tucson; "My Crypto-Jewish Self," a paper by Alberto Omero Lopez published in 1997 by the Jewish organization Kulanu; "Fear and Shadows," an article by Michael Freund originally published in the *Jerusalem Post* (November 22, 2002) and reprinted on Kulanu. org; *New Mexico's Crypto-Jews: Image and Memory* by photographer Cary Herz, with essays by Ori Z. Soltes and Mona Hernandez (Albuquerque: University of New Mexico Press, 2007); and *To the End of the Earth: A History of the Crypto-Jews of New Mexico* by Stanley Hordes (New York: Columbia University Press, 2005).

Any mistakes made are ours alone and not from the any of the wonderful sources cited above.

Sue Boggio and Mare Pearl

New Mexico treasure Cipriano Vigil supplied our musical inspiration.

We thank Barbara Clark (www.bacpastels.com) for her art, which captures the unique beauty of the Rio Grande.

Deepest gratitude goes to UNM Press Editor-in-Chief Clark Whitehorn for his humor, insight, and diligence, and we greatly appreciate all of the hard work from everyone at UNM Press.

Thanks to writer Deborah Rice for her friendship and the phone call that started all of this in motion.

And, finally, we thank our families, who make it all worthwhile. *¡La familia!*

CHAPTER 1

S antiago ran through the cottonwood trees on the well-worn path. He had awakened drenched in sweat from his night-mare, and he was still sweating as he made his way through the chill of the early May morning.

The sun had not yet emerged from the shield of the Manzano Mountains in the east, so the light was gun metal gray. Whether it was because of his sweat or the last of night's precious moisture evaporating around him, the air almost seemed damp. Rain almost felt possible. It had been so long, he couldn't even remember what rain smelled like.

He tried to focus on the branches overhead clutching new leaves like awards they had won or on the sound of his running shoes thudding against the packed soil of the path. Something real, instead of the dark images from the nightmare crouching in the recesses of his consciousness, waiting to pounce if he let his guard down.

Sometimes when he had the dream, he tried to remember it so he could understand why his heart beat so hard and fast. All he knew was, it felt like helplessness and panic and death and no matter how many nights went by with only innocuous dreams, it would come back. It always came back.

Something on the path ahead was wrong. He knew these acres of land as well as his own bedroom and something wasn't right. A tree was down.

It wasn't one of the largest of the stately cottonwoods on their land, but it was at least thirty or forty feet tall. Or had been. Now it was collapsed across the path. He walked around to the base of the trunk and saw it had simply pulled away from the earth. He knelt and placed his hand into the coolness of the gaping wound of it, breathing in the scent. Soil clung to the splintered wood that reached like tiny broken bones from the tree trunk.

A tree this big should have massive roots. He imagined them like thick snakes reaching deep into the soil to nourish it and keep it upright. Nothing like that here. Was it the drought that had killed it? Or hordes of tiny insects, invisible assassins? Maybe a disease had eaten away at it from the inside, even as it had looked perfect and healthy. Its leaves were still perfect. Green, heart shaped, and hopeful. Doomed, though. Nothing could save them now.

He ran his hand along the bark as if he was feeling the side of a fallen animal. It looked like it had merely tipped over and if he had superhero strength, he could reach around it and right it, and no one could ever tell what had happened.

A tree like this must be at least half a century old. It had seen a lot. His eighteen years seemed puny next to that. But he had seen a lot, too. Time was weird. Here he was already graduating from high school in a couple of weeks. A writing scholarship at the University of California, Los Angeles, for next fall. Everything looked perfect.

It had been more than seven years since his crazy, drunk father had killed Bobby, Abby's husband, and she had adopted him. His chest squeezed the way it always did when he thought of it. Abby became his mother. She loved him and never blamed him for what his father had done. He should be grateful. He knew he was, but the feeling that came with it was something else, something without a name. It was a taste in his mouth.

He tasted the same thing now, looking at the fallen tree, its condemned leaves fluttering innocently in the sunlight. It started to sicken him. He looked away, down at his feet planted firmly on the earth. Or were they?

Abby woke to the blast of the shower starting. Six forty-five. It must be Santiago getting ready for school after his early morning run. She hoped Maggie was also getting ready. She rolled over, desperate to sink back into sleep.

It had been one of those nights. Up late with a crabby Maggie, trying to finish her adobe house model they had constructed from mud and straw for her first grade class assignment. Maggie was a perfectionist like her late father. At 10:35 p.m. Abby had irritably pronounced the slightly lopsided house good enough for first grade, sending Maggie into frustrated tears. "I wanted it to be the best!" She had tromped off to bed, dramatically crying loudly enough for Abby to hear for a full ten minutes.

All Abby had felt at that point was relief to be cleaning up the mud and straw mess on her kitchen table and anger toward her dead husband. Bobby was supposed to be here for homework. He would have been patient, and the two, father and daughter, would have put their dark perfectionistic heads together and intently constructed the best goddamned adobe house model ever made for Bosque Farms Elementary School while she soaked in a bubble bath.

After Maggie had quieted and Santi returned from being out with his friends, she finally had her bubble bath, followed by three hours of insomnia. God, no wonder she couldn't get up. She'd walked the floors, listening to her children breathe in their sleep. Maggie's inhalations and exhalations were thick and wet from her tears. Santi's resonated like a grown man's.

It used to be enough. It used to give her peace to hear her children breathing in their sleep. Increasingly, though, it accentuated her loneliness. She felt pathetic. Seven years since losing her precious husband and living the noble widow's life. When she lost Bobby, she had honestly believed she'd never want another man. Now, at thirty-seven, she was beginning to wonder.

She sat up in her widow's bed, kicked off the covers, and got up. In her baggy T-shirt and striped pajama bottoms, she tried to imagine wearing the slinky, sexy silk numbers she had enjoyed when there was a man in her bed. Thankfully she hadn't hung onto any baby weight. She could stand to work out a little more, things maybe weren't as firm as they used to be, but overall she thought she could still pull it off. In candlelight . . . after some wine.

She pulled her auburn hair back from her face. Not one gray hair yet. She peered into her wall mirror. Even in the dim light, her eyes were puffy with prominent dark circles underneath, her complexion sallow. The eyes she stared into were gray and lifeless.

"Momeee!" Maggie's shrill voice made her jump as the door swung open without a knock.

Her daughter was wearing her pastel print Easter dress, ruffled white socks, and patent leather shoes. Her freshly brushed jaw-length hair was a mass of dark contradictory waves that seemed to adopt a trendy, tousled look naturally.

"Wow," Abby said. "What's the occasion?"

"The teacher will like my adobe house better if I'm pretty."

Maggie's big round eyes and earnest expression gave Abby a twinge in her heart. "You're always pretty, honey. Your teacher will be very proud of how hard you worked on your house."

"Come on." Maggie reached for her hand. "Santi made scrambly eggs."

Abby's friend Rachel and her six-year-old daughter, Hattie, came through the kitchen door just as Abby was running dishwater.

"We got to get moving, you guys, since I have to carry that monstrosity into your classroom for you," Santiago teased, jangling his car keys impatiently as Hattie and Maggie raced around the kitchen. With his vintage bowling shirt over some khaki trousers and his sleek dark hair pulled back into a three-inch ponytail, Santi looked the creative, independent spirit he was. Abby was relieved his innate individualism rendered him immune to peer pressure. Yet the less he cared what people thought, the more his peers seemed to deem him cool. They elected him class president, editor of the school newspaper, and captain of the cross-country track team.

Rachel helped herself to coffee and sat at the table. Abby joined her, waiting for the kids to leave and take their chaos with them.

"Let's go!" Santiago boomed, and both girls came to a skidding halt. Rachel's daughter looked nothing like her. Instead of the exotic dark beauty contrasting with light blue eyes, Hattie had curly white-blond hair cascading around luminescent ivory cheeks. She was as petite and waiflike as Maggie was hardy and rough. Hattie looked like one of her grandmother CeCe's garden fairies come to life. People often remarked that it looked like Abby and Rachel had swapped babies. But the truth of it was, each little girl had culled her father's genes.

His backpack slung over his shoulder, Santiago balanced the board holding the adobe house on his palm, as if he was carrying a pizza, and shepherded the girls out of the door. Their chorus of munchkin goodbyes was still audible, long after they'd slammed the door shut.

Abby marveled at her handsome, responsible son. "I don't know what I ever would have done without that boy."

"Just goes to show you how it's nurture, not nature," Rachel said. "Imagine if he'd turned out like his father."

"I don't even think of that man as his father. It's weird, but there are times Santi reminds me so much of Bobby, and they never even knew each other. Like this morning, he was telling me we have a tree down and you would have thought somebody had died. He looked so devastated by this old cottonwood tree, and it frustrated him to no end that I was like, 'See if Charlie will get his chain saw and help you cut it up and haul it away.' I guess I missed something."

Rachel nodded. "If you don't read their minds correctly, they hate you."

"Especially when they're teenagers. But Bobby was like that. He'd go all dark and brooding over something, and it would be up to me to figure out why."

"The sensitive male we claim to want." Rachel rolled her eyes. "Most of the time I'm pretty grateful Charlie is so uncomplicated. He's the original two-button blender, no instruction manual needed."

Abby laughed, but noticed once again how whenever they talked about men, her man was in the past tense. "Charlie *is* . . . Bobby *was* . . ."

Rachel seemed to be peering straight into her. "You've been alone a long time."

Abby shrugged.

"Abby, I know Bobby was a tough act to follow. But I've seen men watching you at the café."

"Yeah, right," Abby said, jumping up to put her coffee cup in the sink and escape Rachel's gaze.

"Seriously, are you going to follow in Carmen's footsteps and turn widowhood into a lifelong career? I need to go, but think about it. You're only thirty-seven. Wake up and smell the testosterone, girlfriend."

Abby went about her morning routine in the quiet of her empty house. Her thoughts kept wandering back to the idea of inviting a man into her life. It wasn't like they were lined up outside of her front door, which needed a fresh coat of turquoise paint. She couldn't think of anyone she knew who was even remotely a candidate. It had more to do with her belief that having a man in her life was first dependent on some sort of agreement she would need to make inside of herself.

She was relieved it was Monday and the café was closed, freeing her from heading over there as she did Tuesdays through Saturdays. She'd be in by nine in the morning to prep for their eleven thirty opening. Starting her soups and sauces, making breads or quiches, the noon special, and a dessert or two. Rachel's mother, CeCe, took care of the chile, both red and green, for their enchiladas and burritos, plus pies and cakes and all the deli items. Rachel helped out when she wasn't busy with the goat cheese end of the business, run from the back of the café. Thankfully, they weren't open for breakfast or dinner.

It was enough but not too much. That and her children kept her busy enough. So where did a man fit into this, and what would Bobby have to say about it?

Abby walked outside into the midmorning sun. Not a cloud in the sky. Was he up there somewhere, her dead husband? Did he watch her? At first it had given her comfort to believe that he did. It was about the only thing that had kept her going when his body was found buried in a makeshift grave after five months of being missing. But then Maggie was born, and Santiago became her foster child and then her adopted son, and her life became about them.

Now Santi was graduating and would be leaving home to go to college. Was that where this man thing came from? A half-empty nest looming?

The ground was utterly dry beneath her feet as she began to jog along the path. She would go look at the tree Santi was so worked up about. Little clouds of dust burst around her ankles. It had been another month without any measurable rain. The mountains looked devoid of color. Their forests, normally a healthy dark green, were now pale and withered, suffering after another winter of little snow.

She was glad Santi had won the scholarship and wanted to go

away for college. Not that she didn't have the money to send him wherever his heart desired. But this he had earned for himself, and as an adopted kid, he seemed to prefer that over her assurances that whatever was hers, was his. She would miss him like hell but wanted to give him wings, let go of him gracefully. She remembered how Bobby's father had clung to him and riddled him with guilt and ended up pushing him farther away. She wanted to be the kind of mother her grown children would willingly flock home to whenever they had the chance.

The fallen tree was up ahead. Sweat was pouring down her face as the sun rose higher and the temperature rose into the high eighties. Already her tongue felt thick and dry against the roof of her mouth.

It was kind of sad to see this majestic tree laying so unnaturally against the earth. But with the ongoing drought, trees were more susceptible to disease, especially these thirsty cottonwoods. Her land, positioned close to the river, had a high water table for the trees to tap into. The surrounding trees seemed okay. It puzzled her why her son seemed so affected by one fallen tree. She examined it more closely, trying to see what he had seen, know what he had felt. It was a loss, and he'd certainly had enough of those. But there were so many other beautiful trees on this path. It must be the poet, the writer in him who felt it so deeply, who made it matter so much. She loved that about him. So like Bobby. Whomever Santi chose to love would be a lucky young woman. Would he find someone to love in California, as Bobby had when he had met her there? She felt a stir of fear that he would be hurt. God, this business of letting go gracefully was hard.

She had already been forced to let go of Bobby when he was torn from her life. It had been a gradual decent into hell. First his disappearance. Her hoping beyond all reason, month after month, that he would miraculously return to her. Then the proof of his death, in its own cruel way only a beginning. From the time she was barely eighteen years old, she hadn't been without Bobby and his all-consuming love. That was more than half her lifetime ago. These last seven years, she had stumbled through some twilight existence, not with him anymore, yet not quite without him either. It was still his memory she turned to for comfort, his name she whispered in the night.

Suddenly she knew with great certainty she needed a new love in her life. A living man to cherish, who would cherish her. The realization came at her with such dizzying force she had to sit down on the tree's trunk to steady herself. She dug her fingernails into its yielding bark and felt its remaining life force give her strength and clarity. She turned her face skyward, squinting into the brightness. Her heart began to speak. It was a prayer. It was an apology. She would love again.

CeCe Vigil knelt on the warming earth of mid-May. Small sprouts of beets lined up soldierlike in two long rows, ready for her inspection. She hadn't bothered planting beets for years. But the day after tomorrow her parents, Mort and Rose Spelman, were arriving from Brooklyn, where they had spent their entire lives, to live with her and her husband, Miguel. In the beginning her father's dementia wasn't that noticeable, not to her anyway, but she kept her communication with her parents limited, the obligatory every-two-week call. So she wouldn't be the best judge of her father's mental health. He had always seemed eccentric to her. Obsessive and moody, even prone to sudden rages. But her mother had lived with the man, what? Sixty years? Rose shouldn't have been the most surprised to find out that he had lost it all—his mind and all of their money. But she was. Like always, too wrapped up in her hoity-toity social crap to have noticed.

That was why CeCe was growing beets. She was really at a loss to respond in any other positive way. She remembered her parents loved pickled beets and borscht. This was part of trying to be a good Jewish daughter.

Each sprout looked hearty. She groomed the soil with her gloved hand, then took the glove off to feel the dirt sift through her fingers. The earth felt dry already. Typical New Mexican soil. She felt guilty about how much water she needed to get her garden going while Miguel agonized over the drought and his chile crop. After a five-year stretch of little rain and decreased snowpacks, the farm was on the verge of failure.

She looked across the yard, where she had thrown scratch to the chickens. Tiny sparrows fell to earth from the poplars, like sprinkles of rain, to get their share, only to fly back up a second later, spooked by an aggressive chicken. Then, once again, the sparrows showered down. If she were to survive her parent's intrusion, she would need the peaceful company of her garden to keep sane. It would get all the water it needed. She looked at the healthy sprouts standing at attention and smiled. Soon, she would be feeding Mort and Rose enough beets to choke a horse. Maybe two.

She breathed in a cleansing breath of perfect May air. The sun was bright, hanging in the vast clear blueness. At the garden gate she saw her daughter, Rachel, let herself in and walk toward her, eyeing the tomato plants as she passed. At almost thirty-eight, Rachel was aging even better than CeCe had. No gray showed in her thick bundles of dark curls, which she still wore past her shoulders. Her hair was pulled back and fastened with an etched silver Hopi barrette, a present from her husband, Charlie. CeCe had seen it glisten when she turned to latch the gate. She wore her usual work attire of blue jeans, T-shirt, and cowboy boots, after a morning of feeding and milking her Nubian goats.

"Hi, Ma." Rachel waved, coming closer.

"Hey, sweetie. Where's Hattie?" CeCe's heart warmed as she said her granddaughter's name.

"She's with her dad. She's at that age, you know, where they want to marry their dads. I'm toad poop these days."

"Excuse me, but aren't you forgetting how you were with your papa at that age?" That age. CeCe went there for an excruciating moment. She herself was never much of a daddy's girl. Mort wasn't that kind of father. He was too busy obsessing and providing. He didn't even teach her to ride a two-wheeler. Never anything in his pocket for her when he came home late from the office, which was almost every night. Just a cigar that he puffed in solitude behind a newspaper. With his short fuse, she was always afraid to intrude.

CeCe stood up and felt her knees painfully stiff from kneeling. The thought of turning sixty this summer was starting to nag at her a bit. Her strong hands ached in the mornings. She knew Miguel's arthritis must hurt more than he let on. He looked thin and worn out more than aged. And heartsick. This wonderful man who loved his land was now beaten down by drought.

She turned to Rachel. "I hope we get some rain this year. Nice and steady, good old predictable monsoon weather. With your grandparents here, I'm not sure what kind of time I'll have to work out here."

"Why can't we just put them in a home or something?" Rachel kicked at a dirt clod with the point of her boot. "This affects all of us, you know. Especially Papa. They've never approved of him. How's he going to deal with having them in his face? I'm half Hispanic, so what's to say they don't hate me, too? We don't owe them anything."

"Don't you think if we had money we'd put them anywhere else but here? Mort lost his and all the rest of the family's money in some investment scam. No one else can stand the sight of him. I'm their only option."

"Have you considered euthanasia?"

"Just for myself."

"How nuts is he?"

"God only knows. But Mort isn't the half of it. Rose still has her senses. That's what's frightening."

"Maybe we can get her addicted to gambling. I could take her to the casino in Isleta and have her play the quarter machines. Old ladies love those things," said Rachel with a naughty smile.

"Maybe she'll win big and buy a fancy-schmancy home some-where far away."

"I don't think she'd let go of a quarter now. She's probably kicking herself that she didn't stick some coal up Mort's butt sixty years ago, to have diamonds today."

"Ma!"

"Don't 'Ma' me. Day after tomorrow my life will change. Never in my wildest dreams did I ever think I'd be the one stuck with them. I'm turning angry, old, and bitter. Get used to it."

"You're such a comfort. I was already depressed this morning and came over to get a cup of good cheer, only to find Lizzy Borden."

"Here I am going on about my woes. What's the matter?" CeCe said, smoothing back Rachel's escaped wisps of hair.

Rachel's mouth gave a little downward twinge. "It's been six years. You'd think I'd be over it by now. But I had a dream I was pregnant. It was so real, Ma. Then I woke up and remembered. I just feel so empty."

CeCe shuddered, thinking how the joy of little Hattie's birth had suddenly become a nightmare when Rachel began to hemorrhage. An emergency hysterectomy had spared her life. CeCe realized they had never really talked about the fact that Rachel could not have more children. "With Hattie in school now, it's bound to hit you. I'm so sorry, Rachel. But you didn't die, that's all I can think about. You have to focus on that. You lost your uterus, not your life and not your baby. You and Charlie will be fine with just that little *pisherkeh*, Hattie." She pulled her daughter by her arm. "Come help me get the invaders' room ready for them. Rose will probably have on the white gloves."

CeCe's heart thumped the whole way to the airport. It had been years since she had seen her parents, and now she was picking them up to come live with her. Miguel's jaw clenched as he drove.

At sixty, he was still incredibly dashing to her, hair thick but almost all silver, like the hatband on his hat. He wore a mustache that had dark remnants of his youth. She knew what he must be thinking, but didn't want to ask. She hated herself for what was happening, what this would do to Miguel.

Charlie, Rachel, and Hattie, who had been following behind, parked next to them in the parking structure. Hattie jumped out of her booster seat, excited to be at the airport for the first time. The five of them stood in a tight circle for a few moments, listening to the sounds of people starting their cars with their freshly reunited loved ones stuffed happily inside.

"Are you all ready?" Charlie asked, as if addressing his troops before battle. He looked at his watch. "Their plane should be touching down about now." He grabbed Hattie's hand as she started to make a run down the long aisles of the parking structure.

"We need to try to make the best of this," said Miguel, sounding as though he was trying to convince himself most of all. He put his arm around CeCe. "You were wonderful putting up with my crazy bruja aunt for so many years. I'm here for you now." The familiar look of love in his eyes gave her the fortitude to move toward the sliding glass doors that led into the airport, with the rest of her family taking up the rear.

She wanted to distract herself by stopping to look at the various glass cases of art and Indian jewelry. The cases displayed fancy beaded buckskin or handwoven clothes tied with belts latched with heavy silver and turquoise buckles, the kind you could buy at exclusive shops in Albuquerque's Old Town, Santa Fe, or Taos. She stopped at the departure and arrival monitors before entering the gate terminal and scanned for Flight 593 from LaGuardia. *LANDED*, it flashed. Gate A20.

A larger-than-life brass statue of an early Native American man almost in flight stood at the security entrance, which they could not go past. He rose on the ball of one foot on the square base, behind an eagle just short of his grasp, and seemed to defy the laws of balance and gravity. Hattie exclaimed at all the new wonders: planes landing and taking off, other children held back by tired parents, announcements on the loud speakers. Rachel and Charlie kept her securely contained between them as they all waited.

CeCe wished they had a few extra moments to stand at the large windows so that Hattie could watch the planes slowly roll to the waiting snakelike connections to the gates. Would she still have enough time and energy for Hattie after today?

Her knees began to weaken as deboarded passengers made their way toward the security entrance. Her grasp tightened onto Miguel's, and he squeezed her hand.

"Do you see them?" Rachel asked as the crowd drew near.

CeCe's eyes searched beyond the gate. She hadn't even seen a recent picture of Rose and Mort, and she didn't know if they had gained weight since the last time she had seen them or if Rose was still dying her hair that red color little old Jewish ladies love. For Christ's sake, you'd think a woman could recognize her own parents. But the people were coming so fast, they, too, looking for loved ones.

She noticed a long line of frustrated-looking travelers waiting at the nearest X-ray conveyor belt. People nervously checked their watches. She could hear them saying things like, "What the hell is she doing up there? She's going to make me miss my plane."

"I demand you find him!" yelled the little old lady to the TSA agents, who, along with the passengers in line, were obviously losing their patience.

"I've called security, ma'am. They'll be here to take care of you as soon as they can. You don't have a boarding pass. This area is for boarding passengers only. I must ask you to leave this line and wait over there for security. We're on high alert. I'm afraid terrorism takes precedence over a lost husband."

"Terrorists? You don't know from terrorists! We fought the Nazis!"

CeCe excused herself up to the front of the line, where the

old woman seemed to be wearing every good piece of jewelry she owned. A pillbox hat sat sassily on top of her red-dyed, pageboy-cut hair.

"Excuse me, sir—," CeCe began.

"Back off, girlie, I was here first," said the old woman through wrinkled magenta lips.

"Rose?" CeCe asked, not believing. Her stomach twisted into a painful knot. A familiar knot. "Ma, what's wrong?"

Rose looked at CeCe. "Oh, thank God! Cecelia! *Gevalt!* Your father's missing!"

CeCe was able to ease her mother onto their side of the security area. She got applause and whoops from the waiting passengers, who could now move forward. "What do you mean, 'missing'?"

"Gone! Not here! What, you only speak Mexican now?"

"Was he on the plane? When did he go missing?" CeCe asked, choosing to ignore her mother's rudeness.

"Of course he was on the plane. I sat next to his snoring the whole way. He's somewhere in the airport." Rose hadn't given any notice to the family entourage huddled behind CeCe.

"Are you my great-grandma?" Hattie asked, pulling on Rose's suit jacket. "Can I try on your jewelry when we get home?"

"Later, we'll talk," Rose said, patting Hattie on top of her blond curls with her bony, bejeweled hand. Her nails were long and impeccably groomed, polished and artificial. "Who is this, anyway?"

"Is he in the bathroom, maybe?" asked CeCe.

"Charlie and I will go check the men's restrooms," Miguel told CeCe. "There's several, so you stay here in case he comes back."

"He's wearing a navy suit, white shirt, and red bow tie. I told him that the navy suit shows his dandruff, but he never listens to me anymore," said Rose.

CeCe could see Miguel grimace as he turned to go. What would having her parents at home do to her marriage? Miguel was already near his breaking point with the farm. Could he live day after day in the same house with people who had shunned him since the beginning?

Rose raised a veiny hand up to her mouth and said to Rachel, "The way Mort's been lately—you might want to go check the women's bathroom."

CeCe and Rose sat down on a nearby upholstered bench outside of Garduño's restaurant. "Remember when I brought Rachel to visit you when she was about ten? This is her daughter, Hattie. Say hello, Hattie."

"Hello." Hattie stared unabashedly at Rose.

"She looks like a shiksa, Cecelia," Rose said.

"Why did Mommy have to go look for Great-grandpa Mort in the women's bathroom? I know what bathroom to go in and I can hardly read. They have pictures. Doesn't Great-grandpa Mort know if he's a girl or a boy?" Hattie asked Rose.

"He knows he's a boy, Hattie, but he doesn't see too well and gets a little confused sometimes," CeCe explained, stroking her corn silk curls.

"Nothing wrong with his eyesight," corrected Rose. "Just every once in a while he forgets things, that's all." She leaned over to CeCe and whispered, *"Er dreyt zikh arum vi a forts in rosl."* He turns around like a fart in a pot.

"I forget, too, don't I, Grandma? Can I sleep with Great-grandma Rose and Great-grandpa Mort tonight?"

Rose went pale.

"I don't think they want to sleep with anyone but themselves tonight. Besides, they don't even know you," CeCe replied.

The color returned to Rose's face.

"I didn't see him," said Rachel, rejoining them.

"Take your hands off of me, you desperados!"

Miguel and Charlie escorted a man in a navy suit, white shirt, and red bow tie between them. "This him?" Miguel asked.

CeCe's father struggled against them. He clutched something tight in his fists. He looked shrunken, especially next to Charlie, who stood six foot two. His nose and ears were much larger than she remembered. His thin white hair stuck out as if he had just gotten out of bed.

"There you are! *Bist meshugeh*, Mordecai?" admonished Rose.

"Where did you find him?" CeCe asked.

Miguel gave her a worried look.

"Found him in one of the men's restrooms way over near the escalators at baggage claim," Charlie said, releasing his grip. "He was handing out folded paper towels to the guys after they washed their hands. Made a buck seventy-five in tips by the time we caught up to him."

"It looks like it's made out of mud," CeCe heard Rose say to Mort as they examined their new home.

"It's adobe. Mud and straw," CeCe explained. "Sun-dried bricks."

"Sun-dried tomatoes I've heard of, but sun-dried bricks? Mort, did you hear that? *Druchas*, Mort. That's where we are," Rose said referring to the Yiddish version of living in the sticks.

CeCe wanted to say to her mother that she should feel damn lucky to have a place to live at all. But she bit her tongue. It remained so ingrained in her, the Jewish tradition of honoring thy parents. Telling Rose off would only result in a harder living situation, and she could not imagine that. Thank God Miguel was out getting their luggage. The less he had to hear, the better.

Mort stood at the picture window overlooking the spring burst of greens and colorful flowers of the front yard. On the cobblestone walkway a peacock stood proudly, his royal blue chest radiant with sunlight and his huge tail spread to impress the peahen pecking at what the birds had kicked out of the birdfeeder. Mort seemed more impressed than she.

"That's Pretty Boy," Hattie told him. She pulled over a reading chair, and he sat down, not taking his eyes off of the courtship in front of him. Hattie squeezed her petite body in next to him. CeCe wished she could have done that at that age. "I like to watch, too." Hattie was the only one of the family perfectly okay with the invasion of the Yiddish people.

Mort looked contented enough. Not angry, like he had when CeCe was young. "Ma, maybe you and Papa would like to rest before dinner," she suggested. "Miguel just put your suitcases in your room."

"I want to help with dinner. I'm perfectly capable of helping."

"I know, Ma, but you've been traveling all day. My friend Bonnie is coming over to help and meet you both. Rachel's already in the kitchen, so everything is under control." Just not under her mother's control.

Bonnie let herself in the front door. She walked toward Rose with a big chocolate-cherry-lipstick smile, her layered maroon hair gelled into perky tufts on top. "It's so nice to meet you." Bonnie held out her hand, fingers lengthened with square-tipped acrylic nails painted dark purple. "I took the day off because I didn't want to smell like hair bleach and perm solution when I met you." Her T-shirt, with three-quarter-length sleeves, clung to her breasts and showed the rolls around her back and thickening waist. Her capri-style jeans were too tight, as usual, especially in front.

Rose hesitated. Finally she reached out her own hand, with her pearly round-tipped acrylics. "How do you do."

"Ooh, girl, nice diamond," commented Bonnie, taking a closer look at the three-carat diamond on Rose's finger.

"N-B-C!" Mort sang from his chair. "Here's Johnny!"

"And you must be CeCe's father," Bonita said, swinging her hips as she walked toward him. "So pleased to meet you, Mr. Spelman."

"Call me Mort," he said, smiling. And staring. "Are you from the agency?"

"No, I'm one of CeCe's best friends."

"Is she a *nafke*, Cecclia?" Rose asked behind her hand.

"Because if you were from the agency, I'd have you cut my

toenails. They're hard as rock," Mort continued. "Shoes don't fit." He held up his foot with its wing-tip shoe.

"She looks like a nafke," Rose insisted. "A prostitute."

"She's no such thing," snapped CeCe. "She's a dear friend. Try to be nice."

Hattie was already taking off her shoes to check her own toenails.

Bonnie smiled and put her hand on Mort's shoulder. "No, I'm not from the agency, but I do pedicures at my hair shop. You're welcome to come and have one, on me. You, too, Rose."

"Mrs. Spelman," Rose corrected.

Bonnie looked at CeCe, who rolled her eyes. "Mrs. Spelman," Bonnie said, giving a saucy curtsy-bow thing, her voluptuous ass pointed right at Mort.

CeCe feared Bonnie and Rose's relationship would end up being like a fifties Japanese monster versus monster movie, gruesome yet entertaining.

"I'll go see if Rachel needs my help. I promised I'd make the tortillas," said Bonnie, making a fast getaway.

Mort watched her round tushy churn its way to the kitchen.

Miguel had long since slipped away to his study. The door was shut tight.

"Where's the bathroom?" her father asked.

CeCe pointed the way.

"I saw you looking, Mordecai," Rose called after him. "You *alter kocker!*"

In a matter of seconds the room was cleared except for the two of them. "Now, Cecelia, what can I do to help?"

CHAPTER 2

"The Araucana hasn't been laying for the past few days," Rachel said, entering through the back door of her kitchen. Charlie sat mulling over the newspaper, absorbed in, from what Rachel could see, an interview with Eloy Sanchez about his farm in Tome. She knew from the farmer meetings at the café that Eloy was more than likely having to sell.

"I wouldn't worry about it," said Charlie, not looking up from the paper. He now wore little round reading spectacles, which would make him an even more believable Santa this Christmas. Would they even have Christmas this year, with Mort and Rose scowling their disapproval? She couldn't imagine CeCe giving up trimming a tall tree and having them all over. Abby, Santi, and Maggie had spent every Christmas at her mother and father's house for the past seven years. The invaders would not take Christmas away from Hattie or stop Charlie from playing Santa for the girls. He lived for that. If they had problems with it they could just stay in their room.

"I miss those beautiful green eggs. Hattie likes them with her ham. I've been having to lie to her because she refuses to eat white or brown eggs. Claims she can taste a difference. I swear, I don't know where she gets her stubbornness," Rachel said.

Charlie's brown eyes peered over his spectacles at her. He hadn't bothered to get a haircut for a long time. Brown salty waves danced all over and curled just below his collar. His worn boots rested on a chair under the old oak table his Grandma Hattie had given him. Grandma Hattie's mother had told her that Billy the Kid sat at that very table and drank a glass of goat's milk when they lived in Las Cruces. Seemed Grandma Hattie's mother's brother, Uncle Ode, was a bit of a bad boy himself back then.

"Sometimes your stubbornness is your best quality," Charlie said, folding the paper solemnly. "You'll never give up the farm."

"Not as long as we live." She worried that Hattie might not want the land. As dramatic as she often was, Hattie would more likely want to become an actress in New York or Hollywood rather than stay home on the farm.

After she had had the emergency hysterectomy, Rachel thought that maybe God was punishing her. She had loved her childhood sweetheart, Roberto, since they were babies together. At eighteen, in her desperation to keep Roberto, she had manipulated him into having sex with her, resulting in a pregnancy. When his leave was up, he went back to the navy—and to his new love, Abby, in San Diego. He told Rachel his name was Bobby now and that having sex with her had been a mistake, that he loved only Abby. So Rachel did not tell him about the pregnancy, which she impulsively decided to end.

It was a late abortion caused by a concoction her crazy bruja great-aunt, Maria, had talked her into drinking. Maria had called it a "remedy." The baby had been a boy. Rachel had agonized and regretted the abortion for so many years. What if she had kept the baby boy . . . at nineteen, would he be working alongside her father now in the chile fields? But Roberto had chosen Abby over her, and all these years later, Abby was her closest friend. Abby mourned him as "Bobby," and Rachel had to admit theirs was the love that was meant to be. She had accepted that years ago, but she would always be haunted by the male child she lost.

"Well, back to work," Charlie said, rising from the chair and giving her a smooch on the side of her face. A light slap on her rear end followed. "See ya, babe," he said, putting on his sweat-stained cowboy hat on the way out.

What a wonderful man, her husband. A loving father. Everything was perfect in their life together; she was smart enough to know that. Why was it so hard to feel it sometimes?

Abby plated the last wedge of low-carb cheesecake and brought it over to her friend Ramone.

"I had to hide this for you, or it would have been long gone." Abby sat with him at their favorite table, which was tucked into an alcove of the café. Potted philodendrons and a tall palm afforded privacy from the last of the lunch rush customers, who lingered over coffee and desserts.

"The sheriff should have a few special favors, no? Or this wouldn't be New Mexico." Ramone winked and dabbed at his silver mustache with his napkin.

"How much have you lost now?" Abby asked.

"Thirty-eight pounds," he said, smacking his flat stomach. "The ladies are all over me these days." With his wavy silver hair, he was movie star handsome.

"I miss your round Buddha belly."

"I don't. I could barely tie my own shoes, let alone chase the bad guys. Now I run three miles every day. And lately, when the ladies are looking, I'm looking back."

Abby felt a pang of possessiveness. Ramone had been her special male friend, her surrogate father, ever since she had lived in Esperanza. Even before being reelected sheriff, he had volunteered to lead the search efforts to find her missing husband. Instead of marrying or leaving Esperanza, he had lived with and cared for his ailing father, who had passed away a year ago. She and Ramone spent a lot of time together, and she didn't want to share him with another woman. Then guilt washed through her; he deserved to date, have some fun, after all the self-sacrificing decades of his sixty years.

The touch of his hand over hers brought her eyes back to his firm gaze. He opened her fist and removed the wad of paper napkin she clenched and lightly held her hand. "Abby, mi'ja, you need to move on, too. You are so young still. Don't let these precious years go by without love in your life."

It was all Abby could do not to jerk her hand away and lecture him about all the love in her full life and who needed a man, anyway. But between them, there had never been anything but gentle truth. "Then I need directions to the Good Man Store, because I have no idea how to go about finding one."

He smiled, let go of her hand, and took a swig of coffee. "I'll let you in on a secret. I believe God has love planted all over the place, but we don't have it until we decide. I hid all those years in my father's house, behind my layers of fat, in my long hours of work. Whenever I did see some woman who looked interesting, I turned away. We give off a scent, no? You don't consciously smell it, but it says: 'Keep away' or 'Come here.' It's some kind of hormone."

Abby laughed. "You've been watching too much Discovery Channel."

"Actually, it was a *Nova* special on PBS. But it made sense." Ramone slowly chewed the last bite of cheesccake and reluctantly put down his fork on the empty plate.

From the clatter of noise and shrill voices bursting through the café door, Abby knew her break was over. The kids were there.

"Mommy! Look what I did!" Maggie ran to their table, dumping her backpack onto the floor as she arrived, pulling out a rumpled sheet of lined paper. "I got an A on my arithmetic test. Maybe I did get Daddy's head for numbers. Hi, Ramone."

"Hola, Magdalena," Ramone said with raised eyebrows. "You need to practice your Spanish, young lady."

"*Si, Señor Lovato. Hola*," Maggie replied before turning back to Abby. "Can I go home with Hattie? Rachel said I could."

"Where is your brother?" Abby asked. Santiago usually came into the café to check in with her and let her know his plans.

"He said he had stuff to do. He's a real crab apple today, so be glad he's not here. Can I go now?" Her dark eyes shone with a hint of challenge. Abby knew she would be seeing a lot more of it as her daughter got older, and she didn't look forward to it.

"Be home by five o' clock. Tell Rachel I said so." Abby watched as Maggie ran toward Rachel and Hattie, who were waiting in the front of the café. Rachel waved before guiding the girls out of the door through a shaft of bright sunlight.

"It's my turn to close today," Abby said to Ramone, who was rising to leave. She glanced over at a man sitting alone at the chessboard table. He was dark and nice looking, maybe forty, and totally focused on his solitary game. He held a rook in midair with his left hand.

Ramone leaned in for a peck on her cheek. "Don't throw any scent over there. He's got a wife and kids in Belén."

"He should be wearing a ring," Abby said.

"He's an electrician. Damn good one, too, if you need one of those." Ramone laughed, enjoying her flush of embarrassment. She knew her fair skin must be ablaze.

"Later, mi'ja." Ramone smoothed his khaki shirt, tapped his badge, and strode away, his black boots striking the wood floor and accenting his swagger.

Abby started to bus the last of the abandoned tables. Three o'clock, and they were officially closed. If she hurried, she would have some time to herself before Maggie came home. An errand? The library? A run?

"We did good today," CeCe remarked from behind the counter. She was going over receipts, bagging up the cash and checks. "Like always," she added with a sigh.

Abby dumped her dishes into the tub, and Leo, their dishwasher, quickly hauled it into the back. She put her arm around CeCe, and the two stood that way for a moment. Abby could feel CeCe lean into her before breaking away and shaking her head. More gray had appeared at CeCe's temples, contrasting with the long dark hair around her shoulders. Weariness was starting to age her normally youthful face. Yet a worry line or two on her brow, a deepening of the lines near her eyes still didn't cause her to look nearly sixty. Even with the stress in her life, she appeared a decade younger.

CeCe smiled. "I love being here, being busy. It's so simple. So peaceful." So unlike home, she didn't need to add.

"How are they today?"

"The day started with my mother complaining that our cheap soap was drying out her skin. Then we argued about how she needs to drink more water here in New Mexico. Then Papa showed up with a ketchup sandwich he'd made, dripping it all over the floor and his shirt, which he'd put on inside out. Thank God Miguel was already out in the fields somewhere."

"Where are they now?"

"Carmen has them today. Her martyr complex makes her perfect for the job. She'll be canonized by the pope before this is over. Santi didn't come in today?"

"I don't know what's up with that boy. He's not home much lately, and when he is he's quiet and moody. Won't talk about it, of course."

"Sounds like love," CeCe said with a grin. "Now you're in for it."

"No, he needs to wait until he's off to school for that. We don't need any last minute relationship derailing his plans." Abby knew even as she said the words how powerless she was to prevent such a thing.

CeCe reached for her purse under the counter. "Good luck. I need to get to the bank and then relieve Carmen. She may be a Catholic saint-in-waiting, but they're a couple of old Jewish *tievels*."

Abby finished wiping down the counter and checked on Leo in

the back. He was hanging up his apron. "Time to call it a day?" he asked in his usual deferring manner.

"Sure, Leo. Say hi to Florecita for me." Abby knew he was on his way to his evening job at a Los Lunas convenience store and it would be long after dark before he returned home to his wife and three young children.

He left through the back door, and Abby locked it securely after him. She wandered back into the front to do a final check and turn off the swamp cooler.

"I guess I better get out of here before I'm locked in for the night." The chess-playing married electrician appeared behind her. He smiled and held his empty coffee cup out to her.

She was so startled she nearly dropped the cup as she tried to take it from him. They fumbled it back and forth until she finally got a secure grip on it, only to find his fingers caught under hers. He carefully reclaimed them. She couldn't believe anyone was still here without her knowing it. But the chess and checkerboard area was tucked around the corner in front of the small stage.

"Sorry, I guess I got so focused on my game I tuned out. Sorry," he said again.

"No, no, that's fine. Come again. Anytime."

He smiled warmly. "Yeah, I will. I'm wiring that new housing development across the highway, so I'll be in the neighborhood. Have a good night."

"Yeah, you too," Abby said, refraining from giving her regards to his wife.

When the door closed behind him, she realized she was trembling. Jesus! What was the matter with her? Lathering over some married guy? Was she giving off some scent? Her heart pounded as defiant hormones coursed through her veins.

Santiago sat at a back corner table in a Bosque Farms fast food restaurant. A carton of half-eaten french fries, cooling, lay in front of him. He took a swig of his soda and felt strangely satisfied to be performing this secret gesture of defiance. Abby hated "fast food joints," as she referred to them, and blamed them for all manner of social and physical ills their society suffered.

Normally he'd be at the Esperanza Café, having an afterschool snack while everybody fawned over him. It was enough to make a guy puke sometimes. "Oh, Santi, I heard your story was published in a real magazine." Or the currently annoying "Have you written your graduation speech yet? We're so proud of you!" Abby looking on, hearing it all, that look on her face.

At least here people left him alone. He looked down at his chewed fingernails, glistening with grease, and wiped them off with a napkin before reaching for his leather-bound legal pad. He'd received the black leather notebook as a birthday gift from Charlie a few years back, and it held his writing stuff, including a killer cobalt blue pen Miguel had given him for Christmas.

He let the fast food frenzy around him recede into the background until he was alone with his thoughts. He jiggled the pen in his hand, fighting a collision of conflicting feelings and flickers of thought fragments that sounded like radio static. It was getting harder to focus, to concentrate. It had never been a problem until lately. He used to be able to pick up pen and pad and the whole world would melt away and his hand and brain were one as sentences seemed to scrawl themselves across the page. He tried not to think about it, afraid the more he tried to figure it out the worse it would get.

Doodling loosened him up sometimes, so he began to scratch his pen around the margins of the page. His hand gripped the pen and pressed hard into the paper. Sharp jagged lines, pointed arrows, angry faces.

For no damn reason his perfect life felt like someone else's. People he knew he loved were bugging the hell out of him. They hadn't changed. He had, and he didn't know why or how to stop it or if he even wanted to stop it. It was dark and powerful and seductive, as if some hidden place inside of him had ripped open and its poison was seeping into his mind, his soul.

When the letter came a few months back, congratulating him on his award of scholarship and admittance into the writing program at UCLA, he was gut-busting thrilled. He'd been so happy. They threw a big party for him.

He grabbed a fistful of cold french fries and stuffed them into his mouth. One minute he couldn't wait to get the hell out of this place, and the next he felt like he was being thrown out against his will, which was stupid and made no sense. He remembered his therapist, back after he saw his dad blow his own brains out, say that feelings didn't have to make sense.

"Hey, Baca, I know you." A guy stood over him, late twenties, maybe thirty. He had on the uniform of a gangbanger, complete with stocking cap and gold chains. But with the hip-hop thing so trendy, who could tell anymore. Even rich white boys got decked out like that.

"Silva," Santiago corrected. "Santiago *Silva.*"

The guy sat down and helped himself to a french fry. He was big, all bulked up, probably spent hours at it in some filthy garage, lifting weights all day with his homeboys. A snake tattoo wound around his thick neck, its beady red snake eyes peered out from under his jaw.

"Can't fool me, dog, I used to hang with your Uncle Manny and your old man. I'm James, remember me? James Ortiz. I heard that white chick adopted you, but that don't make you no Silva. You're Baca."

Santiago felt the lump of greasy fries turn over in his stomach.

"She ain't even no real Silva, she only married Silva. She's just some *guera.*" The guy grinned at him, half-chewed french fries adhered to his teeth.

It was tempting to get pissed off, but that was clearly what the guy wanted. "You knew my dad and uncle?"

"Yeah, I ran with them from the time I was a kid. Just got out of *la pinta*, the penitentiary. I was with your uncle. Manny says to tell you hi and he'll see you in a couple of years."

His Uncle Manny was doing time for his part in Bobby's murder. Accessory after the fact. He had driven Bobby's truck to Juarez to throw off the investigation, gotten some man to lie and say Bobby had been there and was on his way to Baja. Manny would hit Santi for no reason, and after he moved in when Santi was five, their whole life turned to shit. That's when Santi still believed his mom had run away and left him behind. Before he knew his dad had beaten her to death and buried her under the rooster house. They only found her because they were digging up Bobby.

Santiago shook his head. "Manny can go to hell."

James frowned. "*La familia*, Santiago. Manny is doing hard time for helping your dad, his brother. You're all brainwashed. Shit, man! Manny is your blood, *tu sangre*. Your dad killed that punk Bobby in self-defense. He was drunk and threatening and was going to throw Manny, your dad, and your skinny ass out on the streets. You should be grateful they loved you enough to try to protect you! Damn, you don't get it."

"My dad had us there illegally. He wasn't even paying rent anymore. He beat on the old man, Bobby's father, to get him to say we bought the house. He stole it right out from under him, and Bobby knew it." Santiago heard his words come out flat and felt a strange calmness settle into him. He couldn't care less if the guy jumped him or pulled out a gun.

But James did no such thing. He just looked at him a long time. His eyes welled with tears. "I feel sorry for you. I don't even blame you for how fucked up you are. Your dad was a great man who loved you more than his own life. He sacrificed everything for you. Manny, too. But who cares, no? You came out on top, rich woman adopts you, hell, you got it made. Who could blame you?"

James shoved the last of the french fries back toward Santiago and got up to leave. "See you around, kid."

Santiago waited until he was sure James had left the parking lot. Then, he gathered up his notebook and backpack and pushed past the dinner-time crowd getting their fast food fixes. The hot grease smell was making him sick. Pushing open the door, he took a big gulp of fresh air and headed for his car. He stopped short of it, as if seeing it for the first time. The Camry, pearl finish a little worn, but the same car Abby and Bobby had bought right before moving out here from San Diego. He'd been so excited when he turned fifteen and Abby presented him with the title and the keys. Now it seemed obscene. This wasn't his car. It was a dead man's car.

He opened it up and threw his stuff into the back seat. It wasn't like Abby couldn't afford another car. She had bought herself a brand new Volvo wagon. He'd even have taken some old piece of shit; at least it wouldn't have been Bobby's car. Yet he'd been so happy with it at the time. It had seemed like some kind of honor.

He pulled out into the stream of heavy traffic on Highway 47. Commuters coming home for the day. More and more people moved down here from Albuquerque, looking for the peaceful country life, and they were screwing it up for the people who had lived here for generations. He'd written a paper on it for sociology class and gotten an A.

James's face kept appearing in whatever car was whizzing by. James's words were louder in his head than the music from the car radio. Manny was his only living relative that anyone could find, so he'd been lucky Abby wanted him. Manny was a mean son of a bitch, at least when he was drinking, and Santi couldn't remember a time he wasn't. Now he was sitting up in prison. Ten years for driving a truck to Mexico and telling a lie for his brother. Tu sangre.

The turnoff came before he realized it, and he had to do a sudden left turn in front of traffic and blaring horns. He drove fast down the rutted dirt road, the car dipping and jerking, a cloud of dust in his rearview mirror.

He slammed on the brakes when he got to the fork in the road.

Right turn to the Vigils' place and Rachel and Charlie's house. Left for home. Straight ahead, where his old house had been, was nothing. After they dug up Bobby and found Santi's mother, there were two funerals. Then Abby had it bulldozed. Not that it was anything great. It was a dump by the time his family had lived in it twelve years, from even before his birth. Before all the trouble. Bobby and his dad, Ricardo Silva, had built it with their own two hands on half an acre with trees, and it had probably been real nice once. Before all the junked cars and trash piled up and the weeds grew into a tall jungle to hide behind. His dad and uncle had built the rooster house for their cockfighting obsession, and soon there were about a million of them crowing twenty-four hours a day. Roosters still incited bad feelings and memories in him.

He hadn't seen the bulldozers come, but he had heard them. It was like thunder on a clear day. After trucks hauled the debris away, there was nothing left but freshly turned-over soil, like a new garden or a fresh grave. Now it was filled in and covered over with grasses and wildflowers and one scraggly elm tree. As if the house had never been there at all.

The dashboard clock read five thirty. Abby would be wondering about dinner. The inside of his mouth held the greasy taste like a guilty secret. He tried to swallow it away as he turned the car left.

Abby heard the car pull in while still trying to decide how to play this. Tough or casual? Ignore it, or use it to talk about all the other recent changes she'd seen in him?

"Sorry," Santi said as he entered, starting to brush past her with his backpack toward his bedroom.

"Santi, please have a seat. We need to talk." Even as she said the words, Abby was looking at her son with a melting heart. He was getting so handsome, so beautiful with his straight jaw and curved dark eyebrows. She loved his hair long and pulled back in his tight ponytail at the nape of his neck. His brown skin was perfect, never pimply like that of his friends. She took some pride in that, since she'd raised him to avoid fast food.

He nodded but didn't look at her, pulled out a kitchen chair, and sat at the table. "Where's Maggie?"

Abby sat down. "She begged to eat over at Hattie's. Charlie was going to make cowboy food outdoors." Abby smiled. Charlie was famous for his steaks or hotdogs and beans cooked over an open fire. He would be singing and playing old-time cowboy songs for them on his guitar.

"Did you eat?" Abby asked in a sudden maternal reflex.

"I'm not hungry."

"Santi, I'm worried about you. It seems like you've been so down about something or preoccupied. You haven't been your usual self and—"

"Abby, I'm fine." He said it a little too loudly.

She sat a moment. He had called her Abby. Not Mom. Abby. She'd never asked him to call her Mom, but he had started one day, even before the adoption was final, and had never stopped. Until now.

"I mean, Mom," he corrected after a beat.

"I've never forced you to call me Mom."

Santi sighed his teenager sigh. "Look, I'm just busy, all right? I'm graduating in like a week, I've got that stupid speech to do at graduation. Finals, papers . . ."

"Are you sure that's all?" Abby asked as quietly as she could and still be saying it out loud.

"Isn't that enough?" His dark eyes challenged her.

Abby tried to calm herself. Her heart was pounding. It was always so hard for her to have any conflict with Santiago. With Maggie, they could both yell or cry and be over it ten minutes later. Santiago had always been so sensitive, so fragile. Especially in the beginning. "Mrs. Lara called looking for you. She said you missed some graduation committee meeting at four thirty in her office."

"Shit. Sorry." Santiago looked up at the ceiling, his jaw clenched, little muscles twitching in his cheek. "I totally spaced it."

"Where did you go after you dropped off the girls? That was almost three hours ago."

"It's only five forty-five! Jesus! It's not like it's midnight or something. Give me a break."

Abby made herself stop the barrage of knee-jerk lines wanting to spew out. He was probably just exercising a little independence. He'd be on his own in few short months, in Los Angeles of all places.

"You're right about it not being that late. It's just a lot of little things, like your mood lately, changing little habits like not checking in with me, missing your meeting. Put it all together, and it has my mom radar going. Usually we've been able to talk about anything and everything. I want to respect your privacy, but at the same time, I feel shut out. I want to help you."

"Okay! Take my finals, write my papers, and, oh, there's that graduation speech, while you're at it." His sarcasm was like a slap to her cheek.

Abby felt tears start to sting her eyes and struggled to hold them back. "Santi, we have three short months before you go. It's hard on both of us, this transition, anticipating you leaving. After all the wonderful times we've had together here under this roof, I just want our time left to be good . . . for both of us. So we have to figure out how to let go without making it harder for each other."

"It's not like I'm dying. It's just college," Santi said, watching her flick away a tear.

"But it's huge. You won't be here for months at a time. It seems like only yesterday you moved in here with me. Even before that, before they found Bobby, you practically lived here. Remember how fat and pregnant I was? And even though you were barely ten, you took care of me and I took care of you. We were both so sad, but we had each other." She was crying in earnest now, and it felt good. "I know you have to grow up and go away. I just want you to understand how hard it is for me."

Her son reached for her and held her head against his shoulder. She could feel his pulse throb in his warm neck. "I love you, too, Mom."

But even as he held her tightly and said the words another time, she felt as if she were losing him and it had nothing to do with college.

CHAPTER 3

S even years after her Great-aunt Maria's death, Rachel found
it easier to go through her things, which, although meager,
all belonged to her now. They were in a carved Mexican
chest in her closet, covered by the Mexican lace tablecloth Maria
had on the table she had used for her ceremonies and remedies.
She was an excellent *curandera* but had always ventured into the
dark side of things: the gossip, the unfaithful husbands wanting
cures against their wives' curses, and she double-dipping by treating them both at the same time. And besides Rachel's, Maria had
performed her share of abortions in a room next to her wall of crucified Jesuses and a perpetually lit candle. Maria had lied to the
Lord her whole life, but most of all she had lied to herself.

Rachel saw that now, which made her great-aunt's memory
more sympathetic. She felt ready to pan through their relationship
for the gold nuggets and to forgive Maria's trespasses. Her great-
aunt's goodness had become derailed. Maria had been, after all, a
revered curandera in her youth.

Rachel laughed softly as she looked at a photograph she had
taken of Maria with her old goat, Buster, when he was a baby.

Maria smiled while he nibbled at her silver hoop earring. Maria's top gums were almost as toothless as his. She flipped to another picture. Maria was trying to pull her broom skirt from the rotating jaws of Buster, her arms like tanned hide. Big old Nikes on her feet. Buster's tail wagged blurrily in delight.

She remembered that time with Maria. The time before the untreated diabetes and her ventures into the dark side. That time when her *tía*'s laugh didn't smell like stale tequila and osha root, and when right and wrong did not have a fuzzy line between them, and then no line at all. But Rachel had wanted to reclaim Abby's "Bobby," her Roberto, so badly back then, she easily blinded herself to the blackness in Maria's magic. The blackness in herself.

Under Maria's black and red flowered shawl in the chest was a green velvet book that Rachel thought was an old Bible. But when she opened the pages, she realized it was a book of remedies and incantations Maria had written to hand down to her. Maria had taught her about herbs; their smells, their tastes, and their cures. Their danger. How powerful Rachel had felt to hold something deadly in her hands. Only to plead with God, Jesus, the Virgin Mary, whomever really listened, and to give them her solemn promise that if she was born a bruja, she'd always be a good bruja.

Rachel had stuffed the book under the shawl herself when putting away Maria's effects after her death. She had been angry with her and didn't want anything to do with her crazy aunt's belongings. But as she flipped through the pages with the familiar scrawl, she had memories of her tía treating women who wanted to conceive. Some desperately wanting a child to love, and some desperately trying to hold onto their men, who sat too comfortably on a noncommittal edge and eyed other women. She wasn't angry at Maria anymore. There had been beautiful times that created cherished memories, before it had turned so wrong. With a great sadness, she knew the book held no miracles to grow back her missing womb.

Rachel wrapped the black and red shawl around her and tied

it. Then she pulled the heavy chest from the depths of her dark closet out into the sunlight. She put the tooled Mexican silver hoops in her ears and picked up the book with its yellowed pages. Under the cover an inscription read simply: "Mi'ja." And she could swear she heard her Tía Maria whisper the endearment from her grave.

CeCe hurried through the bills from the café. It was late, and she was hiding in her sewing room, where she had converted her sewing table into a large desk. She knew Miguel was waiting for her at their favorite romantic spot in the house, the kiva fireplace tucked in the corner of a sunken room off the kitchen. It was surrounded by finely plastered adobe seating, *bancos*, covered with various Navajo blankets. A four-foot adobe wall separated the room from the kitchen, lending some privacy. A sheepskin rug lay on the floor in front of the fireplace. He probably had the wine open and breathing. She couldn't wait. Her parents had been there a week, and she and Miguel hadn't had any real time with each other, just the exhausted peck goodnight before plummeting into sleep.

When she was done, she slipped into a gauze dressing gown from India and examined herself in the mirror. Although she was almost sixty, things were holding up pretty well. Particularly her breasts, which she attributed to years of farm work. Schlepping equaled perky. But her eyes looked back at her, and in them she saw a dullness, something that created a stranger in the mirror. She brushed out her shoulder-length hair, dabbed some honeysuckle oil on the hollow of her throat, wrists, and the backs of her knees, and hurried to meet Miguel.

The house was completely dark except for the small fire in the kiva. The wineglasses sparkled in the glow. Her breath gave a little catch as she saw Miguel laying there, waiting. She lingered a moment before rushing in. He remained just as attractive to her as when they had met. She knew she was luckier than most women. She bet there was not a woman in Esperanza who did not envy her.

He was more than willing to embrace her as she snuggled up next to him. His arms were warm and comforting. She unbuttoned his shirt and slipped her hand along his hairy chest. The familiar curls greeted the ends of her fingers.

"I've missed you so much," she said and sighed against him. "I'm feeling really needy." He smelled of sandalwood soap.

"Mmm, you feel just fine to me," he said, caressing her breast.

She smiled. "As long as we can have our little world, I know I can get through anything." She could feel his heartbeats thumping against her ear and tried not to think of them numbered. She didn't know what she would do if she ever lost him.

"You have been the most wonderful wife. For forty years you've worked as hard as me to keep this farm going," Miguel said.

She knew the pain that writhed through him as each rainless day continued. She hoped she eased some of his to the extent he did for her. Sometimes she felt his pain more than her own. "I love you, Miguel. I love you more than ever." She had never been more sure of that fact, but still she felt a nagging pull. A sense of dread competed with her lust. Dread becoming fear . . . but of what? Trying to pinpoint it exactly was like trying to catch a slippery, elusive goldfish, so she ignored the distracting worry that throbbed its warning in her mind.

He bent to kiss her. He was already breathing hard as his tongue reached for hers. It tasted like the merlot. His hands held her face, a slight smell of Bag Balm.

She let him ease her back on the rug. Off came his shirt and pants. Up came her gown. She almost started to laugh, thinking that after forty years she still couldn't wait. Her lips met his as he entered her.

CRASH! BONG! BANG! Then a light in the kitchen. They stopped moving. Through the opening of the adobe wall, they could see into the other room. There, a naked Mort bent over, looking in the refrigerator. His cheeks spread before them in silhouette; his testicles dangled halfway down to his knees.

Suddenly the elusive, nagging goldfish jumped right into her hands.

Mort seemed more interested in the farm than Rose did. She sat on the porch and yelled, "Aw, shut up!" to the rooster every time it crowed, which was a lot this particular afternoon. CeCe had found an old pair of overalls for Mort, which he proudly wore out to the garden with her. Although it was the last week of May, it was already hot, warning of a scorching summer.

"See these weeds, Papa?" asked CeCe, handing him a hoe. "All you need to do is just dig them out gently, see?" She gave a few small swipes at the mustard weed, which gave up easily in the well-tilled soil. She didn't expect him to be any good at it; after all, he was eighty-six. But he insisted on trying, and it might be good for him to do something constructive.

"You act as if I've never done this before. I was raising food for my family back in Poland when I was a kid, I'll have you know," he said, going to work.

She had also given him a wide-brimmed hat to protect him from the sun, which beat down through the thin air, and she made sure he wore a long-sleeved shirt under his bib overalls. The only color on his face was liver spots. Sometimes on a day like today the sun could burn a person in a very short time. It was deceiving. She realized he was like having another child around to take care of. He poked at the soil with the hoe, barely missing the delicate new squash plants coming up as CeCe winced.

"Aw, shut up!" Rose yelled in the distance. CeCe didn't even hear the rooster anymore after all this time. But she could hear Rose.

Mort gave a disgruntled wave toward the house. "She drives me nuts," he said. His sixty-year-old wedding band hung loose on his withering hand, which was dotted with various-sized brown liver spots. He reminded her of one of those dried apple dolls sold at the village fairs.

Rachel waved from the goat barn. "Hi, Ma! Hi, *Zeyde*!" she yelled as her friskiest goat, Lily, gave her a side butt to the stomach. "No! Bad girl!" she said and smacked her on the nose. Lily stood up on her hind legs, wanting to engage Rachel in a good butting match. She pushed the goat away several times as Lily refused to stop her shenanigans. Finally Rachel grabbed her around the neck and pulled her into the barn, signaling a time-out for Lily in a stall.

"We had a goat in Warsaw, for milk. Tasted awful. Jumped in our old produce truck and ate the fiber stuffing out of the upholstery. My mother wouldn't let me shoot her. Said the milk would help fatten my *toches* so I wouldn't need cushioning under it. That goat was a *chazzer*!" He made snorting sounds like a pig.

CeCe laughed. He rarely made mention of any other life but the one he had created with Rose in Brooklyn. Then again, he had never talked to her much when she was a child. As far as she knew, he had come from Poland and built a fairly successful tailoring business in New York, like a lot of Jewish immigrants. The generic American dream. And seldom had he ever made her laugh. Or anyone else she could recall. "Did you like Poland?" she asked.

Mort gave a faraway look that turned glassy. "My mother liked flowers. She kept a beautiful garden." He went back to hoeing.

"I never knew that."

"You are like her in ways. I named you after her. Her name was Cecelia, but she was called Chilke," he said and began singing softly, something in Yiddish that had a longing, yet soothing quality—maybe a lullaby? She couldn't quite hear the words. The only time he ever sang was during a *broche*, and even then, he didn't carry a melody.

CeCe knew her grandmother had died young in Poland—still in her late thirties. But what she hadn't known was that it had meant something to him when he named her after his own mother. Did that mean she had meant something, too?

CeCe knew so little about any of her father's family. Rose's family, all of whom had lived in Brooklyn, dominated her early life. She did meet a cousin of her father's once, a skinny, bearded man whose eyes were sadly sunken and dark. He stayed two nights and only spoke Yiddish to her parents, and he always wore a hat, even indoors.

Mort's singing changed. It became pressured and more like wailing. The song was different. He chopped at the weeds as if they were more than just pesky.

"Papa, are you okay?" CeCe asked. She saw the death grip he had on his hoe, his blue veins protruding from the backs of his white hands. "Papa?"

"A *finstere cholem*, a *finstere cholem*," he chanted. A dark dream. A dark dream.

CeCe got to her feet and put her hand on Mort's shoulder. She could almost physically feel him slip away. "Papa!" she said sternly. She gave his arm a little pull back to reality.

He started to fight her off, his weak arms flailing at her. "*Ei! Ei!*"

She barely dodged a smack in the head. She tried to grab him, maybe get him in some kind of basket hold. He was so old and fragile, she wasn't sure what to do.

"*Mameh, Mameh, drigeh nist, Mameh!*" He was yelling at his mother not to worry.

Rachel came running out from the barn.

"Rachel, help!" CeCe screamed as her father tried to get away from her. "I can't get him calmed down." She got hold of his arm again, his skin papery thin.

"Mordecai, Mordecai," Rachel said, continuing to repeat his name until he focused on her face. "It's okay, it's okay now." She smiled, and he smiled back.

There was recognition in his eyes and tenderness in his expression. His body relaxed under CeCe's grip. His face was hot pink from screaming. His chest heaved. They set him gently on the soft ground, crushing some of CeCe's zucchini. But he never took his eyes off of Rachel.

"Nothing he does surprises me anymore," Rose said to CeCe and Rachel, reaching for a piece of raisin cake. "He'll sleep for a couple of hours now, and when he wakes up—who knows?" She was dressed as if someone was picking her up to go play golf at the country club. Her small eighty-two-year-old paunch protruded from under her braided cord belt.

"Does he get like that often?" asked CeCe. Her stomach churned with the thought of things being worse than she had imagined, which was unthinkable.

"Sometimes he forgets what decade he's in. There have been many mornings he hasn't recognized me. But I have the same feeling when I look in the mirror. He's hard to handle sometimes, but what can I do? Put him away at the Jewish nursing home? Who can afford that? Anyway, your papa deserves better. He's from Warsaw, you know." Rose peered over her glasses at them to accentuate her meaning. Genuine pain shone in her eyes.

"Papa always told us that he fled the Nazis, came to America, and met you."

"Your papa never talked about it much, not even to me, his own wife. He fled the Nazis all right. From Treblinka." Her hand was up to God and trembling. "Hid in a railway car under the very piles of clothing he had loaded on after the gassings."

"What? The death camp?" CeCe asked.

Rose checked over her shoulder to make sure no one was around. "His job in Treblinka was to sort through the clothes and belongings of everyone who had gone to the baths. Those usually were the only ones who had a chance to escape, the ones who loaded the railcars. He told me that they didn't care if you filled your own pockets because they planned to kill you and go through

  Sue Boggio and Mare Pearl

your things as well. His pockets were bulging when he escaped, but it still couldn't buy him a place to stay outside the camp. The peasants in Treblinka wouldn't have him. He was only twenty years old." She shook her head.

CeCe stared, mouth agape, as the words caught up to her and registered. "What did he do?"

"He hid for a while outside of Warsaw, then escaped through the sewers. He had the means to be smuggled out from there," Rose answered. "He never told me too many details. But I've heard stories. Makes me sick to my stomach. Until he lost all our money, he donated regularly to the survivors of the victims whose jewels and money he pocketed to get out of Poland."

"What he said just now to his mother. Told her not to worry." CeCe's eyes were filling with tears. What horror for a mother and child to go through. It wrung out her heart. Who was this man she felt tears for? No one she had ever met.

"They shot her right in front of him. A random thing after they lined them up in the street. Too bad it's the short-term memory you lose. When he refers to that time, he calls it his dark dream." Rose didn't cry as she spoke. Her wrinkled, dehydrated face looked as if she had already cried herself dry years ago. "It's mine, too."

CeCe had had no idea. In that moment her mother seemed like a stranger as well. "Rachel was able to reach him during his episode. He seemed to know her as someone else," said CeCe.

"He called me Zofia. That's a beautiful name," Rachel said. "Who was she?"

Rose shifted uncomfortably, as if there wasn't sixty-five years between her and this Zofia. "She was your grandfather's fiancée in Poland. They shot her, too."

Rachel and Charlie's house sat on an acreage closer to the river but still on the Vigil property, which was named *Sol y Sombra*,

Sunlight and Shadow. It was where Charlie's small silver hump-backed trailer had sat when they had been temporarily divorced almost nine years earlier. When they remarried, they built a traditional Texas farmhouse, complete with a wraparound porch. There was something about Charlie that never left Texas, even though Rachel didn't think much of the Lone Star State, a common attitude in New Mexico. Most of the time Charlie kept their horses up at the Vigil barn, but today Charlie's longtime buddy, Sweetwater, and Rachel's strawberry roan, Tie-dye, named for his colors that seemed to run together, were there for shoeing.

Tie-dye whinnied as Rachel entered the barn. "Hi, sweetie," she cooed as she reached to rub his muzzle. Tie-dye snorted in happiness. "How's my handsome man today?" She reached in her pocket and produced a couple of sugar cubes, which Tie-dye scooped up with his curling lips and crunched.

"This handsome man is going to hire a farrier. I'm not going to be able to keep up with the trimming and shoeing this year. I ain't getting any younger, and there's just too much to do around here and at your father's as it is," Charlie said.

He didn't look any older to her, although she knew his forty-third birthday was around the corner. His face seemed more handsome than ever, weathered, maybe, but not aged. She could hardly believe there had been a span of time when she had thought she was better off well rid of him. Thank God for his tenacity.

"Do it, honey, give yourself a break. I came out to let you know that Hattie is over with Ma and Rose. She was determined to have *Bubbe* watch *Peter Pan* with her. Hattie said *Bubbe* reminded her of Captain Hook sometimes and Mort acts like he's from Never Never Land."

Charlie laughed, his dimples creasing his face. "I can see that."

"Zeyde's on some new medication that zonks him out, so he's sleeping."

"Uh-huh," he said, shaving off pieces of hoof.

"So I'll be up at the house for the next couple of hours if you need me," she said.

Charlie stopped and smiled. "Okay, babe. Sure you don't want to stay here with me? This new straw is awful soft. Care to have a roll in it with me?"

She smiled back. That was just like him. "You know where to find me."

As if Rachel didn't have enough to do with the goat dairy, cheese business, and café, when she was home she not only mothered Hattie but also tended her indoor plants, which flourished all over the house. The sunroom was her greenhouse; there she started her cuttings, germinated seedlings for her outside garden, and nursed ill plants back to life. It was her inside sanctuary and her favorite place, next to the goat barn. Rachel had covered the floor with bricks Charlie had reclaimed from an old torn-down schoolhouse in Mountainair, so runoff from watering plants was not a concern. She constantly needed to be creating, growing, and nurturing things in her life.

Her mother's creativity showed in her excellent seamstress skills. CeCe had made Rachel's wedding dress the second time she'd wed Charlie, the real time. She was already gloriously pregnant with Hattie. This sewing thing ran in the family, as Mort had been learning to be a tailor in Poland before the war. It had been his family's business, and it was the business Mort had started in Brooklyn after his escape. CeCe had never worked in the family business, but she had taken sewing classes in high school and was really good at it. Rachel figured it had to be in the genes.

When she became pregnant with Hattie, it happened in the whirlwind of her and Charlie getting back together. Even though they were having sex all the time then, pregnancy had still felt like a miracle instead of something inevitable. She had loved being pregnant with Hattie. Charlie became even more of a prince to her. He had fawned over her so. And over the baby. They included Hattie, the fetus, in everything: music, books, horseback riding. Rachel laughed to herself thinking that they had created this six-year-old child who ended up being way too smart for her own good.

"Yoo-hoo, honey, I'm home!" Charlie yodeled from the kitchen back door in his teasing voice. He opened the fridge and guzzled cold water from a glass pitcher. He had taken his shirt off and was already looking quite tan.

"You're done early," said Rachel, watching him from the doorway.

"You said if I needed anything, I'd know where to find you," he said, grinning with wet lips. "Now don't go tellin' me that wasn't a come-on out there in the barn. Making sure I knew Hattie wasn't home." He shifted hips. "I know that look." He sauntered toward her and grabbed her in an embrace. It was more than his zipper seam pushing against her as he kissed her with a soft tongue.

Rachel reached for his hand and led him to the staircase. He laughed and picked her up, carrying her up the stairs as if they were in her favorite scene from *Gone with the Wind.* She felt his strength as he bounded up the stairs.

And when he laid her down on the bed, she reached for him with joy. But then, for a brief moment, she remembered there would be no baby from this, no matter how hard she prayed. She tried to count the blessings she had, not the ones that were missing. But even as Charlie's love filled her, a small space remained empty.

CHAPTER 4

Even though it was a Friday night and the café was closed, it had never been so packed full of people. Miguel had spread the word through the bosque of the Rio Grande River Valley that farmers and interested community members would meet to discuss the drought and subsequent water shortage. They had held these meetings before, but as the situation became more dire, attendance was increasing.

Tables were shoved back and extra chairs brought in; still, there were people standing in clumps in the back. A din of simultaneous conversations in both Spanish and English heightened the sense of expectation in the room. The small stage served as the focal point. The microphone Miguel or Charlie occasionally sang into would now be a mouthpiece for the farmers.

Abby watched from behind the counter, where she handed out complimentary coffee and iced tea. She noticed not a few folks had walked in with their own bottles of beer in hand.

Rachel stood next to her, a bundle of nerves. "I hope Ma is doing all right at home. Mort was a real handful today, and Rose is no help at all." Her hand absentmindedly reached for the ends of her long dark curls, her fingers twirling at strands.

"Wasn't the cabal coming over to sit with her?" Abby asked. She loved the nickname of CeCe's tight trio of women friends who would do anything for one another.

"Hazel was definitely coming, which is great. Her old nursing skills are coming in handy, I'll tell you. Plus nothing ever ruffles her. I guess she's seen it all. Carmen is good with him, too, though she's wearing a smaller crucifix these days, hidden under her blouse, since Mort tried to yank her big one off and about took her head along with it."

"And Bonnie? Is she coming?" Abby asked, practically having to shout over the crowd's voices, which seemed to be getting louder.

"She and Rose usually end up fighting, so Ma was hoping she'd go out dancing like she usually does on a Friday night. I'm glad Santi could watch the girls. I'd hate to keep track of them in this mob."

"He was going to take them to a movie in Los Lunas. He was actually cheerful about it. You never know with him these days." Just as Abby looked at her watch and saw that it was finally seven o'clock, Miguel took the stage. She couldn't see him, since the stage was around the corner from the counter, but she heard his softly accented voice over the microphone.

Rachel put a hand on her shoulder. "Can you handle this? I want to get where I can see. Charlie saved me a place down front."

"I'm fine. Go." Abby poured herself some iced tea and took a long swig. Getting dehydrated was a simple matter of forgetting to drink something for a few hours. She held the cold, sweating glass against her warm cheek and closed her eyes. The swamp cooler was on full blast, but with this many people and a high temperature of ninety-eight degrees that afternoon, she barely felt it. The crowd quieted as Miguel offered his *bienvenidos*, his welcome.

She opened her eyes to a man staring at her. He was quite tall, so she had to turn her face up. He smiled, put a hand up to the brim of his hat as if tipping it to her.

"I heard a gent might get himself a cold tea here." His slightly raspy voice held some kind of British accent. His face was a day or two out from a shave, his brown hair was shaggy around his sweating neck and face. Brown eyes connected with hers.

"Uh, sure." Abby grabbed a glass and poured too fast. A chunk of ice fell and splashed tea all over the counter. As she reached for a rag, he grabbed paper napkins, and their hands collided. Laughing, they mopped up the mess.

The man held the handful of soggy paper out to her. "Sorry. Do you have a bin?"

She took the dripping wad and tossed it into the trash. "Do you live around here?"

"I'm down from Albuquerque. By way of Australia. Been here a few years now. I teach at the University of New Mexico. I came down to hear how the farmers are coping. Ben Frasier." He put out his hand.

"Abby Silva." Abby gave it a quick, firm shake.

"Pleasure to meet you, Abigail, and thanks for the tea. It's fresh and strong. I like that." He turned and made his way back into the crowd.

Her eyes followed his hat until he reemerged against the back wall. Leaning, taking a drink of tea, looking at the stage and not back at her. She came out from behind the counter so she could see Miguel.

"So there is a lot happening, and if we don't stay informed and get involved no one will look out for us," Miguel was saying over a roar of applause and whistling. "Who would like to speak?"

An Anglo man took the stage. "Hi, most of you know me, Harvey Doyle. I farm a couple hundred acres over by Belén. That land has been in my family since the 1890s, and I'll be damned if I have to lose it on account a some damn silvery minnow! The feds have no stinking right to take our water to save something we ought to be using for fish bait! Endangered species my ass! We're the endangered species!"

He nodded and raised his fist as the crowd went wild. "Aren't we supposed to be the government by the people, for the people? Or is it by the minnow, for the minnow? But here they are, that Tenth Circuit Court, saying they get to use our water to save a fish. We're in a long drought. A double drought—no rain in the summer monsoons and no snowpack to refill the aquifers up north. Even if the Middle Rio Grande Conservancy District says we can have two feet of irrigation water per acre, that don't mean shit if it ain't there!" He handed the microphone over to a man who had joined him.

The elder Hispanic man put the microphone under his arm so he could clap Harvey off the stage. Then he put it below his lips and spoke in a quiet voice. "Friends and neighbors, I'm so happy to see so much unity and energy. We have a tough road ahead of us. I am Juan Armendáriz. My family's farm is east of Tome. I've seen times of drought before, some worse than now. We pray to San Ysidro. We grow our chile and we plant more dry crops like alfalfa. We get through. But now we have cheap Mexican chile coming up from south of the border, cross-pollinating and damaging our pure race strains and keeping prices low even as expenses rise. We have a bad economy. We have all these new agencies and committees from the state or the federal government and the City of Albuquerque making rules and laws and treating water like it is some commodity that can be bought and sold to the highest bidder. I'm frightened. I am eighty-three years old. I remember the Great Depression and the Dust Bowl, and it was bad, but what water we had we didn't fight over. We shared. We didn't talk about putting tiny little fish over human suffering. We didn't have rich upstream city people making thirsty golf courses from desert land or greedy developers building thousands and thousands of new houses without any thought to where the water will come from. They weren't damming up the river and creating reservoirs to stop floods that are a normal part of a healthy bosque. So now we have invasive salt cedars growing like weeds, choking out our cottonwoods and willows. Salt cedar loves fire and does fine in droughts. It increases the salinity of the soil, poisoning it for our native species. We have developers in our own backyards now, eyeing our wilting acres, seeing tract housing and dollar signs. A drought alone is one thing. I pray to San Ysidro for rain. Who is the saint we pray to for the rest of it, no? That is what keeps me awake at night. That is why I am so frightened."

The room was still. No thunderous applause or fists in the air. A sad and chilling silence hung like a visible apparition, and more than the swamp cooler made the fine hairs on Abby's arms rise into goose bumps.

Miguel slowly took the stage. "*Gracias*, Señor Armendáriz. You have given us much to think and pray about. Would someone else like to speak?"

There was a long pause. Some heads bent down; others turned to look around the room expectantly. Finally, Ben Frasier raised his hand.

"That fellow in the back. Come on up here," Miguel said, waving him forward.

Ben stood for a moment in the expectant silence. Abby felt nervous for him and didn't know why.

"Hello, my name is Benjamin Frasier. I'm not a farmer, but I did grow up on a sheep station in Australia, where it's very dry. I became a biologist and teach at the University of New Mexico. One of the things I've been researching is the silvery minnow."

Some unintelligible heckles from the crowd interrupted him.

"Please, I'd just like to correct a misconception. I've been listening to your hardship, and I am truly sorry for your pain—"

"Cry us a river!" Harvey Doyle shouted, and there was a round of laughter and applause.

"I'm sure it's tempting to have something to blame, but the silvery minnow is not the enemy—," Ben said.

"No, the enemies are tree-hugging environmentalists like you who put people out of jobs and kill off the family farmer! Hell, I don't hate the silvery minnows, I just don't give a rat's ass if they all dry up and blow away!" Harvey yelled back.

Ben took a step closer to the crowd and peered into their jeering faces. "You know how in coal mines they used to take down a canary in a cage? If it fell over dead, the miners knew they were in trouble, like an early warning system. That's how you should think of the silvery minnow. If there isn't enough water in the Rio Grande to allow a tiny little minnow to breed and survive, how can it possibly have enough water for all the growing demands being placed on it? When the ecosystem of a river is dying, it means the river is dying. I want there to be water for your farms. Mr. Armendáriz is right about the developers, out-of-control population growth, and golf courses! It's mad to plant sod in the desert! A tree hugger? Yeah, the tree I want to hug is the Rio Grande bosque cottonwood, and trust me, if the silvery minnow is allowed to perish, the cottonwoods will be next." He paused and the crowd was quiet.

"Albuquerque is taking more water from the river every year, and they lose twelve percent of their water to leaks in their system. Twelve percent is just getting pissed away from rotten pipes. That's just one example of something that could be fixed, but I've taken enough of your time. I'd just ask you, for your own good, to realize the problem is so much bigger and more complex than the fate of a lowly minnow. Making it the issue is burying your heads in the sand, and that's all we'll have left if we don't realize that." He handed the microphone to Miguel and tipped his hat to the smattering of polite but cool applause. He seemed to ignore the low booing as he made his way to the back.

After Miguel called up the next speaker, Ben caught Abby's eye and came over to her with a smile. "You got anything stronger than tea?"

"The coffee's strong. That's about it, I'm afraid." Abby smiled back.

"I guess I'm lucky it's too early in the season for rotten tomatoes,"

Ben said, pushing back his hat and wiping his brow with the back of his hand.

"I'm sorry they got a little rude, it's just that—"

"Don't apologize for them. If I were a farmer here, I'd be the first to want to parade a silvery minnow's head on a spike—or a toothpick would do, I guess. No, it's the media and the politicians who want to make it about the Endangered Species Act. That way they can dodge the real issues and the tough choices."

Abby nodded, realizing in some faint recess of her mind that to be seen publicly agreeing with this man she was risking ostracism. She just wanted him to keep talking. She wanted his eyes to keep looking into hers, full of intensity and passion. She wanted to continue to feel her heart bloom in her chest, its crimson petals unfurling in time-lapse photographic splendor.

Abby and Ramone sat under the shade of the towering cottonwood that sheltered her home. Abby looked up through the mass of heart-shaped leaves to the deepening blue of the evening sky and then across the horizon to the purpling mountains. Billowing white clouds settled over their peaks, like perfectly whipped egg whites. Decorative, but holding no promise of rain.

It was quiet with Maggie away on a sleepover with school friends to celebrate the last day of school. Santiago hadn't come home yet from working in the fields with Miguel and Charlie, his summer job since he was twelve.

"I'd offer you some angel food cake I made . . ." Abby trailed off, knowing it was useless.

"Don't even tempt me." Ramone sighed, taking his last bite of steak. Oven-roasted brussels sprouts and a salad made with baby greens, walnuts, diced pears, blue cheese crumbles, and balsamic vinaigrette had rounded out their dinner.

Abby's dinner sat half-eaten. The heat had sapped her appetite. That or the strange way her stomach had been lurching whenever she thought of Benjamin Frasier, which was quite a lot, despite her best intentions. Their encounter had been so brief—why was it caught in her mind like some loop of tape playing over and over? After the farmers' meeting at the café, everyone kept mentioning the big city biologist and his nerve to defend the silvery minnow to a room full of drought-suffering rural folks.

"You're sure off in the clouds," Ramone remarked. "A man could feel ignored."

Abby smiled at her dear friend. "With your busy social calendar, a girl could feel ignored."

"So I date a little these days. Are you jealous?" Ramone smoothed his silver mustache with his napkin.

"Of course I am. We're supposed to be alone in the world together," Abby teased.

Ramone chuckled. "You don't get to hide behind me anymore."

"Good thing, you're getting too skinny." Abby laughed.

"I saw your face that night, when the handsome biologist was speaking. I saw him come over to you afterward so you could dress his wounds."

"You're awfully snoopy, Sheriff," Abby said, picking at a cold brussels sprout. "Besides, I'd probably get lynched around here if I ever saw him again. Which won't happen anyway, so it doesn't matter."

"Don't be so sure. And if you do see him, you have my blessing. I thought the guy made sense."

"You only say that because you carry a *pistola* and no one will mess with you."

"I did some checking on him. He's well respected at the university. He works hard and he's unattached."

Abby shook her head. "Isn't that abuse of power or something, checking up on a guy for no reason?"

"He came down into my territory and incited the passions of my citizenry. It's prophylactic measures." Ramone's tone was full of suggestion, and his eyes twinkled mischievously.

"My passions are not incited, so keep your prophylactics between you and your lady friends."

His laugh was boisterous. It seemed impossible something so expansive could resonate from such a flat belly.

She couldn't help but laugh with him. Abby raised her napkin in white flag surrender. "Okay, I admit it. There was something about him . . . what else did you find out?"

"He's not a U.S. citizen. He's something called a 'visiting professor' on some kind of work visa. But I guess there are visiting professors who have held their posts for years. I also have his office number, should anyone from these parts want to reach him for further discussion."

"My God, did you get his blood type, too?"

"No, I'll let any investigation into his bodily fluids be up to you."

"Shut up! You're terrible! I'm going to wash the dishes!" She got up so fast she banged her legs on the picnic table.

Laughing his incongruous, operatic laugh, he followed with his own dishes. He caught up to her at her double sink, running steaming hot water into a sea of bubbles. "I'm going to wash that man right out of my hair! I'm going to wash that man right out of my hair!" he sang in perfect Mary Martin falsetto. "And send him on his way."

She let him get it out of his system. She washed, he rinsed, still humming his *South Pacific* show tune.

"How could I just call him? That would be so forward," Abby said. Hell, if her cover was blown anyway, why not talk about it?

Ramone helped himself to a low carbohydrate beer he kept stashed in Abby's refrigerator. "Tell him you'd like to hear more about how keeping the silvery minnow alive is good for the river. You see the plight of your neighbors who farm, and you want to better understand the issues."

"That's not bad . . . keeps it on the level of his work. And it's true, I do want to hear more about it."

"And you want to hear it in that sexy Australian accent. Go for it, mi'ja. He'll ask you to lunch or something, and you can see if there is anything worth pursuing. What is the harm, no?"

Her heart pounded just thinking about it. "Give me the number, but I'm not promising anything."

He reached into his pocket and pulled a scrap of paper from his wallet and placed it in her palm. He kept his hand around hers and said, *"Este mundo es un fandango, y el que no baile, es un loco.* This world is a dance, and only fools don't join in the music."

Santiago watched as Miguel inspected the retablo of San Ysidro he had painted. San Ysidro was the patron saint of New Mexico farmers. They had finished their work for the day, and Miguel had invited him into his workshop, where he practiced the Spanish Colonial traditional art of a *santero*, one who hand carves santos as retablos or bultos, wooden representations of saints. They were hung around him on the raw adobe walls. Miguel lit candles to illuminate their faces. He had explained that these retablos, the wooden panels, and bultos, the carved figures, were not idols to worship, as some accused. They were just symbols of the unseen power or holy personage to which people could address their prayers for God.

Santiago could have gone home, but he hadn't wanted to yet. Being with Miguel was the only thing that kept away the dark thoughts, the unnamed feelings that threatened to overtake him.

Miguel held out his bulto of San Ysidro, Saint Isidore. "See his blue coat and breeches? His red vest? His flat, black, round-billed hat? He's dressed like our ancestor farmers dressed. He drives a team of two oxen, just like they farmed back then, and this angel here on his left came to him after he prayed so fervently in his fields. God sent the angel to help him with his labors, and now he in turn helps us."

Santiago thought it was beautiful. It stirred something inside of him, a pleasant memory without form. A wistful nostalgia for something good and pure.

"Okay, mi'jo, now we varnish it in the traditional way. A santero should always follow the tradition, or it has no meaning or power. This varnish is getting as precious as gold. Do you know why that is?"

Santiago shook his head, hanging on Miguel's every word.

"It's made from pure grain alcohol and chunks of resin from the sap of piñon trees; it's what gives my santos and retablos their warm, natural glow and protects the delicate paints I use. The traditional Spanish furniture makers also use it, to give their furniture shine and protect it, just like our ancestors did. But, *mi Dios*, the piñons are dying in droves. I went into the mountains to collect my sap and found whole forests brown and dead from the burrowing bark beetles. It's getting worse every year of this blasted drought. They move in when the trees are vulnerable and dry. The drought's toll on the piñon includes drying up its sap, so it's not like we can go harvest it from the dead ones. I remember my Tía Maria used the sap to draw out splinters and soothe smashed fingers. She also made a tea with the piñon bark or needles to cure respiratory ills."

Santiago had known Miguel's late Aunt Maria and had been afraid of the old bruja, a witch who was rumored to change herself into a raven or owl and snatch children in the night. It was hard to imagine her tending the sick and injured. Good and evil in one entity. For some reason the concept startled him.

"I read in the paper that even if some of the young trees survive the drought and bark beetles, it will take thirty years for them to grow big enough to produce nuts! When I was a boy, we'd go camping in the mountains and collect huge piles of piñon nuts for our winter's sustenance. We'd gather around bonfires to tell stories while our harvest roasted. Mi Dios, it smelled so good! We'd get all sticky gathering those nuts. And our hands would smell like turpentine. We used to have a saying, a *dicho*, that went *Huy mas gente que piñones*, meaning, 'There are more people than piñones,' to describe a crowd. Now it seems true, people will outnumber our precious piñons. I hear it's even worse up north, and it's spreading down here now." Miguel shook his head, muttering something in Spanish that Santiago couldn't catch. "What will we have to pass along to our grandchildren? No? The chain will be broken, and the old ways will disappear."

He reached over to his precious tin of varnish and pried off the lid with a screwdriver. He dabbed his handmade brush into the liquid and began to spread it onto San Ysidro.

The sweet, turpentine-tinged vapors rose to Santi's nose, and he eagerly inhaled them. "I could go with you, and we could gather all the sap we can find and make varnish for the future. Maybe you could teach me how to carve these santos."

"I don't know if we'll have time before you go off to college, mi'jo."

Santiago felt slapped. It was ridiculous, yet he felt tears starting to form in his blinking eyes. He furiously wiped at them, turning his back so Miguel wouldn't see.

The silence hung there while Santi tried to regain his composure. What the shit was happening to him? One minute he finally felt at peace, and then he fell apart for no reason.

"Those were some nice words you said about la familia at graduation. I was very proud of you."

"Thanks," Santi managed to say. He wished he could tell Miguel how he'd been feeling, the nightmares that haunted him without revealing their content to his conscious mind. The darkness that rose in him like a fever. His tongue felt paralyzed in his mouth.

"Are you troubled about something, mi'jo?"

"What? Did Abby say something to you?" Santi heard his own harsh tone and immediately regretted it.

Miguel kept his eyes on his work. "You mean your mother?" he asked pointedly. "I don't need someone else to tell me something my own eyes and heart already know. 'La familia' means we share our burdens. I have just shared mine with you, and you bless me with an offer to help. Now it is your turn."

"I don't know," Santiago said. "It's just weird, thinking about leaving, I guess."

Miguel met his eyes, and Santiago did not refuse his gaze. "The telling of stories, of *cuentos*, is also an important tradition; the power of words and their images stirs our souls. Leaving for college to study story writing is your choice, no?"

"Yeah, I guess. But it's still hard."

"Almost everything worthwhile is hard. But I will also say this: no one is making you leave. If September comes and you do decide to go to college, you must own each step you take away from here, or your future will not be yours."

Santiago nodded. "I see what you're saying." He had a feeling Miguel knew this was just the tip of the iceberg that chilled his soul. But he didn't have words yet for the rest, even though it felt like he was cheating Miguel by not trying. He cursed himself for being such a coward. But he feared the darkness and the power it had. Its grip on him came with a warning not to betray it.

Especially in the presence of saints.

Once or twice a month, Rachel attended the craft circle that her mother hosted to make crafts for the nuns to use in fundraising for their service to the poor. The cabal would be there without fail, as well as Abby, who had joined right after she had arrived in Esperanza. Added to the mix now were Rose and Mort, crafty in their own ways.

They all sat in CeCe's living room. The open drapes let in the bright afternoon sun. Hazel, now close to seventy, could still sit cross-legged on the floor in her usual place in front of the coffee table, carving her folk animals. Her short-cropped hair was now totally white. Bonnie kicked back in a recliner, crocheting a pastel crib blanket lickety-split, and Carmen and CeCe worked on a quilt on the couch behind Hazel. Abby, too, sat on the floor in jeans and a white T-shirt, holding her intricate needlepoint against her raised knees. Rachel reclined in the matching chair near Bonnie, trying her hand at crocheting the afghan Bonnie was teaching her to make. It was all double stitched with not much counting involved, but still her fingers felt spastic as she tried to maneuver the yarn around her needle while holding her left index finger out straight to feed it as she went along. Birthing goats seemed a lot easier.

"I heard Rosetta's daughter gave birth to twins night before last," Bonnie said, starting off the gossip circle. She had highlighted her maroon hair, and chunks of overprocessed straw blond stuck out straight, obviously resisting the hottest curling iron. "The Lord certainly does work in mysterious ways. She's only fifteen and can't even take care of one baby, let alone two. You know Rosetta will be stuck raising them." She shook her head and clucked her tongue, her dark acrylic nails clicking as she crocheted, an accompanying percussion to her spicy tittle-tattle.

"Don't blame the Lord on that one," Carmen said, obviously irked. "He gives us all a brain. He can't help it if people don't use it." Carmen was the only real practicing Catholic in the bunch. Even when her husband was alive, she had spent most of her time working alongside the nuns at the church. Rachel always suspected that to Carmen, becoming a nun was a calling she had narrowly escaped but possibly regretted. Bonnie loved to get her going and shock her "bloomers" off.

"Where is the father of these twins?" asked Rose from a table set up next to the couch for Mort and her. On the table sat a naked baby doll Mort was measuring for small patterns to make clothes. One of the things that did not abandon him was his skill of working thread and cloth. Today he had an old Pendleton wool robe of Miguel's wrapped abundantly around him. Its bold red, black, yellow, and white Native American–style print made him look like the frailest of Indian chiefs, yet for some reason he also wore his green velvet yarmulke.

"Rosetta's daughter is not sure who the father is," CeCe

explained to Rose. "Every guy she knows has left town or is hiding out on the rez."

It took Rose a few blank seconds of looking at CeCe, and then it registered. "Oy vey!"

"My mother started having babies at fifteen," Mort said, cutting the thin paper, his glasses perched on the end of his nose. His hands shook, and Rachel was surprised to see his deftness with the small pattern pieces in spite of it.

"I'm sure that was very different, Zeyde," Rachel said. "Fifteen back then was not the same as being fifteen these days. This isn't turn-of-the-century Poland."

Mort shrugged. "*Enschultig meir!* I was only making a comment!" His saliva-encrusted lips moved beyond his words. His eyes were hazed over and, like a motel vacancy light, seemed to sputter on and off.

"It was an arranged marriage. Your father wasn't some *Chaim Yonkel*," Rose said to Mort.

Abby, Bonnie, Carmen, and Hazel looked at CeCe in confusion. She bent over to them and whispered with readable lips, "Any Tom, Dick, or Harry."

"Babies are hard," said Abby. "When I had Maggie, I had CeCe and Rachel to help, and it was still hard as hell."

Rachel remembered what a relief it was when Hattie got out of the toddler stage. It was different since Hattie had started school. Now there was this gap of time during the day that Rachel could have to herself. Being responsible twenty-four seven had been exhausting, even though she had her family (which included Abby) to help. Yet it was a kind of exhaustion she longed for again. That indelible tie between infant and mother.

"Jorge and I couldn't have children," Carmen said with a yearning. She crossed herself and blessed his departed soul under her breath, as if it were a sensual experience. Rachel had her suspicions as to why Carmen had stayed single after he died so many years ago. Carmen could finally live out her latent nun tendencies;

a real Mrs. *Frum*, as Rose called her, married to Jesus. Rachel tended to imagine Christ as some hippie Jewish guy, not unlike her ex-hippie mother, who still listened to the Grateful Dead and dragged Miguel out to slow dance with her every time "Ripple" played.

"I had a son and then four daughters—bing-bang-boom. All Mort had to do was look at me and I'd be pregnant. Isn't that right, Mort?" Rose said. She dabbed at her hairdo.

"Now all I have to do is look at her and I get a pain in my *bait-sim*," Mort answered. He rearranged the crotch of his pants.

Rose threw a spool of thread at him. "I could have you put away, you know, you alter kocker. Just keep it up."

Bonnie put her blanket to the side and went over to Mort and hugged him from behind, knocking his glasses down to the tip of his fat long nose. Her ample breasts almost served as earmuffs. "I'll take old Mort if you don't want him anymore. Isn't that right, Mort?" She twirled the top of his white hair with her index finger.

"You bet," he replied.

Bonnie kissed his head. "I hear if you do it puppy-style, you have a better chance of getting pregnant and having a boy."

"*Gottenyu!*" exclaimed Rose.

"That explains it," Mort said.

"Pepsi," Carmen said quietly.

"What?" asked CeCe.

"I heard if you drink a lot of Pepsi you'll get a boy." Carmen couldn't look up from the quilt.

"I remember Maria saying that the woman needs to eat more red meat to have males," CeCe added, "but those are all old wives' tales."

"Not all are bubbe *meises*," Rose said. "Sleep to the left of your husband, that's what the yenta always told us. Didn't work so well for me, though."

Hazel laughed. "I had a cousin who was sure if she gorged on salty snacks she would get a boy. She gained about fifty pounds before she finally did get pregnant, gained fifty more, and then it was a girl."

They all laughed except Rachel, who was starting to get annoyed.

"It always seems babies arrive when you least expect them," said CeCe.

Rachel felt her gut tightening with all this baby talk. Especially with how to conceive a boy. Her carefully constructed gratitude for her life was suddenly overshadowed by the fact that she was not even able to dream of having another baby. "How can you say that, Ma? I can't expect one—does that mean one will arrive? It makes me sick that Rosetta's daughter had twins who no one wants, because I would give anything, anything to have another baby, and it's killing me." Horrified, she began to cry.

She felt CeCe's arms around her, murmuring her apologies. Then she looked past CeCe's shoulders to see Charlie standing in the doorway.

The room was quiet as Charlie went to his wife. "Rache? You okay?"

Rachel tried to smile and wiped at her tears. "I'm just being stupid. I'm sorry. I thought I was over all of that. Really, I'm fine." She looked around to see everyone looking at her with such pity that she whispered to Charlie, "Get me out of here."

The next morning, Rachel grabbed a small produce basket and headed for the chicken coop. The hens squawked and fluttered away when she opened the pen. Zsa Zsa, her Transylvanian Naked Neck, sauntered around her quizzically. She already looked half-plucked by design, poor thing, and her feet were more like small dinosaur feet, with extra toes. The breed was also called Turken because the chickens looked like they had small, bald turkey heads. The rooster didn't go near her, there were so many other beauti-fully feathered creatures in the barnyard. In a corner nest were six eggs: four brown, a white, and a green. Rachel smiled. Hattie would be happy to hear the Araucana was laying her green eggs again. Green eggs always brought Dr. Seuss to mind. "Could you, would you with a goat? I could not, would not with a goat!" She held the green one, wrapping her fingers around it, feeling its roundness. It was still warm. Fertile.

The rooster came flapping in, annoyed she was in there rummaging around and stealing his offspring. His iridescent green tail feathers made him look like a Las Vegas showgirl strutting on stage. He flapped loudly this time, like he really meant it. "Urr, ur-ur, ur-ur urrrrr!"

"Aw, shut up," Rachel heard herself say like Rose, and began to laugh.

"Mommy, why don't goats eat meat like dogs and cats?" Hattie asked helping Rachel in the goat barn. Although Hattie was only six, Rachel figured she was not too young to take on more farm responsibilities. Hattie was out of school for the summer, and Rachel's form of childcare involved Hattie working and learning, when she wasn't with Maggie at summer day camp. There was no plopping her child in front of the TV or letting her linger for hours at the swimming pool like some stay-at-home moms did in the city.

"That's just the way God made them, honey. A lot of people believe goats eat tin cans and paper, like in the cartoons. Most things they just give a few chews to and spit out, because they really have very sensitive tummies. "

"Kind of like Great-grandpa Mort, huh? Great-grandma Rose yells at him all the time for eating the wrong things. His poots really smell bad."

"Hattie," Rachel said, "Great-grandpa Mort is old, and he's had two operations on his *kishke*, his tummy. He can't help it."

"When Great-grandma Rose made kishke with the brisket, were we eating Great-grandpa Mort's kishkes?"

"Oh, Hattie, gross!"

Hattie laughed her little munchkin laugh. The laugh that made people at the grocery store turn around and smile. She hugged the goat, Tallulah, while Rachel applied udder ointment. "Remember when you brought my preschool class over to see the goats, and some of them freaked out because their eyes look like they'd been put on sideways, like devil eyes? That was so funny." Hattie giggled.

Rachel laughed with her, even though when it happened she and Charlie feared they'd be paying for therapy for those bedeviled children for years to come. One of the little boys had started to yell that the goats were really devil monsters, and the idea had spread through the group like mass hysteria. Hattie had been devastated when her classmates had started screaming and running to the adults for tight, save-me grasps around their legs. "It sure wasn't at the time," Rachel reminded her.

"No. But we were all just three or four years old, weren't we, Mommy?"

"Yes, just babies."

"I'm going to be seven. Seven's not a baby. Six isn't even a baby. When do you stop being a baby, Mommy? I think when you're five, you're not a baby anymore." She helped wrestle the next goat into place. It gave her a little trouble, and she smacked it on the nose. "Four's still a baby."

"You'll always be my baby," Rachel said, stroking Hattie's hair. She was the most beautiful and perfect child, and Rachel loved her like nothing else. She saw so much of herself and CeCe in Hattie, and now, God help her, a little bit of Rose. But Hattie had her daddy's smile. That little smile he shone on the women who used to gawk and drool over him at the Midnight Rodeo dance bar years ago, usually followed by an ever-so-subtle tip of his hat.

"Are you sad you can't have another baby?" Hattie looked up to her with her searching big blue eyes.

Rachel felt guilt wash through her as she realized Hattie must be picking up on her moods. "Listen, sweetheart. Sometimes I wish I could have given you a baby brother or sister, but there's no way that can happen. I love you and Daddy more than anything. You are so great I could never be sad about no more babies. I promise." She willed her heart to follow her words.

Rachel softly closed the door to Mort's room. Rose stood at her flank, wincing as the latch clicked shut. They had been wrestling with Mort for two hours, trying to calm him enough to take his medicine and go to bed. His "dark dreams" would overtake him when least expected. As Rachel had tried to take off his shoes and socks, he had thrashed at her as if she were preparing him for the gas chamber.

"I thought we'd never get him quieted down," Rachel said to Rose. "It kills me when he gets like this." She wiped away a tear on her lower lid.

"I sometimes ask myself if he really survived that awful place," Rose said.

"Yeah, I know," Rachel said as he snored from behind the door. She looked around. "I guess everyone else has gone to bed."

"Come. I'll make us some peppermint tea. My stomach could use some," Rose said, shuffling her way to the kitchen in her white crew socks and gold sequined slippers.

Rose puttered about, getting the tea ready. She reminded Rachel of her Tía Maria tending her bubbling concoctions, and it warmed her heart. "Bubbe, why don't you sit and let me get the tea?" she offered.

"Nonsense. I'm capable of making my granddaughter and myself a *glezel tai.*"

Rose poured the boiling water right over the dried peppermint leaves in Rachel's cup. From her own fragile china cup she poured her steeped tea into her saucer, popped a sugar cube in her mouth, and sipped from her saucer.

"Why do you drink your tea that way?" asked Rachel, spooning thick honey in hers, as usual.

"I've done this since I was a little girl. It's Russian. My parents did it, so I did it."

"I don't really know anything about where or how you grew up . . ."

"What's there to tell? My parents emigrated from Russia to escape the pogroms. They were kids when they married—arranged, of course. They lived where most of the immigrated Russian Jews lived, Brighton Beach. That's where I grew up," Rose said, slurping tea through her sugar cube. "Your zeyde didn't move there till after the war. A lot of concentration camp survivors came to Brighton Beach after the war."

"What was life like for you?" Rachel did not want to break the spell of this rare moment with Rose, so her question came out barely more than a whisper.

"I remember that beyond my community, there was a hatred of us Jews. On the radio, in newspapers. They said we were greedy and dishonest. We weren't wanted in certain areas or in certain clubs. There were signs that said so. People said we caused both wars and were a threat to the economy. Gangs used to come to Brighton and beat up Jewish kids all the time. I got my arm and nose broken in a hate fight. I must only have been eleven or twelve at the time. After that, I walked around angry, with a big chip on my shoulder, just asking for a fight."

"That's awful," Rachel said. No wonder Rose had it in for other people. She had grown up able to trust only her fellow Jews.

"Awful, shmawful, I lived through it. We still had the beach, hot knishes, and Orange Crushes. My parents use to sit out on the sidewalk in lawn chairs with everyone else and *shmu'es* in Yiddish or watch the tourists. Those were good times. Later it all turned to drek. Non-Jews moved in. Different races. Changed it," said Rose, looking sad. "People moved away. Jewish families broke up." She stopped as if she had wound down and looked into her tea leaves. Rachel could plainly see the hurt child who sat before her. "You know," Rose continued, "I don't mean to hurt anyone. Sometimes I can't stop what's coming out of my mouth. I'm from Brooklyn."

Rachel laughed, remembering her visit there as a girl, when she had noticed the rudeness and how loud and obnoxious everyone seemed. Always into everyone's business and freely putting in their two cents. Right here in her kitchen it had all come full circle. She felt connected now to it all. Especially to Rose.

She looked down to see they had a strong hold of each other's hand.

CHAPTER 5

"I can't believe I left the salt out of the bread. I never leave the salt out of the bread. Beginners leave the salt out of the bread." Abby shook her head, fingers against her temples. The café was quiet. Only two customers since the lunch rush. It was nearly time to close.

"My chickens will love it, don't worry about it," CeCe said. "You do seem a little distracted these days, and since I am the queen of distraction, if your distraction is on even my radar screen, then, baby, you're distracted."

"The scary thing is, I just understood what you said!" Abby laughed. CeCe joined her, the crazy laughter of two tired, stressed women.

Rachel emerged from the back. "I could use a laugh. Justin drove off with only half of the Albuquerque deliveries loaded into the truck. So I'll be getting calls from a bunch of snotty chefs looking for their goat cheese."

That set Abby off again, her indelicate guffaws punctuated by snorts that felt delicious.

"Abby didn't sleep last night," CeCe explained through her own laughter. "You know how she gets. Bonnie says her insomnia is due to her never getting laid."

Rachel's dark, perfectly curved eyebrows raised. "I've been saying she needs a man."

Benjamin Frasier's phone number throbbed in Abby's mind's eye like a neon sign. Ever since Ramone had given it to her a few days earlier and she had stared at it, hoping to find some hidden meaning or guidance from the configuration of its digits, it had been committed to her memory: 268–7192. How could she tell them it was the biologist, friend to the silvery minnow, who kept her pacing the floors at night?

The bells jangled as the café door was opened against the force of the swamp cooler wind. It would be her married electrician in for his coffee, daily flirtation, and game of solitary chess, although he was much later today.

Abby turned her back and headed for the coffee machine. She found if she had his cup ready, it preempted some of his banter.

"Good day. I'd like a tall glass of some of your famous iced tea." The Aussie accent startled her from behind. She spun around.

"You're that guy who spoke out for the minnow at our meeting last week," CeCe said in a tone completely devoid of warmth. Abby had never heard her sound like that.

"Yeah," Rachel butted in. "What are you doing down here drinking our iced tea? Maybe you should keep to Albuquerque water."

It was like a saloon scene from some old western movie. Abby was frozen in place, the cup of coffee in her hand.

Ben smiled. "I deserve that. I should have kept my mouth shut that night and only listened, as I had intended."

"You didn't say why you're back," Rachel said, her piercing blue eyes narrowed in his direction.

Abby knew what it felt like to become impaled by Rachel's glint. She sat down the coffee cup and reached for an iced tea glass.

CeCe put a hand on her daughter's arm. "Rachel, you were going to pick up the girls. You might as well take them up to Albuquerque and finish your goat cheese deliveries; they'll like that. I've got to get over to Hazel's and get the folks. Abby can close."

Abby filled the iced tea glass in the uneasy quiet. Rachel grabbed her purse, and she and CeCe went to the back to exit. Abby could hear Leo finishing his last load of dishes before leaving for his second job. She thought again of the western movie, the scene where the gunfight has been averted and everyone in the saloon resumes his or her activities.

"Thanks," Ben said as she handed him the iced tea. His smile hit her full force, and she realized he was like Bobby in that way. A compulsive, unconscious smiler. Her late husband had smiled to complete strangers every day of his life and never even realized he was doing it. It was just wired into his nature.

"You told me the other night not to apologize for my friends. But they're not usually like that."

"Times are hard. It was daft to speak out about the minnow that night. I get a little caught up sometimes and forget myself. I wanted to hear their views, not spout my own." He took a long swig of tea. "But I am glad I didn't have to explain to your friends why I came back. I don't think they would have bought my story about remembering how good the tea is here."

"The tea is good here. Better than any I've had in Albuquerque." Abby rushed in nervously, sensing where he was heading.

"Oh, right. Great tea, must be the water." He threw a wink in with his grin, obviously finding her amusing.

She had a split second to notice how straight and white his teeth were between his upturned lips before turning in embarrassment. She could feel the warm flush of color rise in her neck and face, thanks to her traitorous redhead's complexion. She poured herself a glass of tea for lack of any other logical reason to have turned her back on him.

"Cheers," he said, clinking his glass against hers, and took another drink.

In the afternoon sun she noticed that his brown hair, now

without his hat, was sun streaked with blond strands. His brown eyes were now flecked with olive green.

"Abby, I came back here to see you again," he blurted. "I'm not very good at this, I'm afraid."

She set her iced tea glass on the counter. "No, you're fine, really."

"Since coming to New Mexico, I've been buried in work. I'm kind of a natural introvert anyway, so it's easy to be on my own. I go hiking or ride my bike or cross-country ski in the winter, all on my own. At home I rattle around with my books or music, talking to myself. Colleagues at UNM will invite me out sometimes, for a pint. At first they tried to fix me up on dates but I never called their lady friends back so they've decided I'm hopeless and I thought I was, too."

Abby hung onto the silence, not wanting to break the spell of his words. She wanted him to keep talking, tell her everything.

"I was married, back in Australia. Teenage sweetheart. About five years ago she divorced me. I'd just completed my doctoral dissertation and hadn't noticed she'd stopped loving me. I thought it was decent of her to wait until I was finished, you know? She knew me well enough to know I'd take it badly and descend into self-pity and never finish my dissertation. So I can thank her for that. Anyway, that's when I went shopping for visiting professorships as far away from Australia—and her quick remarriage to my best mate, Jerry—as I could get. And I landed here." He reached for his tea glass, and it was empty. Abby quickly took it from him and refilled it.

"God, I'm terrible at this. Here I've spilled all this and I don't even know you, but that's the thing. I want to know you."

Abby nodded. Tears filled her eyes, blurring his earnest expression. What the hell, she thought, as her tears spilled over, trailing silently down her cheeks, leaking their salty flavor into her open smile.

Santiago had the rest of the afternoon off after Miguel decided it was too hot to work. They had started at five in the morning and had already irrigated the chile fields with their scheduled weekly allotment of water. Today, the thirsty young chile plants could drink to their hearts' content under the blaze of the June sun. Some of the precious water soaked into grateful roots and rose up through green leaves, even as the rest evaporated molecule by molecule, devoured by the greedy, dry air.

He was exhausted after little sleep and many hours in the sun. He had emptied his liter of water before noon. Despite his faithful use of sunscreen, per his mother's nagging, his skin glowed its summer tone of deep golden brown. His hair, in a single thick dark braid, felt heavy and damp against his neck.

Santiago stood in his yard, watching a cluster of small brown birds battle in the birdbath. His gaze moved to the empty place. The place where his old house had stood, the one he had shared with his mother when she was still alive and his father. And later with his father and uncle and the endless parade of nameless, faceless people who came to party and fight and screw right in front of him.

There had been mean dogs without names who were chained in the yard and tried to bite him whenever he got too close. And the roosters, which were even scarier because they were not chained and sometimes ignored him and other times came at him with their sharp spurs for no reason. He still had scars on his legs. His beloved dog, Besame—Spanish for "kiss me," as in the old song "Besame Mucho"—had tried to defend him from the roosters on numerous occasions, sometimes attacking them first, which led his father to hate the dog. That and the fact that Rachel had given Besame to him in the first place, a pretty little golden retriever puppy, full of kisses. His father shot Besame when she went after a rooster. Santiago's mind went back to the silent film nightmare of that day. Running with bleeding, gasping Besame in his arms to Abby and Rachel, spilling the secret in his anguish, how Bobby had been shot by his father and buried in the rooster house. Rachel took Besame from him to rush her to the vet, but the dog had died on the vet's metal table without him while his father was going to kill Abby in her kitchen. Santiago still remembered the look on his father's face when he realized his son was not going to get out of the way so he could shoot Abby, who now knew too much, thanks to Santi. The police sirens, the sight of his father's head blasted open, blood everywhere. He had felt bad about his father, but even worse about Besame. He thought he might be offending God when his tears were more for his dog than for his father. But she had been a good dog and was not even a year old.

A tree still stood there, a sick old elm tree with half-naked branches. He imagined its roots had drunk his mother's and Bobby's blood while their bodies were still rotting in the soil and that was why the tree had never. looked healthy. The bulldozers should have put it out of its misery.

The sheriff had let him stay with Abby after they took his father's body away. They had gone to the Vigils' house while Ramone scrubbed all the blood and brains from Abby's kitchen. Santi had wished Ramone could scrub out *his* brains and clean away the memory of it. Not even a year of therapy could do that.

For little brown sparrows, they could sure make a lot of noise. They splashed the water right out of the birdbath. No wonder he had to refill it every day.

He could go in where it was cool, but he remained perched on the picnic table, his feet on the bench. If he went in, he would lie down on his bed and probably fall asleep, and then the dream might come, and he was in no mood for that.

A car was coming down the road, too soon to be Abby's. He squinted at it, a dark car half obscured by the hot, wavy air and the cloud of dust it made. Even after it came to a stop not twenty-five feet away from him, he couldn't tell who the driver was behind the dark-tinted glass.

"Hey, *esse!*" It was that James Ortiz. He got out of his car, wearing an oversize baseball jersey, baggy jeans, cap turned backwards, gold chains glistening in the sun. "I haven't seen you around, bro,' what's up?"

"Nothing," Santi said, wondering why he was there.

"Your old house is totally gone, man, freaked me out. Got anything to drink?"

"Water. Iced tea." Santi didn't mention his mother's wine rack.

"Come on. Let's go to my place."

"Why?" Santi asked, feeling as if he had missed something.

"I promised your Uncle Manny I'd look in on you, make sure you're all right."

Santiago hesitated. It wasn't as if he had something better to do. Maybe he should give this James a chance.

"Santiago. I was hard on you that other day. Look, we're like cousins, you and me."

"I could go for a little while, I guess," Santi heard himself say.

"That's more like it." James smiled, revealing a gold tooth.

The ride over to where James lived took about ten minutes. He drove slowly, blasting his rap, the bass vibrating Santiago's internal organs.

James turned down a gravel road, past an unlabeled warehouse and the remains of an old adobe house, now just three crumbling walls. Santi always wondered about those ruins. Who had lived there? Why had they left? Why didn't anyone take care of the house? These things didn't happen overnight.

"Who do you live with?" Santi asked as James parked in front of a small, flat-roofed, cinder block house. It had been badly painted an industrial green in the distant past.

"This is my auntie's house, but she's doing three to five for bad checks. Her daughter Rosalinda lives here, my cousin. Now I do."

Santi followed him to the door, where he could hear a television playing and smell a tantalizing food scent, something with onions and meat that abruptly woke up his stomach.

James led the way. "Rosa! We're coming in."

They entered the darkened house, and Santi noticed there was aluminum foil covering most of the windows. In the narrow living room, a long, ratty sofa hugged the wall, partially covered with a newer Mexican blanket, the kind they sold at the flea markets. A coffee table cluttered with overflowing ashtrays, soda bottles, and candy wrappers sat in front of the sofa.

The television was turned to one of those talk shows where freaks go on to fight with each other and throw furniture. Abby didn't allow them to watch such garbage. Those shows were one of the causes of the decline of civilization, right behind fast food and rap music. Santi figured if he stayed in this house more than five minutes he could nail all three. And maybe even the number one threat to civilization: drugs.

James had moved onto the kitchen, from which the good food smells emanated. Santi stuck his head through the door. A slender young woman tended a cast iron frying pan full of browning crumbled hamburger meat, generously dotted with chopped onions and green chile. A stack of freshly made flour tortillas sat steaming on a plate next to the skillet.

"Sit down, esse. Rosalinda, this is Santiago. You remember Manny and Joseph Baca, those brothers I used to hang with? The cockfighting dudes? This is dead Baca's kid who got adopted by the white woman."

Rosalinda turned from her cooking and appraised him. She was the most beautiful girl Santi had ever seen who wasn't in a magazine. She was long limbed and thin, with long, glossy, straight black hair that brushed against the naked space between where her tank top ended and her cutoff jeans began. Her navel was pierced by a gold ring with some kind of sparkling gem that winked at him.

"Hello, Santiago. What is a nice guy like you doing with my piece-of-shit cousin?" She smiled, her tongue quickly running along her lower lip.

James laughed, helping himself to a tortilla. "Hey, I barely got him talked into coming over here."

Santiago couldn't take his eyes from Rosalinda's teasing smile. She wore no makeup, and yet she looked perfect. Big brown eyes with thick lashes, creamy dark brown skin. "Hungry?"

"Yeah. Looks great," Santiago replied.

"I learned to cook when I was just a kid. My mom kept going away for one thing or another. She used to date your Uncle Manny, that's how James met him. But they're all so stupid they keep getting locked up or dying, right, James?"

"No more, Rosa, I'm done with that shit, man."

Rosalinda handed Santi a plate with two tortillas filled with the meat mixture and shredded cheese. "People who break the law are lazy and stupid, and that includes my whore of a mother who I hope never comes back here, or if she does, I'm long gone."

James laughed, food wadded against his tongue and teeth. "Don't be shy, girl, say what you think!"

She opened the fridge and pulled out three beers, twisted their caps off with her dish towel, and plunked them on the table. "I had to raise myself, cousin, or don't you remember? Who knows where my father is, some drunk Indian in Arizona. I've seen enough to know how not to be." She slammed her plate down next to Santiago and sat down. "I'm sure you'd agree with me, Santiago, since your father and uncle were gangster assholes."

Santi picked up the beer, the bottle running with sweat. He took a drink, not his first taste of beer but the first time he really liked it. "Yeah," he said to Rosalinda, who was staring him down for an answer.

"You judge too much, Rosalinda. People have to survive, and it isn't easy in this world," James said, pointing with his beer bottle.

"I've been supporting myself since I was twelve, bussing tables over at Juanita's Cantina. I worked my way up through the kitchen, and now I'm the night manager and hostess. All it takes is hard work and getting off your lazy ass instead of thinking there are shortcuts, that you shouldn't have to play by the same rules as everybody else. What do you do, Santiago? I bet you don't steal from people or pass bad checks."

"I've been working on the Vigil farm since I was little. I know all about raising chile, taking care of farm animals. I help with their goat dairy, too. Whatever they need. I'm like part of their family." Santiago took the last bite of his burrito.

"No wonder you're so hungry and skinny! I'll make you another plate. James! Get him another beer, this is a thirsty working man. How old are you, anyway?"

"Eighteen. Just graduated. I'm going to college in the fall."

"I knew you were smart. I'm twenty-three already. Finally got my G.E.D. last year, and I'm saving up to go to the Pima Medical Institute in Albuquerque and become a nursing assistant or something. James here is twenty-six and still thinks he's a punk teenager. You have to get your G.E.D. and get a job!" She reached over and smacked his arm.

"I am looking for a job. I might work at Hastings, that would be cool. But I don't know if they'd hire me since I was in la pinta."

"You make it sound all cute, 'la pinta'! You were in the state penitentiary for breaking and entering." Rosalinda rolled her eyes and swigged her beer.

Santiago was on his second beer, and it was just catching up to him. The only other time he'd had two beers was over at a track buddy's house after they placed second in the state meet. Miguel and Charlie sometimes gave him a beer after they had worked hard, but he wasn't supposed to tell Abby. He dove into his second plate of burritos and saw that James had put another round of beers on the table. He felt his head become light and swimmy. He wanted to laugh and tried to think of something funny to say. Then he decided feeling this good was reason enough to laugh, so he did.

Rosalinda leaned over to him, her tank top gapped to expose the gentle swell of her breasts above her black lace bra. "You have a nice laugh, Santiago."

He laughed for her again, listening to himself. He did have a good laugh. He finished his food and third beer, not hearing half of what they were saying, just laughing here and there.

He started to wonder what his life might have been like if Bobby and Abby hadn't come back to Esperanza. His dad wouldn't have had to kill Bobby, so he wouldn't have been adopted by Abby. His dad would still be alive, and his Uncle Manny would not be in the penitentiary. Maybe they would be sitting around the table at his old house, laughing and drinking beers. Maybe Rosalinda's mom would still be dating Manny, so she and Rosalinda would be there, too.

The scene came to life in his mind. It would be like this, only better. "Hey, James," he said. "Tell me about my dad."

By the time Rosalinda drove him home, he was crying and very drunk. Rosalinda told him he needed to go home so his mom wouldn't worry. Since she had had only one beer and James was passed out on the sofa, she told him she was the designated driver. He wept in her arms, telling her how responsible she was and how much he loved her.

He must have dozed off, because when they came to his house he was surprised she knew the way and it was getting dark already. "You know everything, Rosalinda, even where I live."

"You told me, sweetie. Now can you make it inside by yourself?"

He blinked. His house seemed to be moving. "Sure, why not?"

"Okay then, bye now, Santiago. Come see us again."

He fumbled for the door handle, and suddenly Rosalinda was outside, opening it for him and helping him out. He put his arm around her bony shoulders and stumbled along next to her until they reached the kitchen door.

"Keys," Rosalinda commanded, so he reached into his pocket and found some and handed them to her.

He tripped across the doorway and landed on a kitchen chair.

"There's a note," Rosalinda said, picking it up from the table. "'Dear Santi, your sister is staying the night with Hattie. I went out to dinner with a friend. I'll be home early. There is chicken in the fridge. Love, Mom.' Lucky for you. I bet your mom wouldn't like how drunk you are. Let's get you into bed. I need to go home and clean up that mess."

Then he was in bed in his underwear. Everything spinning but Rosalinda's beautiful face, hovering over him. "Sweet dreams, Santiago."

Abby slept lightly and intermittently, her conscious mind unwilling to surrender itself to the uncontrolled realm of dreams. How could it when her waking thoughts were far more rapturous than any dream could be?

She lay there in the early morning light, listening to the insistent call of the piñon jay in the branches of the tree outside her window. A smile pulled at her lips. When was the last time she had awakened with a smile on her face?

"What a difference a day makes, twenty-four little hours." She hummed the old melody, trying to remember the rest of the song. Yesterday had begun as just another day. How could she have known Ben Frasier was about to show up at the café for the second time and change her life with five little words: *I want to know you.*

They had talked for two hours before he had looked at his watch and suggested he take her to dinner. She had called Rachel, who was happy to keep Maggie as long as Abby understood how much she disapproved of Ben Frasier. She couldn't reach Santiago, so she had dashed home to leave a quick note and change out of her food-stained work clothes and into a soft blue sundress and shake out her shoulder-length auburn hair from its clasp. After a quick arm's length spray of a light citrus scent to mask any lingering food smells, she ran to her car and drove quickly down the rutted road

Sue Boggio and Mare Pearl

back to the café, praying he had not disappeared or been some sort of fevered hallucination.

But there he was, leaning against his small silver SUV, his face bursting into a grin when she hopped out of her car and ran over to him. They laughed at their own eagerness and fell into a relieved hug as if their separation had lasted a lifetime, and in a way it had.

Abby had suggested Tiofilos for dinner, a cozy little traditional New Mexican restaurant in an old adobe house in Los Lunas.

At the restaurant, Ben kept his eyes locked on hers the entire time, asking about her life, listening intently to her story. She had spilled it, too, every detail. Her obscenely wealthy upbringing by remote parents in San Diego. Meeting Bobby Silva when she was eighteen and marrying him against her parents' will when she was twenty, losing him after they had moved to Esperanza, widowed by age thirty. Giving arduous birth to Magdalena, crying out for her dead husband. The salvation of Esperanza, most especially the healing comfort of her best friends, CeCe and Ramone, and her challenging yet rewarding friendship with Rachel. Adopting her beloved Santiago, a lost little boy who was as much a victim of his father's drunken madness as she and Bobby were.

Ben understood without her having to explain why she hadn't wanted to return to San Diego for her parents' highly conditional "second chance" to be reinstated as heiress to their fortune. And since she was still half owner of her successful San Diego restaurant, she had her own money coming in, anyway, on top of her large savings and lucrative investments.

He had held her hand in the candlelight, their half-touched plates removed without their noticing, and said, "Of course you didn't go back to your parents, with all those strings attached. That just isn't you."

Their evening had ended back in the café parking lot, where her car was parked. They had sat in his car and watched the sunset's reflection against the Manzano Mountains, shades of purple and pink lighting up the thin strands of clouds hanging at their peaks until gradually fading to dusky blue, then deepening into darkness. The stars twinkled, and a full moon rose from behind the mountains.

"I'd better be going home," Abby had said, not knowing why, except the night had felt so complete at that moment. It was like knowing when one of her culinary creations was finished and any more seasoning would ruin it.

He seemed to know it was not yet the time to escort her home, see where she lived, meet her children. "Abby, thank you."

"Thank you, Ben," she replied as they hugged next to her car. She marveled at how their bodies fit so naturally against each other, yet the physical part of their connection seemed premature and somehow secondary in light of this surprising unfolding. It was the nonphysical, the spiritual connection that took her breath away. The gift of that was so entirely unexpected. Would she actually be fortunate enough to experience that twice in one lifetime?

He kissed the side of her cheek before letting her go, his lips soft and lingering. A wave of longing rose in her center, spreading itself through her deepest self. She nearly reached for him, then caught herself.

"I'll call you tomorrow," he had said as she turned to get into her car.

"Please," she said before she thought and realized she had said it like a question. Her window was open. He bent down to her upturned face and kissed her on her lips in a way that convinced her he would.

Abby watched him get into his car and pull carefully out into the highway traffic heading north to Albuquerque. She had to drive around for half an hour, listening to music, calming herself down, before she felt ready to go home and face her son.

But he had been asleep when she got home, at not quite ten o'clock. He must have been exhausted from his day in the fields. She was relieved in a way; she didn't really feel ready to talk about Ben or name what this was.

Now, she was in no hurry to get up; lounging in bed, reliving the night before, felt deliciously decadent. With Maggie at Rachel's, she might even drift back to sleep.

"Mommy!" She heard Maggie burst through the kitchen door as delicately as a Saint Bernard dog.

Abby jumped out of bed and put on her silky Hawaiian print robe and came out to see Charlie standing in the doorway. Maggie lunged at her for hugs. "I missed you, so I told Charlie to bring me home."

"Well, I hope you asked him nicely instead of commanding him." She gave her daughter a big hug and smiled at Charlie.

"Oh, she was fine," Charlie replied with a tired smile and shake of his head.

"Stay for coffee and some talk?" Abby offered, remembering all of their heart-to-hearts at her table. It had been a while, and she could tell something was on his mind.

Maggie pulled at her. "Mommy, I have to tell you what Hattie and I did in Albacookie yesterday with Rachel."

"You're old enough to say Albuquerque, Miss Maggie Magoo," Abby said.

"I like Albacookie better, Miss Mommy Magoo." Maggie danced over to the fridge, singing a song.

"I'd like that cup of coffee and talk, but you got your hands full, so I'll take a rain check," Charlie said, with a smile that seemed forced.

Abby came over to him by the door and spoke in a low voice, "I need to talk to you, too, so get over here as soon as you can."

"Meet me in the horse barn later, after you get things situated here and Santi gets his butt out of bed. I'll have a thermos of coffee ready."

"See you there," Abby said.

Santiago woke to his sister's high-pitched laughter, which also served to split his head in two. He'd never had a hangover before and was shocked to learn it could be that bad. His stomach roiled with acid; his mouth tasted like dog barf. Attempting to stand, he felt weak, dehydrated, and he had to pee worse than he ever had in his entire life.

He pulled a long T-shirt over his boxers and, using both hands to hold his head together, made for the door. He hoped he could hobble to the bathroom before his mother and sister converged on him.

Their voices were coming from the kitchen, so he had no trouble, even in his compromised condition, making it to the sanctity of the bathroom. Shutting and locking the door behind him, he proceeded to puke not quite entirely in the toilet. Knees buckling, head exploding, heaves wrenching his gut—but at least they were silent and wouldn't summon his mother. One thing to be grateful for. And then he remembered another thing to be grateful for: Rosalinda. Suddenly all the misery was worth it. Suddenly there was a reason to go on living. He cleaned up, gargled mouthwash, scrubbed his face with soap and cold water, and combed his long hair back into a neat ponytail. He surveyed the image in the mirror. Would he pass his mother's inspection? Probably, unless he puked on her feet or something.

Then he tried to look at himself through Rosalinda's eyes. What did she see? At about six foot, at least he was tall; girls liked that. He had heard whispering and giggling girls at his high school refer to him as "cute," but it hadn't meant anything to him then. Of course Abby always said he was handsome, but moms were supposed to say that.

Was his skin as dark as Rosalinda's? Maybe he'd lay off the sunscreen a little. He licked at his dry lips and weaved a moment. He better take some aspirin for the headache and stuff for his stomach and drink a ton of water. From now on, he'd stick to one beer, two tops. God, he'd been such an amateur. Did Rosalinda think he was some dork?

But then he realized the best thing of all. He hadn't had the dream. The soul-sucking, nameless, faceless, black-hole nightmare that haunted him by night and shadowed him by day was gone. He remembered her angelic face floating over his, wishing him "sweet dreams." Rosalinda had exorcised his demons.

"Santi! I gotta go pee!" His sister called and pounded on the door. Why didn't they have two bathrooms, for Christ's sake?

"Stop pounding, dork!" Santi yelled and discovered that yelling hurt his head worse than Maggie's pounding.

"Well, get out, dork!" Maggie yelled.

Santi watched the doorknob twitch from his side of the door as she was attempting to barge in on him. Then came his mother's voice.

"Give your brother his privacy."

"But I'm gonna pee my pants!"

"Santi, I think your sister isn't going to last much longer. All you all right? It's almost noon."

He opened the door. "I'm fine. Can't I catch up on my sleep once in a while?"

Maggie dashed past him and slammed the door.

"Do we have coffee?" he asked. She seemed to be doing that mother examination thing; it reminded him of how mother animals sniffed and licked their offspring. At least she held herself back from going that far. Apparently he passed inspection, because she smiled and reached for a hug.

"I'll have a cup with you and make you something to eat."

"Just toast," he said quickly. "I'm not hungry."

He watched as she cut thick slices from her homemade wheat bread and put them in the toaster oven. She seemed so happy. Her face was different somehow. He felt a moment of tenderness for her. She really had been a good mom, taking him in when she could have just dumped him into the system. He knew how bad those kids sometimes had it, messed-up foster families, group homes, even living on the streets. She really did love him just as if he were her real son.

"Here's your coffee. Want some cream in it?" She beamed at him, her face all full of light, her red hair shiny and loose. Did she look younger, or did he just feel older?

"Thanks, mom, cream would be great." He let her wait on him; she loved to for some unknown reason. But then, he'd love to wait on Rosalinda. He imagined getting her coffee, making her breakfast. There was nothing he'd rather do in the whole wide world. He saw Abby with a new understanding. That was how she loved him.

She set the hot, buttery toast in front of him, and he was astonished to find out he was ravenously hungry.

"Santi, I need to tell you about the friend I had dinner with last night. He's a man and only a friend right now, but I might want to go out on a date with him, you know, like, once in a while . . . if he asks." Her face turned all red like it did when she was embarrassed.

"Cool," he said, realizing she wanted his permission. "You should go out, get a life, Mom. Who is he?"

"He's a biology professor at UNM, from Australia, so he has that accent." She laughed a girlish laugh.

He'd never seen her like this. "I can watch Maggie if you need me to." Unless he had a date with Rosalinda. A date with Rosalinda . . .

"Well, if it works with your plans and he actually calls. I mean, I'm sure he will call, he said he would." She sat down then and took a stiff belt of her coffee. "I tried to explain to Maggie about Ben—that's his name, Ben Frasier. She asked if this means I don't love her daddy anymore, and I told her I'd love her daddy forever but that didn't mean I couldn't be friends with a new man." Her face knitted in worry.

"She'll get over it. She didn't even know Bobby." Santi felt so wise, bestowing advice on his mother.

"Would you watch her for me for a while? I told Charlie I'd meet him in the horse barn for a talk."

"Yeah, I think he's worried about Rachel," he said, knowing for the first time how a woman could matter that much.

Abby walked across the field, wondering how things were going that day with CeCe and her parents and Miguel. She hated to see her friend under so much stress. Before now, CeCe was so consistently upbeat that everyone took her good mood for granted. Optimistic, effervescent CeCe was transforming before her eyes into a tired, edgy woman. She'd go check on her after seeing Charlie. Maybe she could whisk her away for some shopping in Albuquerque.

She found Charlie with his beloved Sweetwater. The horse was out of his stall, tied to a post, enjoying a brisk afterride brushing with a curry comb. Small puffs of dust floated off his shiny coat to hang in a shaft of sunlight. Sweetwater neighed a welcome, and she brought the apple she carried to his reaching lips.

"Hey, Abby," Charlie said and wiped his hands on his jeans. "Have a seat. Here, this chair is cleaner. Want a cup of coffee?"

"I had one with Santi, but I could use another one. Couldn't sleep much last night."

Charlie handed her a blue metal cup with coffee still steaming from the thermos and sat down on the other old lawn chair. Sweetwater, his apple munched and swallowed, bent his brown head to a bucket of water and drank.

Charlie let out a breath like a slow leak and sipped his coffee. "I'm worried about Rachel. And I don't get it. She's been fine for six years since they had to take her uterus. Why is she so broken up about it now?"

"Hattie is growing up fast, right before her eyes. I know how that feels with Maggie. But at least I can fantasize that if I met the right man in time, maybe I could have another one. She doesn't even have that."

Charlie nodded. "It makes me feel so damn helpless. I don't dare tell her I wish we could have had more, too. We built that extra bedroom for a reason. Every time I see it empty, it tears me up."

Abby watched Sweetwater nibbling the hay at his feet and

listened to the soft noises the other half-dozen horses made from their stalls. She inhaled the earthy smells, feeling comfortable and peaceful. Her eyes rose to follow barn swallows as they darted through the rafters on their scissor wings.

"I think you should tell her, gently, that you know how she feels. I think you two should grieve together. You never did deal with it when it happened because you were busy, new, elated parents. She'll be relieved that you can share this and that you understand. I think it will help her move through this more quickly and not stay stuck."

"I guess I've been a coward, hiding behind the excuse that I didn't want to make her feel worse. I'm not always good at this feelings stuff, and I guess it scares me. I knew you were going to say I should tell her how I feel, and I hate that you're right."

"But you still love me." Abby smiled and grabbed his hand.

"I couldn't live without you or your damn voice of reason," Charlie said and pulled her up for one of his big bear hugs.

"Why are you being such a brat to me today? I asked you nicely to pick up your mess in the living room so I can vacuum for Mom," Santi said, struggling to keep his voice even.

Maggie sat in the armchair with her headphones over her ears. She stuck out her tongue at him and made a show of turning up the volume on her iPod. Her legs swung, tennis shoes thumping hard against the chair, something they both knew Abby would never tolerate.

His head still hurt, and the nausea came and went. Maggie had dumped her entire Barbie and Ken collection onto the living room rug. It looked like some miniature half-naked cult had committed mass suicide, clothes strewn about, limbs at unnatural angles, faces frozen.

He turned on the vacuum and began to roll it toward the mess.

Maggie tore off her headphones and started screaming, "Stop it!"

88   Sue Boggio and Mare Pearl

"Then clean it up!" he said, moving the vacuum so close he inadvertently sucked up one of Barbie's skimpy outfits.

His sister began to beat him with her small, tight fists. "Stop it! I hate you! It's all your fault!" Her blows felt like he was being pelted with golf balls.

He turned off the vacuum and grabbed her by both arms. "You don't hit me. Hitting is wrong. What is the matter with you?"

She began to sob so hard her tears were spitting straight out from her red, twisted face. Her wavy, dark hair stuck out in all directions.

"We can get the Barbie clothes out of the vacuum bag. They aren't gone forever." Santi tried to reason with her, his own temper at the breaking point.

"My daddy's gone forever! Your dad killed my daddy! I hate you!"

Santi let go of her and nearly fell over as she rushed past him to her bedroom. She had never said anything like that before. He never even knew she thought about it like that. He stood there, weaving and sick. What the hell was he supposed to do now? He wished Abby would get home. Maggie wasn't his kid.

But she was his little sister, and he loved her. She was barely seven, and after she'd been raised with dead Bobby so present that he practically had a place at the dinner table, her mom had decided to go get a boyfriend.

Her histrionic sobs resonated through the adobe walls of their home, signaling to him he should go in there and try to calm her down.

He knocked at her door, his fist connecting with a painting she had done of their family. Mommy, Santi, and Maggie with dead Bobby hovering over them like the Goodyear blimp.

"Go away!"

"Fair warning, on the count of three I'm coming in. One, two, three." Santi had to push hard against the door to open it. She had piled toys and books in front of it, and the rug was tangled up with the clutter.

"Maggie, we need to talk," he said through the narrow opening he'd managed to make. "Come on, Mom will be home any second. Do you want her to find you like this?"

Her sobbing stopped. With a great deal of sniffling and ragged breathing, Maggie cleared the mess out of the way.

She sat in the midst of it, like some broken misfit doll. Her bony shoulders heaving spasmodically, snot bubbling from her nostrils.

Handing her a tissue, he sat down on a clear place on the rug. "Is this about what Mom told you, that she met a guy she wants to be friends with?"

She shrugged and blew her nose. "We don't need a boyfriend."

"Look, Maggie. She's been without Bobby since before you were even born. People get lonely for people their own age. You have me and Mom, but you still need friends your own age to play with, right? Or it would get pretty boring."

"My friends are all girls like me. Mom has lots of friends, she has CeCe and Ramone and Rachel and—"

"But see, that's different. Mom wants to have a boyfriend. I might want to have a girlfriend—"

"I know about kissing and sex," Maggie said. "It's gross."

"That's not the whole reason. It's about love and companionship."

Maggie pursed her lips, sighing deeply. The fight was leaving her. "I'm sorry I said your dad killed my daddy."

"Yeah, well, he did. But when you're older you'll understand it better. My dad and Bobby were both drunk and very angry, and stuff got out of hand. Doesn't make it right—it was way wrong. You know I'm sorry your dad is dead."

"Your dad is dead, too. I'm sorry he was so bad." Maggie's eyes were huge and wet as she stared at him a long moment before crawling into his lap.

He put his arms around her and rocked her. But even as he felt the tenderness of it, he sensed the darkness emerging like a gathering storm, swirling through his being. He was helpless to stop it. The cold, creeping, nameless enemy had returned.

CHAPTER 6

Abby made her way from the horse barn to the Vigils' house. A gentle breeze swirled around her bare arms and legs, evaporating the mist of sweat already forming in the midday heat. Rachel's goats began to call for her from their pen, a frantic chorus of *mehs*. Long Nubian ears flopped as they converged upon the fence closest to her. A sea of brown and white fur, and black muzzles, pink tongues, and searching golden eyes with the odd horizontal irises. She petted their sleek noses and assured them they were the finest goats anywhere. A pair of babies showed off for her by rearing up on their hind legs to dance for a few beats before diving sideways toward each other in perfect unison.

CeCe's chickens foraged in the yard, clucking their gossip in low tones until something funny sent them into wild cackling. The fenced vegetable garden was thriving, mounds of green divided by straight, well-weeded aisles of moist earth. A garden hose attached to a drip irrigation system fed each individual plant. It was the most water-sparing method CeCe could come up with to save her garden through the drought. Abby remembered when rain could be counted on, an infrequent but reliable visitor.

CeCe met her at the back door. "Come on in. We're just starting lunch." Her smile was wide, but her eyes looked weary.

Abby gave her a quick hug as she passed. "Hello, Rose. How are you today, Mort?" They sat expectantly at the table. Mort looked like he could sit like that all day, his blankness almost serene.

"I'm glad you're here," Mort announced. "I've been telling the board members all about you."

"Only the good things, I hope." Abby smiled.

"I should say so! You're one of our most loyal investors!"

Rose glared at Abby as if she didn't want such crazy talk encouraged.

"Here, Abby, help me slice these tomatoes," CeCe called over her shoulder from the sink in an obvious move to have a few private words with her.

"I want to rescue you today and take you to Albuquerque for some shopping. Can anyone stay with them?" Abby spoke in a hushed tone while CeCe clanked some pans in the sink.

"I'll get Rachel to, she won't mind," CeCe said in a whisper, and then in a loud tone: "We're having Mort's favorite, pastrami on rye with kosher dills and macaroni salad with tomatoes on the side." And then in her whisper, "I can't wait to get out of here. Here, start putting stuff on the table, and I'll call Rachel from the other room."

Abby plated the sliced tomatoes and grabbed the bowl of creamy macaroni salad dotted with bits of carrots and fresh peas. She placed them on the table, which was already set. A vase of CeCe's pink and yellow roses sat in the middle of the table, one her endless extra touches.

"I don't know who she's trying to impress. It's only us here." Rose waved her hand in the direction of the vase.

Abby felt the discomfort of not responding as a knot in her stomach. To think CeCe had to put up with it without any foreseeable end in sight.

CeCe returned, her wink signaling success. "Sit down, Abby. I'll get the rest."

Abby sat next to Mort, who didn't seem to notice her at the moment. Rose leaned around him. "I hear you gave up a fortune to stay here in New Mexico. What—are you meshugeh?"

"There were too many strings attached, and money isn't everything," Abby said.

"You could have fooled me," Rose said. "Before this one lost all of ours, I had a life. I had friends and activities and respect. Now I'm put out to pasture, and I'm not so old. I had a lot of life left to live."

"You still do, Ma. Here, make Papa his sandwich." CeCe handed her a plate of lean pastrami and dark mustard. "Here's the special rye bread I found for you all the way in Rio Rancho."

"And now I'm supposed to feel guilty you did your own mother a favor?"

"No, you're supposed to shut up and eat it," CeCe shot back, pouring tea into ice-filled tumblers.

"Do you hear how she talks to her mother?" Rose muttered but then did as she was told.

Miguel came in the back door nodding hello and going straight to the sink to wash his hands. Abby watched his back, shoulders slumped forward, head bent as he vigorously lathered his hands as if he was trying to wash off more than dirt.

His dark jeans and pale blue work shirt were clean, his mustache was neatly trimmed, and his full head of salt and pepper hair was neatly combed. He paused to kiss his wife and then sat down.

"Nice to see you, Abby," he said before drinking most of his iced tea in one motion. He didn't smile, she noticed, and she realized she hadn't seen the jovial Miguel in a very long time.

"I was in town at the feed store and heard some bad news. The Weavers are selling. Some developers bought all one hundred acres. They're taking the money and moving to Denver, where their daughter lives."

"Oh, no," CeCe sighed. "I've been afraid of that. After Evelyn's cancer and the drought . . ."

"How much did they get?" Rose asked.

"Ma!" CeCe admonished.

"It's a fair question. How much per acre was it worth?"

Miguel didn't look up from making his sandwich. "I expect they got a fortune for it."

"It's not the point, Ma. The Weavers are our neighbors. They farm chile and alfalfa, like we do. It's a tragedy they are giving up and moving away. It hurts all of us. Especially when those developers throw up a couple of hundred houses on the land, and they all need water."

"I think they're smart, those Weavers. They're getting out while the going is good. Instead of starving and going broke here, they can be near their daughter in a nice city and live in style. If you'd married a Jewish man he'd see what I'm saying."

In the stunned silence, the bite Abby was chewing lodged in her throat. Miguel stood up so fast the table jumped. He took his plate and threw it into the sink and seemed about to storm out when he turned around.

"A Jewish man would see what you're saying? A Mexican is too stupid?"

"Ma! Apologize!"

"Jewish people are practical—we've had to be. What's important is to survive and take care of your family, not hang onto land that is not earning a living. Wake up and smell the coffee already. The world is changing—you can't keep farming the way your ancestors did. You should think smart like a Jew, that's all I'm saying. Maybe you could sell off a portion, just enough that your poor wife doesn't have to worry so much and get old before her time."

CeCe tried to speak, but Miguel was too fast. "Pardon me, but wasn't it your smart Jewish husband who lost all of your money? You will not lecture me in my own home! I am the man of this house, and I gave you a roof over your ungrateful head. I will not take your disrespect."

He brushed past Rachel, who stood in the doorway with a tray of cookies in her hand.

"I was only saying—," Rose began.

"Now, now. Everyone just take a breath here," Mort said. "Board meetings can get a little high tempered."

"Did you hear how he yelled at me?" Rose asked.

CeCe snapped out of her shock. "You will never speak to my husband like that again. Rachel, do whatever you want with them—drop them out in the desert somewhere. Abby, I'll meet you at your car in a few minutes. We are getting the hell out of here."

After babysitting Maggie all afternoon, Santiago tore out of the house so fast he nearly knocked Abby down as she was coming in.

"Here, I bought you some clothes for college—," she began to say, rustling through her shopping bags.

"Just throw them on my bed," he said and then, remembering how it was supposed to go, added, "Thanks."

Once inside the car, he realized he didn't even know if Rosalinda would be home from work yet. Oh, well, he could always hang out with James. That was probably smarter. That way it would be more casual when she showed up.

James was home but not alone. There were two other guys, also older than Santi, sitting around in the small living room.

"Come on in, bro', meet some of my homeboys," James grinned, his eyes glassy. "This here is Bones and Carlos. Santiago is dead Baca's kid."

"Oh, yeah. I remember when that shit went down," the one James had pointed out as Bones said. Whenever he got his nickname, it must have been about a million cheeseburgers ago. There were no bones in sight.

Carlos, who should have been called Bones, nodded and sucked on his cigarette. "That was some heavy shit, man, blowing his brains out. That really pissed off the law. They wanted him alive."

Bones began to laugh, his flesh dancing beneath his folded arms. "He was saying, 'Fuck you, assholes! Clean up *this* mess!' How cool is that?"

"Shut up, Bones, his kid is right here and had to see it when he was little." James punched Carlos in the arm.

"Damn!" Carlos scowled and rubbed his skinny arm. "You don't know your own strength, bro'."

Santiago stood, trying to decide what to do. He was close enough to the door to think up some excuse and leave. These were the kind of guys he normally avoided. But they were camped out in Rosalinda's living room. He should stay in case she needed him to help throw them out. He sat down on the carpet in front of the coffee table.

"Get off the fucking chair, Carlos! Let Santiago sit there. He's my guest, man," James scolded.

"I'm okay here," Santi said, but then realized the pecking order was firmly enforced. Clearly Carlos was low dog. Santi claimed the vacated chair with a little pride.

"Hey, any kid of dead Baca is welcome to a chair at least," James said in a nicer tone to Carlos, who shrugged a "whatever" as he lit another cigarette.

Bones began to laugh again. "I remember this one time Baca and his brother Manny got into this fight about one of their badass roosters that got shredded in a cockfight, and Manny lost a lot of money on it and said something, so Baca hit him across his mouth with the dead rooster. Manny was spitting feathers! Pretty soon even Baca was laughing!"

Santiago tried to picture his father, but as soon as his face began to form, it got fuzzy. He'd get a lock on his eyes and then lose his mouth or nose, as if he couldn't see his whole face at once. But he laughed with them anyway.

"I could use another joint, James. Don't be stingy," Bones said.

"It's right there in the box, man. What, I got to smoke it for you, too?" James grabbed the box and pulled out a lumpy white joint and a lighter and proceeded to light it and give it a quick, deep pull before passing it.

Santiago was pretty sure Rosalinda wouldn't like this one bit. He watched as all three took long hits on the joint, and the sweet smell of marijuana traveled on blue smoke to his nose. He recognized the scent from the boys' restroom at Los Lunas High School.

Carlos passed the now nearly roach-sized joint to him. He started to decline but then decided it was easier to pretend to take a little puff and pass it to James. He thought he would just take a tiny bit of smoke into his mouth and then blow it out, but somehow he screwed it up and began to cough the red-hot smoke from his virgin lungs. He pictured them turning black, like in the pictures in his *Health and the Human Body* textbook from junior year.

They all laughed at him like he was their little puppy doing something cute. Carlos had a high-pitched, squeaky laugh that struck Santi as highly amusing, so he laughed too.

Bones picked up an empty beer bottle to signal James, who jumped up and returned with a round of cold ones.

Santi's throat was so dry, he thought he'd have just enough beer to wet his whistle, but he was amazed at how good it tasted. It was the best-tasting beer ever. Some potato chips appeared on the coffee table, and they all dug in. He felt good and then thought about Rosalinda and began to worry. "When does Rosalinda get home from work?"

"Another hour or two," James said through his chips. He stopped chewing, and his eyes bugged. "You got it for her, don't you?"

Carlos and Bones began to cat call and laugh. "Don't bother, man, she's cold. Everybody wants Rosalinda, and she don't want nobody. I'm beginning to think she's some kind of lesbo."

This earned Carlos another slug to his shrunken, tattoo-covered bicep. "Hey—this tat is new! Give it a chance to heal already!"

"As if I'd let you near my cousin, dog. You ain't even fit to be looking at her. Now Santiago here is a good kid, and he's smart. Plus his old lady's rich, so he can go for it. You have my blessing, Santi. But Carlos is right about one thing. She's one picky bitch, so don't get your hopes up. And she's older, so she might think you're just a kid."

Santiago found himself holding another joint that Bones had passed, and this time the smoke wasn't so bad. Part of him was screaming inside to stop, but it was easy to ignore it. Besides, he needed to get more life experience before he went off to college. *If he went off to college . . .*

He'd show Rosalinda he wasn't just some kid. Everybody said how mature he was for his age. She'd see it because she was smart, and she'd love him back. No wonder she didn't want anyone else. He was meant for her, he just knew it.

Pretty soon they were all laughing about something, and Santi couldn't remember what was funny, so he got scared. What if his brain stayed like that? It was like every thought was disconnected from the one that came before it. He looked at the others, and he felt like he'd just been dumped into the room from a spaceship. Then he couldn't remember why he was there at all, and a wave of icy fear clutched at his throat. It paralyzed his vocal chords, and he couldn't speak. He would never be able to speak again, and everyone would call him that dumb Santi kid.

"From now on," Bones was saying, "I'm going to call you Li'l Baca. Cause that's an honor, man, and you deserve it. Li'l Baca is a stand-up dude, man, that's what I'm saying."

"Shit!" James said as headlights shone through the front window. "Move it, man! Rosalinda is home early!" He grabbed a lit joint from Carlos and stubbed it out, throwing it into the box. He ran it into his room while Carlos picked up trash and emptied the ashtray. Even Bones moved, emerging from the bathroom with a can of spray deodorizer, spraying it like he was fumigating bugs.

Santi watched the scene as it seemed to play out in slow motion. Obviously this was a well-choreographed drill.

Rosalinda came through the door, catching Bones still spraying. He grinned at her and said, "Your cousin throws some wicked farts, girl. What do you feed that boy?"

But Rosalinda wasn't looking at him; her eyes were locked on Santiago's. "Hi, Santi, what brings you by?"

His vocal chords seemed to thaw under her gaze. "You," he croaked.

James and the others started to laugh, but Rosalinda held up one hand and they were silenced. She then held out the same hand to Santi, who clasped it and stood. In the silence, she led him to her bedroom. She turned around to say, "James, you and your boys can leave now."

Her room didn't look like it belonged in the rundown house. She had painted the walls sky blue and attached white stars to the ceiling. The bedspread of the carefully made bed was deep blue with gold suns and silver crescent moons. A poster of Van Gogh's *Starry Night* hung over her dresser. The furniture was all in white wicker, including a rocking chair in the corner with moon and sun pillows. The throw rug matched the bedspread. "Wow," he said. "This is beautiful."

Rosalinda was lighting candles that sat on every surface, all white, all sending the sweet scent of vanilla to his nose. When she finished lighting what seemed like a hundred of them, she switched off the ceiling light, surrounding them in a gentle ivory glow.

Without saying a word, she began to take off her short black hostess dress, revealing a black bra and thong panty. She reached up and let down her hair in a sudden dark tumble that reached to her waist.

He waited and watched, afraid to move, afraid to end this dream. She walked over to him and helped him undress down to his boxers. She reached behind his head, her breath soft against his cheek, and removed the round silver clasp that held his ponytail. She put it on her thumb like a ring and ran her hands through his hair.

"I never—," he started to confess his virginity.

She kissed him then, and his arms were around her the way he had imagined. They fell back onto her bed, throwing back the comforter and sheet. All thoughts and worries dissolved as he began to explore her body with light, reverent caresses. Her breasts, the flat plane of her tummy, the curve of her back to her shapely behind. Her thighs were lean and solid under his exploring lips and fingers.

Soft sounds purred from her lips, and she began to put his hands where she wanted them. Suddenly he was on his back and she was on top him and they were joined. So this was what all the talk was about. All the song lyrics, the movies, nothing could have prepared him for the transcendence of their bodies, their spirits, their souls making love. He looked up to her face, dark eyes reflecting a sparkle from the candlelight, and behind her, the ceiling shone with a galaxy of glowing stars.

CeCe had retired early that evening. After her shopping trip with Abby, she'd taken trays into her parents' room and then had a quick supper by herself. Rose had kept her back to her, and Mort had been napping. She had not seen Miguel since he had stormed out during lunch.

She lay in her bed listening to an oldies station on the radio, remembering a time when she and Miguel first started seeing each other. When making love together was new, not better, but new. When was the last time she and Miguel had made love? She missed him.

She got up to wrap a small box with pearly white paper.

"In a white room, with black curtains, at the station . . . ," Eric Clapton sang, pulling her back deeper in time. She remembered her parents had said the cruelest things about Miguel, sight unseen. CeCe's sudden anger felt like a bad case of reflux. They were such bigots. Obviously Rose still felt superior, even after no one else wanted to take her or Mort in. What chutzpah.

But Miguel's family, which was only his father and Aunt Maria by then, hadn't approved of her, either. His father was angry his only son had taken up with a Jewish girl. Miguel's mother had left them when Miguel was still a teenager, when Teresa, Miguel's older sister, went away to college in Arizona. Miguel never talked much about his mother's abandonment, except to say he had been nearly seventeen and hadn't needed a mama anymore. He was closer to his papa and the land anyway.

His father had died soon after CeCe and Miguel married and either had intended to keep Miguel his heir or hadn't gotten around to changing his will. Either way, the newlyweds found themselves in charge of all sixty acres of Sol y Sombra, forty-eight acres of chile, six acres of alfalfa, and the remaining six acres for the houses and barns. His mother had died a few years ago, never having known about CeCe, as far as she was aware. They had received a brief letter from Teresa, who still lived in Tucson. CeCe had urged him to renew his contact with his sister, his only remaining family except for some distant cousins on his father's side who lived somewhere near the Mexican border. But he had taken her into his arms and said he had all the family a man could ever need.

CeCe inspected her gift-wrapped box with the cobalt ribbon and smiled. Miguel would love this surprise. It would be nice to see him smile again. It gave her strength, that dashing smile of his under his Zorro mustache. They desperately needed to reconnect. Form their tightly united front, like in the old days. Miguel only needed to be reminded of that.

Inside his card she wrote: "In our love, we are together. We'll get through this, *mi corazon.*" He always got a kick out of it when she spoke Spanish to him, even after all these years; by now she could speak somewhat fluently, New Mexico style. The peppermint glue was tacky against her tongue when she licked the envelope. She felt goofy for a second as she pressed it to her heart. He truly was her heart. She propped the card against his gift on his end table, his name written in a flourish across the front.

She heard the old metal doorknob jostle just before Miguel entered. Maybe it was her imagination, but he looked a little more slumped than usual. He threw his hat from a distance to the top of his chest of drawers, and it landed where it was supposed to. Nine times out of ten.

"I looked for you. I couldn't find you," CeCe said. Buying a present for him was her way of sending him what she called white light. A powerful surge of love energy. God energy.

"I didn't want to be found," he said flatly, not looking at her. Which was not like him, especially as she sat on the bed in her undies and a T-shirt. "Not bad for a *vieja*," he'd said on more than one occasion. She could tell by the way he unbuttoned his shirt that he was still angry. But deeper yet, hurt.

"Miguel, don't let Rose do this to you. You know how she is," she said. They used to be able to just let this stuff roll off their backs. Rose was the ignorant one, after all. In a way CeCe was thankful for Mort's lack of brain activity. He had forgotten he was a racist.

"It's different when she's in my face doing it. Under my roof! A roof she wouldn't have if not for me! A stupid Mexican!"

"Honey, after almost forty years, what do you care what the stupid old woman thinks?" She could throttle Rose for hurting him. Even after her own husband had been persecuted for being a Jew. You do not humiliate the head of a Hispanic family, especially in front of his family.

Miguel didn't answer her. He stripped his clothes off in silence and went in their bathroom. Why was he so mad at *her*?

"You know, I can't help what comes out of my mother's mouth," she defended herself. It sounded a little loud, almost angry, too. CeCe felt the tears brim to her lids as she heard Miguel turn on the shower. His cold silence was shattering.

She started to go to him, hug him and kiss him and let him know he was the king of all men. Take his pain and wipe it off of the earth forever. But he shut the door.

Her tears came then, like the downpour of rain they all prayed for. She walked to the pearly white present standing out like a smile in the room and stuck it in her dresser drawer along with the card, covering them both with a pair of worn-out panties. A gift somehow didn't seem right, now. Nothing did anymore.

On some level, Rachel knew she was dreaming, but it seemed so real. She was with her late bruja aunt, Maria. Tía Maria appeared much younger than at the time of her death, when her disease and evil ventures had made her look every inch the bad witch she had become.

Her face, though still aged with wrinkles, had softened and glowed with health. Her long hair was dark and shiny, held back by Mexican silver combs with abalone inlays.

She was watching her with one of her clients. She could smell the burning sage bundles and hear the bubbling pots of various curative concoctions on the stove. After the woman left, Rachel's job was to clean up and ready the kitchen for Maria's next patient. Maria was teaching her how to gather and prepare the herbs, even the most dangerous ones. She learned quickly. "A true bruja," Maria said with pride.

"Mi tía, I have missed you so much. Why haven't you come to visit me sooner?"

"Mi'ja, I haven't missed a thing," Maria said with a smile that showed a mouthful of perfect teeth. Her breath smelled as sweet as a baby goat's, not soured with tequila. Her chin whiskers were also gone, and her eyes sparkled clear and bright, emanating goodness. "Your Hattie is my joy, as are you, still."

Rachel felt so peaceful sitting with her now, without the haunting disappointment and guilt she had felt since Maria's death. The last time she had seen her aunt alive, they had fought bitterly. Rachel had discovered that the potion Maria had instructed her to slip into Abby's tea was not to make Abby fall out of love with Bobby, but was the same abortive formula Maria had used to make

Rachel lose her own baby ten years previously. Abby had become ill, but fortunately Maggie had survived within her convulsing womb to be born perfect at the proper time.

As the years went by, Rachel had come to understand Maria had become lost in her severely uncontrolled diabetes and in her misguided mission to give Rachel what she thought she wanted: Abby's Bobby, her Roberto. That seemed like a lifetime ago, especially now as she sat with this transformed Maria. "You look so beautiful, tía. Are you happy where you are?"

"I am very happy, mi'ja," said Maria, putting a smooth hand on hers. "I've come to help you. You need to stop yearning for a baby you can never have. You need to stop regretting not having Roberto's baby. What is done is done. Be thankful for all that you have. Fill your heart with such joy you don't have room for sadness. Please, mi'ja, find your peace."

Maria's hand sent a surge of comfort through her. "Gracias, tía," Rachel said, even as the visitation faded away and she turned over in her bed, drifting back to sleep.

That evening, Rachel poured her father another glass of iced tea as they all sat on the back porch of her house facing the verdant bosque.

A peacock somewhere in the tall trees by the river called to its mate with its jungle cry. Mort was still fascinated by the peacocks, and sometimes he would respond with the Tarzan yell, which came out of him in a high-pitched, wet wheeze. It made Hattie giggle so hard she'd wet her pants.

"You've been coming over more than usual," Rachel said, squeezing a lemon wedge into Miguel's glass as he held it up to her from his rosewood rocker, another salvaged piece from Charlie's grandmother. "Everything all right?"

Stupid question. Not that he would ever tell her things weren't. He would never admit to wanting to strangle Rose or tell her that he was devastated as his chile plants withered under an unrelenting sun.

He smiled up at her before answering. "Sí, mi'ja." She understood why a Hispanic father would lie to protect his children. He would perhaps never see her as an adult.

She poured Charlie tea while their gazes lingered. Since he had shared with her his own sadness that they couldn't have more children, they were even closer. She had felt herself starting to heal with his strong arms around her.

"I pray to San Ysidro that we do not lose the chile fields," Miguel said to Charlie. "We can't afford to buy all of our feed, so the alfalfa helps, but it's the chile harvest that pays the bills."

"We'll do what we have to do. I'll work graveyards as a security guard if I need to. Don't worry about losing the land," said Charlie. He gave her father a reassuring wink. The same wink he gave her when she was giving birth to Hattie.

"And the cheese business and café are doing well, Papa," Rachel added.

"It shouldn't come down to us or the minnow," said her father, gazing out past the trees toward the river. "My family goes back four hundred years in the Rio Grande Valley, to Juan de Oñate. We established the rules of the water and land with Spain, Mexico, and the United States. And now they say there is a danger of us losing these rights and our water. Take away our water, and they take away our lives."

Rachel put her hand on her father's shoulder.

"If the minnow needs a constant supply of water to survive, why not get rid of all that salt cedar that guzzles the river water?" Charlie asked. "We have the technology for that. Hell, Rache can rent out the goats to clean up the bosque. That's not rocket science. But no. We can't do that. What if the flycatcher needs the salt cedar for a nesting habitat? It's crazy. There's a flaw in that Endangered Species Act, all right." Charlie perched in front of Miguel on the porch railing. It was getting later in the evening, and the sunset burned a hot pink behind him, just above the treetops. It was certainly cooler down here by the ever-shrinking river.

"Whether we get the water we've contracted or not, we still have to pay the same tax on it. Ei-ee! The government's double standards! Is that not kicking a man when he is already down? And then, on top of that, we still have to pay for flood insurance. This poor skinny river can't even reach its banks, let alone dream of surpassing them."

"It's their own goddamn mismanagement of the Rio Grande," Charlie said, looking out toward it just beyond the trees. "They overengineered her. She doesn't live up to her name anymore. It breaks my heart."

"But why are only a few of us being forced to bear the burden of the Endangered Species Act?" Miguel emphasized his words with work-worn hands, the knuckles of his fingers ashen.

"Don't the Native American pueblos count as endangered? Their ancient customs and traditions depend upon water, and they were here way before any of us," Rachel said. "Let's see. The silvery minnow, the flycatcher, or thirteen or so pueblos—duh! How do these people lay their heads on their pillows at night?"

Her father took a long swig of iced tea as if he needed a glass of tequila instead. She thought of the added stress Rose and Mort were in Papa's life. No wonder he stayed around most evenings, drinking tea; except more and more lately he and Charlie knocked down cold Mexican beers, tinged with lime.

"I don't think there's anything in the Endangered Species Act that overrides anyone's water rights. But who knows what the federal government can pull off. It's really a matter of federal contract law, at this point," said Charlie. He removed his hat and scratched at his brown waves. He never had expressed much hope of the government helping out farmers. He always said men who lived in Washington, D.C., couldn't quite wrap their heads or billfolds around the notion of independent farming, only corporate agriculture.

Rachel knew Charlie's heart ached for Miguel as much as hers did. Miguel and Charlie had become father and son after all these years of toiling side by side.

Miguel tossed the toothpick he had been splintering in his mouth into the bushes as if flipping a dagger. Just above the tree-tops, Orion was starting to light up in the sky, the three stars of his belt hanging well above the trees. "I heard Hector Gonzales down in Tome was rejected for all five well applications. How do we get supplemental water when our well applications are being turned down?"

"And all the people in Albuquerque who continue to use water for their big lawns and swimming pools don't even get taxed for it. We pay for it," Charlie pointed out. "I swear, an honest man can't catch a break anymore."

Miguel rocked and nodded in agreement.

They were silent for a minute or two. A star fell.

"I've been angry at God," Miguel said. "I've tried to be a good, decent man, and now all of this . . ." He stared down as if God were in the planked porch floor.

Rachel couldn't believe what she was hearing. Her father had never lost his faith in God. Or ever even questioned Him. But now she could see he was at risk of losing an inner battle and slipping away from his foundation, his faith.

"Papa, you always said what doesn't kill us makes us stronger."

His lips twitched in a small, sad grin. "Yes, mi'ja, but the jury is still out on this one."

Abby stood nervously on her front patio in the morning light, watching for any cars coming down her road. Maggie was already off to day camp at the Belén YMCA, Santiago was working with Miguel, and it was Monday, so she had the day to herself. It had turned out that Ben didn't have any classes until evening, so she had invited him to her home.

After changing her clothes three times, she'd decided on jean shorts and the sleeveless white blouse with traditional Mexican embroidery Carmen had made for her. She wore a new matching bra and panties in ice blue satin, just in case. Ben had been very patient with her difficulty in finding private time away from the kids. Although they had dated only a few chaste weeks, it felt as if they had known each other for years. Saying goodnight was getting harder and more prolonged.

She could see a plume of dust before the vehicle came into sight, and her stomach lurched. Here it was, broad daylight, and she was thirty-seven. Ben would be only the second man she had slept with in her entire life, and it had been seven years since she had been in Bobby's arms. This was nuts. She could be reading or gardening or seeing friends or helping CeCe. She could have left well enough alone and stayed a virtuous and celibate widow. But no, here she was, premeditating a morning tryst with a hunky Australian whom everyone she cared about completely disapproved of—but it wasn't his car. It was Ramone's.

"Where's my bouquet of flowers?" he said, getting out of his squad car.

"What?"

"You're standing out here like the welcoming committee," he said, giving her a peck on her cheek. His mustache was soft as it brushed her skin. Then he lowered his sunglasses and narrowed his eyes. "But it isn't me you were expecting, now, is it, Mrs. Silva."

"I'm just standing on my own patio on my morning off. You got a problem with that, Sheriff?"

"You have on perfume and makeup, and your hair is all shiny and brushed out and hanging seductively around your shoulders."

"I may have a visitor coming," Abby said, feeling her cheeks warm at her choice of words.

"Minnow Man?"

Abby smacked his arm. "Let's get inside out of this sun. I can feel my skin getting damaged."

"Do you want me to pull my car around back so I don't scare him off?" Ramone laughed.

"He won't let that stop him."

"Minnow Man is motivated."

"So is Widow Woman, so come in and have your coffee and tell me why you're here."

When they walked in the house, Abby's retinas held onto the white glare of the sun, making it hard to adjust to the subdued indoor light. Her phone was ringing, and she managed to trip over some toys Maggie had left on the floor. She was flat on her ass on the polished wood floor before she knew it, intense pain shooting from her tailbone.

Ramone smiled down at her as he walked past and she sat cussing under her breath. Oh God, he was answering her phone.

"Mrs. Silva's residence. Sheriff Ramone Lovato speaking." Ramone put out his hand to help her up, his wicked twinkle in his eyes. "I'll see if she can get up off the floor to take your call."

Abby stood, grabbed the phone with one hand, and felt her bruised bottom with the other. Ramone doubled over with laughter as he headed to the kitchen for his coffee.

"Hello?"

"What's going on—are you all right?" Ben asked.

"Oh, that's just Ramone being impossible. Are you on your way?"

"Yeah, that meeting took a bit longer than I thought. I'm just heading to my car now. Will there still be enough time to get together?"

Good. He sounded as eager as she felt. "The coast is clear, or will be as soon as I ditch the fuzz."

"I'm on my way, love," he said.

"Be safe," Abby said and then winced. She had to get over her constant anxiety that something bad would happen as soon as she wanted something. Or someone.

"Be there in two shakes."

She carried the phone back to her kitchen, where Ramone had

helped himself to coffee, a slice of cheese, and a small handful of blueberries.

"Do the Vigils know you're keeping company with the silvery minnow savior? How about Rachel—she give you her blessing?"

"I haven't told them yet. I wanted to make sure there was something to tell. I mean, we've only been out five or six times. Besides, you know, he isn't some rabid environmentalist. He's not anti-farmer. He can see their point of view, too. He just thinks that the minnow should be preserved. It's not good for the planet to have species go extinct."

"Man, you better work on your argument. That's pretty lame. I don't buy it, and I'm on your side. But that's not why I came over, and since you're going to throw me out in about two minutes, I better get to the point."

"What, you really did come here on business?" Abby could hear her anxious tone and tried to squelch it. "What's up?"

"There's this guy, James Ortiz. Used to run with Baca and his brother. He's been locked up in the penitentiary the last five years for breaking and entering, grand theft, and a string of smaller stuff. James was with Manny on the inside and showed no signs of rehabilitating his sorry ass. Anyway, he's out and back in Esperanza. A guy told me he saw him with Santi over at the Sonic drive-in."

"Santi? No way!" Abby said. "Must have been someone else."

"Who is Santi hanging with these days? You said he goes out almost every night."

"He's going off to college in a few months. I'm trying to give him some space. I'm sure he's spending time with the same good kids from school he's always hung out with, the track kids mostly."

"I could see the attraction a guy like James could hold for Santi. He's older, was tight with his dead father. Santi might have some curiosity."

"Santi's a good kid—you know he's a good kid."

"I want him to stay that way, that's all."

"You really think it was him with that James person?"

"Just ask him. With your recent distractions, you might be taking too much for granted. Good kids get tangled up with bad ones every day. Don't accuse him of anything, just ask him where he's going and who he's seeing, like you always have. If he doesn't have anything to hide, he won't mind you asking."

"Okay, but I still think you're wrong," Abby said and looked at her watch.

"If Minnow Man is here before ten-thirty, he was speeding and I'm going to have to give him a talking to," Ramone said, pouring himself another cup of coffee.

"Take the cup with you, and don't let the door hit you on the way out," Abby said, giving him a shove toward the door.

He laughed his booming laugh, resisting her shove, and then relented, making her stumble forward. "Ye-owch!" she cried, grabbing her throbbing tailbone with both hands.

"Better put some ice on that thing. Cool it off," Ramone teased before the screen door sprang shut.

She went into her room and pulled down her shorts, expecting to see some hellacious bruise already forming. Her skin was bright red, as if she'd been spanked, and that was how she felt. Like the universe had just smacked her one. She had contemplated pleasures of the flesh, and the universe, using her daughter as its instrument, had injured the one aspect of her body that needed to function without pain. To experiment, she tilted her hips, and in answer, an electric burst of pain shot from her tailbone. Great. Maybe it was broken. What did they do for that? With her luck, a total body cast.

Abby began to giggle as she imagined greeting her prospective lover at the door with an ice pack strapped to her ass.

She heard a car door slam and looked at her watch. It was only 10:25. He had broken every speed limit law to get there.

"Hello?" he called through the screen door.

She came to the door, a bundle of nerves. She could feel the heart-thumping effects of adrenaline pumping through her veins.

Was it too early for a drink? Would adding orange juice to alcohol help her reconcile drinking at such an early hour of the day? Too bad she didn't have Champagne—oh—she did! An unopened bottle left over from Santi's graduation! She could make mimosas!

"Hi," she said, trying to quell the monkey chatter in her head.

"Hi," he said as he entered the door and kissed her.

She kissed him back. They seemed to be getting right down to business.

"Abby," he breathed her name in her ear, "I can't wait to be with you." He was kissing her neck, and just as she started to melt into it, he reached behind to give her butt a squeeze.

She yelped in pain.

He drew back. "What's the matter? Did I hurt you?"

She reached for him. "It's nothing. I fell on the wood floor, so it's a little tender, that's all. No worries," she said, using one of his expressions. She kissed him eagerly—maybe too eagerly, for their front teeth collided.

"Sorry," she said. He had put his hand to his mouth. But he was smiling when he took his hand away.

"I think we're just a bit nervous," he said. "Let's sit down and talk."

"Would you like a mimosa? Orange juice and Champagne? Well, technically it's sparkling wine. I don't normally drink this early, but this is a date, right?" Abby was yanking open the fridge and pulling out the juice and the bottle of New Mexican Gruet Brut.

"Yeah, sounds good," he said, his smile wide against his tan face. His brown eyes looked green in the yellow light of her kitchen. His hair was windblown from the drive down. He preferred open windows to air conditioners. His blue-checked cotton short-sleeved shirt and cargo shorts were the type found in expensive sporting goods stores. His boots were well worn from trekking through the bosque, measuring water depths in the Rio Grande, counting silvery minnows. Sunglasses hung from a colorful woven Guatemalan strap around his neck.

Abby quickly made a cheese and fruit platter to go with their beverages and set it all on the table. She raised her glass; delicious orange scent effervesced from the Champagne flute.

He raised his: "To us." They clinked and drank, he taking a sip and Abby downing half of hers in one gulp.

It hurt to sit, but she tried to ignore it. This was too important. She really liked this man and wanted so much to please him, to take their promising beginning to the next level.

He nibbled at the cheese, a slice of pear, and a sesame cracker. In the quiet she could hear the birds chattering outside her window. She took another drink of her mimosa, needing it for pain control as well as its calming effect.

After they had drained their glasses, Abby reached for Ben's hand and led him to her bedroom.

"We don't have to do this today, you know, with your sore bum and all," he said.

"I want to," she said, kissing him.

He kissed her back and seemed to take the reins now that it was certain. She could feel his arousal and began to notice the lack of her own. Her thoughts kept intruding. What if Santi was hanging out with criminals and she didn't even know it?

Her clothes were off, and she tried to look at his body and get lost in her desire. He was beautiful, fit and tan, and she was pale next to him. The hair on his chest was more than Bobby ever had, but it had lightened from the sun.

She tried to summon the feelings she came home alone with after their dates, the solitary yearning that kept her awake in the moonlight. What if she grew to love him as desperately as she had loved Bobby and he went back to Australia? She never wanted to leave Esperanza. She didn't even want to go as far as Albuquerque— he'd have to live here with her. What if her cherished friends could never accept him? What about her daughter, Bobby's daughter . . .

Her body moved, her lips, her tongue, everything functioned except her libido, which had flown out the window to join the birds. She seemed to watch their lovemaking from somewhere outside of herself. A crushing disappointment began to overwhelm her. She wanted this to be magical, earthshaking, and she was numb. Maybe her fall had damaged the nerves to her nether regions somehow. Served her right, this beautiful man making sweet love to her and she, this lousy mother, this unfaithful widow couldn't enjoy it.

Bobby's face began to appear behind her shut lids, so she opened her eyes and was startled to see Ben's half-hooded eyes staring into her. Afraid he might see her tenseness, she shut them again and tried to feign her desire. Bobby's image refused to vacate the premises. Then came his voice, accusing and jealous: *What are you doing with this guy?*

I want to love him, she told him. *You're gone—you left me, remember?*

She held Ben as he came, shuddering in her arms.

Her tailbone felt like it had broken free of her spine and was piercing her inner flesh. Tears slid from her eyes, and she couldn't remember any recent time when she had felt so alone.

CHAPTER 7

"Maggie—hurry! You'll miss the bus. I see Rachel and Hattie coming across the field." Abby knocked on her daughter's bedroom door.

"I'm coming, but where are my swim goggles? We're going to the pool today, and Karen snooty-pants says she has goggles, and so I have to take mine."

"Why do you want to be like her if she's a snooty-pants?"

The door swung open. Maggie appeared with swim goggles over her eyes, forcing her wavy, dark bob into a gravity-defying Einstein 'do. She carried her fins. "You just don't get it, Mom. But let's just see if she has real Little Mermaid swim fins. Stun her buns."

Maggie paraded past, her beach towel trailing from her bag in regal fashion.

Rachel was letting herself and Hattie in through the kitchen door. Hattie was perfectly attired in an ocean-life print sundress, her swimwear and accoutrements tucked into a matching beach bag. Her fine, snow-white hair was in a french braid, setting off her heart-shaped face and porcelain complexion.

"Who's driving?" Abby asked, looking for her purse and keys. She could feel Rachel's cool, appraising stare and felt like a nincompoop, as Maggie would put it.

"Since we walked over here, I guess you are," Rachel said, herding the chattering girls through the door.

"Duh," Abby said to the empty kitchen as she closed the door.

Rachel was unusually quiet as Abby drove them to the highway and the café. Maggie and Hattie sang one of the camp songs, giggling through the incomprehensible lyrics.

"Rough night?" Abby asked as they unlocked the café. The girls stood in the shade of the front porch, waiting for the camp bus to arrive.

"Mort was having some twilight delirium, so I helped Ma settle him in for the night. But that's not it. I don't mind helping with Mort."

Abby started for the coffeemaker. So they were going to play "That's not it" to her twenty questions. "So what is it then? I can tell you're in one of your moods."

"Oh, I don't know. Maybe it's that I had to hear from my daughter that my so-called best friend has a quote unquote new boyfriend, and he's the minnow guy that no one likes. "

"Oh," Abby said. "I was going to tell you. It's only been a couple of weeks. I didn't want to get everyone all fired up if I didn't end up liking him." She filled the pot with filtered water while Rachel scooped out coffee. The scent of locally roasted *biscochito*-flavored coffee bloomed in the tense air between them.

"How could you? Where do you think you live? What community saved your pregnant, grief-stricken ass?"

"He's not against the farmer." Abby started putting her bread-making ingredients together.

"It's *his* study the environmentalists posted on their website. You are sleeping with the enemy."

Abby was about to say she wasn't even sleeping with him when she flashed back to the previous day's disappointment. She could feel the heat of her embarrassment in her cheeks, something Rachel was bound to misinterpret. "Look, I didn't go looking for the one guy who would set you guys off. We met by accident; we connected. We're starting to get to know each other, that's all. It's not like I picked him out of some eligible, interested guy lineup." She beat her eggs into a frenzy.

"By accident? You met him when he was down here disrupting our farmers' coalition meeting. He came here uninvited and stuck his nose in. He's an outside agitator, and you shouldn't be fraternizing with him."

"You're so melodramatic. You sound like General Patton, like this is war."

"It *is* war—that's what you don't get. We're fighting for our lives here, Abby. You have restaurant money streaming in from San Diego, all your investment income; you're living off your interest while your fat principal sits in the bank. Even without the Endangered Species Act taking our water, we'd be in serious trouble. It's killing my papa—don't you care?"

"Of course I care! I'm closer to your dad than I ever was to my own. Your family *is* my family—at least that's how I feel. But you don't even have your facts straight. Not one drop of water has been diverted to save the minnow."

"But the law says they can, and they will. He's brainwashing you already."

Abby added salt to her dough, trying to give them each a moment to calm down. "Look, I don't even know if this will turn into anything. But he's not some monster trying to hurt the farmer. He grew up on a sheep farm. He's not a politician or part of the government; he's just a teacher. He's a good man who thinks all life is precious; how can that be so bad?"

Rachel shook her head, tears of anger pooling in her ocean blue eyes. "Because he's trying to save some stupid, tiny fish at the expense of my family, my way of life, my father's legacy. He chooses to ignore the human suffering in favor of his precious minnow."

"It doesn't have to be one or the other. What saves the minnow saves the river, and that saves the farmers."

"Is that what he whispers to you in your bed? He's lying to you Abby. He knows better than that. When the irrigation season is cut off by mid-July and our chiles are dying on the vine a full month before harvest and his little fish have all the water they need to make more little fish that are no good to anybody, maybe then you'll see. You'll see your neighbors selling off their land to developers and tract houses covering every square inch of Esperanza. But that's okay with you, right, city girl?"

Abby felt slapped. "I love Esperanza. It's my home."

"You better figure out what you love more: Esperanza or having that man in your bed."

A hailstorm of little fists pelting the front door signaled the bus had arrived. Both women put on their mother smiles and waved good-bye to their daughters.

"I hate fighting with you, Rachel," Abby said after a moment of charged silence.

Rachel's tears began to spill onto her cheeks. "Everyone is fighting with everyone else—Rose and Papa, even Ma and Papa. I just can't take one more thing tearing us all apart. I need you to be my friend."

"Maybe I need a friend right now, too, who would say to me, 'Go for it. You've been alone for over seven long years. You deserve to be happy.' A friend who puts what I want over an ideological argument about a damn minnow!"

"Ideological? You are either for the farmer or against us—"

"Ben is not leading some crusade to put the family farmer out of business. He's not down here working against your family or anybody else's. He just likes me and I like him and we want to date."

"Fine, just keep him away from me and my family. We have enough to deal with right now," Rachel said, dabbing at her eyes with a napkin.

Abby wanted to tell her that would never work. If Ben became a part of her life, he'd be a part of theirs. Their lives were too entwined for them to draw lines like that, or they would lose each other completely. But she sighed and held it back. She'd give Rachel some time to absorb the idea and meanwhile start to work on the others. CeCe and Charlie would never begrudge her a chance at happiness, would they?

She thrust her floured hands into her bread dough and began to knead it. The best therapy she knew.

"I have to get out about a million cheese orders today, so I hope you and Ma can spare me," Rachel said, her cue that they were done fighting for now.

"No sweat. Do you have both Leticia and Jenny coming in today?"

"Yeah, we'll get it done. I'll probably be here late, so I might as well close."

"I could take the girls home with me," Abby said.

"Thanks," Rachel said quietly and left for the back kitchen.

"What are friends for?" Abby said to her bread dough.

When Abby got home with the Maggie and Hattie, she found Charlie and Santiago sitting outside in the shade of the old cotton-wood tree. They were chugging iced tea, the nearly empty pitcher in the grass between their lawn chairs. Even in the shade the grass looked dry and burned from the sun. She hoped the old tree's roots were sunk deeply into the ever-lowering water table. Losing that tree would be devastating. It cradled her entire house with shade. She could feel its benevolent life force and loved it like a member of the family.

"Daddy!" Hattie cried, flying into Charlie's arms.

"Maggie!" Santi said, opening up his arms for Maggie to dive into. Abby put her hand to her heart as she watched how Santi helped Maggie past that moment when it was obvious she had no daddy.

"You should have seen us! Hattie and I were the best swimmers there, and we got to be in the four feet instead of at the baby end," Maggie bragged to her brother.

"See? And you complained when I made you learn how to swim with your face in the water last summer. Admit it, you have the smartest brother in the universe." He tickled her without mercy.

Charlie was laying noisy smooches on Hattie's bare arms as she squealed and writhed in delight. "Where's Rachel?" he asked over the din.

"Catching up on cheese orders. I think the van was about loaded for the deliveries, and she and her girls were cleaning up. Leticia was going to give her a lift back and help her with the evening milking. You two want to stay for dinner?"

"Nah, I'll rustle up some cowboy grub for the little lady and me."

"I want cowboy grub!" Maggie said.

"Tonight I'm frying up some rattlesnake and coyote butt," Charlie said, hoisting Hattie up piggyback-style.

"That's my favorite—can I go, Mom, please?" Maggie held onto her hand.

"Yeah—let—her—come," Hattie said as Charlie jogged her up and down.

"Aren't you two sick of each other yet?" Abby laughed.

"Yeah, right, Mom. See you later." Maggie swatted Charlie's hind end. "Giddyup, horsie." And off they jogged, Maggie galloping her phantom pony beside them.

As Santi and Abby stood watching them, she wondered if Maggie would ever have a horsie to ride of her own. Her eyes drifted to the clouds building up over the mountains, but she knew better than to hope for rain. June was almost over, and then the summer monsoons had a chance of starting. The rains had to come this year. Everything depended on it—and it was completely out of everyone's control.

"What's for dinner? I'm starved," Santi said.

"We have leftover chicken. I could heat it up with some barbecue sauce and make a salad."

"I'll make the salad. Do we have spinach?"

Abby nodded. A breeze began to lift the heavy, hot air. Some clouds drifted over the sun, and she tried to remember what rain smelled like.

"Sure, now it gets cloudy. Not when I'm out thinning chile plants and it's like a hundred degrees."

"You look like you got sunburned. Aren't you using your sunscreen?"

Santi shrugged and held the screen door for her. "It wears off after half a day, and I'm not going to take it out there like some little girl."

Bobby had also been rebellious about using sunscreen in California when they surfed. He always said his Hispanic skin loved the sun. She decided to let the argument drop and instead set out the chicken while Santi dragged out his salad fixings. "You were home pretty late last night. I didn't get to talk to you. It's nice to have some time together, get caught up."

"I made curfew."

"Oh, I wasn't saying you hadn't. I just miss you, that's all." Abby laid the chicken pieces in a baking pan.

Santi was quiet as he expertly chopped peppers for their salad. She had taught him how to use a chef's knife correctly, and he had mastered it by the time he was twelve. "So what did you want to talk about?" he said, reaching for the purple onion.

"Oh, I just haven't heard what you've been up to since graduation. You've been going out a lot." Abby tried to sound indifferent.

"That's what you do when you're eighteen and you've finally gotten out of high school and you work hard all day and you want to see your friends," Santi said good-naturedly, but with the tone of a preschool teacher explaining something to her class.

"What are Josh and Mario up to? Are they working this

summer? I actually miss them coming over after track and eating a week's worth of groceries in one sitting."

Santi laughed. "Remember when Josh and I had that pancake-eating contest and he barfed and blueberries came out his nose?"

"God, that was so gross!" Abby laughed with relief. This was not someone who was hanging out with ex-cons. This was her own sweet Santi, a good kid. "Bring them over some night. I'd like to see them again. And Steve, too. You guys were the four musketeers."

Santi added some grape tomatoes onto his masterpiece of a salad. Abby slid her baking pan into the preheated oven. "It'll be quick—the chicken just needs to warm up. There's bread there to go with your salad. We could go ahead and get started."

Santi tossed the salad with olive oil and balsamic vinegar. Abby sliced some of her herb bread from the café. "So will you invite them over?" she prompted when he hadn't answered one way or the other.

"Sure, Mom. I'll ask them tonight."

He left right after helping with the dishes. It was hard to look at her trusting face when she said to have a nice time. It felt like shit to lie, but the ends justified the means. She would never understand about Rosalinda, and forget about James and his crew. She would freak. Neither one of them needed that. He was sparing her, come to think of it.

They weren't that bad, James and the guys. They were just from a different culture, one that his white mom would never accept. Not everyone had it as easy as she did. People who have to scrape by to survive are different, that's all. They don't always get to stay in school or get fancy jobs; maybe they have to take some shortcuts sometimes. But once you got to know them, they were people just like everyone else. And they liked him and even respected him. Li'l Baca, they called him. It's who he was underneath it all.

As far as his old friends went, he could no longer even imagine hanging out with them. They seemed so juvenile now. Rosalinda would think they were major dorks.

Santi headed for their house, where he would hang until Rosalinda got off work. The setting sun splashed orange soda all over the deepening blue horizon. The Manzano Mountains blushed violet, and a huge moon began to rise like a helium balloon.

He turned off the air conditioner and turned on his headlights. He put down his windows to feel the rush of real air and smell the night arriving. With love burning in his chest and freedom pushing his foot harder against the gas pedal, he glanced up at the moon and gave a quick howl.

Once every two months or so, Rachel and Charlie drove up to the Four Corners area to check on their buyers in Aztec and Durango. The drive on Highway 550 north was a beautiful one, and today Rachel had offered to take Mort along with them to get him out of her parents' hair.

Hattie was off to day camp, and CeCe and Rose were set to pick her up after Rose's hair appointment at Bonnie's salon. They were also stopping by Joe's Pharmacy to get an enema kit for Mort. Luckily for him, this day trip was really an all-day-and-part-of-the night trip, so he was saved from that intrusion and humiliation for one more day. How they could do that to him after he had been tortured by Nazis and Ukrainians was beyond her.

They took the newer truck they had gotten at the car auction in the South Valley two years ago. It wasn't as modern as all the superfancy ones people climbed all over themselves for today, but it could pull the large horse trailer. Rachel sat in the middle. It rode more smoothly than her ancient Ford truck, which nowadays just hauled hay and feed, trusted only to make the shorter, less stressful trips. Besides, the gas gauge still didn't work, and you could only fill it halfway before the gas tank leaked. It made it easily as far as the mountains and back on a half a tank, so she could take it on her trips around adjacent towns. Charlie promised to fix it up good as new again someday, but someday isn't any real day of the week, and so it never happened, especially since the farm had been taking so much extra work.

Papa probably would not be able to afford to hire as many thinners and chile pickers this year, and the extra work from all the corners that had been cut already fell to Charlie, Papa, and Santi. Charlie was worried about Santi, wondered what he did when he wasn't at work and why he came in so tired in the mornings. She just figured he was playing hard his last summer before college.

"Look at that rock with the brown toupee," said Mort, pointing ahead on Charlie's side of the window. Sure enough, she saw, as plain as day, a head-shaped rocky cliff with a low hairline of brown growth. He could be so absolutely nuts at times, and yet at times he was so damn poetic. She had heard CeCe's troubling stories about what he was like when CeCe was a little girl. While other Jewish girls were being pampered and adored by their fathers, little CeCe was starved for an ounce of any heartfelt attention from hers. Sometimes he was so narcissistic he wouldn't acknowledge her for a day or two. He would just come in from work, sit in his den, and read. Read and smoke a cigar. To this day her mother still couldn't stomach cigar smoke. Ma continued to hold all of that against him. Even though that father didn't exist anymore, Ma's anger still did. And Rachel never knew that man. She had only begun to know this Mort—her zeyde. The one who saw perky, pointed hills and talked about the brassieres he said Rose wore in the fifties. She saw the same castles he did in the jutting rocks even before he pointed them out to her.

Rachel looked at this old man-child. Physically he looked like any old Jewish comedian from the Catskill heydays. Rachel could only imagine what Mort had gone through in the Warsaw ghetto and the concentration camp; maybe God was being merciful now by wiping much of his mind away. And even though he still remembered that nightmare, at least he had his good moments as well. Many days he was happy-go-lucky. How does a person survive after watching his mother and fiancée get shot in the head and not being able to move as their blood ran down the very street he had played in as a child? She wondered what other horrors he must have witnessed.

Despite the intrusion he was in all their lives, she could not help but feel a place within her heart warm to him, even love him. Her mother was still too angry at Mort to get to the suffering soul he was inside, but this was her father—she needed to try.

While Rachel could understand her mother's anger toward Rose after her latest nastiness, she wondered about what kind of mother she had actually been to CeCe and her siblings. Surely she must have been nurturing; look how CeCe had turned out. Rachel could feel how much her mother might need her to help her overcome all of the poisonous resentment she held so tightly. But how could she help?

As they drove past the Zia and Jemez pueblos, Rachel noticed ruins of tiny adobe homes that Coronado might have left behind on his destructive trail through their communities. They looked that old. The fog along the mountain ridges resembled floating apparitions.

Charlie had been quiet, and she figured he was lost in his tortured thoughts about the farm. She reached for his hand, and his eyes left the road long enough to give her a tired smile.

She decided to venture out into the land of Mort. "How are you doing, Zeyde?" she asked as he looked so serene gazing out the window. They passed by orange willow branches lining a small arroyo.

She noticed for the first time the numbers tattooed on his forearm in runny, purplish-black ink stain. His thin, dried skin had distorted them somewhat. She couldn't make out all of the numbers. She had been reading about the Warsaw ghetto and Treblinka lately. Seeing the tattoo made her stomach lurch as if she were in one of his flashbacks.

He answered her several beats beyond normal. He smiled at her and said, "My beautiful Zophia," and then tears shone in his hazel eyes, the rims reddening fast. It was clear he had loved Zophia. Really loved her. How different everything would have been had Zophia lived to wed him instead of Rose.

Rachel patted his hand. The cold boniness of it reminded her of Tía Maria's hands and how she missed them. She imagined Mort's hand, this hand she patted, going through all the dead Jews' belongings and, more than likely, the dead bodies themselves, their orifices just more pockets to inspect. Oh, God. She shivered against the brutal images she had seen and read about in her library books.

And he survived when millions of others didn't. Who was this loving, courageous man before Hitler had taken it all away? Took his soul and left this hologram of an old, constipated zeyde?

"I have to *gai pischn*," he announced. He hadn't put in his false teeth. He'd lost his real ones in Treblinka.

They pulled into the parking lot of Freelove's Grocery and Hardware. Charlie gave her a look as he undid his seat belt and resolutely lifted up on the door handle. Mort undid his own seat belt and allowed Charlie to help him out of the truck, which must have seemed like a hell of a long drop to him. He couldn't just fling himself like a little clingy monkey into Charlie's arms the way Hattie did. "You're a good *boychick*," Mort said, poking an index finger striated with age on Charlie's arm and trembling under the glasses he wore, so thick they seemed like magnifying glasses. His yellow nail curved under, making him look like the human fly.

"John's this-a-way, ol' timer," Charlie said, leading a shuffling Mort by the elbow.

Rachel stood, marveling once again at the expansive sky. She had seen enough New York skyline pictures, and no, thanks. How depressing that would be. No concrete buildings in the world could match the intricacy of rock formations that towered over the desert. It could turn anyone into a poet or artist. Even her and Zeyde.

Charlie helped Mort back from the bathroom. She noticed a few wet drops on Mort's pants, near the zipper, as Charlie got him situated in the front seat. Today, Rose had had him put on his tan desert-boot Hush Puppies.

Back on the road she noticed acres upon acres of burned land from recent fires, ponderosas and piñons now unrecognizable except as burned skeletons. She grieved for the poor charred creatures she imagined out in the woods somewhere where she could not see.

"The women burned more easily than the men," Mort said, gazing at the black scenery.

"What did you say?" Rachel asked.

"So their bodies were used for kindling the cremation fires." Mort's face was without expression. "The pregnant women would burst open. Then they watched the babies burn, too." His voice sounded distant, like someone talking in his sleep.

Rachel turned slowly to Charlie, knowing his look of horror reflected her own. "He worked at cremating the dead, too," she explained softly.

"Zeyde," Rachel said, giving his arm a firm but tiny shake, her fingers covering his tattoo, as if she could wake him out of this. She had certainly read enough about what had happened at Treblinka to relive, in some small but humble way, the terror and gruesomeness along with Mort. Whatever love and affection he had possessed before the war had been wrung out of him at that place. Until now. His dementia at least allowed him to get closer to people.

"Don't you see? I am already dead. I never came back. Not really." Mort looked at her like that was just fine by him. "Those tall rocks look like crossed fingers, see?"

No wonder he had been able to stay married to Rose for sixty years. He had been a robot, when he wasn't having a sudden angry outburst. Rose dutifully kept him oiled and maintained and paid up at the synagogue, because no one could have functioned normally again after all of that. Had CeCe ever stopped and really thought about this?

Rachel couldn't believe that her mother had gone a whole angry lifetime without comprehending what her father had been through. Would it have made a difference? Could a child's emotional neglect by a parent ever be justified?

Now Mort seemed to be directing a silent symphony as he watched the scenery fly by. There was a subtle hitch in his shoulders as he led the orchestra. She wondered what symphony it was. Not that she would know it, but she found herself feeling cut out of his loop in some way. "Hum it, Zeyde," she urged softly.

It started so quietly at first that she heard only every sixth note or so. His fleshy lips against his toothless gums muffled what little sound he was making. She imagined it being something gorgeously macabre. Something with begging and weeping violins.

But wait. There were words. Words that sucked back and forth with his lips. She and Charlie leaned toward him to hear. This might be another clue to the mystery of Mort's life. Was it even in English?

"Boop boop diddum and a whattum chew!" he sang.

The ride back home was endless. Rachel was worn out from chatting with her customers at the stores she had visited. In business, it was important to show your face every now and then. Her goat-milk products were great but shouldn't always have to speak for themselves. Some complained that they had not ordered enough cheese or soaps. She had a folder in her briefcase of expanded orders.

Mort sat next to her against the truck window and snored with his mouth completely open. She had given him his medicine as instructed, something to help take the edge off of "twilight time," his worst time with dementia. He was getting more combative during that hour of the evening, when they all turned into his enemies.

Sue Boggio and Mare Pearl

The headlights from oncoming traffic assaulted her eyes. Charlie squinted when a car would whiz past.

"Thank you for today," Rachel said, "It helped Ma and Papa. I love you, you big galoot." She scooped her arm up through his and laid her head against his shoulder.

He squeezed her knee. "Good old Mort kind of makes you put your list of priorities in a different kind of order."

When they finally drove up to her parents' house, CeCe was up waiting for them. They had to wake Mort up, and Charlie lifted him into the wheelchair CeCe had rolled out. Hazel, from CeCe's cabal, knew some nurses who worked at a nursing home and had gotten it for them.

"How'd it go?" CeCe asked. "I owe you big for this. He can be the biggest pain. Thank you so much," she continued, giving them each a kiss on the cheek. Except Mort.

"G'night, Zeyde," Rachel said, making a point to kiss Mort on his forehead. He was awake enough to give a tiny smile. Did he still think she was Zophia? She felt powerful to have been able to draw a smile out of him. Stronger than his enemies, somehow.

"Well, I've got to get him ready for bed," CeCe said. She shook her head. "You spent the whole day with him and lived to tell about it."

"You be sure to tell Zeyde, 'sweet dreams' when he goes to bed," Rachel said sternly. "He lived to tell about a thing or two himself."

The next morning, after milking, Rachel brought a pail of fresh goat's milk over to CeCe. She hadn't slept much the night before, traumatized by what Mort had said about Treblinka. As soon as she would begin to slip into sleep, visions of burning dead pregnant women haunted her. It had made her sick to her stomach all night. It was all so unbelievably tragic, but at the same time she was developing great respect for the shriveled old man she called Zeyde. And for the Jewish half of herself she had turned her back on her whole life.

"Hi, Ma. Brought Papa his milk," she said, coming in the kitchen door. Her mother looked so tired, her eyes vacant with purple circles underneath, lips pale. In the sunshine of the kitchen window, CeCe's face startled her.

Rachel poured them each a mug of tea and placed them at the table so she and CeCe could sit. "Ma, come sit down and talk to me," she said, leading CeCe by her fingertips. "I'm really worried about you."

CeCe sat, elbows on the table, her weary chin dropping on her knuckles. "I've just been so tired lately. Don't worry, honey."

"Ma, it's more than that. You've changed. Like something in you has just given up and gone away. Where's my spiritual, metaphysical, hippie mom who always said we're all here to teach and heal each other? That if something was a pain in the ass, to look at it and see what it is we need to learn. Because I don't see you doing that with Bubbe and Zeyde."

"Too much scar tissue. Things you don't forget. Or easily forgive," said CeCe. "When my brother Sam went missing in action in Vietnam, Mort got even worse. Sam had been Papa's favorite. He didn't try to hide it. They had words when Sam enlisted instead of going to college and getting a deferment. Mort always had big plans for Sam." CeCe swallowed her tears and cleared her throat. "But when we realized Sam had to be dead, Mort withdrew even more and took Sam with him. My god, I was only twelve years old. I worshipped my big brother. It was like Mort had the power to erase him from our lives. We were all grieving, you know? We could never speak of him again. Selfish bastard."

"My god, Ma. Did I ever even know about Sam? That's horrible. But you have to realize, Zeyde barely escaped with his life from his war; then he lost his only son to another war. He was hurting so much, he couldn't reach out to any of you. He was locked away again, in his prison of pain." Rachel paused, trying to find the words that would unlock her mother's heart. "Now that I'm getting to know them and what they've been through, I can see them from a place of understanding. It's changed everything. There are things to cherish about them. Things to learn from them."

CeCe raised a doubtful lip. "Yeah? Name one."

"No, you name one. There have to be some good memories in your heart somewhere." CeCe glinted back at her like a scolded child. "Hey, Ma, I'm only telling you what you'd tell me if the situation were reversed."

CeCe looked down at the table for a couple of seconds, her features softening with a small smile. "We were always at the beach, me and my sisters and Ma. We only lived a block away, you remember?"

Rachel nodded, smiling too.

"We went with Ma almost every day when school was out for the summer. Would you believe she wore two-piece bathing suits? I remember this bright yellow one made of lace. Had those little-boy legs. She had a good figure and was tanned so brown it made her bright orange lipstick look electric, and she smelled of cocoa butter all the time."

Rachel laughed. "I can just see her."

"She and her girlfriends would set up under huge umbrellas, drink their gin and tonics from thermoses, and play mah-jongg while all the kids went wild. They all had huge beehive hairdos that swirled like the cotton candy they sold on the boardwalk. One time me and my sisters found a big, dead horseshoe crab washed up on the beach. We were freaking out. And here came Rose, picked up the scary, pointy tail, made like it was a Hoover vacuum, and pretended to vacuum the beach like Donna Reed. She had us in stitches. She'd tell us to listen for the Good Humor man because we could all have ice cream. He'd walk around with a cooler strapped onto his shoulders like a big bass drum . . ."

Rachel could see the memory held in CeCe's smiling silence. Rachel smiled, too. "See, I knew you had good memories. I can think of a million I've had with you," said Rachel. "What about just with you and Bubbe alone?"

"I can't get past her betrayal when I fell in love with Miguel. I guess I've been too angry and hurt for so long to remember the good times."

"I wouldn't want Hattie to forget me like that," Rachel said sadly. She reached over and rubbed her mother's arm. "You know, they're not going to be here forever."

"I know you're right. Rose was a good mom. And devoted to us kids. If we ever lacked for money, we kids never knew it. Never went without. Pa even made us all the latest fashions in clothes."

"He still does some pretty mean doll clothes."

CeCe's smile lit up her entire face.

"You should see the look on your face right now, Ma," Rachel said. "I'm beginning to recognize you."

"Here's something," CeCe said. "I had scarlet fever when I was nine or so. I remember being so sick, high fever, rash, sore throat. I was really scared because I had never felt so sick before. But Ma stayed by my side for six days straight. I didn't even have to ask her to. She'd sing me 'My Yiddishe Mameh' a hundred times or tell me stories and put cold compresses on my forehead. Do you know she paid Dr. Korn in raisin cake when he came and gave me a shot? Kids still died of scarlet fever when she was a little girl, so I think she was pretty scared, too. She made the best raisin cake . . ." The gleam in her eye continued as she began to hum softly, the way her mother had.

"Sing it for me, Ma," Rachel said.

"My Yiddishe mameh, I need her more than ever now . . . My Yiddishe mameh, I'd like to kiss her wrinkled brow," she sang in a haunting melody, tears filling her eyes. "I long to hold her hand once more as in days gone by, and ask her to forgive me for things I did to make her cry . . ." CeCe stopped abruptly and wept into her hands.

Rachel hurried to put her arms around her. "There you are, Ma. There you are."

CHAPTER 8

"Why do I have to go? He isn't my friend. I want to stay home with Santi or go play with Hattie." Maggie glared at the peanut butter toast on her plate.

"We've talked about this already. He's my new friend, and I want the two of you to get to know each other. He's taking us to the zoo—you love the zoo." Abby filled a liter water bottle with filtered water and set out the sunscreen. Going to the Albuquerque zoo was like going on safari in Africa: you had to be prepared for unrelenting heat, sun, and thirst.

"I don't have to like him if I don't want to," Maggie said, giving Abby the full view of her challenging expression. Bobby came to life in her dark eyes and the set of her mouth. It caught Abby off guard sometimes when he appeared through his daughter's face.

Abby sat down and let the Saturday morning quiet wash over both of them before she spoke. She tried to release her need to have Maggie like Ben. She couldn't force her to. "No," she said finally. "You're right. It's up to you if you like him. But I do insist on one thing."

Maggie cocked her head to the side, her eyes narrowed. "What?"

"You start with a clean slate. Right now you are sitting there thinking you don't like him because he isn't your daddy. Well, he can't help it that he isn't, so that's not fair. It's important in this life to give everyone a chance before you pass judgment on them."

"What's a clean slate?"

Abby smiled. "You know the blackboards at your school? They used to be made out of slate—a big sheet of smooth rock—so the expression comes from that. Erase all the junk off the board and start with a clean slate, get it?"

"Yeah."

"I know it's weird to hang out with someone you know is already important to your mom. I'm still getting to know him, too. This is new; I haven't made any big decisions. For now, he's my friend, and I want us to spend time together."

Maggie stuck her finger into the thick sheen of peanut butter and drew a heart. "Are you going to marry him and he'll come live here like Susie's mom did and she got a stepdad?"

"I'm not even thinking about anything like that. All I'm thinking is we could have a nice time at the zoo together. Today is all I'm thinking about."

Maggie drew an X through the heart on her toast and then began to eat it.

Though they were at the zoo by ten o'clock, it was already eighty-five degrees and climbing fast. Maggie was reserved with Ben, shyly showing him her room when he arrived to pick them up and then saying, "Well, let's get this show on the road," something Abby had said often enough that it made her smile to hear her daughter recite it in the same tone. It was one of those moments when the power of motherhood was so starkly revealed, it made her feel inadequate to have such a profound influence on an impressionable child.

Maggie was in her brave little soldier mode. The same outwardly calm, resigned, never-let-them-see-you-sweat demeanor she'd adopted the first day of kindergarten. "You better be getting to work, Mom," she'd said while her peers wailed and clung to their mothers. Abby had nodded and hugged her stoic daughter, then, on the way to the café, had cried so hard she had to pull the car over onto the side of the road.

The three of them walked through the entrance after Ben bought their tickets. Saturday always brought out the crowds, but it wasn't too bad yet. Teenage couples strolled hand in hand, there more for the romance of the place than out of any interest in animals. Parents in need of getting out of the house, with babies in strollers too young to know where they were. And entire extended families, Navajo, Hispanic, and Anglo, with slow-moving elders and antsy children pointing at pink flamingos standing in a shallow pool, their legs bent backward where their knees should be. Strategically located gift stores were already causing arguments to break out between parents and their kids, who complained they had their own money so they shouldn't have to wait until later.

"Mom, should we start with the cats like we always do?" Maggie said, knowing Abby always insisted they wait to visit the gift stores until they were on their way out. "Whatever you like. Lead the way," Abby said. Albuquerque's BioPark was one of the best in the nation. The habitats were state-of-the-art. The place was so animal friendly, it was sometimes hard to find the animals at all. The grounds flourished with grassy lawns, flower gardens, bronze statues, a generous pond that served as a moat for the amphitheater, and, best of all, a surprising canopy of shade provided by towering elm and cottonwood trees. In this section of the bosque, one would never guess there was a five-year drought in progress. Peacocks screamed, elephants trumpeted, children yelled in their excitement. An interspecies cacophony of sounds permeated the air.

"What's your favorite animal to visit at the zoo? One of the big cats?" Ben asked Maggie.

Maggie shrugged. "It depends on the mood I'm in," she said, looking straight ahead.

"And this is a cat kind of day?" Ben asked.

"So far," Maggie said and skipped ahead.

"She's a tough nut to crack," Ben said.

"You've no idea. Her first grade teacher says she's glad she's on her side because she has no doubt Maggie could take over the classroom if she had a mind to."

"Do you think it has to do with not having her father in her life?" Ben asked.

Abby kept her eyes on Maggie, who, although she was a good twenty-five feet ahead of them on the walkway, turned to look over her shoulder every ten steps to confirm her mother was still in eyesight.

"I never really thought of it that way, but yeah, she may have some sense that she needs to be tough. Although it could just be genetics—I see so much of him in her."

The Siberian tiger exhibit came first, an expansive pit with a moat separating it from a wall that slanted up steeply to meet the railed observation area. One tiger lay on his back in the sun, his tail swishing over the compacted soil. Another climbed the stripped branches of a dead tree positioned as play equipment. A young cub batted a beach ball around a small grassy circle under the tree.

"I can't look at these tigers without thinking of the childhood story about Little Black Sambo. I loved that story. I was so distressed when I got older and learned how racist it was," Ben said.

"The title is, and his name, of course, but the story itself wasn't so bad, was it?" Abby said. It had been one of her favorite stories also, especially the part where the tigers ran so fast they turned into butter.

On they went, past the lions, cheetahs, and leopards, Maggie studying each with serious scrutiny and saying little.

"Is she hating this?" Ben whispered.

Abby looked into his brown eyes, shaded by his brimmed safari hat, and saw such concern her heart melted. "No, she's fine. She'll just take a little time to loosen up."

Ben smiled with such relief Abby leaned up and planted a quick kiss on his lips.

"What was that for? I want to be sure I keep doing it, whatever it is."

"You really care about her, if she's having fun or not."

Ben looked quizzical. "Of course. That's the point, yeah?"

"Yeah," Abby said, mocking his accent.

"I want to see the polar bears now," Maggie announced when they caught up to her.

The polar bear exhibit had viewing areas both below water level and above to capture all of their wild antics. A waterfall poured onto a slippery, steep slide that could plunge the bears back into the pool. Molded, undulating surfaces mimicking rock along the back and sides of the pool were perfect for sunning and lounging. A crowd of people obscured the underwater viewing windows, so they headed up the winding walkway to the larger observation area.

The polar bears were putting on quite a show with their Volkswagen Beetle–size water blocks and toys, so it was quite congested there as well. More people were arriving, drawn by the *ahhs* and laughter of the crowd, while the ones in front were not about to yield their choice spots.

"I can't see," Maggie complained, craning her neck and standing on tiptoe. "Don't they know they're supposed to give turns?"

"I could hoist you up on my back if you like," Ben offered.

Maggie looked him up and down. Abby wondered what she was basing her decision on. His height? Whether she felt comfortable enough with him to get that close?

"Okay—like a pony ride—not clear up on your shoulders—you're too tall for that," she said, hands on her nonexistent hips. Her jean shorts sagged a bit, and her gold Esperanza Eagles T-shirt had already become grimy in spots. Wild dark waves fluttered from beneath her Albuquerque Isotopes baseball visor.

Ben crouched down and reached behind to assist her. She put her arms and legs around him, and he stood in one fluid motion, as if they'd been practicing this move forever. Abby couldn't tell which of their grins was wider until she felt her own.

Now Maggie was walking between them and directing her conversation to Ben. "So why do you like minnows so much?"

Ben laughed. "I like all animals; that's why I became a biologist. I'll show you one of my favorite animals I used to see where I grew up in Australia."

"Mom showed me on my globe where Australia is. It's awful far. Don't you miss your mom and dad?"

"My mom died of cancer when I was your brother's age, so I miss her wherever I am. My dad is still working the sheep station with my two brothers. I go back and visit, but yeah, I do miss them all. It's winter there now, did you know that?

"You're pulling my leg." Maggie rolled her eyes.

"It's true; ask your mom if you don't believe me. It's below the equator, in the southern hemisphere, so our seasons are opposite. Besides, pulling your leg would be like this." He reached toward her leg, which sent her into a squealing run.

He ran up to her. "I'll race you to that building over there!"

When Abby caught up to them, they were in front of a cage just outside of the building. A large, speckled, brown-and-white bird with a massive bill hunkered on a naked branch.

"Kookaburra," Maggie read. "I know a song about Kookaburra."

"So do I. Think it's the same song?"

"Kookaburra sits in the old gum tree. Merry, merry king of the bush is he. Laugh, Kookaburra! Laugh, Kookaburra! Gay your life must be." They sang at the same time, their voices only needing a few beats to match keys.

"I guess kookaburras are gay, like our friend Edward in San Diego," Maggie said.

"Is that right?" Ben grinned at Abby, who was trying not to laugh. He pointed to the adjacent building's entrance. "Inside there is one of my favorite animals of all time. When I get homesick for Australia, I come here and visit them," Ben said. "We have to be quiet when we go in—this is the middle of the night to them."

"It's the koala bears, only they aren't bears," Maggie said as if she'd heard it all before. "But why is it night to them—is it because they're from Australia and everything is upside-down and backward there?"

"Right again," Ben said. "See?" He handed Abby his hat and then took a step forward and placed his palms on the ground, legs flying upward. He began to walk on his hands. "Upside-down and backward." Gravity pulled his shirt down, revealing his tan, taut abdomen.

Maggie giggled as he took three more steps and then righted himself, doing a quick bow. Maggie and Abby clapped their hands, as did a family behind them on the walkway.

"Thank you. Next show in an hour," Ben said.

"He's kind of goofy, Mom," Maggie whispered. "But don't tell him I said so. I don't want to hurt his feelings."

"Sixty is a big one. I can't believe CeCe's turning sixty," Bonnie said, picking at the lime green polish on her artificial nail. Her hair, now dyed cherry mocha, was sprayed into a gravity-defying bouffant. Her eyebrows and lips were drawn in the same color.

"Sixty is a great age. Try getting past seventy—that one will get your attention," said Hazel, who didn't look or act a day past a fit sixty herself. She was still participating in 5K runs for charity events.

"It doesn't look so good on her though, mi Dios! She's aged ten years since her parents got here. *Pobrecita!*" Bonnie looked heavenward, her view obstructed by Abby's kitchen ceiling.

CeCe's cabal had gathered to plan her sixtieth-birthday surprise party.

Carmen nodded in rare agreement with Bonnie. "I help her as

much as she'll let me, and those two require the patience of Job," she said in her best martyr tone, touching her crucifix.

Abby put a tray of snacks on the table. She poured iced tea and sat down. "What do you think we should do? For the party, I mean."

"I thought Rachel was coming," Bonnie said.

"Rachel will be here," Abby said.

"Before she gets here, I heard some disturbing *mitota* at the salon. They say Miguel has been drinking," Bonnie said. "Not that I'd blame him, *hijo la*! The drought, his crazy Spanish-hating in-laws—"

Hazel groaned. "Put a lid on it, Bonnie. We're here to plan a party. It's none of our business."

"We're CeCe's best friends. If it's true her husband has been hitting the cervezas, that's more stress on her, and we should know about it."

"Mitota is dirt, and it has no place in Abby's kitchen," Carmen decreed.

"What about a private party at the café? It's big enough to hold a lot of people, and we could think of some excuse to get her there. Like the power went off and we need to save food from the refrigerator," Abby said. "And the stage is there for music and dancing."

Rachel burst through the screen door. "Sorry, one of my goats is sick, and I had to wait for Charlie to stay with her. What did I miss?"

"Abby said we should have the party at the café instead of one of our houses," Hazel said.

"A full dinner, or just cake and ice cream?" Carmen asked. "If not a sit-down dinner, then at least a buffet. Turning sixty is at least worth a nice buffet."

"We could do a *matanza* at my place," Bonnie said. "We keep a pit dug, and my brother-in-law is always up for slaughtering a pig."

"My grandparents don't eat pork," Rachel said.

"Okay, so we give them hamburgers. It isn't *their* birthday,"

Bonnie said, taking it personally. "At a matanza we could be out-doors, enjoying the night air."

"What if it rains?" Carmen cautioned.

"We'll be so happy we'll all strip naked and roll in the mud! What do you mean, 'What if it rains?' It ain't going to rain." Bonnie laughed, her heavy breasts looked like they were trying to make a run for it.

"Oh ye of little faith." Carmen wagged a serious finger at her.

"I like the café idea," Rachel said. "It's a safer place for my bubbe and zeyde and closer to home if they get tired."

"What about what your mom would like? You're just agreeing with Abby. I remember when you two didn't agree on anything," Bonnie said, popping another strawberry in her mouth.

"We still have our disagreements, trust me," Rachel said, help-ing herself to iced tea and some Brie on a cracker.

Bonnie wiggled with excitement. "Like what?"

Hazel's retired head nurse voice broke in. "I say we vote on the café and be done with it. I'm not getting any younger here."

"Abby's dating the minnow-loving biologist, the one who dis-rupted the farmers' meeting. The one who thinks none of us matter as much as a four-inch fish," Rachel said with her old evil glint in her eye.

Abby's hands went defensively to cover her face. "Oh, great, thank you, Rachel."

Bonnie grabbed her hands and pulled them down to squeeze in her excitement. "Look me in the eye and tell me it's true."

"It's true," Abby said.

Bonnie's scream brought everyone's hands to their ears. "Hijo la! Girlfriend, are you finally getting laid?"

Abby felt the crimson tide flood her neck and face.

"Bonnie, behave yourself. No one wants to hear your smutty talk," Carmen said without sincerity. She scooted her chair closer.

"Let's vote on the café so those of us who don't give a flying fig can go home," Hazel said. "All those in favor of CeCe's sixtieth-birthday surprise party being held at the café with a pot-luck buffet, BYOB, say *aye*."

A chorus of *ayes*, including Bonnie's, rang out.

"Any nays?" Hazel asked.

Dead silence.

"The ayes have it. Now, next time we meet we'll hash out who's bringing what so we don't have ten green chile chicken casseroles. And bring ideas for a guest list. Especially you, Rachel, ask your dad for folks from their past we can invite. Bonnie, will your cousin's band provide the music?"

"Sure, yeah, okay already. Can we go back to the subject at hand?" Bonnie whined to Hazel.

"Not before I say this, and then I'm going home to soak my feet in Epsom salts. Abby, you date whomever the hell you want as long as he's good to you. And it's nobody else's business, so don't let yourself be bullied."

Abby stood when Hazel did and put her arms around the tall, skinny old bird who could probably take anyone in the room.

"I'm not staying. I'm totally against her on this," Rachel said with her usual drama.

"Get over yourself. Who made you the hall monitor?" Bonnie said, with her drawn-on eyebrows arched so high they disappeared behind her cherry mocha bangs.

Rachel flipped her off before following Hazel out the door, and Bonnie returned the gesture with a flash of lime green polish.

"Now, go ahead. All the details. Oh, you better go, too, 'Sister' Carmen, your ears might get burned," Bonnie said.

Carmen refilled her iced tea glass. "And let *you* be the only influence? Go ahead, dear, we're listening."

Rachel rode Tie-dye down to the river. Tie-dye was good at tracking Sweetwater, whom she knew Charlie had taken out for a ride. The mulberry trees held fistfuls of ripening berries, but it looked like it would be a good season for CeCe's syrup and preserves, if she had the time to make them. There was a high demand last year, and all of her jars sold out at the café. There was always such a limited supply and it went so fast, Rachel thought of upping the price a bit. Anywhere a little extra money could be made would help. Grasshoppers catapulted out of the high, dry weeds as she rode through them. Some buzzed and flew with red wings. The mosquitoes hung thick in the rare moist areas, and she worried about the horses getting West Nile virus this summer, even though they had been vaccinated. More and more cases of the virus in humans had been reported, so people had started slathering on DEET lotion.

They were lucky last year, but a few of their friends had lost horses to it. And one elderly woman in Belén had died from it. Most now, including themselves, kept goldfish in all the water tanks to help eat the mosquito larvae. It was Hattie's job to check on them and make sure there were no floaters and then to take a sieve and skim the leaves and debris off the top.

Rachel had Leticia and Jenny doing the late afternoon milking, and CeCe had Hattie over visiting Rose and Mort. Charlie had taken off on a solitary ride earlier.

She heard Sweetwater neigh from behind a group of Russian olive trees. Tie-dye snorted in reply. Charlie sat on a dried log, aimlessly whipping a foxtail weed across sandy dirt where water used to be. She got down off Tie-dye, who joined Sweetwater munching grass.

"Hi, ya," Rachel said.

"Hey."

She sat next to him on the log. The river seemed sad, flowing out there beyond her grasp. He did, too.

"I was thinking about your dad. After you went to bed last night, he showed up with a bottle of whiskey. He was pretty drunk."

Rachel felt her stomach twist. "I've never seen him drink like this."

"It's not like I can tell him to relax, it'll be all right. He's got those in-laws, the chile plants. . . . If we don't get some rain soon and if they don't extend the irrigation past July, the whole crop will be a bust. I might have to pick up the bottle, too."

"We have to have faith, *mi amor.* Somehow, we have to believe it will be all right."

He looked at her with a quizzical expression. "Who are you, and what have you done with my wife?"

"The more I read about Jewish history, all they have been through, and not only do they survive, they thrive. And being with Mort and hearing about his past, I guess I've finally accepted the part of me that I've denied all these years. So I feel more whole than I've ever felt, and that gives me faith."

He looked into her eyes, and she could feel a charge of electricity when their gazes connected. He kissed her, and for once it was just them, and all the rest seemed to blow away on the hot, dry breeze that ruffled their hair.

CHAPTER 9

S anti and Rosalinda lay in her bed after making love, the glow-in-the-dark ceiling stars spread out above them like the entire universe. Santi felt like he was piloting a spaceship into space, had jettisoned his old life and was rocketing into the vast yet thrilling unknown. He and Rosalinda could find a new planet and claim it for their own.

She stretched like a cat, her lithe brown body glistening with sweat in the candlelight. The sight of her breasts only inches from his hand caused his groin to stir, even though they had already been at it for hours. He had no idea what time it was and didn't care. Abby was sleeping better these days and didn't notice when he crept home after curfew.

He wished Rosalinda would talk more, open up about stuff. There was so much he wanted to say to her, but they spent most of their time having sex. Not that he minded. He wrote long love poems to her when they were apart, and he was pretty sure they were good. "Rosalinda, are you awake?"

"Sort of." She curled into him.

"I love you. I'm never going to leave you," he said without planning to.

"You're going to college in the fall," she said sleepily and with as much emotion as if she were referring to him going on an errand.

"No, I'm going to stay here with you."

"You'll go," she said like an order and then smiled up at him and pinched his cheek, which made him feel like a little kid.

"Don't you love me? Don't you want me to stay?" Santi said, a stabbing in his heart.

She sighed and sat up, punching her pillows so she could lean against them. "This is only barely July. We have the whole summer yet. Why are you bringing this up?"

"Because I think about it. Because it's out there like some dead end for us, and I don't want that. It's like when you're at the state fair and you're on your favorite ride and you never want it to end but that's all you think about. It's going to end, and you have to get off."

She began to laugh. "So that's all I am to you—some carnival ride? Come here, little boy—I'll give you a ride!"

She tickled him, which he didn't like, but he laughed involuntarily. With a quick, strong movement, she pinned his arms over his head and mounted him, looking him in the eye.

He got hard, and she guided him into her, and all of his thoughts and worries flew into space, and he held on for the ride.

He felt himself start to fall asleep afterward and didn't fight it. But then the dream came. It was dark, and he was powerless. Someone was going to die, maybe him. He tried to shout, to warn people, but his mouth wouldn't open, words couldn't come out. He couldn't move, and he knew a terrible thing was going to happen unless he did. He couldn't even move his lungs to breathe, so they collapsed like empty sacks. His smothered heart beat wildly in his chest, like a trapped animal looking for a way out. He would die if he couldn't breathe—his heart would explode—

"Santiago! Wake up!" Rosalinda shook him by his shoulder, and he jerked awake.

"I'm sorry," he mumbled, rubbing his face and looking around, trying to bring himself back into reality.

"Jesus! I thought you were going to kill me or something—you were flopping and punching—"

"Did I hurt you?" Santi asked, mortified.

"Nah, but shit, that must have been a hell of a dream," Rosalinda said.

"I get it all time. It's like I'm paralyzed and I need to defend myself and I can't. It's terrifying, like I'm really going to die. I don't know what it means or why it won't stop. Maybe I'm going crazy." Santi couldn't believe he was telling her, telling anyone about his private hell. He was consumed with shame and self-loathing.

"That's too bad," she whispered. "I used to dream about this one boyfriend my mom had who kept messing with me, you know? That he was going to kill me, like if I told or didn't do what he wanted. I had the dream for a whole year after he was out of the picture."

"You were abused?" Santi said, forgetting his own pain.

"Yeah, it was pretty gross. I was only eleven. Twelve by the time he left."

"Didn't you tell anybody? Your mom?"

"You can't do that, or they really hurt you or your mom. It's no big deal. I just brought it up because of the nightmare thing. Did something bad happen to you?"

"My dad killed himself in front of me. You already know the whole story," Santi said. He'd dealt with all of that years ago, over and over again in therapy until it got boring. So he didn't think it was giving him nightmares now. Why would it, this late in the game?

"You were little. It was a huge thing, so it got stuck in your brain. Go to a curandera. There's a good one in Tome I heard about."

"Would you go with me?" Santi asked and then felt ashamed. Here he was, trying to be a man in her bed, and he was acting like a scared little kid.

"On my day off, I'll take you." Rosalinda yawned. "Are you

staying all night or going home? Because I have laundry to do in the morning."

"I better go. What time is it?"

"Two thirty," she said and rolled over, putting the pillow over her head.

Santi got up and found his clothes. He blew out each of her candles to keep her safe and then left.

When he drove into the driveway, the gravel sounded loud under his tires. He turned off his headlights so they wouldn't shine into the house. There was no moon, and it was very dark, but the stars shone bright in the dry, clear sky, and he thought of Rosalinda's ceiling and felt better.

He had less than two hours to sleep before getting up to help Miguel with the irrigation. It would be a sixteen-hour day. They should just do it at night—it wouldn't evaporate as fast—but Miguel said he was too old for such nonsense.

He let himself in the kitchen door and closed it quietly behind him.

"Where have you been!" Abby sat in the dark at the kitchen table.

He about jumped out of his skin. "God—you scared me!"

"I scared you? Where the hell have you been? I've been terrified. I was about to call Ramone," Abby said, her voice a forced whisper so as not to wake Maggie.

"I was with my girlfriend," he said wearily. "I'm sorry, I fell asleep on the couch watching a movie. Tomorrow is irrigation day—can I get to bed?"

"You have a girlfriend?"

"Yeah, I'll tell you all about it tomorrow. We both have to work. Let's just do this later."

"You've been lying to me, Santi. I ran into Mario, Steve, and Josh at the grocery store, and they said they haven't seen you since graduation. What is going on with you?" Abby's voice cracked, and he could hear her start to cry. "Are you hanging out with that James Ortiz? Is that why you're lying?"

How did she know about James? "He's not bad. He did his time and turned it around," Santi said, giving in to the truth. There was no point in trying to lie. He was too tired to think of anything that fast.

"He's a lifelong criminal and what, thirty years old? Why are you doing this?"

"He's only twenty-six. He looked me up because he was friends with my dad and my uncle and knew me when I was little. At first I wasn't sure I wanted to hang out with him, but I got to know him, and he's a nice guy. He's had a hard life, but he's a good person. His cousin's my girlfriend. Rosalinda."

"You're to stop hanging out with those people, do you understand? They'll get you into trouble. You have to trust me on this! You are jeopardizing everything you've worked for."

"I'm eighteen, Abby. You can't tell me what to do. You aren't even giving them a chance. It's not fair. Just because they're different from you, you're jumping to all these conclusions. What about trusting me?"

"Ramone says James is bad news and the guys he hangs out with are nothing but trouble. They all have records. Why can't you see that this is not good for you?"

"People aren't perfect, Abby, not even you! You want Maggie and me and all of Esperanza to give your boyfriend a chance, and now you're some hypocrite and won't give my friends a chance. Rosalinda is who I hang out with, and she's never done anything wrong."

He could see, now that his eyes had adjusted to the darkness, Abby wiping her eyes and trying to calm herself. He could hear her ragged breaths, and he felt like shit.

"I should have told you about her. I'm sorry. I figured you'd decide you didn't like her because of her cousin, but she can't help that. She's hard working, she's a hostess at a restaurant and is saving her money to go to school. She's trying to help her cousin out so he stays out of trouble. He lives in her house—that's why I see him."

"What about her parents?"

"Her mom is . . . away, and she doesn't have a dad."

"She lives alone? How old is this girl?"

"Twenty-three."

"She's not a girl, she's a grown woman! What are you doing, Santi? This is crazy!" Her voice began to rise.

"Look, Mom, what's crazy is fighting about this right now. When you meet Rosalinda you'll see how great she is. Let's just get some sleep . . . please!" Santi said.

She got up and came over to him and put her hands on his shoulders. "I'm still your mother, and even though you're eighteen you still have to listen to me. This isn't over." She released him and made her way to her bedroom.

Santi retreated to his room and dove into his bed fully clothed.

The air that hot July morning still smelled like smoke, and the sky cast a gray smog as Rachel helped her father open some irrigation turnouts. The cement in-ground troughs created a grid around the forty-eight acres of chile and another six acres of alfalfa. River water flooded sections of their fields one at a time, channeled first from canals, then to ditches that were opened up. The process of opening turnouts, or diverting the water flow in the cement ditches, was a twenty-four-hour endeavor, every ten or twelve days. The Middle Rio Grande Conservancy District had put all the farms on a rotation schedule, and it was up to a person called a "ditch rider" to control the water and keep the schedule.

Rachel had gotten up earlier than usual to come out and help irrigate. She didn't have to worry about morning milking. It was still far from easy, but she was saved a lot of trouble now that she had milking machines, as well as Jenny and Leticia, so she didn't have to worry about getting it done by herself. She often wondered how many gallons of goat's milk she had hand milked over the years.

"Hi, there!" she greeted as Santi came riding up on his mountain bike. He looked like shit. There were purple circles under his eyes, and he was thinner, she was sure. "You look half-dead. Are you okay?" she asked.

"I didn't get any sleep, okay?" he snapped.

"Excuse me for caring."

"I've already gotten enough shit from my mother," he said, yawning wide in her face. His breath smelled sour.

"You know, why don't you just go and get a couple of hours of sleep? Come back when you're nicer," she said, giving him a push toward his bike. The back wheel kicked up a small cloud of dust as he sped off.

She met back up with her father at the old black walnut tree by the access road. Hard-shelled nuts from last year still lay strewn about its circumference. Seemed like such a waste. A wind gusted and rustled its full green leaves like a mop of thick hair.

"I called the ditch rider three days ago to make sure we'd get our water on time," he told her. "He was complaining about how so many families are still holding out on installing cement ditches. They still have dirt ditches, which is crazy. They know it would save them close to half of their irrigation water, and even with the feds kicking in seventy percent and loans for the rest, they still don't do it. It loses water for all of us." He looked out to his lush green chile fields. The plants seemed to wave back at him in a sudden breeze, their swaying green skirts revealing young fruit underneath. Water began to pool in the trenches between the rows, glittering like gold in the sunlight, but worth more.

"Charlie was out all night fighting the bosque fire on the rez," Rachel told him. "There's not many volunteers left since they've put so many obligations on them. Like they think volunteers can afford to leave their day jobs to get training and take tests. It's scary to think how fast those fires spread, and it was just up on the north side of Isleta—what's that, about ten miles? It's even scarier to think Charlie was out there somewhere working on an under-staffed fire."

"It was better in the old days when the *viejos* could get together and figure it out. They had it covered without all the complications and regulations." Miguel took in a deep whiff of scorched air.

"He came home while I was out milking this morning, flopped on the bed, and fell asleep. Hijo la, Papa," she said, "this fire season will do him in."

"I wish I could help, but mi'ja, your papa's not what he used to be. It's all I can do to take care of things around here."

He looked so sad at that moment, his dark eyes haloed by broken red veins. And as if he were shrinking, his old faithful cowboy hat started to look too big for him. It shocked her breath away to see her father getting old. She had never noticed it until this moment. Not that sixty was old, but circumstances had aged his body and soul. He looked so different.

A roadrunner darted, stopped, darted, stopped in front of them across the road. It made them smile. Roadrunners did that to people, little unexpected clowns. Papa's grayed mustache curved up like two tiny silver arrows. When did that happen?

"You put in your years to the fire department," she soothed, pat-ting his arm. "Don't you dare feel guilty."

He took her hand and gave it a sandpapery little squeeze, then let go. "You're good company for me, mi'ja, do you know that?"

"I hope so, Papa," she said.

They scuffled along slowly back toward their trucks. The rows of green chile stood at a healthy salute as they suckled water from the ground. She knew he was giving a silent thanks to San Ysidro as he passed each row.

She was well aware of the strife going on between her par-ents, but she whittled her question down so that her father could hear it without a knee-jerk reaction. Sort of like sneaking in the side door of a house. "It must be really hard for you and Ma to stay connected, what with the Spelman invasion on top of the other plagues of the Bible," she said.

They walked a few steps in silence.

"Your mother and I . . . ," he stammered, "we just don't . . . we can't . . . she makes me so . . ." he puffed in exasperation. He finally just shook his head as if giving up. He shoved his hands into his jeans pockets. "I don't know, mi'ja."

This was more than Papa had ever confided in her about something so personal. Her parents had never needed her intervention before now. She had always needed theirs. There had never been obstacles too big for them to overcome. He told her the redness in his eyes was from the smoke and ash in the air, but she knew it was also from his drinking.

She wanted to help her parents through this hard time in their life, be there for them as they had always been there for her. These days, Ma and Papa leaned tentatively on her and her on them like a house of cards. La familia.

After Rachel ordered his exhausted ass back to bed, Santi had slept another four hours. Luckily his mom was at work and his sister off to day camp, so the house had been quiet, with only the monotonous drone of the swamp cooler to lull him to sleep. He woke feeling refreshed, if not a little guilty, Rachel's scolding still ringing in his ears. But at least now he could function and contribute his share of the work. He'd start following curfew again, vowing like some reformed drunk to stay on the wagon. Hopefully his mom would mellow out today and he could reason with her.

He left his house after applying a generous slathering of sunscreen and filling a recycled milk jug with water. There was still a long day of irrigation ahead of them. His shirt flapped open in the dry breeze, any sweat evaporating before his skin could even sense its presence.

The mountains looked dusty, reflecting subtle orange patterns where there should be green, stands of dead piñon trees visible even from this distance. He missed having a pocket full of sweet piñon nuts to munch during the day. He thought of Miguel's santos and retablos needing the piñon's sap for their finishing lacquer. But lately Miguel wasn't spending much time on his meditative, sacred artwork. San Ysidro was turning a deaf ear to all their prayers for rain. One night Santi had found Miguel drinking beer in his workshop; he had turned all his saints around to make them face the wall. He told Santi, "*Si rezas que caiga agua, pero no cae, castigate a los santos y llueve.* If you pray for rain and none comes, punish the santos and they will respond." But even Miguel's time-honored dicho had not helped.

When Santi was ten, he believed in San Ysidro like some kind of Santa Claus and swore up and down to Miguel that the saint had made an appearance in his bedroom one night, just before he had fallen asleep.

Miguel had laughed and ruffled his hair. "You were already asleep, mi'jo!"

Santi made his way across the fields, hiking along the raised ditch banks, watching the water flow through the two-foot-wide channels that delivered precious sustenance to the chiles. The first four sections, each six acres, had already been flooded, the coffee-colored water rapidly soaking into the soil around the brilliant green plants with their fledgling fruit. At least he could still help with the last half of the work. Miguel was usually in a better mood on irrigation days. The pungent smell of the wet earth filled Santi's nose. It was almost his favorite smell. Topping that was the smell of freshly harvested green chile pods roasting over a fire, accompanied by the hiss and pop of a few stray seeds, their emerald flesh gradually charring until the magic moment when they were tumbled into heavy plastic bags to steam. The peels would then slip right off between his fingers, and he would suck the fiery fruit straight into his salivating mouth.

He slowed up a minute when he saw Miguel and Charlie turning the valves on the next section of six acres. Charlie was pointing at something, their heads together as they talked. He could hear Miguel's laughter in between birdsong. They were like father and son, despite how different they looked, their livelihoods joining them at the hip, their love for a mother and daughter making them family. Was he a part of it? Their familia? They all said he was, after his father died and Abby took him in. There had even been talk about whether the Vigils should take him, but Abby was determined. It seemed like one extended family anyway back then, not perfect, but united. He realized he missed that feeling and tried to think what had changed. The drought putting pressure on all of them, CeCe's parents arriving, his mom dating Ben, who didn't seem like a bad guy but just by what he believed in managed to divide them all even further.

And then there was Rosalinda. His love for her, all the time he was spending with James and his friends when he would have been goofing off with Maggie and Hattie or listening to Miguel and Charlie play their guitars around a little fire after dark.

"Hey, sleepyhead, done with your siesta?" Miguel hollered as he drew near.

"Yeah, sorry. But I'm good now." Santi put his hand on Miguel's shoulder, and they stood watching the water spread evenly over the laser-leveled field. No part of their sixty acres varied more than one-tenth of an inch, promoting an even flow of irrigation water and preventing water from standing in lower places, which encouraged disease. Although Miguel followed the old ways, he wasn't above using science to improve upon the methods of his elders.

Charlie tipped his cowboy hat. "Get your beauty sleep? Or were you sleeping with a beauty? I heard there might be a girl to blame."

Santi grinned. "I stayed too late at my girlfriend's house last night. Mom caught me, so I'm in for it."

"There's sandwiches in a cooler under that cottonwood over

there," Miguel said. "Let's have some lunch and hear all about your misbehavior."

They sat in the shade, where sparse grass seemed determined to grow despite the lack of rain. Miguel passed out thick turkey sandwiches that CeCe had wrapped in wax paper because she knew he wouldn't tolerate plastic wrap. There were also apricots and cherries from their trees and fingerling carrots picked that morning from CeCe's vegetable garden.

Charlie nudged Santi's tennis shoe with his worn boot. "So who's the girl?"

"Rosalinda Ortiz. I met her through her cousin. She lives in Los Lunas and works at a restaurant down there. She's twenty-three, so Mom is freaking out."

He saw Miguel and Charlie exchange a look. "It's not like that. I think I love her."

"Uh-oh, boy, you are in some deep shit now." Charlie laughed.

"Tell us some more about this young woman. Why is she spending time with a wet-behind-the-ears, barely-out-of-high-school boy?" Miguel asked.

"I don't know. She likes that I have goals and want to go to college. She wants to take classes up in Albuquerque. Her cousin and his friends have been in trouble and are kind of lazy, I guess, so maybe I look good compared to them. That's the other thing Mom is worried about. It's like she thinks I'm going to turn into some gangster all of a sudden. She doesn't even trust me. Rosalinda is a real good person."

"*Dime con quien andas, y te dire quien eres.* Tell me with whom you travel, and I will tell you who you are," Miguel said, pointing his carrot at him.

"But I'm my own person, and I'm not going to suddenly get stupid and do stuff I know is wrong. It's Rosalinda I care about, anyway, not her cousin or their friends. She's just nice enough to give her cousin somewhere to live, that's all. So he can make a fresh start."

"She must be a real beauty for you to want to get tangled up in that mess," Charlie said.

"She's beautiful," Santi admitted. "But that's not why I love her."

"Love is always physical for a man, at first anyway," Miguel said, and Charlie nodded. "You can't separate it that easily and have anyone believe you. Have you taken this woman to bed?"

Santi choked on the apricot he was chewing.

"That's a yes." Charlie laughed.

Miguel nodded, smoothing his mustache with his finger. "I assume you are using protection."

Santi took a swig of his water. "Of course. You've been drumming that into me since I was thirteen. I'm eighteen, not some ignorant little boy."

"Not anymore, anyway. Not with an experienced older woman leading the way," Charlie said. "Whatever happened to that cute little girl you took to the prom? She looked like more your speed."

"She was just a friend. I didn't have any love for her, not like Rosalinda. I don't know, why do you love Rachel? Or you love CeCe?"

There was a brief pause, and then both men began to laugh. "You got us on that one, boy," Charlie said. "Love never has and never will make a lick of sense. In fact, sense goes right on out the window."

"I will say this about love," Miguel said. "It is easily confused with pleasures of the flesh, especially to the young. Love stands the test of time. Love is never selfish. Love never demands you compromise your integrity, your honesty. It makes you a better person and never lowers you."

Santi nodded and tried not to think about the pot and the drinking. His lies tumbled in his gut like sharp rocks. None of that was Rosalinda's fault. He'd just have to figure out how to ease back from James, Carlos, and Bones without making any enemies. He knew guys like that would never allow any disloyalty or disrespect. They'd kill you first.

# CHAPTER 10

After taking Maggie to her friend Sara's birthday slumber party, Abby walked across the field to the Vigils' property. The sun was beginning to lower, casting her long-legged shadow far to her left. The dry stubble of weeds and grass crackled under her sandals, and she missed seeing the usual plethora of wildflowers along this well-worn path. A few stunted orange globe mallow and purple broom dahlia held token blossoms. Her eyes traveled, as they always did, to the sickly elm tree where the Baca house had once stood. Where Bobby was murdered and had lain buried so many months. She still ached for him, his face, the feel of him remaining fresh in her memory. That torturous summer when she had carried Maggie. The pain she had suffered, the tears she had cried—it seemed a miracle her daughter was born so full of joy.

She thought also of little Santi carrying his horrifying secret even as they grew to love each other. She held his innocence and fearlessness close to her heart, remembering how he'd put himself between his gun-wielding, drunken father and her, willing to die for a woman he'd known less than five months.

Last night's episode in the kitchen invaded her mind's eye, wiping out the vision of little Santiago and replacing it with teenage Santiago, angry and rebellious. Was she merely overreacting to some normal stage? He'd always been so compliant, so approval seeking, so good all through his adolescence—until now. Maybe he'd saved it all up for one big blowout right before he left for college. Something was wrong; she could feel it in the cold center of her bones. It was as if his dead father in the form of James Ortiz was somehow battling for control of her son. Or was this every adoptive parent's worst fear, that latent genetics could override all the positive nurturance in the world? Was what she saw of her Santi, the lovable, healthy kid she'd been raising for more than seven years, a fragile veneer that was weakening against the weight of his first ten formative years with the Bacas?

Suddenly she was standing in the Vigils' driveway, remembering how she'd come to them the morning after Bobby first disappeared. CeCe was her compass, her touchstone, and she needed her now.

Cicadas struck up their vibrating chorus overhead, obliterating the gentle evening murmurings of various farm animals. Offended, CeCe's rooster took on the challenge with a round of crowing.

Abby admired the vibrant blooming in CeCe's fragrant rose garden in the courtyard as she passed. All of her flowers belied the drought. Through the careful use of drip hoses, CeCe had gauged the minimum amount of water necessary to keep her gardens healthy and producing.

She found her in the vegetable garden, pulling opportunistic weeds that were springing up along the drip line.

"Hey, girlfriend," Abby called.

"Oh good, I need a break." CeCe rose, one hand on the small of her back as she straightened. "I hope you're ready for more tomatoes and cukes. Can I get you some soda or something?"

"Get me whatever you're having."

CeCe returned with two diet root beers, and they sat in the old green metal lawn chairs. The goats in the corral were hunkering down after a short burst of hopeful bleating.

"What's up?" CeCe asked, her intuitive radar functioning despite her own problems.

"I don't even know where to begin," Abby said, trying to triage her worrisome topics. There was her son and there was her new boyfriend, each their own meaty cans of worms.

"Hit me. Whatever you got is a pleasant diversion from the circus in my head. Just no bush beating; I'm too tired to hunt for it."

Abby laughed. "You make me feel better already. Okay, two topics. Topic number one, I'm dating a guy who's public enemy number one in Esperanza. I'm begging you to give him a chance, though, because he's wonderful and kind and even Maggie likes him. He got off to a bad start down here last month at the farmers' meeting, but he's really not some rabid environmentalist out to destroy—"

"I heard all about it from Rachel and the cabal. At first I was all set to try to talk you out of it. But then I saw how selfish that was. I didn't want you to date him because it could cause me some aggravation? Life is too short, Abby—I don't have to tell you that. Don't care so much what people think, even me. Go for it. I trust you. Have some fun. Somehow it will all come out in the wash. And if it pisses off my husband, well, he's pissing me off these days, so he can get over it, or not. Next topic." She swigged her root beer and belched like a truck driver, wiping the back of her hand across her lips.

"This one is harder. I'm worried sick about Santiago. He's given up his old friends from school in favor of an ex-con who used to hang with his father and uncle. And he's breaking curfew because he's hooked up with this guy's cousin, a twenty-three-year-old woman named Rosalinda."

"Oh, boy. You must be beside yourself. What are you going to do?" CeCe asked.

"I busted him last night at, well, nearly three in the morning when he finally came home. Said he'd fallen asleep on her couch watching a movie, like I believe that. He was so . . . unlike himself. It scared me. I tried demanding he stop seeing these people, and he informed me he was eighteen and could do what he wanted. Called me a hypocrite because I wanted him to give Ben a chance and I wouldn't give his precious Rosalinda a chance. He swears up and down she's not like her cousin, but this gangbanger is living right there in her house. No parents anywhere. Maybe I'm overreacting, but all I can see is trouble."

"Maybe Ramone could talk to him. Maybe it would go down easier from a man, not his mother."

"I thought about that. I even have this fantasy that I have Ramone grab up James Ortiz and threaten him to stay away from Santi."

CeCe paused to think, her fingers absentmindedly combing through her dark hair, which was streaked with shiny silver strands that began along her temples and cascaded through the length of her hair to her shoulders. It was thick and youthful hair, not wispy old-lady hair. Though everyone said they could see her stress in her face, Abby thought her strain shown as tiredness, some dark circles around her eyes, and no permanent damage was being done to her alabaster complexion with its fine tracing of lines. CeCe was timeless and beautiful, her signs of age giving her a wisdom and grace. Abby hoped like hell she looked half as good turning sixty.

"This is what I think," CeCe said, leaning forward and looking deep into Abby's eyes. "It's rebellion. Santi has been almost too good, you know? He's going away in the fall, and he has to test those ties that bind, see how strong they are. I raised Rachel, the queen of 'Screw you, Ma'—and what I learned from that is it takes two to play tug-of-war. You make demands; he'll have to see you and raise you to save face. Call his bluff, invite this Rosalinda over, welcome her. I bet the attraction wears right off if mother doesn't disapprove. Meanwhile, make damn sure he's using condoms. She may see him as a good catch and try to trap him. As far as the cousin and his criminal record, maybe Ramone could keep a close eye without any of them knowing about it. Stake him out. Catch him breaking his parole and send him back up the river where he belongs."

Abby blew out her tight breath. "You're so smart. What would I ever do without you, CeCe?"

"That's okay, sweetie. Now all you have to do in return is solve all my problems."

CeCe decided it was time to take Rose to get her hair colored and set. Rose refused to switch over to a curling iron, claiming her hairdo didn't stay as long as it did if she sat under the dryer. CeCe also brought Hattie along for the distraction.

Bonnie's beauty shop was a small addition onto her house, which sat off of the main highway through town, Highway 47. It was next to a great takeout New Mexican restaurant, the cause of Bonnie putting on a few pounds over the last couple of years. She insisted on squeezing into the same clothes she'd worn before the weight gain, putting rubber bands through the waistband button-holes of her pants and around the buttons for additional mileage.

The shop was painted pink with white trim on the outside, and in a large window a sign that read CLOSED was stuck up under some miniblinds. On the door hung one of those little card clocks with a "will be back" message. It was after hours, but Bonnie was expecting them.

"My favorite customer!" Bonnie said to Rose as if going for an Academy Award. "Did you get your hair spray brushed out real good?"

Hattie skipped in ahead of them in her new western-style sun-dress with a colorful cowgirls-and-horses print.

The air held the smell of leftover perm solution and cigarette smoke from Bonnie's customers. She wouldn't have any customers left if she refused to let them smoke. Most of them were her old high school friends. Along one wall were three hairdryers that looked secondhand from the sixties, chairs covered in pink vinyl with gold flecks, and two sinks for hair washing and rinsing. A stack of mismatched frayed towels were folded neatly above each sink.

Rose held her hand to her overprocessed, thinning hair, which looked like Larry's of the Three Stooges from the brushing. "You think I always go around looking like this? Of course I brushed it."

"You look funny, Bubbe Rose." Hattie laughed and pointed. "You look like my stuffed koala bear Maggie gave me from the zoo. He's got hair like that coming out of his ears."

Bonnie sat Rose down in the chair and draped a burgundy plastic cape over her. Her long purple nails sifted through Rose's fuzzy hair, pulling it straight so she could see the growth. "Hijo la, it's grown," Bonnie whined in sympathy. "*Bueno*." She took the gray plastic bowl and some tubes of color and began mixing with a stiff, flat brush.

"Ma, maybe you could tone down the red a little," CeCe said to Rose. "It's kind of orange for your skin tone." CeCe looked in the vanity mirror beyond her mother and hardly recognized herself under the harsh lights. She could barely discern her lips from that distance, they were so pale. When did she stop wearing lipstick?

"You father likes my hair red. I'll just change the tone of my makeup," Rose said.

"Ma. He wouldn't notice if you came home in a *shaitel*."

"Oy! My mameh use to wear one of those ugly wigs! She was from Lithuania, you know. Escaped the pograms," Rose whispered as if the Russians still lurked nearby.

"Maybe Zeyde Mort likes your hair red so he can see you from a distance," offered Hattie.

"Hattie, sit like a lady. I can see your flowered *matkes*." Rose crossed her legs under the cape, exposing seersucker pants striped in blue and white. The collar of her blue polo shirt had been tucked safely down into the cape, covered over by a towel around her neck fastened with a toothy hair clip.

"I've always said women should please themselves about hair and clothes, not men. What do those *gallos* know?" Bonnie added, still vigorously stirring the creamy paste and probably hoping to stir up a lot more.

Rose always referred to Bonnie as the *platke-macher* behind her back, or gossipy troublemaker. "What did the platke-macher say about that?" Or, "Is the platke-macher coming over to try to seduce my husband again?"

"Bubbe Rose, do you hate me and my mom?" asked Hattie, running her fingers through a plastic bin of tiny blue perm rods.

"*Tumler!*" Rose exclaimed to Hattie that she was being a little noise maker. "I don't hate you or your mother! Where in the world would you ever get that idea?"

"You act like you hate everybody, even Zeyde Mort sometimes," said Hattie, trying to wrap a blond curl around the small perm rod as her blue eyes crossed. "But not more than my grandpa. You hate him most because he's all Hispanic."

"CeCe, what are you telling this child?" asked Rose's baby doll pink lips.

"Me? She observes this for herself, Ma. Maybe you should listen."

"I have Hispanic in me, and Bonnie's Hispanic. You're going to have to hate a lot of people around here if you hate Hispanics," Hattie said.

"I don't hate anyone," Rose insisted. Since Bonnie was now applying the hair dye, her face and her hair were reddening at the same time. She reached back to reassure Bonnie. "I just grew up with some ideas that aren't right anymore, and sometimes things come out the wrong way. I'm from Brooklyn, it happens."

"You're just under a lot of stress, Mrs. Spelman," Bonnie soothed.

"Call me Rose, dear."

"Rrrose," Bonnie let it roll off her tongue.

"Besides, Hattie," Rose said, "according to the Talmud, you

are Jewish because your mother is Jewish because her mother is Jewish. See?"

"Who's Talmud?" Hattie asked.

"It's not a who, but a what," explained CeCe. "It's like the big Jewish book of rules."

"The strictest definition of a Jew according to the Talmud is one whose mother was Jewish. Period," Rose said.

"Why is that? Why is it that if your mother's a Jew, you're a Jew? What about the father?" Bonnie asked, now combing the color through to the ends with a wide-toothed comb. "Twenty minutes," she said, winding an egg timer and sitting it on her vanity top next to the Barbicide.

"Because a child's mother is always known. There's such a long history of Jewish slavery and oppression, and it wasn't always known who the fathers were, if you know what I'm saying," Rose said, looking over the rims of her glasses. "Instead of casting out the woman and her child, the Jewish community took them in by considering the child to be Jewish. Babies just weren't left in garbage cans like they are today."

CeCe had never heard this before and realized that when she was growing up, her parents had never really talked about their faith much. They just did things a certain way without ever explaining where the traditions came from. She wondered what else she didn't know.

"We go to church with crosses, not stars," Hattie told her.

"To me, you are Jewish. You're born what you are, and you'll die what you are," Rose said. "So you were born a what?" quizzed Rose.

"A girl," said Hattie.

Ben spread the map out across the hood of his freshly washed silver Honda CR-V. Usually the vehicle held a few layers of bosque dust and mud caking the tires from his forays onto the riverbanks and drying riverbeds. The early morning sun slanted over the mountains and filtered through the overhead foliage of the cottonwood tree, dappling his map with dancing light.

"We'd take I-25 north to Bernalillo here, just north of Albuquerque, and get off on 550. We'd take that over to San Ysidro. We'll pass Santa Ana and Zia pueblos, then take Highway 4 through Jemez Springs, past Jemez Pueblo—really gorgeous through here with the Jemez River and Jemez Mountains. We'll be climbing up out of the valley until we hit Highway 6, and then we go east past Los Alamos, and then we're at Bandelier National Monument to see the ruins and take our hike, grab lunch. How does that sound so far?" Ben grinned, excited as a kid playing hooky.

Abby couldn't believe she had actually pulled this off. Thanks to Santi, CeCe, and Rachel, she was actually going away with Ben for two whole days, with one glorious night sandwiched in between. "Great," she said.

"Because nothing is set in stone—it was hard to pick a one-night getaway. This state has a million possibilities. So some of this we can play by ear. Anyway, after Bandelier we hook back up with I-25 at Pojoaque Pueblo and go up to Española—that's only about twenty minutes. Then on the other side of Española we take 285 to Ojo Caliente, another twenty or thirty minutes, and stay there at the hot springs for the night. Soaks, wraps, massages, dinner . . . and a bed in the old hotel. No phones, no TV, no radios. Just nature—and us."

"The 'us' part sounds very nice," Abby said, handing her overnight bag to him. "Let's get this show on the road."

After an hour they were driving through the Jemez Mountains. The village of Jemez Springs was tucked into a narrow canyon along the Jemez River and boasted hot springs also. Bed and breakfast establishments had sprung up to accommodate city folks looking for a nearby place to unwind and enjoy the incredible scenery, fish, day hike, or visit the funky shops. There was a monastery tucked away for those looking for more serious retreat.

"Would you like to stop?" Ben asked as they crawled along through the traffic in the twenty-five mile per hour speed zone.

"Some other time," Abby said, noting his constant thoughtfulness. "It's enough just to see all of this. I want to get on to Bandelier and Ojo Caliente." As the highway ascended through the mountains, Abby could feel more and more relaxed. Maggie was in good hands and didn't even seem to mind she wasn't going along. She and Hattie had big plans to camp out in a tent Charlie was putting up in their backyard. She had taken CeCe's advice and told Santiago that she would trust him to use good judgment and condoms and to stay out of trouble. She had also talked to Ramone, who had assured her James Ortiz and his boys would be surreptitiously watched. For the next forty-eight hours she would do what everyone had been telling her to do: get a life.

"This is so incredible," Abby said as they wound down the steep, curving, mountainous drive to the floor of Bandelier Canyon. Bandelier National Monument marked the place where the Anasazi, the Ancient Ones, had formed a thriving community and culture a thousand years previously. Some four hundred years after that, they migrated from Bandelier and Puye settlements to the river bottoms, eventually becoming the present-day Pueblo Indians.

"Yeah, I love coming here. I can't believe you've never traveled much in New Mexico. We'll have to remedy that. Good, the parking lot's half-empty, shouldn't be crowded."

Abby realized that Esperanza had been her entire world these last seven years and how even that small place had seemed vast without Bobby to fill it. She and Maggie had gone back to San Diego a few times to visit her dear friend and restaurant chef, Edward, and check on her restaurant, but it was harder than she had anticipated to face it without Bobby. Occasional trips to Albuquerque or Santa Fe seemed to take her as far as she needed to go, and she was always relieved to get back to her little house under the huge cottonwood tree.

Ben pulled into a parking spot, and they emerged to go through the visitor center to see artifacts and pottery excavated from the site and read about Anasazi life. After a quick tour of the exhibits, Abby was anxious to explore it on her own.

Ben wore a day pack on his back, holding their water bottles and some snacks for the hike. Abby slathered on some additional sunscreen and wore one of Ben's hats. The sunlight was intense after the cool semidarkness of the visitor's center, with its adobe walls and stone floor.

"Rio de los Frijoles, meaning 'Bean Creek,'" Ben said, consulting the self-guided tour brochure, "attracted the ancient Pueblo Indians suffering from a disastrous drought in the thirteenth century. So they farmed the floor of this canyon, Frijoles Canyon, growing corn, beans, and squash."

They walked toward the path that would lead them up to the cliff ruins, where she could see wooden ladders leading to the caves carved into the northern wall of the canyon. "Talus villages extended along the base of the canyon for approximately two miles. These houses of masonry were irregularly terraced from one to three stories high and had many cave rooms gouged out of the solid cliff. The cliff of compressed volcanic ash, or tuff, was worked with tools of harder stone. The plateau this canyon is cut into is called Pajarito, or little bird." Ben looked up. "Am I boring you?"

Abby took her gaze from the tan cliffs and pulled her sunglasses down so Ben could see her eyes. "No, it's fascinating. So a drought brought them here to this oasis. What made them leave?"

"Another drought, soil depletion, famine, disease—take your pick," Ben said. "But they lived here for centuries, building villages, honeycombing the cliffs with caves, tilling the soil of the valley and the mesa top, trading beautiful black and white pottery to obtain cotton they wove into clothing. Then the drought cycle returned, and it was time to move on. That's why there's eight present-day Indian Pueblos within an hour of here who all have oral histories tracing themselves back to this canyon."

The trail cut across boulders and formations of tuff, leading them up to the ladders. Abby climbed up one, Ben right behind her. They crouch-walked into the mouth of the cave, its low ceiling and walls burnished black from ancient fires. It was quiet and cool, their shoes against the soft, grainy surface sounding amplified. They sat down in the dim light. The mouth of the cave was like a large picture window opening onto an incredible view of the maze of excavated ruins below, the green of the valley and the forested mesa, all under an azure sky. Billowing white clouds were building along the periphery of the horizon, as if forecasting an afternoon monsoon shower.

Ben took out a bottle of water and passed it to her. She drank several long swallows and handed it back. Words seemed intrusive in the space, but so much seemed to emanate from the ancient walls surrounding them.

Abby imagined living here seven hundred years ago, rebuilding the multistoried buildings and plazas in her mind. Crops thriving, children playing, a peaceful farming community with rich cultural and spiritual practices. The drums and song, the laughter and stories, the dances celebrating and appealing to their gods. Thriving here for so long until having to disperse, move, surrender to the forces that threatened their existence. Living links survived, and she caught a glimpse of them at the state fair whenever the Pueblo Indians took turns competing with drums and songs and dances in their arena. It always transported her to some other time and place.

Approaching voices, those of excited children and their cautioning parents, caused Abby and Ben to move to the ladder and relinquish their cave home.

After they explored more caves and various kivas—underground round rooms entered and exited by ladders through a single hole in their roofs, once used for religious practices and training—they explored the Tyuonyi ruins. Tyuonyi Village, or pueblo, once had more than four hundred rooms and had been three stories high in places, but the ruins were now only a few feet high. Abby walked through the large interior open plaza, the ruins encircling it, trying to see it as it had once been, a bustling city center. Three large circular holes remained where three kivas had been. Even with her sunglasses on, the sunlight was nearly blinding as it reflected from the tuff floor, and she could feel its hot rays soaking into her flesh. They shared some water and moved on to find relief in another kiva.

Snake Kiva was built into a cave carved into the base of the cliff. When they entered its silent semidarkness, Abby could see painted designs on its back wall. As her eyes adjusted she could make out a zigzag snakelike creature with a plume flowing back from its head.

"Awanyu," Ben said so quietly at first she thought he was saying, "I want you." "Feathered serpent. He brings the water and rain. I imagine a lot of desperate prayers were chanted in here."

They hiked back to the visitors center through the shady canyon floor, along the gurgling, fast-moving stream. Pausing on a footbridge, Abby peered into the pristine water, the rocks along its bed shimmering with refracted light.

Conversation had been limited to occasional hushed comments. Piñon jays' piercing calls, the single scream of an eagle when it flew high overhead, the chatter of squirrels, the rustle of the growing breeze through the branches overhead seemed to say it all.

A thick, prolonged rumble of thunder resonated through the canyon as the peripheral clouds began to mass overhead. Their undersides darkened, and lightning began to shoot as if from

Sue Boggio and Mare Pearl

unseen fingers, cracking and crashing nearby. Before they could say a word, pea-sized hail began to pelt them. Ben grabbed Abby's hand, and they jogged the flat trail, laughing as the cold rain came, still punctuated with hail.

Their jogging strides matched in rhythm, Ben's muscled, tan thighs contrasting with Abby's pale, freckled legs, their clothing flattened against their bodies, hats limply hanging over stringy wet hair. Ben's wide smile met Abby's, and she was filled with warmth even as she shivered from the freezing water streaming over her.

After changing into some dry clothes in the visitor center restrooms and grabbing green chile cheeseburgers and coffee at the snack bar, they headed for Ojo Caliente, their destination for their long-anticipated night alone.

Returning to the packed interstate was a jarring trip through time. The clouds dissipated, rolling away like unwanted rugs, the rain stopped as suddenly as it had arrived, and the conquering sun tried to erase any evidence that the rain serpent had visited at all.

The road to Ojo Caliente wound through another canyon north of Española, steep jagged mesa on her side of the road, a drop into the green Rio Chama Valley seen from Ben's side of the car. The back of the Jemez Mountains were visible in the east. Below, in the river valley, modest houses and trailers were surrounded by neat rectangles of farmland, and even though Abby knew the drought was here as much as at home, she was struck by how green everything seemed. A glance along the perimeter revealed the reason: a grid of narrow irrigation ditches carrying the crops' lifeblood.

"They call their water ditches acequias up here. You don't hear that as much farther south," Ben said. "But this area has stayed more traditional, more Hispanic. You find small family farms mostly raising chile and alfalfa for their own families or neighbors, not for big commercial purposes. Very close-knit communities, trying to resist the changes of time. They elect a mayordomo, a ditch boss, and he stands at the appointed place every morning at six, and anyone wanting to irrigate that day must present himself and ask permission and work out a schedule with his neighbors."

He turned left at the large wooden Ojo Caliente Mineral Springs sign, faded from the sun, old paint curled and chipped. The narrow road descended rapidly as it passed some small horse corrals and homes tucked under large cottonwood trees, then a few tourist shops appeared, colorful natural clothing hung along their porch overhangs like flags. They reached the compound and pulled into the gravel parking lot. Ben parked in the shade of a cottonwood and smiled. "Here we are."

After checking in, they found their room in the small one-story hotel. It was cool despite no air-conditioning or swamp coolers, owing to the thick adobe walls and ceiling fans. A colorfully quilted queen-size bed, antique dresser, nightstand, and vintage green leather chair appointed the clean, simple room. The bathroom held a commode and a sink set comically low to the floor. Crammed between the two, Ben peered down to the sink near his knees. "This should be fun." His laugh echoed in the tiny space.

Abby sat on the edge of the bed, her legs tingling from all the climbing and hiking at Bandelier. The large wood-framed window looked out over the flower gardens and walkways, shade ramadas and buildings clustered at the base of the volcanic tuff cliff and rising mesa. A handful of guests in bathing gear and shorts walked back and forth at a leisurely pace in the afternoon sun. The entire scene was so relaxing, she could feel herself begin to unwind.

Ben sat next to her. "What do you think? All right for the night?"

"I love it. I'm ready to be completely hedonistic."

"You've come to the right place for that. Seven mineral pools, all kinds of massages, wraps, facials, you name it. And after all that pampering works up your appetite, the dining room has great food and wine."

She put her hand on the side of his face and looked into his light-filled eyes. "Thanks, Ben. This is wonderful."

"I've been up here twice on my own, watching the couples, wishing I had someone to share this with."

"I'm glad it's me."

Feeling naturally high after an hour-long massage, Abby met up with Ben at the cliffside iron and arsenic pool. It was a good twenty-five feet across, cement with a tile border. The tan cliff rose dramatically seventy-five or eighty feet to a flat, scrubby mesa top. The cliff face was eroded in vertical tentlike formations. Horizontal striations marked the progress of ancient lava flows as they had constructed the cliff layer by layer.

Abby stepped down into the pool where Ben and a few others were soaking. She sat down into the three feet or so of warm water, which was fed by a small waterfall situated at head level on one end. An older man sat under it, turning his neck from side to side to catch the full force of the stream.

"There's a hike up there to the top of the mesa, where the Posi ruins are," a dark-haired, twenty something woman next to Ben was saying. "I hiked up there this morning. It was a huge pueblo, like a thousand people lived there, and they soaked in these same hot springs. I could show you where the trailhead is . . ." She trailed off as Ben turned to give Abby a kiss.

"I'm sorry, you were saying?" Ben said to the attractive woman who had been speaking.

"Uh . . . that's okay. I need to get going. Have a good time." She rose out of the water, her minuscule bikini barely attached to her perfect figure. She paused to wring the water from her long hair and looked back as if to say, "See what you're missing?"

"I didn't mean to scare your little friend away," Abby said, lolling against him, enjoying how her body felt slippery against his skin.

"I never know how to handle those situations," Ben said.

"You handled it fine," Abby said, wondering how many times Ben had to contend with "those situations." Probably a lot, she figured—a handsome Australian professor, young, eager female students.

"Let's go over there," Ben suggested, pointing to the adjacent mud pool. It was fenced in low wrought iron to discourage people from leaving the area before showering under one of the three open-air spigots. Variously shaped people, all covered in the light brown mud, lay in plastic patio recliners, their skin drying in the sun. They looked like a collection of Mud Heads, Zuni Pueblo kachinas.

Abby and Ben stood over the large terra-cotta flowerpot that held the mineral-rich, pure mud dug from nearby clay pits; next to it was the rinsing pool. She thrust her hands into the mud, and it felt like smooth, cold pudding. She began to smear it all over herself, as Ben did the same. They covered each other's backs and carefully painted each other's faces until they were ready to join the anonymous ranks of the other mud people drying in the sun.

"I feel like a piece of pottery," Abby commented after twenty minutes or so, feeling the mud tighten against her skin as it dried. Her face had transformed into a tight mask that resisted subtle movement. She gazed overhead at the brilliant blue of the sky streaked with a solitary wispy white cloud. The sun was starting to lower near the cliff top.

"Yeah," Ben agreed. He started to flex his arms and legs, and she did the same.

Her thin pottery slip began to crack as she moved, flaking into small, powdery pieces. She felt like a new life-form emerging from a dried, dead husk.

"It's alive!" Ben mimed the awakening of the Frankenstein monster.

Abby laughed, brushing the dried surface flakes off with her fingers. They got into the mocha-colored waters of the warm rinsing pool, lathering the wet clay from their bodies. "My skin feels so soft and smooth," she said, as if she were in a soap commercial.

"The mud sucks out toxins and impurities," said a large Hispanic woman solemnly as she rinsed the mud from her copious flesh. "It might stain your swimsuit, though."

Abby noticed the pigment wanted to cling to the tangerine and lime swirls of her swimsuit fabric.

"OxiClean," the woman leaned over and whispered as if revealing the secret to the universe. "That'll take it right out."

"Thanks," Abby replied. "I'm new to this."

"I'm a local. Come here all the time. My whole family has yearly passes—a lot of the locals do. I like how they keep it rustic, not all fancy. The Santa Fe snobs can go somewhere else."

"Right to that," Ben said.

"Are you from England?" the woman asked.

"Australia."

"There's always foreigners here. Japanese, Germans, all kinds. I don't know how they find out about it, but they come and spend their money, so that's all right."

"Shall we?" Abby asked.

"Yeah, we have our private tub and then our Milagro Wraps to do before dinner."

After showering off the remaining mud, they headed over to the coed bathhouse, where an attendant filled a private bathtub for two with hot spring water. She laid fresh towels on the wood slat bench and before closing the door said, "I'll be back to get you for your wraps in twenty minutes."

They eased into the hot water, clouds of billowing steam filling the small room. It was completely quiet save for the trickle of water from the spout. Abby floated on her back against Ben in the deep tub. He caught her and pulled her toward him so that her head was against his jaw and her body rested lightly over his. His arms gently encircled her waist, and his fingers wandered over her belly.

She closed her eyes and melted into him, hearing his soft breath against her ear. He ran his hands lightly over her body, over her breasts, her throat, her abdomen. She felt herself become aroused, and instead of tensing, she surrendered to it, the hot, soothing water creating a dreamlike departure from reality.

One of his hands lingered over her right breast, and her breath caught as he lightly ran his thumb against her jutting nipple. His other hand slid slowing down her belly and onto the top of her thigh. She moved her hips slightly, inviting him to explore further.

He kissed her throat as he continued his tender caresses, and Abby could feel her insistent flesh subdue all thought. Her back arched, and she grabbed his hand with her own, directing his movement with a final, startled gasp. Her body convulsed with pleasure, and tears of relief flooded her eyes. Ben's arms enveloped her as she curled up against him, her head against his chest. He cradled her in the hot water, slowly rocking her, humming a soft, nameless tune while she listened to his heartbeat.

After a sumptuous dinner of local trout and wine, they strolled the grounds under the stars. A crescent moon smiled down; the compound's cat accompanied them for a time. Then they walked down the hallway, carpeted over creaking wood, to their room.

"It's your turn now," Abby whispered as Ben put the key in the lock.

He smiled as he opened the door. "Let's see if I can make it worth both our whiles."

The next day, after a morning soak and a hike to a nearby defunct mica mine, they ate a late brunch in the dining room and checked out. Back in Española, Ben took a side trip to Chimayo, only ten miles east of their route home down Interstate 25.

"The Santuario de Chimayo is a famous old mission church, dating back to the early 1800s. It has sacred earth that will heal the faithful. Or so it goes," Ben said. "People come from all over the world to pray for a miracle cure and apply the sacred dirt to their ailing bodies. They leave their crutches and braces behind to demonstrate it worked."

It was a short and beautiful drive to Chimayo, the Sangre de Cristo Mountains to the southeast seeming close enough to touch. Adobe homes, their tin pitched roofs catching the sun and reflecting it like blinding searchlights, were interspersed with chile and alfalfa fields.

"The chile up here is called 'land race' because they use the seeds passed down for generations from the same chile that the early Spanish explorers introduced in northern New Mexico centuries ago. The chiles are smaller and have thinner skin, and they tend to have a sweeter heat than the varieties down south. I buy the powdered form here, great for cooking with."

The village of Chimayo itself was centered around the church and the tourists and pilgrims who visited. There were a few shops with hand-lettered signs in the windows: "Genuine Chimayo Chile Sold Here."

The entrance to the church, or *santuario*, was through an open gate under an arch in an adobe wall. Pink hollyhocks, yellow climbing roses, and other flowers bordered the flagstone courtyard between the gate and the church's heavy wooden doors.

Ben opened the door, and some elderly Hispanic pilgrims walked under his arm as they were leaving, smiling at Abby as they passed.

The sanctuary was small and lit only by candles and natural light from the few windows placed high up on the walls. The old gilded alter was framed in an intricate design of bloodred and turquoise and featured a magnificently carved and painted crucified Christ. Although Abby was not Catholic, she felt the spiritual power the thick walls radiated. It was cool and silent, the twittering birds outside the only sound she heard. She began to remember the only two times she had stepped foot in the Esperanza mission church. The first was with Bobby, to attend his father's wake and funeral, when she felt so useless and foreign to her husband's soul-wrenching guilt and grief. And then, six months later, she was back to hold Bobby's funeral. The scent of the hot candle wax, the light flickering against the shadowy walls, the musty old adobe smell sent her reeling back through time. She felt the pain rise fresh in her unprepared heart.

Ben led her through a side doorway near the altar where the sacred sandpit, or *El Pisto*, was. He whispered, "Believers rub the sacred earth where they need to be healed."

She looked down at the neatly circumscribed hole with loose earth churned to a tan powder. She knelt down and put her hand into its cool softness, cupped a little into her palm, and pulled down the scoop neck of her tank top to rub the healing powder in the place over her heart. She closed her eyes and prayed for her heart to be strong and brave, to be freed from the pain of the past. She wished Bobby peace and told him she would always have her love for him safely tucked away, even as she moved on to a new love in her life.

Abby opened her eyes, blinking back a few tears, to see Ben rubbing some healing earth over his own scarred heart.

CHAPTER 11

Rachel's lungs were about to burst. She swam toward the top of the water, where she could see light faintly glistening. Her arms and hands pushed and pushed themselves tired, her feet kicked, but the water felt like mud. She didn't think she'd be able to hold her breath a second more and wondered how it would feel when she sucked her lungs full of this thick muck and floated up to heaven. Finally she broke through the surface, gasping for air. She could not see. A baby cried in the distance. Her baby. She must save him—

She sat up suddenly. Her armpits were wet, her T-shirt clinging. It was still dark in their bedroom. Charlie snored lightly next to her. Not one of those window-rattling kind of snores, but more like an oscillating fan in summer. His wide muscled back was to her as he hugged his pillow.

Careful not to wake him, she slid out of bed. He had been so exhausted for so long, every wink of sleep he got was a godsend. And bless his little heart, he still had the energy to make love to her that evening.

She slipped on a pair of moccasins and padded to the bathroom.

They had made the master bath large but rustic, with wood plank floors, a claw-foot tub, and painted-Mexican-tiled vanity and double sinks. They had traveled down to Juárez in the old truck, no less, to pick out the sinks and tiles and to get a good deal. She was very pregnant with Hattie, and they had to stop every hour so she could pee and adjust her bra straps, which were having a rough go at keeping a tight rein. She had been so damn uncomfortable, amazing she had had such a good time.

Charlie babied her silly on that trip. Even on the smooth interstate, the truck jostled her and fetus Hattie; a wonder the baby didn't suffer intrauterine brain scramble. And when her ankles swelled, he carried her. Boys on fast bicycles guiding tourists to the *mercado* swerved around them as Charlie carried her across streets. Men stared and women giggled as they passed by. She imagined that this was not a usual custom in Juárez, or anywhere. But she didn't care. She had been proud to be with a man who loved her that much. His love was as big as this house; she was reminded of it every day.

On her way to the stairs, she peeked in on Hattie, who was sleeping peacefully. Charlie had wanted a traditional farmhouse, and so they had a second floor where their bedroom, the extra bedroom, and Hattie's bedroom were. Hattie had a half bath off of her bedroom, but used their bathroom for her baths in the big old tub.

For Hattie, pulling out the stopper by the bead chain was one of the highlights of bath time. She stayed in to watch the last little bit of bathwater spin its tiny tornado and suck loudly down the drain, her bath toys looking like flood victims washed aground.

The plank wood floor ran throughout the house. On the staircase, a long Indian rug flowed down the center in a colorful geometric waterfall. Indian rugs also hung along the top railing along the second floor hallway, and there were more scattered throughout the house. The rugs had been Grandma Hattie's, too, and

Rachel hated to use them to walk on; but Charlie said this was what he had kept them for all these years. For his dream home with his dream girl.

Seven years ago, when they had gotten back together after their divorce, she had become pregnant right away. Building this house became another pregnancy and birth. They had not built it entirely themselves—it would have never gotten finished—but she and Charlie had worked with the builders whenever they could. They had handpicked every single feature of the house or made it themselves. Charlie had shaved and shaped the stocky wooden balusters on the stair rail himself, and he had helped cut and nail the planks of the floor. Rachel had laid the brick on the kitchen and sunroom floors in a Mediterranean style, with a brick mosaic in the center of each. Family and friends had come out to lend a hand on the house when they could, which pumped that much more love into its inception. To this day, this house, her home, was still a continual labor of love. Here, with her family, she felt centered in God's hands.

She decided she and Hattie would have girl's day this upcoming Saturday in Albuquerque. Have a big girl lunch after hitting the flea market at the state fairgrounds. Or maybe she'd take her to Old Town to the puppet theater after having lunch at Le Crêpe Michel. Next door was Old Town Cat House, where the extreme cat lover could find every kind of cat paraphernalia you could imagine. Hattie loved going in there to visit the shop's cats.

No way would she go back to sleep. First, the dream disturbed her. And now, her mind was awake with a parade of thoughts and memories.

Oakley trilled and rubbed up against her leg as she stood at the stove and made tea. Oakley was always in the kitchen these days, staring and laying patiently in wait for the mouse he suspected lived under the stove. Rachel had rescued him as a tiny kitten last summer from where he had been abandoned at the large ditch and presented him to Hattie, who bottle-fed him and weaned him to solid food. To Hattie, being Oakley's mom was not a game. She devoted herself to him.

One of her and Charlie's best finds was the late-thirties enameled stove. It was that mint green from the era, with black piping. She had always wanted one. Roberto's *abuela* had had one in her house, but it was white. Basic but functional. Just like the cooking fireplace, where Charlie cooked some good beans from time to time. Sometimes he made a little tent in front of it, and he and Hattie pretended to be cowpokes on the open range. Or Tom Sawyer and Becky. That was what he had been reading to her lately at bedtime.

She smiled remembering the distance she had to stand away from the stove when she was nine months pregnant with Hattie, she was so huge. Charlie had to get the long barbecue utensils for her to reach the sizzling food. He'd nicknamed her Haystack.

Oakley heard them before she did. Steps. Dry, crunchy steps, then clomping on the back porch right up to her back door. She and Oakley looked at the door with perked ears. A knock followed.

"Mi'ja! Is that you? Are you up, mi'ja?" It was her father.

She ran to open the door. "Papa! What are you doing out here at this time of night?" He smelled of whiskey. His eyes were bloodshot. Had he been crying? He wore yesterday's shirt.

"I'll tell you, mi'ja, what I am doing," he said, holding up a finger.

Rachel helped him to a chair, from which he looked at her with bleary eyes.

"I saw your light on and thought maybe you were awake. Your mother kicked me out. Said I was drunk." He tossed his head indignantly.

"You are drunk. I'm going to make some strong coffee," Rachel said, fetching some fresh beans to grind. "You're scaring me, Papa. I've never seen you like this."

"What does a man do when his faith is failing him? Whiskey dulls the pain, mi'ja. It is not so much that I need to be drunk, but that I need to be numb. It's been taking more and more lately."

Rachel sat with him at the table while the coffee sputtered and brewed. She scooted her chair closer. He looked down into his leathered hands.

"I can't live with the thought of losing this farm," he said in an exhausted voice. "Every morning I wake to clear skies or, worse yet, promising cloudy skies that give nothing. I don't know which disappointment is more torturous." He laughed so it seemed he would not cry and shook his head. "Where are my beloved saints now? They are only my bultos that stand there and do nothing! Painted retablos with fish-eyed stares! Your mother, she doesn't understand."

"You're wrong, Papa. About your saints and about Ma. She's going through her own stuff, you know, turning sixty. I know you don't see it as a big deal, but we women feel differently. And come on! Day in and day out with Rose and Mort? She probably feels her faith wavering, too."

"Yes, *her* faith. Where is her benevolent universe now? Why would such a universe allow us to lose our land, our love of this life? Yes, right now we have a crop because we have irrigation water, but we don't know about next week. Now is when we need water more than ever up until harvest. It's the limbo, mi'ja, that is wearing me down. Here it is middle of July, and still no monsoons. And if we get the monsoons, it only takes one hailstorm to destroy our plants, mi'ja, you know that." He stretched out his arms in front of him on the table, hands clasped, fingers wrapped around tightly. "The farm probably will end right here with me. I'm not sure I can manage it anymore. It's not fair to Charlie to keep working him so hard." He took his bandana out of his pocket, blew his nose, and wiped his eyes, then stuck it back in his pocket.

"I miss your mother. Ever since her parents came, she and I have haven't had time for each other. And at the end of the day, I feel so beaten down by the sun and dry earth. She's beaten down by her folks, and then working the café . . ."

"You need to stop drinking, Papa. You'll never get close to Ma if you're still drinking. She's feeling old enough without you acting like one of those drunken *viejitos* at Pablo's every night."

He took in a deep breath and blew it out slowly. His eyes widened to reveal how difficult this was going to be for him.

"Look, Ma's birthday is coming up in a couple of weeks. You can do this. You miss her, she misses you. I'm sure everything will feel better when you and Ma are back in sync. Join forces again and cope," she said, pouring him a second cup of coffee.

"How did you get to be so wise, mi'ja? Must take after your mama." He stirred in some half-and-half from Mickey's Dairy. "What would Teresa say if she saw me now?"

"Your sister?"

"Sí, my big sister, Teresa. Remember she left for college from this farm, and I haven't seen her since. Mama took the opportunity to leave when Teresa did, going off to Tucson with her. Mama was not cut out for farm life. I missed them so much, but I didn't dare tell Papa." He took another quick gulp of coffee, brushing away his tears. "The tears of an old, drunken fool, mi'ja. I apologize."

Rachel knew the story about his mother and sister leaving when he was still a junior in high school. She knew that even the death of his mother had not brought his sister and him together again.

"Is Teresa still in Tucson?"

"I suppose, but how would I know? Strange how the years can separate two who were once so close as children. She was wise to go away, get an education." He yawned and rubbed his eyes. "Well, you don't have to worry, mi'ja, I take what you say to heart. I will lay off the whiskey and mend things with your mother."

"Want to crash here?" she asked.

"No, thanks. I think I'll go sleep this off in my hammock. Maybe your mother will wake up and take pity on me. I will take some ibuprofen if you've got some."

Rachel took the bottle from the cupboard and shook out four pills, which he downed with the rest of his coffee.

"Thank you, mi'ja, for listening." He hugged her and kissed her forehead. His soured breath brought tears to her eyes.

She watched for a while as he walked back into the night. She had never seen him so fragile, so hopeless. She felt all the more uneasy. He means what he says now, but what about tomorrow, when he sees his crops wilting in the heat?

She could still hear his crunching boots on the access road even after she could no longer see him. When she couldn't hear him anymore, she shut the door.

"Do you think Leo and Florecita love each other?" Jenny asked, referring to the married couple at the café who washed dishes and cleaned. She was hooking a milk machine up to two goats for the five o'clock milking. The goats fussed on the stands until they began eating from the food trays.

Jenny prepared the goats by washing their udders in a disinfectant. "She looks like she's frowning all the time, and he barks at her a lot in Spanish. She never says a word back."

"He's only telling her what to do," explained Leticia. "It's easier for him to bark at her in Spanish than for her to not understand him in English. That doesn't mean they don't love each other."

Jenny shrugged. "How long do you think Florecita's braid is that she keeps wrapped around her head?"

Rachel sat at the small desk in the milking room, trying to catch up on her milking records. She smiled. Jenny had just graduated from high school with Santi but had been working for Rachel and the café for the past three years. She had been an early transplant to New Mexico, since grade school, but not a native. Her family came from the Midwest, and she was not foreign to farmwork. She felt more comfortable here than working at the restaurant. Her last name was McCarty, so she figured Jenny was of Irish descent; her coppery red hair and translucent complexion supplied more evidence.

Jenny had taken on the two mechanical milking machines Rachel had bought when she hired her. You still had to have a special touch for attaching the inflations. Goats were not like cows when it came to milking, and the new machines were designed especially for goats, meaning the vacuum levels were lower, the pulsation ratio set correctly at 50:50. If the time when the inflation was open to milk or closed to rest was higher, it would cause mastitis.

At about fifteen hundred dollars apiece, Rachel almost went broke buying two milking machines at once, but now they could milk four goats at a time, saving time and money, not to mention wear and tear on her arms, hands, and fingers. They quickly paid for themselves, and she was able to expand her herd to twenty goats. Each goat produced about three quarts of milk a day, so even after bottle-feeding the kids, she still had plenty to make her cheeses.

Leticia, though the same age as Jenny, was already a young mother with a mechanic husband. Her talent was working in the kitchen making the cheeses. She was a petite girl with long, dark hair that Rachel hardly ever saw down. Leticia loved coming out from the back to talk to the regulars, usually because they knew the same people from church. She tried to be a good mom but often lacked good judgment about whom she left her baby with during working hours, so Rachel, CeCe, and Abby insisted that she bring the toddler and playpen to the café or the farm if she couldn't find reliable help.

Jenny and Leticia were still on the conversation of love.

"I just broke up with my boyfriend, who I thought I would love forever. I was surprised when I didn't. How do you know? How can you know?" Jenny asked Leticia, who had been married since she was sixteen so was therefore an authority.

Jenny removed a cluster from another goat's teats and ran her index finger and thumb down the teat to squeeze out the last drops. Then she put a disinfectant on each teat, which also helped close the milk orifice. Leticia filtered the milk into sanitizing jars and then placed the jars in the ice water bath.

"I thought of leaving Cisco before, like when he's being a butthead about something. But I think of the baby and my life, and I realize that I don't want it to change, and then you decide to hang in there and work things out. Money's a big problem for us. Mostly that's what we fight about," she said, scratching the sides and belly of the goat she was disinfecting on the stand. It bobbed its head, sticking out its tongue, pleading for her to continue. "Cisco wants me to have another baby, but I tell him it's hard enough with one and we should wait until Pedro is a little older. Hijo la, we fight about that, too."

"Have them while you can," Rachel said. "There's never a right time, and it only gets harder the older you get. Then when you want one desperately, you can't."

"You're still young, Rachel," Leticia said. "You'll have another baby."

Rachel almost told them about her hysterectomy. And that she wasn't that young. She could be their mother. Her son would have been their age now. She tried to breathe and remember she was working through the pain. With Charlie's help she thought she was farther along in letting all of this go. It amazed her how something as innocent as Leticia's well-meaning remark could throw her back into her regret and grief.

After they were done, Jenny and Leticia cleaned all the milking utensils with warm water before boiling them. If milk residue wasn't rinsed off immediately after milking, water that was too hot or too cold glued the proteins and fat onto the utensils. Rachel was glad they were so thorough. Bad help could cost plenty.

CeCe kicked off her shoes and felt the coolness of the brick floor on her bare, aching feet. It had been a day! She had gone to work early and gotten everything ready to open the café, preslicing a larger-than-usual amount of corned beef, roast beef, breads, and a few cheeses for the lunch rush, which she would miss.

Instead, she had taken her father to a couple of thrift stores to find him more suitable clothes for him to wear while dabbling on the farm. Polyester pants and shirts didn't cut it outside in a New Mexico summer. This July was like last July and the July before that. So hot and dry that when there was a gust of wind, it would feel like a blast from a raging fire. She couldn't understand why he wanted to come out and do things around the farm at his age. Then again, he didn't know what age he was half the time, time traveler that he was. Rose was happy sitting in Miguel's recliner watching "The Price Is Right" with the swamp cooler on high. Just as well.

But Mort wasn't too bad with a hoe. There he'd be, out in her garden wearing the extra-large-brimmed straw hat she had scrounged for him, looking like a migrant worker. He movements were small, but his strokes with the hoe were steady and deliberate.

Mort had started taking a new medication, and she thought he was doing better. His lucid moments were more frequent. Nights had been easier, too, although there were still times she needed Rachel's help to calm him.

She thought they'd start at the Salvation Army way up on Juan Tabo Boulevard, near the foothills of the Sandia Mountains east of Albuquerque. It was a long drive, but it was the largest Salvation Army in the city, and she knew there would be a large selection of men's clothes.

The traffic wasn't too bad. For once they weren't working on the freeway. She pulled into a handicapped parking space and displayed the sign she had gotten to use when she schlepped her parents around. Thank God they had installed the steps on the passenger's side of the truck. She was worried that one of them might break a hip.

The store was having a clearance sale. Piles of clothes were strewn on tables, and pairs of shoes were lined up along a double wooden shelf that ran half the length of the store. Women's shoes, men's shoes, and children's shoes, in all shapes and sizes.

"Over here, Papa," she said, leading him to a clearance table of men's pants. "We'll just start sifting through looking for your size; something in cotton." CeCe rummaged like a pro through the stack. "What are you, Papa, about a thirty-two?"

"Inseam thirty," he said, nodding his head.

"We won't worry if they're too long. We can fix that. Help me, Papa."

Mort reached into the clothes and began to go through them.

"Any luck?" CeCe asked.

But her father stood frozen now, staring blankly.

"Papa? Papa. What's wrong?" She thought he was having a stroke in the Salvation Army.

But Mort continued to stare off as he slowly started going through the pockets of the pants. His hands shook as his fingers reached in to scoop them out swiftly. His hands came out empty every time.

"Papa, come sit over here," she told him, pulling him over to a chair by the display of shoes. "Just sit and rest and I'll go look, okay?" But while she went through racks now, she saw him picking up shoes and shaking them out. What the hell?

"Papa, let's go," she said pulling him by the elbow. A eeriness crept over her. She dumped the shirts she had hanging over her arm onto a rack as she passed. "Let's get out of here."

As soon as she got him home she called Rachel, made her drop what she was doing to come right over.

"It was the strangest thing," she told Rachel. "He was this shell of a man in front of me. He couldn't hear or see me. Just when I had high hopes for this new medication, he's going through pockets and shoes like a homeless person looking for a dime."

Rachel gave a shudder.

"What's wrong?" CeCe asked.

"Ma, I think it's time you educate yourself on what Zeyde has gone through. I did, and I can see why a person could go through the rest of his life and not act normal. You know what happened in the Holocaust, but you have no idea all that happened to your own father. There were only about sixty who lived to tell about Treblinka. Don't you see? The thrift store triggered that trauma. Remember Rose said he was enslaved by the Nazis, who forced him go through the belongings of gassed Jews? Can you imagine?"

"That explains what happened at the thrift store, but . . ."

"And when we took him to Durango, remember I told you what he said about the burning bodies? He keeps going back to that hell over and over. How can you possibly hold a grudge now? You've got to let this go," Rachel said. "Get over it."

Many times CeCe wished she could have been more like her sisters. It seemed much less painful for them. She never recalled them tediously making Father's Day cards with lace doilies, hearts, and fake money or learning a new tap dance to cheer him up when he was exceptionally foul. They never wrote poetry to him in hopes of breaking through the glacier around his heart. They just steered clear of him. Sam never had to try; he was Mort's chosen child.

"You have no idea how it was for me."

"But Ma, had you known about what happened to him, wouldn't it have made a difference? You're a grown woman—it has to make a difference now."

"Look, you're free to have whatever kind of relationship with him you like. I'm not against that. But you can't tell me what kind I'm going to have."

"No, but come on, Ma. You sound like Tía Maria! Old and spiteful."

CeCe gasped. Rachel's words punched the air right out of her like a goat butt to her chest. It was the most hurtful thing anyone could have said to her. Being compared to that crazy bruja! Besides, she didn't know what bothered her more: old or spiteful.

"And what about la familia? Only when it suits you?"

"You just don't understand how long and deep this pain goes," CeCe said, shaking her head.

Rachel rolled her blue eyes. "What I don't understand is why you don't try to love him for the quirky guy he is now. He needs it more than ever, Ma. Half the time he's still going through the most horrendous experience anyone could imagine. Flashbacks are just as real as being there. I think of that now when I'm with him. Especially when he calls me Zophia. I feel I need to respect his memory of her. He watched her be murdered, Ma. " Rachel reached into her bag and produced some literature she had printed from the Internet. "You have to look at these."

CeCe took the papers, but turned them away from her. She had read Anne Frank and seen the documentaries on TV. It all made her sick. She knew as much about the Holocaust as she wanted to know.

Everything about Rachel's idea of forgiveness scared her. Probably the minute she fell in love with the alter kocker was when he'd decide to die and hurt her all over again. At this stage of the game, angry distance was less threatening.

CeCe remembered the time she and her sisters were practicing their instruments, hers being the clarinet, and he came in to scream at all of them about something trivial and ended up shattering her clarinet against the wall because he thought she wasn't paying attention to him. Cutting her hands as he ripped it from her. They were always walking on eggshells around him, tortured by the unpredictability of his rage. It never made any sense. He was impossible to please.

Her mother had a large, close family in Brooklyn. When Mort was in one of his rages, she took her kids and escaped him by fleeing to her mother's house. CeCe remembered the large Seder dinners at her bubbe's. Aunt Sylvia always brought the *lokshen kugel*, a baked noodle pudding with butter, sour cream, eggs, sugar, cinnamon, and raisins, one of CeCe's favorites. Rose never put on the graham cracker crumb topping, but Aunt Sylvia did. Auntie Gussie would bring her *tsimmes*, sugared diced carrots baked with meat, and knaidel, a kind of matzo ball. Auntie Gussie's breasts were so large, CeCe dreaded hugging her when she was little, for fear of dying of suffocation. Uncle Milt never failed to do his corny magic tricks. And all the male cousins and Sam would find unrelenting ways to tease her and her sisters. She had been closest to her cousin Eli. He had the curliest short red hair and teddy bear button brown eyes. They would talk about deep things and vow to change the world someday. He became an orthodontist. Those were her good childhood memories. That was her family. Her father had no part in it.

"Forgiving Mort isn't just for him. You need to do it for yourself," Rachel said.

CeCe had a host of arguments but held them back. Even with the pain of her past lodged in her like a stake in her heart, she knew her daughter was right. But knowing wasn't feeling, not yet.

Rachel looked at her long and hard, with tears forming in her eyes. "If you have the guts, you'll do what is right," Rachel said as she disappeared out of the screen door, which snapped shut like a slap.

CeCe looked through sudden tears at the stack of papers she was holding. Her hand shook so much she couldn't read them. She started to bury them into the drawer of her Art Deco buffet, under a stack of vintage linens. But her hand couldn't let go of them. So she pulled them back out and smoothed a wrinkled edge. Her daughter was right. She summoned all the courage she had and began to read.

Mort readied the card table for what had become their weekly night of cards as CeCe watched, amused, from the kitchen door. He must have positioned the dish of peanuts and spice drops ten times on that little table, trying to make everything perfect.

Rose came in dressed in her robe, fresh from her evening bath. From her terry cloth pocket she pulled out the old deck of cards, their backs faded and creased from years of shuffling.

"Let's get started. I'm not getting any younger here," said Mort, clapping his hands together. He looked healthier with every passing week, and CeCe took pride in that. In the reading material Rachel had given her, there were pictures of Holocaust Jews who were just skin on bone. She knew—not just intellectually, but from her heart now—he had been one of them.

Rose counted out the cards, flipping them perfectly facedown in front of each of them. "You're first, Mort. Pick up a card. Throw down a card."

"Don't rush me. I haven't even looked at them yet," he said, scooping them up and fanning them out. "What game are we playing?" he asked, scratching one of his large ears.

CeCe laughed, which made Mort laugh. "Gin rummy, Papa."

Bonnie had convinced Rose to tone her hair down to a brownish red, which was more how CeCe remembered her. Rose's skin was nearly free of any wrinkles, and even without makeup, her face glowed.

Mort discarded a five of spades and peeked over his cards to see if CeCe was going to pick it up. CeCe pretended at first to reach for it but took one from the deck at the last second. She giggled to herself watching Mort deflate with relief. She discarded the card.

"You know, I was thinking of canning something for the farmer's market," Rose said, picking up CeCe's card. "Better than sitting around watching my soaps all day. I need to be productive. Maybe even bring in a little gelt here and there."

"That's a great idea, Ma. There's lots around here to choose from. Peaches are almost ready. Cherries, too." She used to win ribbons at the state fair with Rose's canning recipes. She had learned to can as a child at Rose's knee.

"We ate your canned goods you'd send us for the holidays," Rose said. "Didn't we, Mordecai?"

"Down to the last drop," Mort said, secretly taking the card he drew from the deck and tucking it in his hand.

"Really? I never knew if you even opened them," said CeCe.

"What? And miss out on my CeCe's canned goods? You're much better at it than I ever was."

It amazed CeCe what she saw now that she could peek around her curtain of anger. What she invited in. "We could do it together. Maybe we'll make a good team."

"You know, Mort and I were talking, and we need to start over. That's what Jews have done for thousands of years. We're not dead yet. Thought we'd put on our straw hats, schlep to the farmers' market like Ma and Pa Kettle, and start from scratch," Rose said, reaching over to pat Mort's hand. "Yes, sir, Ma and Pa Kettle."

"Which one do I get to be?" Mort asked.

CeCe and Rose burst into laughter. Living in the now and not the bitter past. Could they all start over? It was tantalizing, this glimpse of hope she saw in their eyes. Hope soothed her. She allowed herself to feel it.

CHAPTER 12

"I've got the steak in strips, wrapped in foil, on the warming rack of the grill. I think the chicken is about ready. The red snapper filets and shrimp are standing by," Ben reported from his post at Abby's large gas grill, her Mother's Day splurge this year.

"Great. They should be here any minute. The beer is on ice in the cooler." Abby stood at the picnic table, slicing avocadoes and shredding lettuce and cheese for her fajita bar party. She'd invited Rachel, Charlie, Miguel, and CeCe for an adult informal dinner party, designed, of course, to introduce Ben into the fold. Santiago had agreed to watch the girls at Hattie's house until ten, when Rosalinda got off work. Hazel and Carmen were hosting Mort and Rose for spaghetti night at Hazel's place. Carmen had even donated her homemade soft corn and flour tortillas for Abby's party.

She spooned out sour cream into a small bowl to accompany the dish of *pico de gallo*—diced onion, tomato, and jalapeño—and a bowl of last year's roasted green chile from her freezer, thawed, peeled, and in strips. Everyone could assemble their own fajitas, adding whatever combination of ingredients they wanted. Guacamole, salsa, and tortilla chips rounded out the meal. "Oh, the cilantro! I almost forgot the cilantro." She began to dash back inside, but Ben caught her in his arms.

"Everything looks great. Thanks. Even if I'm not a hit, the food will be," he said, giving her a kiss that tasted of smoky meat.

"I want you to just be yourself, Ben. They will like you, I know they will."

Abby smoothed his vintage Hawaiian print shirt in shades of aqua and tan. He was freshly shaven, brown hair shiny clean, brown eyes twinkling above his wide smile.

A light breeze and the shade under the cottonwood tree created the perfect picnic spot. Ben lit tiki torches of citronella to repel mosquitoes around the perimeter.

Right at seven, Abby could see the four figures approaching across the field. Rachel and CeCe were walking together, followed by Charlie and Miguel. Not a good sign that the couples were divided. She could only hope that an all-adult party might ease some of the stress on all concerned. Maybe the romantic environment she had worked to create might rub off in the right places. Flowers, candles, torches, sunset, icy beers, and sensual, fiery finger food.

"The grilled peppers and onions are ready—want them left on the grill?" Ben asked.

"Sure, just pile them on some foil and leave the tongs handy," Abby replied. "Wait to start the fish until they're actually here." She felt like she was back at her restaurant in San Diego, choreographing the preparations. Luckily, Ben didn't take offense, even though he must have thrown plenty of "shrimp on the barbie" back in Australia.

Abby walked to meet her guests as they entered her yard. Rachel managed a small smile. CeCe hugged her. "What a nice thing to do! A dinner away—I can't tell you how great that is. I don't care if you have Jack the Ripper here, I'm going to have fun."

"He's hardly Jack the Ripper." Abby pulled back.

"Ben the Greenie, then," Rachel said with her sarcastic tone. "But we won't go there."

"Of course not. It was just a bad joke." CeCe shrugged and reached for her hand.

Miguel cleared his throat. "Everything looks beautiful, and what a lovely night. We thank you, Abby."

Charlie gave her a wink. "Which way to the beer and grub?"

Ben waved from the grill as if on cue.

The men clustered around the grill as the fish and shrimp were cooking. Abby and the women set out glasses and a pitcher of freshly squeezed lemonade. She was going to make a pitcher of margaritas, but after CeCe's complaints about Miguel's drinking, she decided to keep it to beer and lemonade.

"He's handsome, I'll give you that," CeCe said.

"He's as beautiful inside, too. Really a gentle and sweet man," Abby said, worried that she was selling too hard.

A burst of laughter from the grill, and Abby saw them clink their beer bottles.

The women sat in lawn chairs, Abby and CeCe with beer, Rachel with lemonade.

"Santi tells me the chile crop looks great," Abby remarked.

"We're waiting to hear about a possible water sale from the San Juan–Chama to the Middle Rio Grande Conservancy District that would extend our irrigation season by two weeks. Otherwise we run out by the end of this month, and we could lose it all before we can get it harvested," Rachel replied.

"When will you know?"

"Supposedly by July 20, so I guess that's in just a couple of days. If we don't get that water, we'd better start getting some monsoons. The rains are already two weeks late, and all we've been getting is dry lightning storms, which scares the hell out of me because of the fire danger. There's already a big fire in the Gila Forest from lightning. It's so dry I'm almost afraid to even walk in the bosque for fear of my shoes somehow causing a spark," Rachel said.

"At least they've restricted all access up and down the bosque. All it would take is one careless cigarette from a fisherman or someone," Abby said.

"Enough already!" CeCe said, swallowing her beer. "Tonight we lighten up, forget our woes, and make peace. I affirm in front of God and everybody: The rains will come, the crops will survive, and love will conquer all!"

"Amen, sisters," Abby said quickly and clinked her beer against Rachel's glass and CeCe's nearly empty bottle.

"Everything is ready," Ben called.

They milled around the picnic table, constructing their fajitas before sitting down.

"This is great," Charlie said through his mouthful, steak juice and salsa running down his chin. Rachel dabbed at him with a napkin.

"Lots of extra napkins here," Abby said.

"I have juice running down to my elbows, I think," Ben said with a laugh.

"This chile tastes so good. Are you about out of last year's?" Miguel asked.

"I only have one small bag left in the freezer, so I'm looking forward to the new crop," Abby said, grabbing up a shrimp that fell out of her tortilla. The combination of cilantro, chile, and avocado with a spritz of lime juice was heavenly with the seafood.

"God willing," Miguel said.

"Tell us about your life in Australia, Ben," CeCe said, changing the subject.

"I grew up in the state of New South Wales, southeast part of the country, coastal. Gorgeous place. On a sheep farm near Goulburn, small inland town with a nice old beer brewery and a huge statue of a merino sheep—no kidding, it's several stories high. The visitor center is between its legs, under its belly. The region supplies the best merino wool in the world, so it's a big deal. Australia is very arid place, so we have a lot of the same water concerns there as here."

"How many head of sheep on your ranch?" Charlie asked.

"Varies between two and three hundred these days, a good-sized mob. My father and two brothers still run it. My mum, a schoolteacher and animal lover, died of cancer when I was eighteen. I was closest to her, a big influence in my life. Funny how families sort of divide up. Me and Mum and my brothers with Dad. Anyway, I had enough of sheep shearing to last me a lifetime. I used to escape to the beaches in Nelson Bay to surf or go backpacking into the Snowy Mountains. I went to university in Sydney and lived there while I was married."

"You were married?" Rachel asked.

"Eight years, although the last one shouldn't count. Sherrie was already hooking up with my best mate. Came as a shock to lose them both at the same time. So I packed off to America after landing the job at UNM three years ago. Haven't looked back."

"But you will go back someday, at least to visit?" CeCe asked.

"Yeah, I'll visit. Whether I'll live there again, well, never say never, but I have no immediate plans. My contract is up for renewal next spring, so who knows?"

"You didn't tell me that," Abby blurted, the familiar fear of loss tightening her throat.

"Didn't think of it until now. I'm enjoying the present too much to be too concerned with the future." Ben smiled, oblivious to her growing panic.

How could you separate them, the present from the future? Abby couldn't. Her enjoyment of the present was dependent on her knowing there was a future. They'd never discussed it, she realized with a start. She had been assuming they were building something that had no foreseeable end. Now there were contracts to renegotiate and a homeland to consider.

"I read somewhere Australia has less than ten percent of its land able to be cultivated, it's so dry. The whole interior is desert land, isn't it?" Miguel asked.

"Yeah, another twenty percent is usable for grazing. Australia is roughly the size of the United States, but the only place more dry is Antarctica. Even Africa is wetter. The population is only around eighteen million and clustered around the perimeter where the water is. There's been a big emphasis in recent years to look at water and land management because of all the degradation and chronic drought, wind erosion. Back in the late seventies the government established the NLP, National Landcare Program, to try to shift things from crisis management to long-term sustainable resource management. Farmers and other groups have participation in it."

"I'd like to hear more about that sometime," Miguel said. "Sounds like there are a lot of similar issues."

Ben smiled. "Anytime. Look, I know I got things off to a bad start with my minnow lecture. But I want to correct a misconception that came out of that. I'm very pro-farmer. I care very much about your chile production continuing and thriving. I'm just a bloke who studies animal life in the river, as an indicator of its overall health. We all agree we don't want our river to die out. The real threats are uncontrolled development and overengineering, the shrinking underground aquifer, and politicians who like to pit the farmers against the ecologists. Did you ever think about why they don't want us to join forces? They can beat us better if we're divided. There's a movement called wild farming; it's bringing together farmers and the ecology folks who agree about taking care of the land and, let's face it, share a common love for the land. There's so much common ground and power in joining forces and looking out for each other."

"You've seen this work back in Australia?" Charlie asked.

"A lot of progress is being made. I went to the Common Ground Summit, they called it, last April in Albuquerque. Dan Imhoff was there, author of the book *Farming with the Wild*, and he talked about ways we can all work in partnership, increase our dialogue

Sue Boggio and Mare Pearl

for the land's sake. I figure, as long as the environmentalists and farmers are feuding, no one wins except the developers and the politicians in their pockets. Anyway, I don't mean to talk your ears off."

Miguel put out his hand, after wiping it off with his napkin. "I appreciate your talk, and I'm listening—see, my ears are still attached. Old dogs can learn, no?"

"So can young ones—or middle-aged ones, maybe I should say." Ben laughed and shook his hand. "I look forward to learning more from you, Miguel. I'd like to visit your operation, see how you do things. Help out if I can."

"Sure, if you have time while you're saving all those little fish. I read in the paper about that program they have down at the BioPark. Are you a part of that?"

"Yeah, the refugium. We're having some success in raising silvery minnow from eggs and even breeding them with hormone introduction. We sent 300,000 minnows back to the U.S. Fish and Wildlife Service to return to the river. How they do once they're back in the river is part of what we're studying now."

"All that for a little fish you can't even eat." Miguel laughed and stood up. "Abby, I must have more of your very edible fish—"

He trailed off as a car approached, coming up Abby's driveway around the side of her house. It was a dark lowrider car with tinted windows. Loud bass music thumped a rap beat.

"More guests?" Rachel asked.

"I don't know who that is. Maybe they're lost," Abby said, getting up from the picnic table bench.

A man emerged from the driver's side of the car. "James Ortiz," he said. "I'm here for Santiago."

"My son isn't available. He's helping out his family tonight," Abby said.

"He was supposed to meet up with us tonight. We've been waiting on his sorry ass. Tell him we don't appreciate his disrespect." With that, he turned and got back into his car and executed a quick turn out of there, gravel flying in all directions.

"I'm calling Ramone—," Abby said, nauseated with her fury.

"Hold on, Abby," Charlie said. "They already left, and Santiago is safe over at our house—they won't go looking for him over there."

"But you heard—he threatened Santi." Abby felt her impending angry tears choking her.

"I agree with Charlie," Miguel said. "Don't put gasoline on the fire. Let us talk to him about it calmly when we go back there tonight. We'll learn more that way."

CeCe smiled her encouragement. "It's just how those tough guys like to act. Let's not let it ruin the party."

For Abby the party was ruined when Ben acted vague about his future. She could hardly listen to anything anyone was saying for all the alarm bells going off in her head. Now this. But her guests were having a nice time, and she was too good a hostess to give into her fears. "Okay, I guess you're right. More beers all around? There's still a ton of food—"

"I ain't even got to my seconds yet," Charlie said with relief. "There's at least two more fajitas with my name on them."

"Go for it, mi amor, you'll need your strength for later," Rachel said. "Bring me some chicken?"

"Sure, babe." Charlie leaned over and kissed her.

Miguel leaned over and kissed a surprised CeCe. "It's contagious, I guess. What can I bring you as long as I'm up?"

"Steak and shrimp," CeCe said. "And another beer. I don't want this night to end."

"Oh, I think you might like the ending I have in mind," Miguel said.

Ben beamed at Abby as he joined her where she was still planted. "This is going very well, don't you think?"

Abby looked at him like he'd lost his mind. "For you, yeah, it's a regular lovefest."

"What's the matter?"

"Oh, I don't know. Maybe that my son was just threatened by an ex-con gangster and you don't know where you'll be in a year.

Other than that, everything is hunky-dory!" She flounced away to get herself another beer, or maybe she'd get out the tequila and do a few shots.

"Hunky-dory?" Ben called after her.

Rachel teetered on the rickety wooden stepladder as she strung the lights around the café for her mother's surprise birthday party. She had already hung plastic multicolored Chinese lanterns around the stage area, with tiny white lights along the rim of the elevated stage floor. In front of the stage was the dance area, the wooden floor cleaned and lightly oiled and buffed by Carmen. She made it shine like the pews, stair rails, and balusters at Our Lady of Fatima Church, where she had cleaned and polished faithfully for the last thirty years, in the name of our Lord, Jesus Christ—again, the cleanliness-godliness thing. But she had the old wood floor looking like a twenty-five cent spit and shine.

"It's beautiful, Carmen. I hope it's not so slippery that Mort or Rose falls and breaks a hip. That's Ma's worst fear," commented Rachel with a teasing smile.

"I don't think I put a dent in this tired old wood. It must be a hundred years old," said Carmen, situating herself upright and straightening her sleeveless blouse and crucifix. There was something about Carmen that seemed, at times, to be at odds with her piousness. Rachel had heard her on many occasions gossip and banter innuendo with the best of the cabal, then seen her blush at her own hypocrisy.

Friends started to stream in with hands full of potluck dishes and presents. Rachel knew the minute Mrs. Herrera had gotten there because she could smell the hot green chile chicken enchiladas she held with an oven mitt. The best in town. Mrs. Herrera always made two casserole dishes of enchiladas, one green chile and one red, the red meatless with cheese and onion. The thought of sinking her teeth into them made Rachel's stomach growl.

Abby manned the food tables, taking the dishes and arranging them. She smacked Ben's arm when he stuck his finger into the dripping caramel of Angel Martinez's flan. Angel was shaped like an apple now, with skinny little legs sticking out of a short jean skirt. Her breasts had surrendered to gravity long ago, but she showed them proudly. She was still searching for a husband.

Abby had been looking good lately, even with the sleepless nights Rachel knew she had been having recently over Santi. Or with Ben. Rachel had to admit, she liked his funny stories of his surfer days, and Abby was so Gidget-and-Moondoggie over him; obviously he appealed to the old California girl still inside. Ben seemed to keep her afloat in the midst of her stress over Santi, and who wouldn't want to cling to him rather than a life preserver? Rachel could see how enamored he was of Abby.

Hattie had heard the locals talk in the café about the environmentalists, calling them bait lovers. "Is Ben a bait lover, Mommy? I don't like putting worms on hooks. Does that make me a bait lover?" Her blue eyes questioning. Children had such an affinity with small, defenseless life-forms.

Bonnie was filling helium balloons and letting them rise and hug the antique tin ceiling. Hattie squealed as Bonnie sucked helium and sang "Ave Maria," tying expert knots at the ends of the balloons with her long nails before sending them ceilingward. Sixty of them, that was her plan. It was beginning to remind her of the colorful polka-dotted plastic rain hat Rose always carried in her purse but never needed, like an old condom.

"Mommy! Bonnie sounds like the Lollipop Guild!"

Bonnie was now well into her rendition of "I'm a Soul Man."

"That's how you sound all the time," Rachel replied. "Like a little imp." She tweaked Hattie's nose.

"I took a message for you little while ago," Bonnie said, her voice sliding back down to normal. "The band is on their way now to set up and do a sound check. I told them okay, okay? Too bad my cousin's band broke up at the last minute." She tied and snapped the rubber umbilicus of a blue balloon. Her dexterity came from holding the phantom hairs of viejitas and wrapping them around teeny yellow or blue perm rods. So tying an overblown balloon was nothing. She handed it to Hattie, who pulled at the knot and snapped it to rise to the ceiling.

"This band is great. They can do it all: country, bluegrass, Beatles, the Dead. Ma's going to flip. Wait till you hear their fiddle player," Rachel said.

"Girl, I'm going to leave scorch marks on that dance floor," Bonnie said, "after I've had me some beers." Her midriff moved like a python as she danced in place.

"You better not hurt Carmen's floors," Hattie warned.

The present table over by the deli case was starting to be covered by a small, colorful skyline of wrapped boxes of different sizes. Hattie's eyes grew wide as she inspected them. Maggie came out from under the food table Abby had draped in white cloth (no doubt her imaginary tent) to help Hattie sniff around the presents.

Charlie appeared and playfully slapped her butt. He was especially good humored, as was everyone the last couple of days. The farmers had just found out that the Middle Rio Grande Conservancy District and the City of Albuquerque had agreed to let the district borrow 15,000 acre-feet of water from the San Juan–Chama river water in Abiquiu Reservoir. Two more weeks of water. A reprieve.

"This is going to be one hell of a celebration. We're going to blow the roof off of this place," he said, hugging her from behind. She could tell he was freshly shaven and had dabbed on some English Leather. "I just talked to Miguel. He called from the hardware store, where he's holding CeCe hostage with his browsing. We've synchronized our watches. Said he'd have her here in forty-five minutes on the dot. Then I called Hazel over at your folks' house. She'll have Mort and Rose here at the same time."

"Hey, Charlie," Ramone called out. He stood by a portable

bamboo bar from the fifties, complete with lobster and fish tiles on the front. Little parrot lights were hung in the plants to give it a more tropical feel in the middle of the desert. A neon martini glass with an olive sat on the bar's black and pink linoleum top. "Come help me set up the bar."

Charlie gave her a wink before turning to join Ramone. "Gonna be a hot time in the old town tonight," he said over his shoulder.

"Let's stop and get something to eat," CeCe said to Miguel on the road back to Esperanza from Albuquerque. "All that waiting for you made me hungry."

Miguel looked at his watch. "I thought we'd get home and I'd grill something for dinner. Can you wait?"

That made her suspicious.

"Besides, I told Charlie I'd meet him to help load his air compressor onto his truck. He's probably been waiting for me as it is. Needs new bearings."

The traffic on I-25 south was not too heavy, but it was manic. Drivers would rush upon the car in front of them and practically touch bumpers, trying to intimidate the car in front to go faster. Then it turned into a game of wills. Miguel hated the foolish and dangerous behavior. He always tried to be a courteous driver. Let people in when they needed. Used his turn signals. Didn't pull out a gun.

Sometimes a police car whizzed past their truck, red light twirling, to attend to a rear-end accident pulled over at the side of the road with distraught motorists, a common sight along this long stretch of highway, along with couch cushions and whatever else decided to take a flying leap out of the back of a truck.

When they were nearing the turnoff to their farm, Miguel checked his watch again. Something fishy was going on . . .

"It looks like the café is open. What are all the cars doing there?"

CeCe asked as they approached. He swerved into the parking lot too fast. Her waist muscles strained trying to hold herself upright in her seat.

She knew now. A surprise party. Well, a surprise up until this moment. And although she didn't feel like celebrating being sixty years old, a big celebration needed to be had by all. They had enough water for this year. Farm life was spared. Miguel was spared. Her marriage was spared.

"Surprise!" everyone yelled as she walked in. The band started to play "Birthday" by the Beatles. A large cake stood in the center of a table, its frosting as perfect as new snow. Rachel, Hattie, and Charlie greeted her.

"Happy birthday," said Rachel, kissing her cheek. "I hope I'm as beautiful at sixty. Any words of wisdom from your sixty-year-old mouth?"

CeCe looked around and saw all her friends and family. The band played on, driving that wild beat. A joy welled up from her toes and out her lips. "Let's party."

Several frozen margaritas later, CeCe and Rachel had Charlie on the dance floor. They each had one of his arms like a rope in a Maypole dance, as he twirled them around him. Rachel looked festive in her western-style calico sundress and cowboy boots. Rarely did CeCe get to see her in a dress. And Rachel's thick, curly dark hair billowed out full in a high ponytail, with fugitive tendrils hanging haphazardly around her face and neck.

Bonnie was snaking around, dancing with every man who was not her husband. CeCe was flattered to see Bonnie's husband there at all, as he never ventured out of his house to socialize. She had seen him only a handful of times in the years she and Bonnie had been friends. He was sitting at a table with Ramone, reminiscing over beers. By the way his belly spilled over his belt and compromised the buttons of his shirt, she guessed beer was his drink of choice. He seemed to enjoy watching his wife flirt innocently with the men, her voluptuous roundness bandying back and forth among them like a pinball. But as far as CeCe knew, Bonnie had never strayed.

In the mix, wearing his best jeans, boots, and Scully cowboy shirt, was neighboring farmer Harvey Doyle, happily handing out cigars like a proud papa, congratulating everyone for their extra irrigation water. With his smiling Irish eyes and rosy cheeks, she couldn't help but think of a big old leprechaun cowboy.

CeCe watched Hattie dance with Rose, pulling her arms back and forth doing the twist. Rose's gold bauble bracelets were like hula hoops on her bony arms. The music lifted CeCe. She closed her eyes and swayed. The intoxicating tequila had picked her up like a flurry of wind. She didn't know where she would land and didn't care. She felt herself be swept up in familiar arms, smelled a scent she had longed for like rain. Miguel danced with her slowly in one spot, his body rubbing against hers.

"*Feliz cumpleaños*," Miguel whispered in her ear.

She cradled him to her. She felt ageless, and they went back through time, dancing at a Dead concert in the middle of a huge crowd as if they were the only two in the stadium, while Jerry Garcia sang just for them. Nothing had changed between them. Not really. Time had become this mystical bird they had learned to ride together, no hands.

It turned out Ben was a dancer. Abby's high-school swing dance lessons finally paid off. As they jitterbugged, two-stepped, and spun around the tight dance floor, she began to wonder if there was anything he couldn't do.

"Take a breather?" he asked when she collapsed into his arms.

"Yeah—a cold beer sounds nice," Abby said, leading him back to their table.

"Be right back," Ben said with a smile, kissing her hand in

farewell. After her fajita bar party the previous week, they had survived their first argument. Abby had confronted him on his casual mention of his future's tenuous nature, the fact that his contract as a visiting professor at UNM expired the following June. She smiled, remembering her fury. She had felt so suckered to have fallen in love with a man who had an expiration date. Again. Only this time, instead of the impending end being the result of unpredictable violence, it seemed completely premeditated on his part. What a stupid lack of self-preservation on her part. Duh. *Visiting* professor. What part of *visiting* could she not understand?

After her ranting tears and accusations that he should have known better than to have involved himself with a widow if he was only going to abandon her in one short year, his stoic demeanor snapped. He began to yell that he never had any intention of leaving her, he loved her, and he would stay with her no matter what. After that had gotten her attention and silenced her, he went on to explain he understood from the beginning of their relationship that Esperanza was her home and he would need to make it his home if they were to be together. If for some unforeseen reason UNM would not renew his contract, he'd simply find another job. With his resume, U.S. Fish and Wildlife and various other agencies would consider him a hot property. Or he would become a chile picker or scrub the floors at the café—anything to be near her. He apologized for not assuring her and her friends of his intentions, but had felt it was too personal to discuss in front of them. He was wrong; he was a complete and total jerk. Would she ever forgive him?

It amazed her how conflict had only brought them closer. How anger and recrimination and pain somehow added depth and truth to a relationship. Conflict was not only unavoidable with two strong people in love, it was somehow a necessary ingredient. In balance, of course, and conducted within the bounds of decency.

The band started a slow one, and she watched as Rachel and

Charlie melted into each other, their eyes locked. Her eyes wandered over to Miguel and CeCe, also dancing in each other's arms, Miguel leading in an elegant box step, CeCe's eyes closed, her expression the very definition of peace as they floated as one.

Abby felt a wave of gratitude to share such a night and see her friends happy after such a stressful time. There would be irrigation water to see them through to the harvest, and love still overcame the divisions—at least this one night—which was no small feat. She could sense them all recharging, drinking deeply from this pool to carry them forward through whatever lay ahead.

"Mom, we're taking off," Santi said, interrupting her reverie. She could even feel a little goodwill toward Rosalinda, whom, she had to admit, seemed to put a new kind of smile on her son's face. Abby had taken CeCe's advice and was no longer fighting Santi about dating Rosalinda; she had told him he could invite Rosalinda to CeCe's party to meet his family and friends. But he was so smitten it broke her heart. She couldn't quite see that Rosalinda mirrored his rapture. With her veil of long hair and impassive expression, she was tough to read. Abby had to restrain herself from taking the young woman aside and threaten her within an inch of her life to never hurt her precious and innocent son.

"All right then. Thanks for coming, Rosalinda." Abby managed not to remind him about curfew or tell him to be safe. She knew he was hearing her say it in his head, and he smiled in apparent relief when she didn't say it aloud.

"Thanks for inviting me," Rosalinda replied, connecting with Abby's eyes for the first time. "It means a lot."

"Come by the house. You're always welcome," Abby said, exceedingly proud of herself. Santi rewarded her with a quick squeeze of her shoulder.

Abby watched them weave their way back through the tables to the door.

Ben reappeared with two beers and Maggie. "I found this poor little urchin girl all on her own. Can we keep her? Please, can we?"

Maggie sat herself down on her mother's lap. Abby put both arms around her waist to hug her tight. "Just what I needed! A little urchin girl of my very own."

"Careful, Mom, you're going to make me puke up cake and ice cream. Hattie's dancing with her Bubbe Rose, see?"

Ben put down his beer. "Where are my manners? Would the lovely Maggie care to dance?"

Maggie giggled and then looked to Abby. "Go ahead if you want. He's a great dancer."

"But I'm not very good," Maggie said, biting her lip. "Nobody ever taught me to dance."

"They're starting a fast one. All we have to do is bop around. In fact, I'll follow your lead and do whatever you do."

"What if I get really silly?" Maggie's eyes bugged with the possibilities.

"Then I'll be forced to become really silly, won't I?" Ben said.

Maggie jumped off of Abby's lap, her bony bottom denting her thighs.

Hazel plunked herself down at Abby's table, a dishcloth over one shoulder. "He's good with her, isn't he? He looks like he's in love with her, too."

Abby nodded. "Sometimes it seems almost too good to be true. I keep waiting for the other shoe to drop, the hidden bad thing to show up, or the cruel hand of fate to . . ." She trailed off as an avalanche of unspeakable fear took her breath.

Hazel grabbed her hand and rubbed it between her soft fingers. "You got dealt a real bad hand with Bobby. It takes guts to lay yourself on the line again. But you got to risk your neck if you're going to have any of the good stuff. You've played it safe for seven years. Perpetual loneliness can hurt worse than coping with loss of a loved one. At least in my career as a nurse that's what I saw."

Abby nodded. She wondered about Hazel's solitary life. Had she never been in love? It was an unspoken rule never to pry with Hazel. Behind her brusque cheeriness, her tough exterior hiding the huge heart, Abby thought she could sometimes detect the familiar scent of loss. She wondered if that loss was the fuel stoking the fires of Hazel's driving energy and relentless activity.

"It's hard to trust," said Abby. "I know I need to, or I'll screw it up. It's just my hard thing to learn, that's all."

"CeCe looks happy," Hazel remarked. "Does my heart good to see that. It's important to have a good sixtieth birthday. It's one of those threshold birthdays, starts off a new phase in your life."

The band wound down the rockabilly tune, and the dance floor thinned. The band's leader spoke into the microphone as the crowd applauded. "Thank you. We're going to take a short break for a little liquid refreshment—if you guys left us any. Miguel Vigil has a special song he'd like to do. Come on up here, Miguel."

Miguel took the stage and grabbed his acoustic guitar. "Most of you know how much I love Cipriano Vigil—no relation, I'm sorry to say. For those of you who don't, let me tell you about my idol. He is about my age and lives in northern New Mexico, where he was born and raised. I think he knows every traditional folk song ever sung in this land, and he keeps them alive through his teaching and performing. He also writes songs in the traditional way about things that make him angry, about predatory forces that hurt our people. His new songs, his *nuevas canciónes*, are a form of protest. The song I want to sing now is a traditional song that I first learned listening to Cipriano when he was performing with Los Folkoristas. It is called '*El Labrador.*' I dedicate it to my beautiful wife on the anniversary of her birth, with all of my love."

He began to strum and pick a combination of chords, establishing a refrain, and then sang, first in Spanish and then in English:

> *Yo me alimento con*
> *la cosecha.*
> *La tierra se*
> *alimenta con*
> *mi labor.*

Llevamos una buena
vida juntos,
cultivando
alegría y pasión.

I nourish myself with
the harvest.
The land
nourishes itself with
my labor.
We have a good
life together,
cultivating
happiness and passion.

"Everyone, sing with me now," Miguel said and reached for CeCe to join him onstage.

All their voices joined, at first tentatively to secure the words and melody, and then rising with confidence. Tears streamed down CeCe's face as she leaned forward into the microphone to sing alongside her husband.

CHAPTER 13

After leaving CeCe's birthday party, Santi and Rosalinda argued.

"Let's just go somewhere and be alone," Santi pleaded.

"No! I told you we have to show up. It's my cousin's birthday party, too. I promised him we'd come. He's already pissed at you for avoiding him. This will make it up to him."

"It was always you I wanted to be around. James and his guys, they're just not into what I want to be into, okay?" Why couldn't she get it? She always acted like she disapproved of James. Why was she pushing it?

"You just don't cozy up to someone like James and then drop him cold after you get what you want. You're important to him; you just can't blow him off on his birthday. That would be really stupid. Come on, Santiago, we're going. I went to your dumb-ass party. This will at least be some fun."

Her words stung. He thought she had had fun meeting his family, his friends. They had all been nice to her. With a sick feeling, he let her drag him over to her car. She drove aggressively, grinding her clutch. He felt the dark presence of his nightmare taunting him from the recesses of his consciousness. It had been torturing him more regularly again, robbing his sleep, his peace. It invaded his waking life, a specter shadowing his every thought and move. It sapped him of everything and left behind a sense of dangerous foreboding, and once again he was caught in the ambivalence of wanting to know what it all meant and never wanting to know its ominous secret. It seemed to be growing, gaining power and strength as it feasted on him, and he was more and more afraid that he was powerless to stop it.

Rosalinda turned onto a dirt road leading back to the river. She crossed an old wooden plank bridge over the main irrigation ditch. The moon seemed to float on the silent black water. Her headlights bobbed as the old sedan hit ruts in the makeshift road, which was becoming little more than a path through the trees of the bosque. They were in "no man's land," the border between Isleta Pueblo land and Esperanza village limits. The Vigils' property was the first privately owned land south of there.

Santi could see a clearing ahead where cars were parked and, beyond that, the rosy glow of a bonfire. Laughter and music floated toward him.

He had heard about these parties by the river and knew Ramone was always trying to bust them and had even been successful on occasion. "The bosque is closed, on account of the fire danger," he said after she parked and cut the engine. "Even a spark from a hot car engine can ignite the grass."

"God! You know, Santi, your Boy Scout crap is getting boring. Do you want me to drive your crybaby ass home, or do you want to be with me and wish James a nice birthday?"

Of course he wanted to be with her; he loved her. It was just getting harder to pay the price. "I'll wish James happy birthday, and we could stay for a short while," he said, feeling like he was selling off a little more of his soul.

She smiled and pulled him to her for a lingering kiss, her tongue teasing his lips. "You will be so glad you did."

After a short tromp through the trees, they reached the river-bank, where at least forty, maybe fifty people were partying hard. Coolers of beer, open bottles of hard stuff, and bags of snacks crowded a card table someone had set up. Joints and pipes glowed in the dark. Rap music throbbed from a boom box parked under a tree.

Santi didn't see anyone he knew, but everyone knew Rosalinda. She didn't bother introducing him as they wove through the throngs of loud-talking, drunken people. Some were teenagers, but most were a lot older. Flashes of elaborate tattoos adorned bulging biceps, cleavage, necks, and backs. Less professional prison tats lined cheeks in the form of teardrops or small crosses. He was in the middle of a gang party, and at the center of it, feeding branches to the bonfire, was James.

"Hey, bro', you came! Li'l Baca, you have redeemed yourself!" James clamped him into a tight hug, smelling of body odor and booze. The fire rose a good six feet into the air, blasting a furnace of heat into the already warm night. "Hey, this is dead Baca's kid—Li'l Baca!" James hollered, causing a few nearby people to raise their drinks and nod his direction.

Rosalinda handed him a beer and clinked hers against his with a smile. "See, this is great, no?"

Carlos and Bones appeared with a couple of skanky women on their arms. Bones put a clench on the back of his neck with his strong, fat hand. "Hey, Li'l Baca, about time we saw your ass again. James was starting to wonder about you." He pulled him closer and spoke into his ear. "Don't make him question your loyalty, man. Especially with how tight your mom is with the sheriff. Not cool, bro'. I'm only telling you this one time."

Carlos had a long box in his hands. "For James. Help me, Baca. We're going to surprise his ass with some fireworks. He loves that shit!"

Santi stood, weaving from the heat, the beer he'd chugged to get through this, knowing how an animal felt caught in the steel jaws of a trap. What were his choices? Lose Rosalinda? Never to have gotten in James's car in the first place? Not to have been born a Baca? "I'm not good at that stuff," he said lamely.

Carlos laughed his breathy hyena laugh. "You crack me up, son. All we have to do is light them up and aim them at the river. Come on!"

Rosalinda actually stepped in. "Go find someone else, Carlos. I want Santi with me." She pulled him away, and they made their way to a more secluded place near the water's edge. She was carrying a bottle of tequila and half of a lime.

They sat down in the soft soil. Pure, fertile mulch, you could plant anything here and it would grow, he thought, watching the river as Rosalinda took a quick shot and sucked at the lime. For these people the bosque and the river were a place to party; for him, it was a sacred place. How did he get here?

Rosalinda smiled and put her perfect lips on his. He felt himself turn into a wax figure. "What the matter? Are you pouting?"

"I just don't belong here. As much as I love you. This is wrong." His eyes were on the river; it gave him courage. Even as it ran shrunken from its banks, even as patchy strips of scrubby land rose like the backs of primordial beasts above its meager waterline, he thought it was more beautiful than any woman. He knew she nourished them all. Even as thirsty mouths and greedy fists multiplied, even as the stingy heavens refused to replenish her with rain or melting snowpack from the mountains, she had never forsaken them. Her waters ran dark as blood in the moonlight, and he felt them course through his own veins to give him strength. "I have to go now."

"I'm not leaving," Rosalinda said. "And if you leave me here, I will never forgive you. Ever. And neither will James."

Santi nodded. "I know. But if I don't leave, I'll never forgive myself, and that's worse."

He got up and walked away, making his own path through the tangle of salt cedars poisoning the bosque. Fireworks burst behind him, and he felt them as a shower of bullets in his back, and yet he didn't fall. Voices cheered as he broke into a run. It might take half the night, but he was going home.

He followed the irrigation ditch bank south for an hour. It was only a few more miles until he reached the northern boundary of the Vigils' land; if he ran he could be home in no time at all. But he was not in any hurry, it was only ten o'clock, and putting one foot in front of the other was all he wanted to do at the moment. He could smell the chile before he saw the fields, a spicy green freshness just beginning to ripen, his nose as trained as any chile farmer's. In another three or four weeks they would begin harvesting. That was as far ahead as he wanted to think. In fact, he mentally rewound back to the present moment, the cooling night air on his skin, the hooting of an owl overhead as it hunted mice.

He would write when he got home. He hadn't written anything decent all summer except for love poems, which he now planned to trash. The sights and sounds of the night inflamed his senses, and he craved the release of scratching words on paper.

His nose picked up the scent of smoke. Shit, his clothes must reek of it from the bonfire. But as he lifted his T-shirt to inhale, the stench grew stronger. He looked to his right, where the bosque thickened along the river about a half mile west. From the raised bank of the ditch, he saw an explosion of orange flames and black smoke riding the treetops. He froze there for a moment, watching fire engulf the bosque faster than he ever could have imagined possible. In seconds it raced past him, moving south, riding the river like the horsemen of the Apocalypse.

He began to run. No cell phone because Abby thought they were a scourge to civilized public behavior. No homes or businesses close enough out on the highway, several miles east. It would be faster to run to the Vigils' house and call in the fire from there.

He ran as fast as he could, chasing the fire like a dog after a racing fire truck and with just as much chance of catching it. He couldn't let himself realize the fire would beat him there or wonder if it might be able to jump the ditch and ruin the chile fields and spread east, toward the barns and houses. And then he remembered. Charlie and Rachel's house was between the ditch and the river, right in the fire's path.

He prayed as he ran, out of shape since track season ended, never good at long distances anyway, more of a sprinter. The smoke, which was burning his lungs and stinging his eyes, didn't help. Why didn't he hear sirens? Didn't they know the world was on fire? Were they all still dancing at the café, safely out on the highway, oblivious?

Fire was spreading fingerlike toward the ditch where he ran. The smoke became thicker, and he stopped long enough at a turnout to kneel down and soak his shirt in water and wrap it over his nose and mouth. He ran on, still hoping by some miracle it would skirt Rachel's house. He remembered watching them build it, helping sometimes. It seemed to take forever to be completed, and it could be gone in an instant. Charlie had cleared a perimeter yard around the house for a fire buffer—maybe that would work. They had left some towering cottonwoods, though, for shade, which could create a nice bridge for the flames to cross.

Rachel brought out another bucket of ice for the bar. Charlie was manning it, making Shirley Temples for Maggie and Hattie. They squealed at him when he pretended to forget the extra cherries he had promised. She saw Rose coming at her like a crab trying to walk straight, elbows hitching for more speed.

"Have you seen your zeyde?" Rose asked. "He went to use the bathroom and never came back. I checked, but he's not in there, but I sure surprised Bonnie's husband when I walked in on him. Acted like I never saw one of those before. And I haven't, since he isn't circumcised."

"I haven't seen Mort lately, either." Rachel's eyes darted around the café.

"I'll go look in the kitchen," said Charlie, wiping his hands on a towel and tossing it on the bar before he left.

"Jesus, he could have just walked out. There's a back door to this place out of the kitchen. He could get hit by a car," Rachel said.

CeCe and Miguel walked up arm in arm for another beer, an unlit cigar dangling from Miguel's lips.

"Mort's missing," yelled Rachel, grabbing each one of them by a shoulder.

"We just came in from outside. He wasn't out there," CeCe said. She turned to Rose. "How long has it been?"

Rose looked confused. "Well, let's see, I've been dancing with Hattie for . . . and for a while I didn't think anything of it, because I never know how long he's going to sit on the pot, so . . ." She acted like this was the sixty-four thousand dollar question as Charlie came careening out of the kitchen.

"I just got a call," he said, pulling Rachel along. "The bosque behind our house is on fire!"

The mile ride down the road to the house was endless as the smell of burning wood began to choke her. Rachel could hear the crackling and whooshing of the fire as it spread. The sounds became deafening as they drove up.

She sprang from the car before it came to a stop, with Charlie right behind her. Nothing felt more angry and punishing than fire. How it lashed out to kill anyone who got in its way. And there it was in the treetops next to her house. A defiant dragon licking its lips with its red and orange tongue, devouring everything around it.

By now everyone had caught up to them, except for the cabal and a few others who split up to look for Mort along the highway near the café and grounds. CeCe, Miguel, and Hattie huddled around Rachel and Charlie as they watched helplessly.

The branches of the dry pecan trees and the cottonwoods sputtered like a kitchen match, spreading, reaching toward the second floor of their home. It took only seconds for the house to ignite, but it didn't give into the fire as quickly as the dried skeletons in the woods. The blaze came alive as it took over Hattie's room and everything in it. CeCe clutched Rachel's shoulder.

Hattie let out a piercing scream, pointing up to her blazing room. "Oakley! Get Oakley out!" she cried and dropped down, face in the grass, not able to bear to watch.

Charlie took off toward the house. The first floor had not caught fire yet. Rachel screamed at him to stop, but he couldn't hear her or refused to obey. He burst in the door and disappeared in the eerie calmness of the first floor. The front door puffed out a couple of smoke rings behind him.

A large branch in the burning cottonwood gave way and fell onto the roof. Everyone around her screamed as the roof held a few seconds, then caved in, taking half of the second floor with it.

Hearing Abby scream Ben's name kept Rachel from fainting. Her wooziness cleared enough for her to catch a glimpse of Ben pulling his shirt over his mouth and entering the house.

Abby and Rachel gripped each other's hands until Rachel could feel Abby's thumping pulse. Each second became an hour. This couldn't be happening to them again. Not now. Hadn't Abby already lost someone she loved? Hadn't *she*?

The rest of the second floor came down, causing a huge burst of flames, and hot ashes shot up like fireworks, creating smoke so heavy Rachel could barely see, especially through her tears.

Then she saw Ben come out from what was left of the house carrying Charlie on his back, taking him out a safe distance. She found herself already running toward them. All she could think was Charlie was dead. She slid down next to him like she was stealing home base.

He moaned in pain. Alive, thank God. He wheezed and went into a short fit of coughing.

"What in the world were you thinking?" Rachel cried. Her salty tears dripped onto his scraped and burned cheeks. There were cuts on his forehead that would need stitches. The blood trickled down like tears as he moaned in pain. "I almost lost you," she whispered.

She accidentally touched it before she noticed it. Felt its wet stickiness on her fingertips, smelled his metallic blood. His leg was broken midthigh, and the bone stuck out of him and his pant leg like a piece of splintered wood.

"Keep her back!" Rachel yelled to her parents as they restrained Hattie from running to her daddy.

She cradled Charlie's head, careful not to rub his sooty, seared face as she heard the sirens arrive.

Behind them the house continued to burn. Beyond saving.

Santiago approached where he thought Rachel and Charlie's house must be, but the flames and smoke obscured his view. "Help!" a raspy voice yelled. He wasn't even sure he heard it over the roar of the fire. But the wind shifted, and he could see a man in front of him crawling along the ground next to the ditch, a handkerchief over his face.

"Hey!" Santi called and waved. The figure waved his handkerchief in surrender. It was CeCe's father, old Mort.

"Where's my cigar? I was smoking my cigar, and I lost it," Mort yelled as Santi reached him and helped him up. The old man's hands were blistered, and he clutched a book of charred matches. Fire popped and exploded in the trees not thirty feet away.

Santi grabbed his arm and helped him walk away from the fire, toward the side of Rachel and Charlie's yard. The smoke parted, and he could see the house was in flames, the second story already gone. He heard voices and commotion as they made their way slowly through the perimeter of trees, Mort stumbling along weakly, talking incoherently in his foreign language, Santi trying to get him to keep his handkerchief over his nose.

Santi struggled to walk across the yard, Mort hanging onto his neck, blinded by the headlights of everyone's cars parked randomly in front of the house, the cars' doors hanging open, dome lights on, illuminating them like little spaceships.

He pulled down his T-shirt and began to yell. Mort chimed in with his weak voice, surely inaudible to anyone but Santi, whose ears were only inches from Mort's cracked and bleeding lips.

No one noticed them as they collapsed onto the ground.

"You okay, Mort?" Santi panted and coughed.

"Water would be nice, if our rations permit," he replied, the book of spent matches still in his hand.

"Stay right here. I'll get help." Santi stood up, dizzy and coughing again. He could see everyone in a cluster, closer than he thought. As he walked near, he saw Charlie on the ground, covered in blankets, his face distorted in pain. Rachel cradled his head in her lap, crying for the ambulance to get there.

Miguel was directing people to clear away their cars for the approaching fire trucks. Abby's face turned, and her eyes zeroed in on him. "Santi!"

He pointed back at Mort, sitting where he had been told. Abby and Maggie ran to Santi, engulfing him in one big, undeserved hug. Ben was patting his shoulder. Santi was so relieved to be there and grateful they were unharmed, he hung on for a minute before remembering. "Get CeCe—her dad's over there. I found him in the bosque."

Abby went to CeCe and Rose, who stood by Rachel and Charlie. He saw her point and say something, but the sirens were closing in. Miguel noticed and joined them as they all ran to Mort.

"I lost my cigar. Dropped it out there somewhere. Got the matches, though; never know when you might need matches." He handed the charred packet to Rose as if it were a treasured gift.

"I thought you were dead, you old tievel! Dead on the highway from a truck!" She helped him stand up, strong for an elderly woman, and then hugged him to her, crying and saying things in their private language.

CeCe seemed to take in what he said and then startled Santi by yelling, "You stupid, selfish, crazy old man! You burned down your own granddaughter's house with your damned cigar! You nearly killed Charlie! They lost everything! All for your goddamned cigar!"

Miguel pulled her back. "He can't help it, CeCe. He doesn't understand!"

Three fire trucks pulled up, and firefighters swarmed the area with hoses, blasting water at the fire. Paramedics jumped out of an ambulance and ran to Charlie, obscuring Rachel and him with their flurry of activity.

Ben directed a pair of them to Mort. "We'll check him over in the truck," one said, and they carried him between them back to the ambulance.

Santi and the others watched as the team of paramedics working on Charlie got him loaded into the back of the first ambulance. They let Rachel climb in, also. A crying Hattie was left behind in CeCe's arms as the ambulance sped away.

Maggie began to cry in sympathy, so Ben lifted her up in his arms, where she clung on like a baby monkey. Abby brought a paramedic over to Santi.

"Are you all right, kid?" asked the paramedic, who didn't seem much older than him. "You look a little sooty around the nostrils. I better check you out."

Santi let him lead him over to the same truck Mort was in. They were giving the old man oxygen through a mask as he lay on the gurney with his head elevated. They had started an IV drip to give him fluids, and EKG leads dotted his naked chest. "Is he going to be okay?" Santi asked while the paramedic was taking his blood pressure and listening to his lungs.

"Yeah, he's doing good. A few blisters on his hands. We're just taking precautions on account of his age. You sound good, too. All clear."

Santi coughed and spit onto the ground. It felt as though there was grit or ash scraping his eyeballs every time he blinked. He started to rub them when the paramedic stopped him and squirted liquid from a squeeze bottle into each eye, obscuring his vision but relieving the irritation.

"Normal saline. Here, keep the bottle. Irrigate, and don't rub or you'll scratch your corneas," the paramedic said. "I guess you're one of the heroes here tonight. That Australian dude saved the guy who ran into his burning house for a cat. You saved the old man. Hey, sheriff, give this kid a medal."

Santi blinked the dripping saline from his eyes and tried to focus his blurry vision.

"That right, Santiago? You save Mort Spelman tonight? Should I arrange a parade in your honor?"

Even half-blind, Santi could tell Ramone wasn't smiling. The sheriff clamped his large hand on Santi's bare shoulder, making him feel naked, and walked him away from the paramedic van.

"He was a little turned around. I walked him back to the yard. No big deal," Santi said. "I hear Ben's the real hero."

Ramone nodded, still staring with his squinty eyes, chewing a toothpick. "How did you happen to find Mort out there by the ditch? Abby said you'd left the café party a few hours ago with your girlfriend, Rosalinda Ortiz."

"I did, but we had an argument, and I guess we broke up, so I was just walking." Santi began to catch on that Ramone believed he had something to do with the fire. And then he realized, maybe he did. What if he'd gone straight to Ramone about the bonfire and the fireworks instead of meandering home? Could the fire have been prevented or at least controlled before it reached Charlie and Rachel's house? He knew the answer, and it made him retch on his tennis shoes.

"Smells like beer. You sneak a beer at the café? Or did you have a little nightcap somewhere else?" Ramone handed him his handkerchief.

"Rosalinda put some beers in her purse when we were at the café. We came back here and had the argument after drinking them. She's over twenty-one."

"So I hear." Ramone threw his toothpick down. "Right now people are assuming poor old Mort and his cigar started the fire. There will be a full investigation, of course. Fire marshal and his team will be gathering evidence, interviewing witnesses who will be able to say how far upriver the fire started. No lightning tonight, so it's a man-made fire. Arson. Amazing how they can determine the exact cause and the exact spot a fire started. But you probably know that, smart a kid as you are."

Abby, Ben, and Maggie came over to them. Maggie looked a little big for Ben to be carrying around, but she seemed to be soaking it up. His mom grabbed him in another hug. "Thank God you're all right. I would have had a heart attack if I'd known you were in the bosque! Why were you out there, anyway?"

Santi shrugged and tried not to look at Ramone, who stood with his arms folded over where his fat gut used to be. "Rosalinda and I drank some beer she took from the café, and then we had an argument and broke up. After she left all mad, I just started walking along the ditch out to the chile fields. Just to think. That's when I saw the fire and came upon Mort."

"I'll be taking down your formal statement tomorrow, Santiago. I'll be checking in with Rosalinda, too, since she may have seen something."

"She left way before the fire," Santi said a bit too quickly. "I just mean she lives down in Los Lunas, the opposite direction of the fire."

Ramone paused as though he was going to say something, but didn't. Instead, he gave Abby a hug. "I'll be checking on Charlie at the hospital, and I'll give you a call if anything happens. Looked like a bad fracture, but that can be fixed." He reached over and squeezed Maggie's knee, which was dangling from Ben's embrace, bringing her glassy expression back to life. "Hey, that tickles," she said, kicking her foot out to him in defense.

"See you tomorrow, Santiago," Ramone said before he turned to talk to some of his men.

They rushed Charlie into surgery after a quick exam in the ER. The look on the doctor's face when he saw Charlie's leg worried Rachel.

They had given Charlie some morphine, so at least he wasn't moaning and writhing as much. She had never seen living human bone before; it looked surreal as it protruded out of his erupted flesh. Would he be able to walk again? What if they were cutting his leg off in there? Certainly they would come tell her. She and Charlie had just talked about taking Hattie on a hiking trip after the harvest. God, how long before he'd be able to ride? Be himself again?

Someone else in the waiting room changed the channel on the TV. Oh, great, monster truck racing. She hadn't even noticed there were other people there. A handwringing family of all ages. Two toddlers sat on the floor, ripping pages out of magazines; the adults were probably relieved they were occupied.

How long had it been? Three hours? She had chewed several coffee stirring sticks.

Why was it taking so long? She imagined electric paddles jarring Charlie's limp body. She stood up and paced a small circle. Stop it. People don't die from broken legs, do they? She had to pee but didn't risk being out of the room for a second. The surgeon might come in. She sat back down. Holding it was easier that way.

Finally a surgeon emerged from the double doors with his green surgical cap on, still in his paper boots. Her heart thumped hard as he approached, his face blank.

"Mrs. Hood?" he asked in a soothing voice. "I'm Doctor Brock.

I worked on your husband's leg. It was a very bad break. We had to put a rod in it, plates and pins. He'll have to use crutches for six to eight weeks, and he'll need extensive physical therapy after that. But things went as well as could be expected in surgery. We're optimistic. It will take a while to heal, of course."

She nodded in agreement, shook his hand, and thanked him. It would be okay if God never answered another one of her prayers. She thanked Him over and over for answering this one.

CHAPTER 14

W ithout wind, without so much as a breeze, the smoke hovered like an apparition. Santiago sat in his room as if it were his prison cell, pacing and waiting for the house to become silent. At around one thirty in the morning, people finally had dispersed from the fire scene. The fire had been put out, and there wasn't much to do except assure the Vigils they would help out in any way they could. Rachel was at the hospital with Charlie. Rose and Mort had taken their shame and gone to bed. CeCe was hugging and crying angry tears with her friends. Miguel sat without expression, Hattie asleep on his lap, staring in the direction of his spared chile fields.

Abby, Ben—carrying a dozing Maggie—and Santi had walked home, relieved and feeling guilty that they had homes at all. Ben poured Maggie into bed. He and Abby had sat up for a time. From his room, Santi could hear her crying, "It just isn't fair. Poor Rachel and Charlie and little Hattie . . ." He couldn't make out his words, but Ben was talking in a low, soothing tone, Abby's "I know" and "You're right" interspersed as repeated refrains.

Finally they went to bed.

Santi tried to think clearly and stay calm. The good things: The fire marshal said the fire hadn't spread beyond a narrow strip of about thirty acres right along the river. No other structures were damaged and no other injuries were reported, thanks to the lack of wind and the combined forces of the Esperanza, Bosque Farms, and Isleta Pueblo firefighters. His mind repeated those positive statements like a droning news report, but it couldn't come close to drowning out the bad things.

Rachel and Charlie's home was gone; everything in it was ruined or burned into nothingness. Charlie had a broken leg. His thigh bone had fractured with such violence, it had not only punctured his muscle and skin, but had ripped his jeans from the inside out. They were inserting steel rods and plates to put him back together. What were they going to do without Charlie for harvest? He was Miguel's right hand. They already had fewer pickers coming. Santiago vowed he'd work around the clock to help make up for Charlie's absence. If he wasn't in jail.

What the hell was he going to do? James and his friends would kill him if he ratted them out, but Ramone wasn't buying the Mort's-cigar-and-matches hypothesis and seemed to realize Santi knew something. Poor Mort getting yelled at by CeCe, looked at by everyone as the crazy, dangerous old fool, when he was probably innocent. Science would reveal the truth; the fire was started by a bunch of idiot assholes who didn't care about anybody but themselves, partying around an illegal bonfire, shooting off illegal fireworks, throwing lit cigarettes and joints onto the ground, trespassing in the closed bosque. They might as well have run through the bosque with lit blowtorches. His so-called friends. His so-called girlfriend. Him.

He had to get out of there.

Once out in the night air, he only felt worse. Maybe if he could cry or something. But all he seemed to be able to do was shake and tremble as though he had the chills, gag and nearly puke, stumble around not knowing which way to turn. How did everything get so bad? It used to be just some vague nightmare that tormented him. Now it was like the bad dream had leaked out of him and taken over his life and hurt innocent people he loved.

It was all his fault; somehow he should have stopped it. He looked up to see he was standing in front of where his old house once stood. The only home he knew for ten years. And then he realized, everything had turned to shit because he was a Baca. It was his tainted blood. It was a curse uttered by his father just before he blew his own brains out. The nightmare was his legacy, and now it was his endowment to the good people of Esperanza, whose only crime had been to love him and save him from his father.

But giving him a new name, a new family, a new house couldn't change anything. Inside of him, the Baca genes waited until it was time, then awakened to their true nature, gravitating to James and Rosalinda, willingly seduced by their familiar darkness.

Headlights came up the road, illuminating the particles of ash suspended in the air like moon dust. Was it Rachel coming home? The car didn't turn right to the Vigils' or left toward his own house, but instead came directly at him. He stood there in its path, unable or unwilling to move. The car slammed to a stop inches from his body.

The door opened, and James Ortiz stepped out, calmly closing the door behind him. As he walked over to him, Santi suddenly heard every noise of the night there was to hear. Barking dogs in the distance, the cry of some nocturnal raptor scanning the fields for rodents, insects singing as if this was any other night. He smelled everything, too. Past the lingering smoke, it smelled like the earth aching for rain, chile pods drinking in the cool night air, the sweet sweat of people struggling to save their way of life. It smelled like hope in the face of ugliness.

"I was coming for you," James commented, leaning against his car, apparently satisfied Santi was not going to run.

He could have outrun lazy, baggy-pants James without

breaking a sweat. Santi just stood, smelling the smells, listening to the sounds. Everything so real and so unreal at the same time.

James jumped forward, grabbed Santi's arm, and twisted it behind his back, sending a burst of pain exploding from his shoulder into his brain. Just as quickly, James flicked open a blade and pressed it into his neck. Santi could feel his pulse throb against its cool steel.

"You stay quiet about me and my friends at the river, and you get to live. You talk, and you die. But only after you watch what I do to your little sister. Got it?"

Santi tried to nod but only succeeded in causing the blade to pierce his skin. "Yeah."

James released him and pushed him down into the dirt and held him there with a heavy foot to the small of his back. "'Cause if that sheriff looks my way, Baca or no Baca, you will pay."

Santi lay in the dirt and thought he was about where his old living room would have been. Phantom walls appeared before his eyes, grungy broken furniture, flying beer bottles, echoes of drunken yelling, slaps against tender flesh.

"I'm giving you a chance, Santiago, only because you are a Baca. Otherwise I'd kill you right now."

"I get it," Santi said.

"Then I'm through with you," James said. "For now." But he must have thought better of it, because as he lifted his shoe from Santi's spine, he reared back and kicked him hard in his side, catching his bottom rib or two.

"That's for Rosalinda."

He must have passed out from the pain, because when he came to, James and his car had vanished. His thoughts were confused; everything was running together. He wouldn't have been sure James had really been there at all if he didn't have the souvenir of blinding pain in his right side. His phantom house still wavered around him like a hologram, and an ocean of smoke drifted above him, backlit into an eerie gray-green glow by the moon.

His brain became an onion, layer upon layer of disjointed memory peeling away until his nightmare stood naked and bold in front of his mind's eye. He didn't want to know its contents, but he had no defenses left to protect him from its secrets. Helpless, he became little boy Santiago Baca once again, on that very spot on earth.

Despite the loud thunderstorm, he had fallen asleep on the sofa. The TV droned, his father drank. Someone was at the door, yelling for his dad. His dad, cussing, got up to see who it was. The stranger pushed his way into their home, drunk and angry. "You get the hell out of my father's house," the man was shouting. "You never bought it, you lying rat bastard! This is my property now, and I have the papers to prove it, so get your ass out of here tonight, or I go get the sheriff."

"Roberto Silva, you are one stupid *pendejo*," his father replied calmly, motioning him inside.

As soon as the man walked past him, dripping wet from the rain, Santi's father picked up the baseball bat he kept by the door and hit him across his upper back, knocking him to the floor. Santi cowered on the sofa, peeking over its arm to see what would happen next.

The man groaned on the floor and began to get up, so his father gave him another whack. While the man lay still, his father got some duct tape and used it to bind the man's wrists behind his back. He put another strip over his mouth, muttering and cussing that this would shut him up.

The man began to move again. This time his father just watched him flail around like a fish on the bottom of a boat.

Santi had seen his dad fight plenty of times. He'd even seen him use the bat. But he'd never seen him use the duct tape before and realized something really bad was going to happen. He felt small and helpless. He didn't know what to do. So he watched.

"I knew you were going to be trouble. As soon as your father died, I knew I'd have to deal with you," his father was lecturing, rolling the bat between his hands like a rolling pin. He slurred his words and swayed as though a huge wind was trying to blow him away. "Your father was a fair man. We had reached an understanding: This house was mine, or he had hell to pay. Ricardo was smart enough to know this little piece-of-shit house wasn't worth the kind of trouble he would get from me, and in exchange, we would leave him in peace."

The man on the floor growled behind his tape and managed to right himself into a sitting position. He sat there breathing hard, his saliva beginning to loosen the tape on one side.

His father lay the bat on the man's shoulder and leaned in to rip the tape from his mouth. "Move an inch, and you get it in the side of your head, and that would be lights out, mi amigo."

The man seemed to have sized up his father as someone to fear, which Santi gave him points for. He didn't move an inch, but he did begin to talk. "Please, I have a wife and a baby on the way. We just want to live in peace."

"Did I come busting into your house and threaten your family? You came here, Roberto Silva, and threatened me and my son. Now you want peace? You have some nerve, asshole."

Roberto Silva shook his head. "I buried my father today. I argued with my wife and went out and got drunk. Can't you cut me a break? I was stupid—you're right. We can work something out."

His father tapped the bat lightly against Roberto's shoulder as he thought. "No, it won't work. You're an arrogant son of a bitch, and now you think you can outsmart me. There's no way you're going to let us stay here. I saw your pretty guera wife. You did very well for a Mexican kid from Esperanza, no?" He laughed his harsh cigarette smoker's laugh and picked up his whiskey glass, raised it to the man with a smile, and drank it down.

"Stay away from her! I mean it, Baca, I'll come back from hell if I have to—leave her and my baby alone!"

"You know I have to kill you." His father sighed. "It gives me no pleasure."

"No, please, for my baby—let me live. I promise I'll leave you alone, I swear," Roberto said. "I was stupid, it was a mistake— here—the deed for this house is in my pocket. I'll sign it over to you, all legal. You'll own it for real."

His father reached over and pulled out the folded, rumpled paper and looked it over. "Stay here," he said and went into his bedroom.

Santi was alone with Roberto. He wanted to help him up, help him escape, because he knew if he didn't, his father would kill him. But if he helped Roberto, his father would kill *him.* So he sat on the sofa, listening to Roberto's futile whispered prayers, knowing his father had gone for his gun. He had to pee so bad, but he couldn't move. He was too ashamed. He didn't want Roberto to see him and know he wouldn't help him.

His father returned without the paper and now holding his gun. "I'm sorry, but I can't believe you. You'd find a way to take back my house, say I forced you to sign it over, some bullshit like that, and the law would believe you since you're a hotshot navy dude and I'm just a poor single father on unemployment."

"Swear to me you won't hurt my wife. She has no idea about this, I swear it on my baby's life. She doesn't know where I am or anything about this house," Roberto said, his voice sounding like he was trying not to cry.

Santi knew how hard it was when you needed to cry but you couldn't or it would make things worse. He was feeling that way, too.

"Come on, we're going out to the rooster house. I don't want to mess up my carpet. If you want your wife to be safe, you'll stand up and walk out there with no trouble. Try something stupid, and I go get your wife next."

Roberto stood up with some difficulty from his pain and his arms being tied back, but he didn't try anything. Santi was relieved about that.

"Come on, Santiago," his father commanded.

"Why?" he said, trying not to cry or wet his pants. "I want to stay here."

"I'm doing this for you, so you have a roof over your head. You will come with me in case I need your help," he said.

Santiago followed his father, who poked his gun into Roberto Silva's neck. He poked him toward the rooster house, which came alive with crowing. The cold rain hitting his bare feet made him want to pee even more.

Inside the rooster house, stacks of cages holding fifty or more birds encircled them. Their beady eyes, cocking heads, and bursts of crowing and flapping made Santi think they were like the rowdy spectators at cockfights. Only now, his father and Roberto Silva were the roosters, and just one would come out alive. Thunder crashed nearby. The roof was leaking down one wall.

"Get on your knees," his father ordered.

"Swear to me on the head of your son you will leave my wife and child alone," Roberto said.

"I swear to you on the life of my son, Santiago, if you told me the truth and your wife knows nothing and doesn't come after me, I will spare her and your child. Now get the fuck on your knees."

Roberto got on his knees, but as he did, the wet duct tape began to unwind from his wrists.

"Shit! What are you trying to do?" His father said.

"Nothing—I'm not doing it," Roberto said. "It's all wet and falling off."

"Shitty Walmart tape! Santiago, hold the gun for me. I don't want him getting any ideas and ruining my aim. When you have to kill someone, it should be done right, not all half-assed and messy. One clean shot is all it should take."

Santiago stood motionless. His father had taken him shooting, had taught him to hold the gun. But he hated it. It scared him, and it was heavy and loud.

"Get over here, mi'jo! I need to tie his hands better."

Santiago walked over, and his father put the gun into his small hands.

"Hold it like I taught you. Aim it at his chest." His father stood behind Roberto, bent over, whispering curses as he tried to secure the wet tape. When it wouldn't stick, he began tying it in knots. Roberto flinched as his father pulled it tighter.

Santi's arms were shaking. He tried to think of a way to set Roberto free, but he didn't want to shoot his father. He closed his eyes so he wouldn't have to see Roberto's lips moving in prayer, the tears streaming down his face, his eyes pleading with him to do something, anything.

A bolt of thunder crashed, and Santiago jumped. His finger jerked against the trigger, and the gun fired. He opened his eyes to see the hole in Roberto Silva's stomach, his eyes looking at him in shock before he crumpled against the earthen floor.

"Fuck, Santi, you could have hit me!" His father said as he got down to check Roberto. He rolled him over and watched the blood soaking his shirt. "Still alive, you stubborn pendejo . . . Santiago, what did I just tell you about a clean kill?" He took the gun from Santi and fired a round into Roberto's skull. "That's how you do it."

Santi couldn't speak. His ears rang from the gunshots. A flinty smell filled his nose. He couldn't take his eyes from what used to be Roberto's face. A gush of warm urine flowed down his legs, but there was no relief.

Santi now held the truth in his mind for the first time since that night. His father had told him he was not guilty of murder, since Roberto was going to die anyway. His father said he took full responsibility because as the father, it was his job to keep them safe no matter what. Killing Roberto Silva was ugly, but necessary, because family, la familia, always came first. God understood that.

He remembered going to bed in shock, still wearing his pee-soaked pants. He slept and when he awoke, he couldn't remember anything. He knew something bad had happened, but he didn't know what. Maybe it was some bad dream he couldn't remember.

When his father saw how blank his mind was, he told him he'd left him in the house and taken Roberto out to the rooster house and did what had to be done. He had buried him under the rooster house floor, and Uncle Manny was driving Ricardo's old truck down to Mexico to get rid of it. They would pick Manny up later and eat in the restaurant they liked in Juárez. It would be fun.

Santiago found the tears he'd been missing and began to sob into the dirt, which made his ribs hurt worse, but he could only cry harder. He gagged and vomited frothy mucus and cried some more. Even though his father had finished him off, it was he, Santi, who had shot Roberto Silva, Abby's Bobby. He had killed Maggie's father.

He looked through his tears at his shaking hands in the moon-light, the hands of a murderer. Somewhere in his soul, he must have known. Even as Abby fed and clothed and loved him, he must have known. But he hadn't. It was sealed inside his dream. And now that he did know, how could he live?

He sat up, holding his side, biting his lip in pain until he tasted blood. Dying was too easy and cowardly, like his dad's suicide. He knew what he had to do. He would tell them all. Tell them every-thing. How he had shot Roberto instead of saving him. How he had seen the seeds of the wildfire that burned down Rachel's house and nearly killed Charlie and had done nothing. How he had let a frag-ile old man take the blame. There would be relief in their hatred.

He got up and walked through the cool, smoky night air. His watch said 3:05. He walked down the road to the north, the road to the Vigils.' He would confess to the man he loved and respected more than any other. He would bear Miguel's abhorrence first.

Santiago was not surprised to find Miguel awake, sitting outside on the porch as if waiting for him. Miguel did not seem surprised to see him, either.

"This is not a night for sleeping, mi'jo, is it," the older man said. "I thought it might be a night for drinking, but the beer tasted like dog piss, so I threw it out."

"Miguel," Santi said and knelt on the ground before him. He hung his head and began to cry. He had no pride left in him to feel embarrassed, so he cried freely.

"What is it, mi'jo? Is that blood on your neck? Are you hurt?" Miguel reached over and lifted Santi's chin, putting his finger to the wound.

"No, it's nothing. I have to tell you things . . . you'll be angry and never look at me again, but I have to tell you."

"What is it, Santiago?" Miguel leaned closer, and Santiago tried to meet his eyes. He owed Miguel that much. His tears ran down his face, stinging the cut on his neck. His ribs were on fire, but none of his physical suffering could touch the pain in his soul. This is what damnation felt like, he realized, the relentless, searing fires of hell. Then, he told Miguel what had happened, what he remembered, what he had done.

"Mi'jo, you were a little boy. Your father was going to murder Bobby. It was an accident. You never meant to harm him, and you were too little to stop your father."

"I killed Bobby. I should have killed my father."

"You should never have been put in that position. It was tragic, but your father's soul must bear it, because he had the intention of murder, and it was his shot that completed that intention. You were as helpless as Roberto. I'm glad you are facing this; it can't be healthy to hold such a secret from yourself. I am honored you came to me."

Santiago shook his head. "No, don't say that. I have more to tell you. The man who cut my neck started the fire last night. Rosalinda's cousin James was having a party up the river with a bonfire and fireworks, and I was there. It disgusted me, so I left, but when I was walking home I saw the wildfire, and it was spreading too fast. I couldn't get there in time. He came to me later and threatened me not to tell or he would come after Maggie. That's when I remembered killing Bobby. See now? Everything is my fault, I'm so sorry, I'm so sorry . . . I don't know what to do," Santiago cried, digging his palms into his eyes, rocking in misery at Miguel's knees.

Miguel leaned forward and embraced Santiago, hugging him tightly. "I forgive you. We will all forgive you, mi'jo, because we love you and you are part of our family. Nothing that happened was your fault. You will stand up and say what you know to be true, because that is what a decent man does. We will keep little Magdalena and everyone else safe. James Ortiz and his friends broke the law and caused the fire, and they will pay. Your father killed Bobby when he put the gun in your little trembling hands. You can torment yourself over whether you could have stopped him or not, or if you could have outrun the velocity of a wildfire like some kind of superman. But I have news for you, mi'jo: You weren't a superhero at barely ten years old, and you aren't a super-hero now. You're a man, and men make mistakes, we screw up, we make poor choices. But only a good man does what you did tonight. A good man takes responsibility and tells the truth. You are a good man, Santiago Silva."

After Santiago's confession, he and Miguel watched the sun turn the sky from black to seashell, and even before it fully rose from behind the mountains, they called Ramone's cell phone. He told them he already had James Ortiz, Carlos Salazar, Daniel "Bones" Ceballes, and three other men in custody for negligent arson, drug possession, and related charges. The fire marshal and his team of investigators had found a wealth of evidence at the scene of the party, including gifts for James with his name still on the tags. Rosalinda had provided a statement to seal their fates and was willing to testify against them in court. In her statement, she had sworn Santiago Silva was never there.

"You're not going to contradict my star witness are you, Santiago?" Ramone asked.

After a night of truth telling, Santi hesitated, listening to the static on the phone.

"No?" Ramone said for him. "Glad to hear it."

Miguel and Santiago walked the chile fields as the sun climbed over the mountains. The light was hazy, filtered through the remaining smoke, which had dispersed into a fine, nearly invisible veil overhead. Santi could smell the chile again, spicy and green.

Miguel bent down to feel the fruit between his experienced fingers. He picked one and cracked it open, examining the seed formation, placental tissue, and inner flesh. He put it to his nose to inhale and then licked it several times. "God willing, no hail, one last irrigation, we'll be harvesting within two weeks. It could be a great crop. A huge crop. The hard part will be getting enough hands to get it all picked in time. We could have two pickings of green and still have plenty to turn red for late September, early October, depending on how long we want to play chicken with the first frost."

Santiago nodded. He was still in shock, trying to process what he had remembered, his guilt barely containable. Then he pondered the news about Rosalinda stepping up and doing the right thing about the fire. He realized that her protecting him from any involvement was to spare him, not from the law, but from the violent retribution of James's gang. She was saving his life and keeping his loved ones safe. It consoled him somewhat that she felt she owed him at least that much. When he began to worry about her safety in testifying, he realized he didn't know anyone more capable of taking care of herself than Rosalinda.

Santiago took the broken pod Miguel handed him and performed his own examination. He knew that as Miguel inhaled and tasted, he was performing therapy, the best therapy he knew, the therapy that had seen him through his sixty years of life.

"What if I stayed here? I don't need to go to California. I could stay here and harvest. Maybe go later or something," Santiago said.

Miguel put an arm around Santi's neck the way he had been doing since he was ten, only now he had to reach up to do it. "As good as you are, you are only one set of hands. I'll work you so hard between now and September, you'll be glad to go to college."

Santi smiled, yet felt immense sadness well up inside of his bruised chest. How could he ever leave this place, this man? "What if I decide I want to be a chile farmer?"

"Mi'jo! We will first get your head examined! Then we will call in the curandera for a healing and the priest for an exorcism. And after that, if you still want to be a chile farmer, you are welcome to it. There will always be a place here for you here on Sol y Sombra. 'Mi'jo' is not your nickname—it is who you are. My son."

Abby woke with a start when the knowledge of the fire infiltrated her dream. Ben was still sleeping behind her, his arm around her waist. In the aftermath of the fire, in the middle of the night, it only made sense for him to stay. It felt so right for him to be there, next to her, under this roof. When without a word he had bolted into the burning house to save Charlie, even in her terror she had prayed for him to come out unharmed. After all she had been through, it was good to know she still had faith.

She slipped out of bed and found her robe. It was only seven thirty, but she needed to find out how Charlie was doing, be there for Rachel and CeCe.

As she made coffee she pondered how even the smell somehow gathered one's resolve, filled one with fortitude for whatever one faced. She phoned the Vigils' as soon as she had cup in hand.

"Hello," CeCe answered.

"It's Abby. How's Charlie?"

"I just got off the phone with Rachel. Surgery went fine. They put in a rod and hardware, and he'll be good as new after he mends. He's in a regular orthopedic unit and will be home in a few days on crutches. Thank God!"

"How's Rachel?"

"Relieved. Strong for Charlie. Not dealing with the house and everything they lost yet. I tell you, Abby, I don't know how I can cope with Mort being responsible. I mean, I know it's the illness, but yet it's still so like him to smoke those damn cigars, be so selfish."

"Yeah, but you can't really afford to go there, can you? It was an accident, and you have to find some way not to blame him. He could have been killed," Abby said and then took a big gulp of her elixir.

CeCe sighed loudly into the phone. "I know. We are so thankful for Santi bringing him out of the fire, and my God! Ben going in after Charlie while the rest of us stood there all helpless. The whole house caved in as soon as they came out. Thanks just doesn't begin to cover it. He saved Charlie's life."

"You know Charlie would have done the same. Good men don't think of themselves at a time like that."

"Or the women who love them," CeCe said. "I guess it's good they don't. Oh, Ramone is here. What if he's here for Mort? Would they arrest an old man with dementia? I'll call you back."

Abby, Ben, and Maggie were at the kitchen table finishing up the blueberry pancakes and turkey bacon they had made for breakfast when Abby saw Miguel and Santiago walking toward the house.

The morning air was still tolerable, so they were not running the swamp cooler yet and had the kitchen door open, except for the screen, to let in the light breeze. The air was fresh, with no hint of the smoky inferno from the night before.

"I was thinking maybe Maggie and I could go do something special up in Albuquerque today, free you up to help out your friends," Ben said, scraping the last bit of syrup with his fork.

"I think they're your friends, too, after last night," Abby said, watching Santiago come closer, the stoop of his shoulders, Miguel's hand on his back.

"I want to go to Albuquerque with Ben for something special. What are we going to do, Ben?"

"Lady's choice. A movie, miniature golf, or I could even take you to the refugium, where we are growing all the baby minnows. That's pretty neat. We have all these fish tanks in our laboratory and outdoor pools where they go when they get bigger. Do you have roller skates?"

"Yeah, I'm good at it, too, aren't I, Mom?" Maggie said.

"Another idea is we go see my office at the university and then roller skate all over the campus and visit the duck pond."

Maggie considered the possibilities. "Here's what we do. First we go see the fishes. Then we go to campus and see where you work, then we roller skate and feed the ducks some bread. Then we go for sandwiches and ice cream. Do you have roller skates?"

"I have some roller blades, and I'm quite terrible, so you'll have a good laugh," Ben said as Santi and Miguel reached the door. "I'll bet I can be ready to go before you are."

"No way! Hi, Santi, I get to go to Albuquerque with Ben," Maggie said and then jumped up and tore off to her room.

"Thanks," Abby said, squeezing Ben's hand on her shoulder. "I can really use the time."

"I figured," Ben said. "Hi, Miguel, Santi. How's Charlie?"

"Came through the surgery fine," Miguel smiled. "My whole family thanks you."

"Not necessary. I'm just glad everyone is all right. Sorry about the house, though."

Miguel shrugged and nodded. "A house can always be rebuilt. I hope they'll agree to come up out of the bosque a ways this time, though. There's a nice site on the other side of the horse barn I tried to get them to consider last time. But you know Rachel, had to have her house in the woods."

"She might feel different now," Abby said, watching Santiago the entire time. He had some kind of deep scratch on his neck she hadn't noticed last night. His eyes were avoiding hers. She could feel his distress in the pit of her own stomach, and it didn't sit well with the pancakes.

"I'm going to clear out with Maggie, so good luck," Ben said and kissed Abby quickly on her forehead.

He and Miguel shook hands.

"Bye, Ben," Santi managed.

"Coffee, Miguel? Santi? I could throw on some more pancakes and bacon," Abby offered.

"Coffee sounds good," Miguel said, "and then we need to talk."

They made small talk until Ben and Maggie had rounded up her skates, helmet, and knee pads, grabbed some stale bread, and headed off for their day.

Abby sat expectantly, hoping for anything but more bad news.

"Santiago came to me in the night, and we've been talking. He has some things to tell you, and it's pretty hard for him, but I know he can do it. I've told him you love him and will support him, as I do."

"Of course. Always," Abby said, trying to get Santi to meet her eyes. When he wouldn't, she looked to Miguel, who nodded his encouragement to her.

"I've been having nightmares for a long time now. Maybe since . . . you know, after Bobby was killed. But they got a lot worse, and I never knew what they were about—they just scared me and messed me up real bad. Anyway, after I left the café with Rosalinda, it's true we fought and broke up, but not until she took me to her cousin James's birthday party. I didn't want to go. He and his friends have been creeping me out lately, so I was trying to avoid them. But they didn't like it, and Rosalinda said if I didn't go the party it would only get worse. So I went."

There was a long pause while Santi collected his thoughts and took a gulp of orange juice.

"So the party was up by Isleta. In the bosque. And there were a whole bunch of people there, drinking and stuff. And James had a bonfire going. I didn't like it, and that's when Rosalinda and I started to argue even more. And this guy Carlos was going to set off fireworks and wanted me to help, and it all made me sick, so I left, and Rosalinda was really pissed off, but I didn't care anymore. I just wanted to get home, get away from there. I was worried about a fire starting, but Carlos said he'd shoot the fireworks out over the water, and the bonfire was in a clearing, so I just started walking for home."

"I'm glad you got out of there, Santi," Abby said and tried to reach for his hand. He slid it off the table into his lap.

"I should have run as fast as I could and reported them, but I was just walking for a while, so I'll never know if I could have stopped it. About as soon as I saw it, the fire was exploding all around me and racing past me. I ran as fast as I could. The nearest house was the Vigils', so I was trying to get there, and then I realized Charlie and Rachel's house would be in the way of the fire, but I couldn't get to it fast enough. That's when I found Mort. I knew the main fire had started upriver a ways, but I didn't know what he was doing with matches. I was just so freaked out about it all, I couldn't think straight. I shouldn't have let him take the blame, but I knew if I told on James and his gang, they would retaliate, and I was really scared they would hurt you or Maggie to punish me."

Abby sat in stunned silence. The words *I told you so* were echoing through her mind. With great self-control she held her tongue and waited.

"After you went to bed, I snuck out to think and stuff. I was feeling bad. You told me to stay away from those people, and I fought you on it. I was feeling the nightmare come again, only I was awake, scared, and all weird—it's hard to describe. I went over to where my old house used to be, and James showed up and told me to stay quiet about the party or he'd come after Maggie." His voice began to quiver, and his breaths were ragged. He fought for control. "He had a knife to my throat the whole time and said he'd leave us in peace if I stayed quiet, and I guess I got cut. He knocked me down and kicked me in the ribs, and then he left."

"Oh, my God!" Abby said as Santi's tears began to trickle down his dirty face. She felt her own tears trying to escape, and she pressed her hand to her lips.

"I was laying there. It hurt like hell, and then it was like my mind opened up and showed me this movie, only I was in the movie and it was the night Bobby came to our house, during the storm." As he spoke, Santiago's voice became slightly higher and younger.

Abby trembled, and her tears started to come uncontrollably, but she remained silent, knowing she had to hear what Santi was about to tell her.

"He was all mad, telling us he was kicking us out of the house, that it was his house now and he had the papers to prove it. My dad hit him in the back with a baseball bat and knocked him down and taped him up. Then he got his gun and told Bobby he'd have to kill him. That's when Bobby tried to make a deal, told him to take the paper out of his pocket and he'd sign the house over to us, but my dad didn't believe him, and he took him to the rooster house. Only he made me come also, and I never remembered that part. That's when I saw Bobby was kneeling on the ground, and I wanted to help him so bad. My dad noticed the tape was coming off his wrists, so he made me hold the gun." Santiago was weeping now. The tears and snot ran down his face unchecked as he went on with the story.

"The gun was so heavy, and he had me point it at Bobby, and I wanted to stop my dad but I couldn't, and Bobby made my dad promise on my life to never hurt you or his baby because you didn't know anything about the house not being ours. So my dad agreed, and he was trying to tie Bobby up better, and Bobby was staring at me, pleading for help with his eyes and praying to God. That's when the thunder crashed so loud, and I jumped, and the gun went off. It hit Bobby in the stomach, and he was bleeding bad. Then my dad shot him in the head to finish him off." Santiago's head was in his hands, and he sobbed. "I'm sorry, Abby, I never meant to hurt him. I never remembered I did. I should have saved him. I had the gun. I had a chance to save him, and I didn't."

Abby saw the movie in her own mind, and it was nearly too much to bear. Her beloved Bobby, her beloved Santi, both terrified and doomed. Connected in this unspeakable way, the bullet leaving the gun in Santi's hands, embedding in Bobby's body. She remembered the thunder that night, how she had been startled with every crash. One of those thunderclaps was when he had lost his life.

"I told Santiago, it was his father's intention to kill Roberto. That the gun was in his hands for that moment was a cruel accident," Miguel said.

"Santiago, it wasn't your fault!" Abby cried, putting her arms around him. Miguel's words snapped her out of her nightmare and into her son's. "You couldn't have saved him—you were little. Your dad would have hurt you and still killed Bobby."

"I had the gun—don't you get it?" Santi yelled. "Maybe if I'd held the gun on my dad and gotten the tape off of Bobby's wrists, we could have overpowered him or called the sheriff or something."

"Bobby was a stranger to you," Abby said. "A stranger who was going to kick you out of your house. You only knew your dad, and you loved him. It was only later that you got to know me and learned who Bobby was. You couldn't save him. I want you to trust me on that and believe it. But you did save me, remember? Maggie and I would be dead right now if you hadn't protected me from your father. You were only ten years old, and you stood in front of me, pregnant with Maggie, and you wouldn't let him harm me. Remember how brave you were? You saved us!" She held his head between her hands, "Look at me, Santi. I mean it. I love you. It wasn't your fault—it was a terrible, terrible thing that your father did."

"He killed himself when he knew I shot Bobby first. I can't figure that out," Santi said. "Was he protecting me?"

"He knew he was responsible for Roberto's death and that any court of law would convict him. The sheriff and his men had him surrounded. I think he was just getting out of the consequences," Miguel said. "I don't believe he was capable of protecting you. But we'll never know what was going through his sick mind when he pulled the trigger."

Santiago began to calm down, reaching for a paper napkin to blow his nose.

Abby was overwhelmed with her love for him. Eight years his young mind had kept this horrific secret from his consciousness. Until it leaked out in nightmares and then revealed itself when he was being threatened yet again to keep silent about another's wrongdoing. "Are we in danger from James? Have you called Ramone?"

"Ramone already knew. There was enough evidence at the place where the party was, and Rosalinda is testifying against them, and she swore I was never there. I was going to tell Ramone I was there, which he already knew, but he wouldn't let me say it."

"We don't want to shoot any holes in Rosalinda's story," Miguel explained. "I'm proud of you, mi'jo. You did good telling your mother what happened. You did good hearing it, Abby. I better get back home. CeCe needs me, and there's an old man to let off the hook."

"I imagine she's already heard it from Ramone. I was talking to her when he showed up. She's probably feeling pretty rotten about now. She was rough on Mort," Abby said. "Thank you, Miguel. I don't know what we—"

"Abby, la familia. *Amor primero, amor postrero,*" he said, heading for the door. "Love first and last."

CHAPTER 15

The few hours Charlie had spent in the recovery room were hard for Rachel. She had never seen him laid up before, tubes and bags hanging off him, the strong smell of anesthesia wafting on his snores. The nurse trying to rouse him from his unnatural sleep. The reality of the long, bulky splint on his right leg. He had always been the one to take care of her when she needed it, and now he was going to need her in a way he never had.

He was in an orthopedic unit, still hooked up to an IV, in a room he shared with an elderly man who had just had a knee replacement. An antibiotic-laced bag of fluid dripped into Charlie's body, but because of a urinary catheter, he was spared having to use the bathroom. Soon the physical therapist would be here to get him started on his crutches, and the catheter would be removed.

"Does it hurt much?" Rachel asked, adjusting his blanket. His leg seemed twice its normal size, obscured by the bulky splint, propped up on multiple pillows. His toes were all that were visible; the nurse came in regularly to check them for proper circulation and amount of swelling.

"Not so much. They have me dosed up on some pain medications," he slurred.

"Hattie wants me to sneak her up here to see you. She's pretty freaked out by all of this."

"I don't want her to see me like this. It'd just scare her more," he said. He reached for his cup of water with a straw and knocked it off the tray instead. The plastic cup went bouncing across the linoleum floor, waking up the knee guy with a snort.

Rachel ran to retrieve it, smiling and apologizing to the roommate, whose blankets had fallen down and hospital gown had ridden up. She pulled the dividing curtain farther between his area and Charlie's.

She set the cup where Charlie could reach it. "Well, then, how about we call her?"

Charlie pressed his palms against his burned cheeks and eyes. There were little blisters forming on his nose. "I really fucked up," he said. "Your poor father . . . I'm useless now. I won't ever forgive myself."

"The harvest will happen. Leticia and Jenny are going to help out. There will be things you'll be able to do. All you need to worry about is getting better," Rachel said.

She knew their pain about losing the house was too devastating to talk about yet. All the hard work. All the love that had gone into it. Possessions that were tucked away in chests or scrapbooks, things that could never be replaced, gone. Everything lost. She knew that for her to get Charlie through this, she would have to put all that on hold. Besides, none of that stuff really mattered anymore now. She was spared losing what she loved most.

CeCe sat in an Adirondack chair on the bricked patio outside her bedroom, sipping a cup of tea. So her father hadn't burned down Rachel and Charlie's house after all. Some gang punks with no regard for the law or other people had set the fire. She was going to apologize. Not only should she apologize, she wanted to. For so many things. The shock of all that had happened had finally stripped away the last of her resentments, and she could see her father for the victim he had been. Even though he had escaped Treblinka, there was no escaping the damage done.

She had said some terrible things to Mort, and it sickened her now with this perspective. But what were any one of them to think, seeing him coming out of the woods looking scorched and sooty, holding a package of burned matches, obsessing about his cigar? She could not forget the blank look of devastation on his face when she accused him, the look she had seen on the faces of the victims in pictures Rachel had given her of Treblinka. Her shame made her nauseous.

A piñon jay in the tree branch overhead reprimanded her about the empty bird feeder. His piercing call and angry stance seemed to scold her for more than her negligence.

Mort was innocent. She needed to tell her parents. Not that it couldn't have just as easily been him. She had been worrying he would end up burning down her house. But it wasn't his fault, and she must forgive him, finally, for the father he had been. Accept that the pain she had suffered as a young girl was not his responsibility alone. The past must be relegated to the past. She took in a huge breath and blew it out for as long and as hard as she could, willing all her negative thoughts and pain to dislodge themselves from the deepest part of her and leave her in that moment.

She took in a new breath, praising life, grateful for second chances, feeling her forgiveness as redemption.

Now she could face him and set him free from his guilt. And Rose from her shame. They had all suffered enough.

She found Rose and Mort burrowed in their room. Rose had made a tray of food and coffee, but it sat on their dresser untouched. They were in their robes, disheveled. Mort's charred hands lay in his lap. With his glasses off, his eyes seemed embedded deep into his head, above his prominent translucent cheekbones.

CeCe gave a quick prayer that she would find the right words. "How are you two? Can I come in?" she asked, peeking in the door.

Rose wore a hairnet that kept her fuzzy hair contained. Her varicose veins in her calves showed from under a flowered cotton robe and seemed to run like blue ink down into her terry cloth scuffs.

"You have enough on your mind. Don't worry about us," Rose said. Her nostrils were deep pink, and so were the rims of her eyes. "Let me know if I can do anything, anything at all," she added. A second later she burst like a balloon. "A *kappore*! I feel so terrible!" She pulled some tissues from the inside of her sleeve, wiping away sudden tears. Then a scant blowing of her nose.

"I need to talk to you two," CeCe said, leading Rose back to her chair next to Mort's. CeCe pulled up the vanity chair.

She looked her papa in his eyes and hoped he was coherent enough to understand and to feel the softness in her heart as she said it. She took a deep breath. "You didn't set the fire, Papa. It was a bunch of gangsters having a party at the river. You didn't burn down your granddaughter's house. *Farshtaist*, Papa?"

"*Danken Got!*" Rose cried, slapping her hands to her mouth, her fingers devoid of rings.

A tear or two escaped down her father's cheeks. "I wouldn't have wanted to go on," he said after a couple of hard swallows. Saliva pooled in the corners of his mouth. "I have survived when others didn't. I've seen and been forced to do the most horrible things and lived with it, but thinking I did that to our Rachel . . ."

She wanted to erase his tortured look. "But you didn't, Papa," CeCe assured him. "It was all a misunderstanding." It killed her to watch his tear make its way slowly down his cheek, diverting back and forth in his dejected, wrinkled face.

"But *a nahr bleibt a nahr*. A fool remains a fool. I could have.

I think I better go to a nursing home. We can sell Rose's jewelry to help with the costs. It doesn't look so good on her anymore, anyway."

Rose sobbed into her spent tissue. It was plain she wasn't crying over her threatened jewelry.

"I don't want that, Papa," CeCe said, putting her hand on his. She meant it. She was so ashamed for not having grown up sooner. All the time she had wasted. "There are new medications all the time. I haven't lost hope." She cried freely in front of him, putting her forehead against his burned hands.

"You've always been a good daughter, CeCe," he said, cupping her jaw and wiping a few of her tears. "I kept every card and poem you ever wrote me; they're stuffed in with my socks. And now that little blond girl is making more cards and pictures for me, and soon there will be no more room for socks. But now that I threw away all my cigars, I have room to spare, and who needs so many socks anyway? I only have the two feet. Keep those cards and letters coming!"

CeCe gave a laugh of relief. "We will, Papa. I promise."

"I've been in touch with the nuns, and they're launching a fundraiser for Rachel and Charlie," said Carmen, sitting at CeCe's kitchen table. The afternoon sunlight poured like hot butter onto the tabletop. "And you know how those nuns feel about Miguel; he's practically one of their saints. Oh, and they sent these toys for Hattie," she said, bending and reaching under the table, where she had stowed her purse and the bag.

"Hazel's out gathering up a few things from her Red Cross buddies," said Bonnie, taking a bite out of a chewy green chile bagel. A Bud Lite sat to the right of her, a heavy brown lipstick print under the rim. The FBI would never have a hard time tracking Bonnie down.

"Maggie has a lot of clothes she's outgrown. I'm still going through them, but I'll bring them over tomorrow," Abby said, picking up her iced tea glass and taking a long swallow, the lemon wedge hitting her nose. "And I can give them however much they might need if the insurance money isn't enough or it's taking too long. Remember, we're family, CeCe."

CeCe felt like crying. Not for herself, but for Rachel, Charlie, and Hattie, and for the intense pain she felt watching her daughter's life incinerate into a pile of black nothingness. Luckily Rachel had never moved the dairy or horses down to their property, so all of them had been spared the horror of losing any of the animals. Even Oakley had appeared the next morning.

"I don't know how I would get through this without you guys," CeCe said, her voice straining against a flood of tears. "You've all helped so much. I love you guys." She finally let herself sob, her teardrops feeling as foreign in her hands as rain. Abby jumped up to hold her. "I finally apologized to my father," CeCe cried. "And I feel like I'm the one who was forgiven."

"That's the way it works," Carmen said.

Rachel kicked through the ashes where her house had once stood. Funny how the birds still sang and the sun still shone, as if a disaster had never happened here. It was only her world that had changed.

She poked through the ashes with a twig she had pulled from a tree murdered by the fire's heat. Amazing how certain things were able to survive the inferno, with no reasonable explanation. A plastic spatula, of all things, looked barely burned at all. And standing there before her was their old enameled stove, charred around the edges but still a vivid vintage green, shining like hope in the bright sunlight.

Safely away from Charlie, she felt free to mourn the home they had conceived together. And now, almost every single thing was gone forever: documents, stashed savings, Charlie's collection of western books, and all she had left of her Tía Maria. Not to forget the old oak table where Jesse James had put his feet, the wood floors Hattie had taken her first steps on. Rugs she had been afraid to use were now the ashes on which she stood.

She couldn't talk to Charlie about this, not yet. He hadn't been himself since the accident. His anger seeped out of him. Anger toward James Ortiz for burning down his home. Rachel knew Charlie had wanted to kill James when he first found out. Thank God, Mort had had nothing to do with it. And when Santi had come to him, Charlie had listened to his guilt by association and absolved him. He loved Santi like a son.

It was Charlie's anger at himself that boiled his insides. And shame that when Miguel needed him the most, he was useless. He sometimes took it out on her. Like yesterday, when she had brought him his medicine. "I'm not a cripple!" he'd muttered as he swung himself up on his crutches to meet her halfway, then grabbed it out of her hands. Men were never good patients, the nurse had warned her. Too much dependency. He was such a proud man, but his feelings of helplessness and guilt got the better of him. Except with Hattie. He put on a good face for her.

"Here, Daddy, kiss Oakley. He wants to make up with you," Hattie had said, carrying Oakley like a small sack of potatoes. His whiskers had been singed off, his ears burned at the tips. Hattie had him wrapped up in gauze like a Civil War soldier after battle.

Rachel had seen Charlie's lip trying not to smile as Hattie carried Oakley to him. "How ya doin', Oakley," he said, patting the cat's head.

"Oakley wants you to kiss him. That's how I always know I'm off the hook," Hattie said, using the new phrase she had learned from Rose talking about Mort. She was always letting him off the hook for this or off the hook for that. "Maggie says you and Ben were like Batman and Robin."

"Is that so? I've never seen a superhero kiss a cat. Have you?" he asked.

Hattie tried to hold Oakley up to Charlie's lips, but Oakley squirmed and wormed his way out of her arms like Pepé Le Pew's cat-mistaken-for-skunk girlfriend and darted out the door. Charlie had looked relieved.

Rachel bent to pull Hattie's pink piggy bank, now pitch black, from under a mound of ashes. The coins thudded inside instead of clinking when she shook them against the glass body. But she could see through the small slit the sooty coins were still viable.

Hattie seemed to be holding up pretty well, considering she had to wear hand-me-downs and play with secondhand toys. She still had her mommy and daddy and Maggie and the rest of the family, in that order. In the world according to Hattie, she hadn't lost a thing. Grandpa had promised to take her shopping for new toys after the harvest. She looked forward to that.

Rachel said a prayer, wiped her nose with the back of her hands, and stuck the overcooked piggy bank in her backpack. Right now every penny counted.

"Hattie fell right to sleep after I read to her," Charlie said, joining Rachel on their bedroom patio at the Vigils' later that evening. He hopped into his chair, putting his crutches next to him.

"Beer?" she offered, handing him one.

The sun behind the remaining trees shone pink, purple, and orange as it began to disappear. Colors that she and Charlie had watched many nights from their own house, their own bedroom window. From their own bed.

They both stared in silence, taking swigs of beer every now and then. She didn't want to start a conversation, especially about her excavation through the remains of their house. She wanted to tell him that all of this had created a different, better woman. She didn't know why or exactly how, just that it had all erupted something in her, like mountains reforming, becoming taller and more majestic than before. Some issues in her life that had seemed huge before now seemed minuscule from her new vantage point.

She could feel his heart wince as he soaked in the colorful

pulled-taffy twilight and hoped he was not dangling himself over hell, as he had the last few days. Harvest, especially this harvest, was a time for rejoicing. The fact that he was alive deserved rejoicing. She hoped his leg healed quickly. She hated to dance this new dance alone.

He broke the silence as a tear trickled down his face. "I was only trying to save the damn cat for Hattie. I can still hear her screaming. A father's impulse," he said. "I wish I had it to do over."

She put her hand on his as he reached for his beer, which stood sweating on a small table between them. "No do overs. That's the hardest rule of this game for me to swallow, too," she said, entwining his fingers with hers. "At least we're here to move forward."

He squeezed her hand in response.

"This may sound crazy, but I've never felt more grateful, for you, Hattie, our lives together on this land. I don't need anything else," she said, shrugging as her own tears came.

Charlie leaned over and tipped her chin to him. His kiss told her he felt the same way.

Rachel found her father in his study, sorting through a stack of bills. "Hey, mi'ja," he said, looking up.

"We'll be harvesting soon. Then we can start catching up," she said. "There's also the money the community raised for us, if you need to dip into that—"

"That's for you and Charlie to rebuild. Insurance won't cover everything. We'll be fine," he said, even though the worry still clouded his eyes.

Rachel knew the harvest was still in question. It was good the crop had made it this far, but a hailstorm could still wipe it all away. And would they be able to hire enough pickers to get the job done? But she was holding a secret and it was time to share it with him.

"Papa, I did something, and I hope you will approve," she began, suddenly worried that he may not see her actions as the gift she had intended.

He looked at her with obvious worry. After all, most surprises lately were not good ones.

"You may not remember, but one time, when you came to my house in the middle of the night, you talked about your family. You mentioned your sister Teresa."

"I was drunk, no?" he said with a shake of his head. Another proud man in shame.

"Self-medicated, yeah, a little." Rachel smiled. "I got online, and you'd be amazed. It took, like, five seconds to have her address and phone number. I hope you don't mind, but I wrote her a letter, and she wrote back. We've had a few phone calls, too. She sounds so wonderful, Papa. She misses you and has been wanting to get back in touch ever since your mother died. But then her husband got sick, and he just passed away a few months ago. She wants you to call her, Papa." She reached into her pocket and pulled out a folded square of paper. "She's still in Tucson."

Miguel was tough to read as he took the paper and stared at it in silence.

"Are you angry?" she finally asked.

"No, mi'ja." He put the paper in his breast pocket.

"Will you call her?" Rachel asked, urging him to talk with her, share his feelings. She knew she already loved her Tía Teresa and wanted to meet her, here on their ancestral land. But it all depended on what her father decided. "I don't claim to know what's best for you, Papa, but how can it be wrong to reconnect with your sister? La familia."

"You don't think we have enough la familia around here already?" He smiled to soften his gruff tone. "*Todo en la vida se puede recuperar, pero el tiempo nunca se recupera.* You can recover everything in life, but time."

Rachel considered the meaning of his dicho and decided it was time to leave him to the privacy of his thoughts. She had done all that she could. For now.

CHAPTER 16

S ol y Sombra chile fields supped their last irrigation water on July 31. The summer monsoons were more than a month late. A few showers had visited the mountains but petered out before reaching the river valley. The long-range weather forecast was predicting a storm that could contain high winds and hail for the second week in August, so Miguel decided harvest would begin August 3, giving time for the surface ground to dry after irrigation and allow a week of frantic picking before the potentially crop-damaging storm hit.

Miguel's loyal and experienced crew of eight workers appeared a few days early with the surprising addition of four more young men, nephews and sons, ready to learn the trade. Even with twelve pickers, Miguel's forty-eight acres of chile loomed large. His plants were heavy with shiny, fat, long green pods. Ten fast pickers could handle maybe an acre a day. The plan was to pick as much green chile in the next week as possible, see what happened with the storm, and, he hoped, be able to continue picking throughout August and September. In the last weeks of September, as the chile continued to ripen into red, Miguel's eye would be on the nighttime low temperatures and the deadly first hard frost.

With the growing demand for red chile, both as fresh pods for roasting and to dry into red chile powder, he hoped to have 200 tons of red out of his predicted 576 tons of total yield. If all went well—still a long shot at that point, but statistically possible—with chile prices staying flat at $300 per ton, Sol y Sombra could make the Vigils about $172, 800. Subtracting the pickers' wages of $3 to $4 per forty-pound sack picked each day of the harvest, plus all of the other enormous bills stacked on Miguel's desk, they would have enough to support two families and livestock, pay taxes, repair tractors and other equipment, and see them all through one more year, God willing.

With the possible hailstorm looming, all hands were needed on deck. CeCe, Rachel, and Abby closed the café for the week. So that she could suspend goat cheese operations for the harvest, the previous week Rachel had doubled up orders to her vendors and restaurants, freeing up Leticia and Jenny to lend a hand, except for the milking, which could never be postponed. Leo, the dishwasher, and Justin, her part time delivery man, both agreed to help with the harvest as well.

Since hailstorms had been known to completely decimate hundreds of acres of chile in less than ten minutes, even the slightest chance of one coming was a guillotine poised over their heads. With everyone pitching in—the inexperienced pickers moving more slowly, hands to aching backs—they might be able to pick fourteen acres in a week, leaving the remaining acres of perfect chile vulnerable to the storm.

The other threat was the possibility of no rain at all. With the Middle Rio Grande Conservancy District's irrigation season officially over, they were now at the mercy of Mother Nature. Mature chile plants needed even water more than growing plants to remain viable—a good rain once a week over the next eight weeks, until they could all be picked. With no measurable rain since March, the chances of moisture seemed slim, despite the fact that July and August were supposed to be the rainiest months of the year. With July a bust, all the chips were on August.

Miguel's chile fields had avoided common diseases like curly top virus, alfalfa mosaic virus, blossom end rot, bacterial leaf spot, powdery mildew, pepper mottle virus, pepper weevil, root-knot nematode, and a host of others. It had thrived despite the devastating drought. Now all it needed was to be picked before it dried up or became shredded by hail. The loyal troops were gathering to get the crop in or die trying.

Abby, Maggie, and Santi were up by five in the morning to eat a big breakfast, pack snacks, lunches, and water, and slather on sunscreen. Sun hats, work gloves, and a bag of books and activities to keep Maggie busy were also gathered. They met up at the first field by six o'clock.

"Good morning!" Miguel greeted them. "It's a beautiful day to pick chile, no?"

Santiago gave him a quick handshake instead of his usual hug, looking a little shy in front of the Mexican pickers, who had been teasing him since he was ten. Miguel introduced him to the four new guys, who were his age or younger.

Abby saw Rachel and CeCe over by a table shaded with a canvas canopy. Charlie was able to begin light weight bearing on his broken leg, but his crutches were still needed for balance and most of the weight bearing. Determined to be useful, he was briefing the workers in Spanish and English and would also serve as tally man, recording who picked how many sacks and the overall totals.

Hazel, Carmen, and Bonnie were going to switch off picking duties with babysitting Mort and Rose back at the house.

"I took off my fake nails for this. Hijo la! I feel naked!" Bonnie said. In her skimpy red halter top and short blue jean cutoffs, she was as naked as Abby hoped ever to see her.

Hattie and Maggie were racing around in the cool morning air.

They dumped their activity bags under the shade of the table and wanted to stay outside, where the excitement was. Abby knew they would be inside the swamp-cooled house by midday with Rose and Mort.

Rachel greeted her with a hug and a brave smile. "Did you see how cheerful Papa is? I haven't seen him like this in so long. I think he's actually starting to believe everything will work out."

"Yeah, he looks good. How about you, Rachel, how are you holding up?" Abby asked. It seemed they hadn't had a chance for a real talk since the fire, eleven days and a lifetime ago.

"The bulldozers were here yesterday, and the trucks hauled away all the debris. You should see how bare it looks now. Just the flat, charred ground where it had been. It looks so much smaller than the house was. I don't know. Maybe since all the surrounding trees are gone, we could still rebuild there and be safe. We're going to wait until spring to decide, get through the winter at the folks', let Charlie heal. The insurance company came through but said if we rebuild on that site our rates will go up bigtime. So maybe we'll come up closer to Ma and Papa's house. That's what they want us to do."

"Might make sense," Abby said.

They stopped talking when a long University of New Mexico van pulled up. Everyone watched as Ben emerged from the driver's seat and ten other people began to climb out. Six men and four women, varying in age.

"We're here to help, if you'll have us," Ben said to Miguel, who broke into a wide grin. "Students who thought picking chile sounded better than writing a paper and a few colleagues from the biology and botany departments. I called a colleague down at New Mexico State, where they have the chile institute, and he gathered a half-dozen more volunteers, who should arrive in a few hours. They'll actually know what they're doing."

Miguel clasped hands all around, giving his thanks. "I'll pair each of you up with an experienced picker. Just remember to squat or sit to save your backs, and drink plenty of water. The pods closest to the ground will be the ripest. Learn from the pickers how to pick without damaging the plant and leave the immature pods for later. You'll fill these five-gallon white plastic buckets and then carry them over to the flatbed truck, where you'll dump them into the burlap bags. The truck will follow you up the field. Take breaks when you need them. And before we start, let's take a moment to thank God, San Ysidro, Mother Nature, or whomever you believe in for this bountiful harvest and the good hearts and strong hands who are making it possible." He repeated this in Spanish for his workers.

Abby squeezed Ben's hand as they stood in the moment of silence, a gentle breeze ruffling the chile leaves.

"Thank you," Miguel said. "Let's get started!"

The days went by in a blur. A few sunburns, more than a few aching backs—since chile picking demanded one nearly stand on one's head—and the quiet, steady efforts of more than thirty sets of hands enabled them to make progress through the fields.

Word spread at UNM, and the *New Mexico Daily Lobo* newspaper ran an article about the project, and long-haired kids driving old Volkswagens with environmentalist bumper stickers began to show up and work hard. Miguel gave them plastic bags of chile to take home to roast, despite their protests that they were there for "the *cause*, man."

On the eighth day, at three thirty in the afternoon, while the workers napped in the bunkhouse, CeCe roasted a turkey in the oven to make huge trays of enchiladas for the troops, Rachel and Charlie gingerly made love for the first time since his injury, Miguel played cards with Santi and Hattie, Mort and Rose watched Dr. Phil, and Abby and Maggie rested on her bed reading books, it began to rain. The dark clouds opened their stingy fists, and the water began to pour down in silver torrents.

It pounded roofs and chased the goats inside their barn. Mad wet hens found the collective sense to retreat into the henhouse. Sweetwater and Tie-dye pranced around their corral, their sleek backs twitching in delight.

Every human in Esperanza and beyond stopped whatever he or she was doing to go outside and remember what rain felt like.

Abby and Maggie raced over the soggy, slippery ground, shrieking with laughter to the Vigils' house, where they found them all dancing in it, except for Mort and Rose, who watched from the safety of the covered porch. Even Charlie stood grinning in it, without his crutches and with a plastic garbage bag taped around his splint to keep it dry, a hand on Rachel for balance.

"I knew it was going to rain because I dreamed it!" Hattie yelled. She and Maggie jumped in the puddles. Their wet hair was flattened against their skulls, ears sticking out, eyelashes pointed in clumps as they blinked back the rivulets coursing down their foreheads.

Maggie held her mouth open, catching drops. "I forgot how good it tasted." Santi lifted her up on his back and galloped across the yard.

CeCe hugged Miguel, who was playfully catching the downpour in his hat as the *canales* on his roof drained the precious water into rain barrels.

"Do you think it will hail?" Abby asked him, wondering if it was even raining where Ben was. Low thunder rumbled in the distance.

"Nah, these aren't hail clouds, and there's no wind," Miguel said. "We got lucky this time."

Every morning the picking continued under clear blue skies. Billowing white clouds stacked themselves over the mountains and assembled overhead by late afternoon for a monsoon shower that lasted a few hours. Evenings were cooler, even after the sun reappeared. The volunteer numbers dwindled, and the café reopened after the initial threat of hail passed and the normal rhythm of harvest ensued.

Despite the late appearance of the summer monsoons and the relief that rain brought, weather forecasters and experienced farmers alike cautioned that the pattern of drought was not over. Ben told Abby hydrologists were saying it would take fifteen years of above-average rainfall and snowpack to refill the reservoirs to their normal levels. But that didn't mean they wouldn't celebrate while they could.

Santi spent his late afternoons with Miguel, who had returned to his workshop to finish his long-ignored retablos and bultos.

He held his carving of San Juan Nepomuceno, Saint John of Nepomuk. "See this guy, Santi? He was martyred by his king back in Prague, Bohemia, for refusing to break the secrecy of the confessional. From there his cult spread to Mexico. In New Mexico, he caught on as a symbol of secrecy for the *Penitentes*."

Santi heard about the top-secret cult of Penitentes, which was found in northern New Mexico in small, very traditional Hispanic communities. He'd heard they flogged themselves to repent their sins. Miguel's figure held a cross in one hand and a palm leaf in the other.

"My faith was sorely tested this summer, and I fear I didn't do so well," Miguel said. "For that I need to repent. I don't want to have a fair-weather relationship with my God, or there is no need for faith. I failed the tests to my faith when I needed it the most."

Santi put his hand on Miguel's shoulder. "You're always telling me not to be so hard on myself when I screw up. So I don't think you should be beating yourself up either. Shouldn't we just be grateful for the rain, the harvest, and that we survived all the bad stuff?"

"So, in other words, what you're saying to me is: *La mierda, entre mas la escarban, mas hiede.*"

After Santiago translated the dicho in his head, he burst into laughter. "Yeah, the more you sift the shit, the worse it smells. So stop sifting the shit!"

"I will if you will, mi'jo," laughed Miguel, wiping off his hand before offering it to Santi.

As the harvest continued, Abby could feel a sense of normalcy return. Santiago was working long hours in the chile fields and returning home tired and dirty. After a shower and a nap, he was spending his evenings at home with her and Maggie and with Ben, when he was there. She was letting herself become accustomed once again to her son's company and fought to live in the present, not count down the remaining weeks until he left for college.

One night Santiago and Maggie were painting with watercolors at the kitchen table after dinner. Santiago used a dry-brush technique and was attacking the paper with rapid staccato strokes. Abby could see a chile field emerge from the chaos, the mountains in the background. "It's going to illustrate a story I'm writing for Miguel. Like a present for when I leave."

"It's beautiful, Santi. He'll love it. Will I get to read the story?" Abby asked.

"Sure, when it's done. Where's Ben tonight?"

"Yeah," Maggie said. "It's boring without Ben here."

"Ben had to meet with his graduate students about their research projects tonight," Abby said, realizing it was beginning to feel more natural when Ben was part of her family activities than when he was absent.

"Stop it, Santi, you're splattering on my picture!" Maggie said, her paper curling under because of her liberal use of water with the colors. "This is my present for Hattie. It's her house before it got burned down, so she doesn't forget. Our house won't ever burn down, will it?"

"It's a very scary thought, isn't it?" Abby said. "The Silvas built this house farther from the bosque to protect it, so I would say the chances are very slim of that ever happening."

The phone began to ring. "Maybe that's Ben!" Maggie said.

Abby answered it while Maggie watched her expectantly, paint dripping from her brush onto her lap. "Hello?"

"Hi, Abby, it's CeCe. We just got a phone call from Miguel's sister. She's up in Albuquerque at the airport. She's here for a visit, and he hasn't even seen her in more than forty years."

"I didn't even know he had a sister."

"She left with the mother when the mother left his father. Or the mother left with her when she went off to college. Something like that. Miguel was in high school at the time. Never saw his mother again, and we heard she died a few years ago of breast cancer and was buried in Tucson. Anyway, turns out Rachel got in touch with her last month, and then Miguel called her and invited her to visit. So here's the big favor: Can she bunk at your place? We're filled to the gills over here. She's only staying a couple of days."

"Sure," Abby said. "Santiago has the neater room, so he can either sleep on the couch or go join his compadres in the bunkhouse."

"I'll take the couch," Santiago said quickly.

"Thanks. I owe you," CeCe said. "Tell Santi I'll bake him those chocolate brownies he loves. Miguel just left to pick her up. God only knows what Teresa will be like. She's two years older than Miguel. He remembers her being real quiet, a bookworm type. But I think it's so good for him that they're having this reunion. Oops, gotta run. I hear Rose yelling something about Mort's medicine."

Abby hung up the phone. "Miguel's sister, Teresa, will be staying with us for a couple of days. Sleeping here, mainly . . . I guess."

"Starting when?" Santi asked, casually blowing on his finished painting.

"About an hour from now," Abby said, surveying the mess on her table, Maggie's toys strewn all over the house, laundry in the basket next to the refrigerator. Santi jumped up to change the sheets on his bed and straighten his already compulsively clean room.

Maggie looked up from her painting, blue and yellow paint running down her forearm. "Don't worry, Mom, it's called the lived-in look."

Before the hour was up, CeCe arrived with cut roses for Teresa's room. "It's good I can meet her here and not at our three-ring circus. I'm a little nervous. You know, his family didn't want him marrying a Jew any more than my parents wanted me to marry a Mexican. Now we get to sit around the Sunday dinner table together tomorrow. Will the fun never end?"

Abby put the vase on Santi's bedside table, along with a few current magazines and a novel she'd recently enjoyed. Thanks to Santi's minimalist style of decorating, it looked comfortable and uncluttered. "Sorry I won't be there."

"Oh, but you will, my friend. You would never let me go through that alone. Bring the kids, and Ben, too, if you like. We'll set the huge long table in the dining room, and there will be plenty of space. The more people, the less likelihood of cold, stony silences."

Abby nodded. "I see your strategy. Okay, Team Silva is on board. I'll invite the Aussie, too; he's good for distraction. Can I bring some food?"

"You know that Asian fruit salad you make with the ginger-sesame dressing? Would that be too much trouble? That would go well with the baked chicken dish I'm making with sweet potatoes. That, plus whatever green vegetables I grab out of the garden, and Rachel said she'd make flan."

"Sounds good," Abby said, placing a fresh powder-blue bath towel set on the foot of Santi's bed.

"Should be interesting." CeCe looked around the quiet comfort of the bedroom and sighed. "Plan B. I'll hide out here with you, and she can sleep with her brother. How does that sound?"

"I don't think she'd be visiting if she wasn't ready to accept you. Look at how far Rose and Mort have come with Miguel."

"Mom, they're here!" Maggie's shriek from the living room reached their ears without any problem.

"Gulp," CeCe said, smoothing her hair and blouse.

"Stop. You look gorgeous."

"I look Jewish, and to her, that ain't good."

Abby grabbed her hand and led her down the long, polished-wood-floor hallway to the living room. Maggie had made a successful sweep of toys, and her bedroom door was shut to hide the mess. She stood with Santi by the front door, a white bow clipped in her wild, dark, wavy hair. Abby had a moment to admire both her children, a little paint streaked and disheveled, but with welcoming smiles on their faces.

The sun was setting in riotous colors. Miguel went around to his sister's side of the car to open the door for her, a small brown leather suitcase in his hand.

Teresa emerged, wearing a pale pink suit. Her silver-streaked dark hair was swept up in a French twist. She was a handsome woman who bore a slight resemblance to her brother.

Abby opened the screen door. "Welcome to my home. I'm Abby, part of the extended family around here."

Teresa smiled warmly and reached for Abby's hand. "Miguel has been filling me in on everything—I appreciate you letting me stay here. I guess I've come at a bad time."

"No!" CeCe said quickly as they entered the house. "We're glad you came. I'm CeCe, Miguel's wife."

Teresa opened her arms, and CeCe stepped into them. "I've let too many years go by. I'm so happy to finally meet you."

Miguel stood, blinking quickly as he watched their embrace.

"I'm Magdalena, but you can call me Maggie, unless you get mad, and then I'm Magdalena."

"Oh, aren't you a cutie?" Teresa said. "And you must be Santiago. Miguel has been bragging about you."

"Can I make some coffee? We could all sit down," Abby said.

"I think I'd like to pass on that. I'm a little tired. One of those early to bed, early to rise old ladies these days. We can catch up tomorrow, Miguel. Is that all right?"

"Sure, Teresa. I just can't believe you're really here," Miguel said, hugging her and giving her a peck on her cheek. *"Buenas noches, mi hermana."*

"Buenas noches, mi hermano," Theresa replied, returning the kiss.

"Great to meet you. See you tomorrow," CeCe said, linking her arm through her husband's.

"Goodnight." Teresa smiled.

"It's been a long time since we had twelve around this table," CeCe said.

"I remember it seemed like it could hold fifty when we were kids—right, Miguel?" Teresa said. "But Mama insisted we eat at it together, every meal, no exceptions."

"Another thing Papa hated." Miguel smiled. "He always thought she was too formal about everything. One of her uppity northern New Mexico customs."

Teresa smiled. "Those two were oil and water. I have never understood how they ever got married in the first place. We must have been mail-ordered."

The long table was laden with food, baskets of bread, and wine. CeCe had made an arrangement of white roses in a simple antique turquoise crock. The midday light lent the hand-plastered adobe walls a golden glow.

Mort and Rose ate quietly, following CeCe's directions, thus far. Hattie was shyly ducking around Charlie for glimpses of her mysterious great-aunt.

"Aunt Teresa, tell us about your life in Tucson," Rachel said.

Teresa took a sip from her water glass. "I'm a librarian at the University of Arizona. I love my work; the students keep me young. I graduated from there, goodness, forty years ago. When I was accepted to college there, Mama packed up and announced she was going with me. Miguel and I were not that surprised that she would leave Papa. The surprise was she was tagging along with me."

Everyone laughed. Abby caught Santi's eye and raised her eyebrows. "No way," he mouthed in reply.

"So instead of my getting to live in the girls' dormitory, Mama rented us a little house near campus and promptly enrolled herself in some classes. She could finally pursue her dream and get an education. It was actually a good time in our lives. We became closer, and she began to open up about her family, whom we never knew."

Miguel leaned toward her. "Her people were from up north, near Mora. I think they visited here when we were very small. I remember they were not very talkative."

"They didn't like Papa. They thought she had married beneath herself, since all the Vigils were farmers. Her papa was a real estate attorney, and her mother was a schoolteacher up there."

"I never knew even that much," Miguel said.

"Do you have a husband?" Maggie blurted. "Or kids or anything?"

"I did have a husband. I met him at college. We never were able to have children. Alberto was a wonderful man. I lost him six months ago to pancreatic cancer. We had a lot in common, and we had a wonderful life together. Mama loved him, too, and she lived with us until she passed a few years ago. His name was Alberto Lopez. He grew up in Tucson; his family had been there for several hundred years. Researching his genealogy was his passion and also his vocation. He was a historian, specializing in ethnological studies of the Southwest. He chose that field because of some interesting customs his family had. Like shunning pork because it was a dirty animal, and there were a lot of other rules about food. They strenuously emphasized obtaining advanced education and professional careers. They were very political and intellectual and would not participate in the Catholic community; instead they kept to themselves. There were no crucifixes or saints in their home. When someone died, the mirrors were covered for weeks on end. Friday evening dinners were always special—his mother always lit candles, and they dressed in their best clothes. The list goes on . . ."

"They were Jews. You married a Jew!" Rose exclaimed, sounding like she had the winning answer on a game show.

"Yes. Alberto discovered his family were Sephardic Jews who had escaped the Spanish Inquisition, only to have the Inquisition follow them to Mexico City. They were castigated as *Marranos*, meaning "filthy pigs." They witnessed friends and family put to death in unspeakable ways. They tried to practice their faith in secret, pretend to be conversos, converted Catholics. But it was a witch hunt. They migrated north, settling in what would eventually become Arizona. Where, over time, the practices were handed down, the secret from mother to daughter, and eventually even that knowledge was lost. Until Alberto began his research and discovered records and letters tucked into an old family Bible, the Old Testament, in Hebrew. He committed his entire life to researching the crypto-Jews, the hidden Jews in the New World."

"I never knew the Inquisition came to the New World," Rose said, her hand on her forehead. "That there could even be Mexican Jews. But it makes sense. They've run us out and killed us all over the world."

Miguel had put down his fork and stopped eating. "What you described, Teresa. It sounds familiar. Mama would never eat pork or cook it or use the lard in her baking or make blood sausage for Papa. She said she was allergic, that it would make her sick. That's one of the things they fought about. Her stubborn, strange ways."

"Mi hermano, *somos Judios*," Teresa said, blinking tears.

A brief, confused silence was broken by Rose, her hand clutched to her heart. "You're a Jew! My son-in-law, the Jew!"

All eyes were on Miguel, whose face reflected a rapid sequence of emotions. Finally he put his linen napkin against his eyes, and it seemed as if he was weeping, until he burst out laughing. He laughed so hard he couldn't breathe, tears streaming down his face. He waved his white napkin in surrender, and his feet stomped the saltillo tile beneath his boots.

"I knew there was something I liked about you!" Rose cried.

CeCe stammered, "But your father, he wasn't a Jew."

"He hated the Jews!" Miguel said through his hysterical laughter. "He never forgave me for marrying a Jew, and he had married a Jew and never knew it! Oh, mi Dios! She got the last laugh!"

"She revealed her family's secret to me as soon as I brought Alberto home. That is why she never returned to Esperanza. She was tired of keeping her faith a secret. We joined the Jewish community in Tucson, which has several Sephardic Jewish families, and we attended synagogue. Mama still made me swear never to tell you; she thought you would think less of her because of Papa's attitudes. Remember, we never knew you had married into a Jewish family. But after she passed, and then I lost Alberto . . . You can still be Catholic, Miguel—no one is expecting you to change your religious beliefs. I thought you had the right to know the other half of your ethnic heritage. And I got tired of secrets. Secrets only bring harm. They separate people. Divide families. Look at all the time we've lost. I've missed my little brother."

"Oy vey! Such a tsimmes!" Mort said. "We all came from Adam and Eve, so what's the big deal? Now that we have all of that straight, can I have some more chicken, or what?"

CHAPTER 17

CeCe loosely french braided her hair in front of her dresser mirror, her fingers working deftly. She had on a simple, long gauze skirt and a Mexican embroidered blouse. Around her neck she wore a small-beaded silver necklace with a slice-of-green-turquoise pendant; in her ears, silver hoop earrings. She draped a black crocheted shawl around her head and shoulders and went to meet the others.

Earlier that afternoon Rose, Rachel, and she had worked hard together preparing the evening meal. CeCe boiled some egg noodles for the lokshen kugel and was in charge of the chicken soup for Rose's matzo balls, which Rose patted softly into shape like baby's bottoms over at the counter. She stuck a dozen of them in the fridge to chill.

"Club soda instead of water," Rose told Rachel. "That makes them real *geflufkeneh*, fluffy." She carried the bowl to the kitchen sink and rinsed it out. The day before Rose had spent cleaning the entire house. Rose reminded CeCe of the mother she had had when she was young and her own bubbe and zeyde were still alive. A mother with a purpose.

"Racheleh, how are you doing over there with the chopped liver? You know, in my day we didn't have those fancy-schmancy machines to grind or chop everything. You're all lucky. It's much easier to be a Jew today."

Rachel gave CeCe an amused look. Finding out Miguel was half-Jewish had changed Rose. She saw it as a sign from God, and it renewed her faith in her religion. As the eldest female in the family, she had a function to perform. She was a Woman of Valor, the kind King Solomon sang about.

"I'm almost done already due to my handy-dandy food processor," replied Rachel with a few pulsating *vip-vip-vips*. "Don't want to make it too smooth. I like it coarse and spread on some challah. I remember having it like that on that trip to Brooklyn I took with Ma when I was a little girl."

"The brisket sure smells good, Ma," said CeCe, mixing the sour cream, cinnamon, sugar, and raisins in the egg noodles for her lokshen kugel and then transfering it into a glass dish to stick in the oven.

"I'm starting the kishke next," said Rose, hitching up her apron like a holster before a big gunfight.

Yum, kishke. CeCe's mouth watered with the thought of her mother's stuffed cow intestines. She loved when it popped open its pasty bready stuffing while it baked. Made it easy to steal a bite every now and then. Rose would always nestle it in with the brisket to bake. The tsimmes with knaidel she tucked in with the chicken. Luckily, CeCe had two ovens.

The challah, or braided egg bread, she was able to buy at La Montanita Co-op in the little shopping area near the university called Nob Hill, which saved a lot of time. Although Rose might be a little stuck-up about it. No poppy seeds. But she and Rose could not have whirled themselves around the kitchen any faster, let alone have baked bread. She bought the gefilte fish and horseradish, too.

CeCe entered the dining room, where Miguel waited. He was

done up with his new Stetson perched on his head, boots polished, silver Hopi *bollo* tie pulled up lazily under his loose collar.

She wondered how he would adjust to all of this in the long run. His sister had told her that some people have a very hard time adjusting after finding out this part of their heritage. She couldn't help but think that on an unconscious level maybe Miguel had sought her out, a predestined Jewish bride who seemed so comfortingly familiar. It felt God had given them to each other. Being a Hispanic Catholic would always be his true identity, but he was open to augmentation. He had said that, as a chile farmer, he couldn't have too many roads to God.

Rachel, Charlie, and Hattie joined them, Hattie bursting out of their room in a pretty flowered dress and patent leather shoes.

Sunset approached. The dinner smells from the kitchen made CeCe's mouth water. She handed Rachel a black lace scarf to put on her head. Rose and Mort should be out any second.

Rose came out of their bedroom escorting Mort on her arm, she in a simple hat and dress suit, Mort wearing his green velvet yarmulke and the navy suit he had had on when they picked him up at the airport. He looked so different to her now. A man of respect. Her papa.

On the dining room table sat the two loaves of challah, covered by an embroidered tea towel, and Rose's silver candelabra, which she had packed between her clothes when they moved out here. It held three white virgin candles awaiting their sacrifice.

Mort began to sing in Hebrew, which CeCe recognized as the praise for the lady of the house. "Strength and honor are her clothing . . . she openeth her mouth with wisdom . . . her children arise up and call her blessed; her husband also, and he praiseth her." With his eyes closed and the way he piously rocked from toe to heel, CeCe knew he meant every word. He loved his Rose.

This was the beginning of *Shabbes*, God's day of rest and in olden times sometimes known as "the Queen of the week," for it gave them respite from their bone-weary labor. According to the

Torah, Jews were only allowed to break the Sabbath to save the life or relieve the pain of a person or an animal. Otherwise it was commanded by God to keep the Shabbes holy. A night with the invited angels filled the room with excitement and the possibility of miracles.

CeCe nudged Miguel, the *baleboost* or head of the house, reminding him to set a few dollar bills on the table to go to charity.

Rose struck a wooden match, which hissed in the air. She lit the candles, passed her palms over them, and beckoned the light toward her as if dousing herself in it as she said the broche. Then she covered her face momentarily with her hands, only to open them to look at the light anew. Old hands now that had once engaged CeCe in peekaboo, one of CeCe's first remembered images. It had been so hectic lately that CeCe hadn't noticed Rose didn't have on her fake nails, but her natural working-length nails. The simple gold band she got married in had replaced her gaudy diamond set.

CeCe looked at Rachel, who had her arm through her Zeyde Mort's, watching her Bubbe Rose turn into the priestess she became while performing the mitzvah reserved for Jewish women. Charlie stood next to her, the only real gentile in the whole house, holding Hattie's hand. How different Rachel had become because of Mort, embracing his pain and his culture and striking a vein of gold within herself. After Rachel's years of disdaining her Jewish half, it was remarkable to see her find the balance and whole-ness that reconciliation brought. What would Rachel's Tía Maria have said about all of this? For so many years Maria was a wedge between CeCe and Rachel. If only Maria could see Rachel now, her silver crucifix sharing its chain around her neck with the Star of David. CeCe chuckled inside, the last laugh feeling a bit naughty but delicious.

CeCe had changed, too. Had it not been for her father's demen-tia, she would never have gotten close to him. Time with him had become a precious commodity. Even the anger at her mother had dissipated and been replaced with a newfound respect that Rose had stuck with Mort and shielded her children as best as she could from his now-explained dark moods.

Miguel stood respectfully in attendance with a curious gleam in his eye. He took her hand in his and held firm.

"When do we get to blow out the candles?" Hattie whispered loudly to Charlie, who gently hushed her, while Rose continued to ask God to preserve her family's health, peace, and honor. A prayer to unite them once and for all. Amen.

Rachel and Rose headed to the kitchen to bring the food to the table as Mort poured into the kiddush cup the wine that would sanctify the Sabbath.

And although CeCe was aware a Jew was not to think or speak of anything that would make one cry on the Sabbath, she knew God forgave her tears of joy.

Abby finished her early morning jog and decided to walk it off in the direction of the Vigils'. The sun was cresting over the mountaintops, washing the valley in golden light. The last day of August, the day Abby had dreaded all summer, had arrived. Santiago's last day at home before leaving for school.

She stretched her burning quadriceps; she still loved to run, but her muscles liked to complain more these days. The chile fields would be empty of pickers today. The green harvest was essentially completed as of the previous afternoon, and it would be another week or two before the remaining fruit was red enough to pick. Miguel always had a few small special orders for the half-red, half-green chile, called the *pintado*, or painted chile, prized for its marriage of the two distinct flavors.

At least Santi could feel like he'd seen most of the harvest through to some kind of closure. He would miss the Esperanza Harvest Fiesta in two weeks, though. He would miss a lot of things. Not nearly as much as she would miss him. It was astounding to think she didn't even know him nine years ago and yet his leaving was as wrenching as if she'd carried him herself and given birth to him eighteen years ago.

The delicate smells of late summer were as scintillating as the first robust smells of spring. She walked under the shade of the cottonwoods on the border of the Vigils' property. She smelled the sweet scent of fresh-cut alfalfa, the more pungent lower notes of the reddening chile, the pleasantly earthy smells wafting from the horses and goats. CeCe's lone rooster crowed, and her chickens went clucking about their pen, seeming to grouse among themselves about his arrogant strutting. The goats ran toward the fence as she came nearer, ears flopping, bleating a welcome. Was there anything more hopeful than a goat?

Charlie came out of the horse barn to see who was approaching. He waved and limped a few feet toward her, his crutches absent. He was exactly whom she was hoping to find up and around as early as she was. She petted a few goat noses, tugged on their silky ears.

"How's the leg?" Abby asked as she climbed over the rail fence. Sweetwater trotted over from his breakfast of alfalfa, in case she might produce something more exotic. He snuffled her empty palm and allowed a little nose stroking before rejoining Tie-dye for seconds on alfalfa.

"Can't complain. I could, but it wouldn't do any good." Charlie smiled when she recited the tired joke along with him. "It lets me put a little more weight on it before it squawks lately. I'll be starting physical therapy this week to build the muscles back up. Can I get you some coffee?"

"Something cold sounds better," Abby said, wiping sweat out of her eyes.

"I'll grab you some water in the barn," Charlie said.

She walked slowly alongside his limping gate. "How do you think Santi is doing, about leaving and everything?" she asked.

"He talked to me about what he remembered after the fire. Poor kid, my heart about broke for all the suffering he's had. But honest to God, Abby, I think he's good. There's a peace about him now that's never been there before. As hard as this summer was on him, it grew him up real fast, and that'll be good for him out at college. He learned some tough lessons, and he kicked that damned skeleton out of his closet. He's got to feel a ton lighter."

"I hope so," Abby said, watching him rinse out her cup three or four times and letting the water get nice and cold. Her mouth salivated as she reached for and brought the tin cup to her thirsty lips. As the water spread its coolness through her, she marveled at how anyone could take a simple drink of water for granted.

Charlie sat on his chair and refilled his coffee mug from his thermos.

Abby sat, too, feeling her leg muscles twitch as they cooled down. "So he seems ready to go that far away?"

Charlie smiled. "This is more about you not being ready to let him go. The boy will do fine."

"Yeah, of course it is. I worry, you know? It's not like he's going up to Albuquerque or something. What if he needs us?"

"He'll call. He'll have new friends and professors and advisors and all that stuff. He's a resilient kid. Look at all he's survived. And you, you've got Maggie and Ben to keep you occupied. Is this thing with Ben getting serious?"

"I think if we were younger and hadn't been through what we'd been through before we met, we'd stand a better chance of screwing it up. I think we both realize how special this is, and we're determined to hang onto it. We love each other," Abby said, enjoying how it felt to say it so directly to someone else.

"I'm happy for you. He's a decent guy."

"So you won't mind if he spends a lot of time in these parts?" Abby mimicked Charlie's twang.

"Nah, I'll even drink a beer or two with him when he can tear himself away from you."

"Things seem good with you and Rachel."

"Yeah, nothing like almost dying and losing all your worldly possessions to make you feel grateful for what you have. Even though we knew when Hattie was born that we couldn't have more kids, we had to finally face it and get over it."

"What a summer." Abby sighed. She wasn't sure how to bring up her real reason for seeking him out at the crack of dawn. It made her nervous to search for the words, even though she could talk to Charlie about anything.

"Yeah, we got through it, alive and a few dollars ahead," Charlie said. "That's all we ask. Miguel is pleased. Even though the drought ain't over and with what Ben says, the water situation will only get worse. Hell, even I can see that. Still, you got to take your victories when you can."

"I heard two more farmers were giving up and wanting to sell. The Shafers and the Abeytas."

"No, really? Shit. I knew the Shafers were getting tired, but the Abeytas have been here forever. Where'd you hear it?" Charlie pushed his hat back up on his head and chewed his lip.

"I was doing some checking at Darnell's real estate office; Jack has been in talks with both families about handling it for them. Tell me if you think this is crazy. I want to buy them both before a developer can get them." Abby said it all in one breath.

"You got that kind of cash?"

"Let's say I do. If I buy them out, it keeps more than a hundred acres from becoming over four hundred houses. I can lease it to farmers, dairies, or leave it fallow for a while. It could be for my kids someday. Or just an investment. Of course if this place does go into a major water crisis years from now, it won't be worth much. But I feel like I should take the risk." Abby tried to read his eyes in the soft light of the barn. Time seemed to cease passing while he thought.

"It's a gamble if it's about the long-term investment, but I got to think land is always worth something. I just can't buy in to all the doomsday shit about running out of water. When you opened your restaurant back in San Diego all those years ago, that was a huge risk, and you made a fortune off it, and you still are getting those checks, right?"

"Right. Staying on as a partner was smart. People still associate my name with a quality operation out there. I still get offers to do a cookbook, and I might, to give any proceeds to my new ventures as a real estate magnate." Abby leaned toward him. "Charlie, I want to know what you really think. I don't want to do it if I'll be resented as some rich woman buying up Esperanza piece by piece. Maybe people want houses and growth like that. Maybe they want a Walmart to move in so they don't have to drive so far."

"Nobody I know wants that. Maybe the people moving into the new housing developments do, but who cares what they think? I think the farmers who have to give it up would rather get your money than some developer's. Especially if it gets to stay farmland. Hell, some of them might turn around and lease a part back from you. A lot of farmers down south have done that; much cheaper enterprise to rent some land without near the operating costs of owning it. Now whether anyone will still even want this way of life in fifty years, who knows. You and Ben could turn it all into a nature preserve, let the natural grasslands come back, buy a herd of buffalo."

Abby laughed. "And live happily ever after."

"Sounds like a plan."

Santiago packed his car the night before he was leaving. Abby had cooked him green chile chicken enchiladas from the new crop of chile. It was the best-tasting crop he'd ever had. He didn't let her hold a big goodbye party. He said his goodbyes to everyone one at a time. Miguel was hard. He seemed to like his painting and the story he wrote about the farmer, though. He said he liked that it had a happy ending.

He lay in bed waiting for the four o'clock alarm he'd set to go off. He wouldn't be back in this bed until Thanksgiving. He wanted to get an early start, since the drive going west would be hot and long. His mom was worried about him going by himself, but he wanted it like that. They would be out to visit him on parents' weekend in a few weeks anyway. Even Ben was coming, which was cool.

Santi got up and threw on his running shorts and shoes. He crept outside and stretched in the moonlight. A big, fat, chalky white moon hung overhead, surrounded by stars. He thought briefly about Rosalinda's ceiling and then wondered about the girls he would meet at school. That made him smile.

He began to jog at an easy pace, drinking in the cool night air. He would miss seeing the cottonwoods turn gold, amazing under the stark blue autumn sky, the mountains purpling in the distance. He'd have the ocean, though. Ben said he'd teach him to surf sometime.

It was easier to leave knowing Ben would be there for Maggie and his mom. For some reason, the place needed a male around, though his mom would never like hearing that. Even when he was ten, he felt like he had an important job, helping Abby with the new baby and making her scrambled eggs after she had been up all night.

Up ahead on the path was the place where the cottonwood had fallen last spring. Charlie had come with his chainsaw, cut it up, and hauled it away. The empty space had continued to nag at him even after his recovered memory had vanquished the nightmare.

So a few weeks ago he'd transplanted a little cottonwood sapling from the riverbank to this spot, and after hauling out a five-gallon bucket of water for it every day, it was thriving.

He reached out to feel its young, heart-shaped leaves, slippery and shiny in the moonlight. It was a healthy little thing and should do just fine without him.

As he ran on, he thought about families and how the best ones seemed not to be like the ones on television. The best ones were sometimes put together in odd ways, but they held together as sure as the stars in the sky did. It didn't have anything to do with blood or religion or race or being on the same side of something, as long as you were there for each other, no matter what. People who didn't know that missed out on a lot.

But you could learn it even when you were old, like Rose. Or only ten, like he had been. Even when he had almost forgotten it this summer, everyone was there to remind him, to catch him when he fell.

He looked up to see a falling star and then another one. The sight made him stop in his tracks as a whole shower of meteors burst like diamonds across the black velvet sky. Tears welled in his eyes, transforming the falling stars into cascading streams of brilliant white light. He blinked them away, but more tears came. It was all so beautiful.